The
UNFORESEEN

To Linda MacWhinney

The
UNFORESEEN

Dorothy Macardle

With an introduction by Luke Gibbons

TRAMPPRESS

First published by Doubleday & Company, Inc, 1945

The Unforeseen © copyright The Beneficiaries of the
Literary Estate of Dorothy Macardle, 1945, 2017

This edition published 2017 by Tramp Press
www.tramppress.com

Introduction © copyright Luke Gibbons 2017

A CIP record for this title is
available from The British Library.

1 3 5 7 9 10 8 6 4 2

ISBN 978-0-9934592-4-5

Thank you for supporting independent publishing.

Set in 10.5 pt on 14 pt Minion by Marsha Swan
Printed by ScandBook AB in Sweden

The Unforeseen: An Introduction

Luke Gibbons

Like all people whose future has suddenly been obscured, they
longed for an oracle.
>   —Dorothy Macardle, *The Seed Was Kind* (1944)

AT ONE POINT in *The Unforeseen*, Nan Wilde, a young artist home from London to stay with her mother in County Wicklow, goes for a walk in the mountains with her new friend, Perry Frank. A recently qualified doctor, Perry mentions he is thinking of continuing his career in the United States, to which Nan responds: 'I thought it was usually to Germany or Austria that doctors went for special study.'

'So it used to be,' Perry replies, 'they had great teachers. But those are the sort of men the Nazis have scattered.' He then adds that the most advanced work in surgery is being conducted in the United States: 'The thing about it is, if there's a world war these treatments may make quite a difference. So you see!' '"I see," Nan replies. She wanted to know whether he thought war was coming, but that was not a question to ask a man in the prime of his life on a hilltop in June.'

Later, however, Nan has second thoughts: 'For our generation, life is not going to be a summer holiday ... [but] frightening and terrible... we *must* face that.'

The Unforeseen is set in Ireland during the summer of 1938, but it was written by Dorothy Macardle on her return to Ireland from war-time London in 1945, when it was clear that Nan's worst fears about impending war had indeed been confirmed. The novel, titled *Fantastic Summer* on its British publication in 1946, was Macardle's fourth book of fiction, preceded by a collection of stories *Earth-Bound* (1924), published originally in the United States; *The Uninvited* (1942), adapted for the screen in an acclaimed Hollywood version (1944) and re-issued by Tramp Press in 2015; and *The Seed Was Kind* (1944), a depiction of life set in Geneva in the run-up to World War Two and the extreme conditions in London during the war. Macardle's career as a writer and activist flew in the face of conventional categories: a pioneering feminist who was also a radical republican in Irish politics; a universalist civil liberties humanitarian who was also a nationalist; a defender of Irish neutrality during World War Two who moved to London to participate in the fight against the Nazis; a brilliant lecturer who held no teaching position; a journalist and historian who was a critic and novelist of distinction; a psychological rationalist who also put in a good word for ghosts and extrasensory experiences.

Born in Dundalk in 1889 to the wealthy Macardle brewing family, Dorothy Macardle was educated at Alexandra College and University College Dublin, where she graduated with a B.A. degree in 1912. Steeped in a love of literature from the outset, she moved to Stratford-upon-Avon to pursue her Shakespearean interests, before returning to teach English at Alexandra College. This period in her life provided the milieu for several of her publications, including an edition of *Sir Philip Sidney's Defence of Poesy* (1919), *Selections from Sir Thomas Malory's Le Morte d'Arthur* (1922), and the posthumous *Shakespeare: Man and Boy* (1961). As in the case of the 1916 leader Thomas MacDonagh, this love of all things English did not prevent her from gravitating towards Republicanism in the Anglo-Irish war, and taking the anti-Treaty side in the bitter Civil War. Dismissed from her teaching post at Alexandra College, she was imprisoned in Mountjoy and Kilmainham jails, and led a mass hunger-strike protesting against conditions in the prisons. She published 'Kilmainham Tortures', an exposé of the ill-treatment she received with other female prisoners, which was soon followed by her first exercise in investigative journalism, a chilling account of atrocities in County Kerry during the Civil War, *Tragedies of Kerry 1922–1923* (1924). In the 1920s, Macardle's creative energies were devoted mainly to theatre, writing eleven plays, many of which are lost or survive only in manuscript form. Three of her plays were produced at the Abbey Theatre – *Atonement* (1918), *Ann Kavanagh* (1922–32) and *The Old Man* (1925) – while one, *Dark Waters*, was produced at the Gate Theatre in 1932. This interest in drama led to her appointment as theatre (and sometimes film) critic for the new *Irish Press*, launched in tandem with Fianna Fáil's accession to power in 1931/1932. Throughout this period, she worked on the monumental history of the Anglo-Irish and Civil Wars for which she is best known, *The Irish Republic*, published originally by Victor Gollancz/the Left Book Club in London in 1937, republished by the Irish Press in 1951, and re-issued in a paperback edition by Corgi Books in 1968.

Macardle's novel *The Unforeseen* bears witness to the relative calm of neutral Ireland following her homecoming in 1945, and is a comparative rarity in Irish fiction of the period in that it deals with the lives of well-to-do middle-class Dubliners, characterised by tennis clubs and swimming, sports cars with hoods, telephones, radiograms, cameras, books, cocktail-shakers and salon-style dinner parties. The story centres on Virgilia Wilde, an Irish author who leaves Manchester and London following the death of her husband to begin a new life in a restored cottage in the tranquil setting of Glencree, County Wicklow, with her long devoted home-help, Brigid Reenan. Virgilia's daughter Nan, an artist working in London, returns to spend the summer with her mother, partly to help her work as an illustrator on a fantasy book, *Puck and the Leprechauns*, but also to escape the attentions of an impulsive Sicilian artist, Carlo, who smashes a bust of her in a fit of pique. Nan's visit is welcome, for her mother has been feeling unwell and has consulted various doctors to find out what is wrong, including a Dublin psychiatrist Dr Franks, whose son Perry, embarking on his own medical career, takes a romantic interest in the newly returned Nan.

The tranquility of the novel is disturbed, however, when it emerges that Virgilia's condition displays symptoms not of a medical disorder but of 'second sight,' a paranormal ability to catch glimpses of the future, usually, but not always, presaging danger. This, not surprisingly, is initially greeted with skepticism, including by Virigilia herself, and Dr Franks is inclined to interpret it as a troubling case of mental projection. When Perry brings his friends, the recently married Garret Ingram and Pamela Fitzgerald, to bear on the proceedings, however, the response shifts from psychology towards the unexpected interest in paranormal experiences of 'prevision' and 'precognition' in scientific and wider cultural debates in the anxious interwar period. Pamela is no stranger to uncanny visitations, having featured with her brother Roddy as a main character in Macardle's first novel, *The Uninvited*, set in a haunted house off the wild coast of Devon: on Pamela's mention of a house-warming party in their new home in Donnybrook, 'Her husband, giving her a quizzical grin, said he hoped she would have no uninvited guests'.

But there are also other ripples on the surface calm of the settled community in *The Unforeseen* in the form of a Traveller family, The Vaughans, who camp for a few weeks in the district on their grounds as tinsmiths, and as horse, pony and mule dealers, in the Wicklow countryside. Though archaic, they are not out of touch with the modern: they travel to the accompaniment of gramophones, showing a particular aptitude for the music of Grieg. Going against conventional prejudices, moreover, the disruption associated with them has less to do with danger on their part than the intrusion of state violence on Traveller family life: the threat of incarcerating the Vaughan's wayward son, Timeen, in an Industrial School, represented by the grim edifice of the nearby Glencree Reformatory (closed by de Valera's government in 1940). The famished Timeen has escaped from one such school, and his nervousness has much to do with the prospect of his being caught again by the police. The theme of precarious or damaged family attachments is central to the novel, relating the plight of Timeen in one of Virgilia's flash-forwards to the terrifying fate also awaiting her daughter Nan in another ominous 'prevision' of the future.

Macardle's pioneering commitment to children's rights was already evident in the campaigning articles she wrote as a crusading journalist for *The Irish Press* in 1931, dealing with the impact of poverty on working class family life in 'Some Irish Mothers and Their Children', 'Children and the Law: A Test of Civilization', and a classic piece of reportage, 'The Newsboy as Breadwinner'. This concern with the emotional consequences of deprivation and abandonment led to her wide-ranging investigation, drawing on the research of Anna Freud among others, into the devastating experiences of orphaned and refugee children across 20 countries in Europe after the Second World War, *Children of Europe. A Study of the Children of Liberated Countries: Their War-time Experiences, their Reactions, and their Needs, with a Note on Germany*, published in 1949. In the immediate aftermath of the War, her energies were translated into direct involvement in the massive social reform programmes that attempted to pick up the pieces of a devastated continent. In 1946, Deputy Robert Briscoe informed the Dáil that the Irish government's main contact in Europe was, in fact, Macardle, who in her travels across Europe, also sought to ensure that Irish governmental aid got to its proper destinations.

Gypsies and tinkers have long been imbued with second sight and fortune-telling in the popular imagination, and it is not surprising in *The Unforeseen* that following the infliction of 'a tinker's curse' by Sal, Timeen's mother, she is described by Garrett Ingram as 'The perfect Shakespearean witch. I'm sorry I could not hear her curses. I bet they were eloquent.' Nan thinks that Sal's curse may have something to do with her mother, Virgilia's, strange behavior, only to find out that the exotic has no monopoly on witchcraft: "And Sal didn't … it wasn't Sal?" asked Nan: Virgilia smiled: "It is I who am the witch I'm afraid."

Wild landscape and mountain scenery conventionally provided the mise-en-scène for those possessed of second sight, as in the witches in *Macbeth*, a play that comes to mind when Nan reflects on her mother's condition: 'What her mother was doing came from a sick mind… It was shock that made her think "so brain-sickly of things"… Macbeth: I seem to be haunted, she thought, by Macbeth. The little red volume was among the set on her chest of drawers. She opened it.' *Macbeth* points to another link in the chain of unreason – the extensive historical literature locating second sight in the Scottish Highlands and, more generally, the Celtic periphery, from the late seventeenth century.

The occult powers of an endangered Gaelic culture formed part of the pre-history of the cult of Ossian and Celtic antiquity that emerged in the mid-eighteenth century, closely followed by the aesthetics of the sublime and 'Romantick' landscape. But another connection is also important: the association of a preternatural ability to look into the future with those who have no actual future. The political background to the rise of interest in second sight in the 1690s was the defeat of the Stuart dynasty by Williamite forces in Ireland and, as such, it has affinities with the more overtly millenarian longings of the *Aisling* genre in eighteenth-century Ireland. The persistence of the Jacobite cause in Scotland, culminating in Bonnie Prince Charlie's invasion in 1945 and the disaster of Culloden, re-activated interest in second sight, and the phenomenon was given a sympathetic hearing in Dr Johnson's *Journey to the Western Islands of Scotland* (1775). Not surprisingly, however, glimpses of the future in these circumstances were often bound up with fearing the worst: not only intimations of mortality, but predestination, the inevitability of the fate awaiting those, whether individuals or 'doomed races,' facing extinction.

The cultural milieu *The Unforese*en is one of foreboding, as storm-clouds gathered over Europe in the late 1930s: 'London might be wiped out any day,' Macardle wrote in October, 1938: 'gas-masks, newspaper scares, incessant wondering as to what was likely to happen'. When refugees gather in London, as recounted in Macardle's wartime novel, *The Seed Was Kind*, the longing for news from the European mainland was pressing, as the young protagonist Diony discovers when she returns from Paris: 'They wanted her to talk to them about France; interpret the mind of the Russians, prophecy about the future of Austria. Like all people whose future has suddenly been obscured, they longed for an oracle.' Faced with these prospects, it is not surprising that second sight re-emerges in the fiction of the interwar period, assuming centre-stage even when there is little mention of the 'international situation' (though much about India and empire), as in Neil Gunn's *Second Sight* (1940), set among an English hunting party stalking deer in the Scottish Highlands. Gunn's novel stages a series of discussions and disagreements among characters as to the nature of a fateful premonition revealed to one of the Highland guides, Alick, and while the mysterious power to see into the future is interpreted by one of the party as a vindication of mind over matter, the very fact that the gift is 'passing out' under modernity ensures the ultimate 'triumph of the material over the spiritual.'

This does not settle the argument, however, for in a shift of register echoed in *The Unforeseen*, the terms of debate in Gunn's novel are switched from 'survivals' and residues of superstition, to the highly contemporary topic of Einsteinian relativity, particularly the concept of 'prevision' formulated by the startling reconfigurations of time in the writings of the eccentric Irish aeronautics engineer, J. W. Dunne. Traces of Dunne's controversial *An Experiment With Time*, published in 1927, found their way into the work of James Joyce, TS Eliot, Flann O'Brien, Jorge Luis Borges, John Buchan, JB Priestly and, not least, Neil Gunn and Dorothy Macardle. Elaborating somewhat selectively on Einstein's theory that time was not absolute, but an objective relation between things, Dunne contended that it was therefore a mental construct, a subjective condition of interpreting the physical world. If subjectivity were suspended, as Dunne believed was the case in dreams or unconscious, trance-like states, then time could also be circumvented, and the future opened up to the present. It is no coincidence that Virgilia's experiences of precognition in *The Unforeseen* occur in trance-like states, catching momentary glimpses of the future through windows, mirrors, or Nan's glittering 'witch-ball.' When Virgilia sees on one occasion what was earlier prefigured:

Perry said, his eyes never leaving her face: 'You saw what you were going to see.'

'Exactly,' she replied.

'Paranormal precognition,' Perry said.

'Precognition?'

' "Prevision", to be exact.'

.... '– This requires a revolution in our ideas of causation.' [states Dr Franks, Perry's father]

'It does,' Perry said, bluntly.

'It requires,' the doctor continued, 'a new concept of time.'

'Dunne has worked that out.'

The new ideas of causation involved 'retro-causation,' the counter-intuitive idea of an effect coming *before* its cause: Virgilia's premonitions are, paradoxically, 'effects' of causes that have yet to come. Leaving aside plausibility, this poses an insuperable difficulty for the mind's putative ability to transcend matter, for no sooner has it extricated itself from 'times arrow' – the successive cause/effect chain of events – than consciousness is faced with a further dilemma: if the future is determined, then human choice and freedom are illusory. The very moment of affirmation turns out to be the end of free will and the autonomy of the human spirit. Much of the formal structure of *The Unforeseen,* and Gunn's *Second Sight,* is devoted to resolving this dilemma, for if a story is predictable, or the outcome easily determined, then it loses all suspense – and its readers – along the way. That this is one of the pre-eminent concerns of the novel is clear from the 'Authors' Foreword' in *The Unforeseen,* construing the action as a report along psychological or scientific lines, with only the facts changed to protect the innocent: 'We know that our friends will excuse the elements of this fiction on this record, which in no way diminishes its psychological validity, and we trust other readers will overlook the limitations imposed by the elements of fact'. It then goes on to address the issue of free-will: 'Some of those who shared in these events hold that free will played no part in them from first to last. With that idea the writers do not agree.'

The problem of free will and determinism presented itself historically to Western thought in the theological guise of reconciling God's foreknowledge, as an omniscient being, with human agency and responsibility – the philosophical task of countering predestination to which St. Augustine dedicated his labours. In the modern era, the prospect of human freedom being foreclosed by blind physical causation (whether forwards or backwards) is no less inescapable, and to this JW Dunne proposed an imaginative if facetious solution – human intervention is comparable to a musician playing on a pre-programmed instrument: 'The intervener, in fact, is analogous, not to a skilled musician composing with the aid of a piano, but to the amateur user of a pianola, whose interferences with the complex performances of that instrument is limited to the changing of one perforated roll for another.' The desire to intervene is not just a theoretical problem but an urgent necessity in the case of Virgila's previsions, for they spell impending disaster, in keeping with the fatal vision of second sight in the Scottish Highlands in Gunn's novel. To be forewarned is to be fore-armed, according to conventional wisdom, but to receive dire warn-ings without any possibility of averting tragedy is a crippling fate – the plight of Maurya in JM Synge's *Riders to the Sea*, and the source of Virgilia's pathologial anxieties in *The Unforeseen*. 'If you had warned her,' Pamela remonstrates to Virgilia in one case, 'it wouldn't have happened; but it *had* to happen; you only foresaw it because it was going to happen.' Virgilia tries to explain that chance also played a part in developments, but Garrett is not convinced: "Aren't you assuming free will, Mrs Wilde? I think we musn't do that." "Not to assume it, would," Virgilia said, hesitantly, "make one's responsibility seem less." "You had no responsibility," Garret declared.'

Not least of the sleights of hand of *The Unforeseen* is the unas-suming but deft plotting through which the conundrum of free will and determinism is negotiated, for as the novel suggests in its own structure, it is through narrative that contingencies of time and place disrupt predetermined outcomes. "'In fact, not a bus, but a tram,'" declares Perry, quoting Maurice Hare's notorious put-down of human delusions of freedom, but so far from running on tram-tracks, history is continually thrown off-course by chance. 'There are accidents; there are wars', notes Dr Franks, and accidents direct the course of the action, often against Virgilia's better judgment. Hence her recalling the mazes sketched by Milton in *Paradise Lost*: "'... fore-knowledge, will, and fate, / Fix'd fate, free will, foreknowledge abso-lute, / And found no end, in wandering mazes lost.'" "'[D]on't let us begin running around these mazes again,'" she pleads later, but it is in fact the unpredictable (at least in a good story) turns of narrative that cut across time's arrow in the end.

Previsions flash up in moments of danger but they are *images*, vivid in their intensity but with no anchoring context or narrative grounding. Images do not speak for themselves: their meanings, as

Roland Barthes has reminded us, are indeterminate and relatively open-ended until secured by a caption, title, or – the issue at stake in *The Unforeseen* – narrative input. 'It had been a mere flash. It remains in my mind like a picture,' Virgilia notes: 'You see, I wanted so much to think that a vision need have no meaning at all'. The mistaken belief that images yield their meaning at a glance encourages a tendency to rush to judgment, and to read more into the picture than is there. The fragmentary and inchoate nature of flash-forwards adds to an inclination to join dots that is not, strictly speaking, warranted by the evidence. The 'Authors' Foreword' alerts us to the possibility that the human world follows not only iron laws of cause and effect (or as we might now say, the logic of the algorithm), but is also open to chance: 'It seems to us that on the narrow track of individual destiny there are forkings and cross-roads where choice is free, and that the whole sequence of things could have been different if a different decision had been taken at this or that critical moment'. Insofar as it makes sense, chance is rendered intelligible through narrative, and in a reflexive passage, Virgilia notes that a flash-forward is like a film-still, devoid of narrative force: 'But looking back, now, I see that moment as static. Have you even been watching a film when a still photograph was suddenly shown? It's like that in my memory; as if even a torrent had ceased to move. But I may be imagining this. I certainly didn't *remark* it the time'. When certain events happen, the vague feeling of being there before but not remarking it at the time prompts the feeling of déjà-vu, noted by Dunne in his experiments with time: 'what about the curious feeling which almost everyone has now and then experienced – that sudden, fleeting, disturbing conviction that something which is happening at that moment *has happened before*?'

To account for swerves and bends of narrative, Macardle looks beyond the supernatural and the natural, superstition and (para) science, to *history*, that which intervenes between mind and the physical world. Proponents of Dunne's work were adamant that the past exerted no influence on previews of the future, just as Dunne himself was determined to keep psychoanalysis at bay, and to set the clock forward in the realm of the unconscious. That history presides over

Macardle's fiction, however, is apparent from the first use of the device of second sight in her short story, 'A Story without an End' (1922), set during the Irish revolution. This recounts how, in a dream, a young woman, Nesta (a name that recurs in *The Unforeseen*), learns that a wounded IRA officer, given refuge by her husband Roger from British forces, would end up executing her husband in a civil war: 'In this dream I was not present myself – I knew in a way I was asleep – there was a mad feeling that if only I could wake – if only I could cry out – but I had not power.' Macardle wrote the story while she was imprisoned as a Republican activist in Mountjoy jail, and its date, 'December, 1922,' reveals that it was written in the shadow of actual executions of Republican prisoners in Mountjoy by the Free State government.

In *The Unforeseen*, superstition is approached not from a laboratory or cognitive angle but in anthropological terms, acknowledging cultural differences and non-western traditions: '[T]here is a vast reservoir of inherited knowledge in all corners of the world,' Perry explains: 'we have dismissed far too much of it as superstition.' Garret further elaborates: 'You see,' he says, 'we have to admit the powers of witch-doctors in Africa and Polynesia and Haiti, haven't we? How can we assume that the western countries were always immune, or even that they're quite immune now? We just mustn't make these assumptions; it's unscientific. Hasn't Perry convinced you of this?'

Inherited knowledge extends to County Wicklow, the location of Virgilia's home but also of stories haunted by the past in Macardle's earlier collection, *Earth-Bound* (1924). In *The Unforeseen*, Garrett and Pamela's visit to the ruins of Glendalough recalls the cover remote hiding places gave to insurgents in 1798 rebellion (and perhaps the more recent war for independence): taking shelter during a storm in a smoke-filled room, Pamela attempts to open a window: '"It would be a pity to let the smoke out: it's historical," Garret remarked. "Pipes of peace that turned into fumes of war. No end of underground meetings were held here in the troubled times."'

The transformation of pipes of peace into pipes of war in late Summer 1938 evokes 'the Prime Minister's return from Munich' described in Macardle's *The Seed Was Kind* (1944), that horrifies the young protagonist of the novel, Diony: to the injunction 'Come on … and drink to "Peace in our Time!"' Diony replies 'wretchedly, "peace at that price?"' As Paul K Saint-Amour has shown in *Tense Future: Modernism, Total War and Encyclopedia Form* (2015), the late interwar period was subject to a sense of trauma from the future as well as the past, as dread and apprehension intensified in the build up to a second World War. 'Life has changed into a timeless succession of shocks,' wrote Theodor W Adorno: 'nothing is more ominous for the future than the fact that … for each of the returning combatants, each shock not inwardly absorbed is a ferment of future destruction.' Total War also applied to non-combatants, as civilians combed the skies, scanned coastlines or scrutinized neighbours, for signs of aerial bombing, invasion, or betrayal. Northern Ireland was clearly in the firing line, but south of the border, Ireland's legal immunity and formal neutrality hardly compensated for its minimal defences and vulnerability to attack from both sides.

This impotence in the face of the 'inevitable,' whether as threat or actual event, echoes the apparent powerlessness of second sight, and it is difficult not to suspect that, as in the case of its earlier Jacobite variant, prevision provided a 'structure of feeling' (in Raymond Williams' phrase) for the anxieties of an age. Whatever about its predictive value, premonitory experiences may act, as Jung suggested, as potential shock-absorbers for the jolts to the system described by Adorno, preparing an individual (or a culture) for grave, imminent danger: 'One would know what to expect,' exclaims Nan: 'One could prepare oneself.' The power to intervene is based on a sense of history and justice in Macardle's fiction, and it is these that prevent the foreclosure of the future. It is striking that as present-day events gathered momentum to impel Donald Trump towards the White House, the powerful film *Arrival* (2016), based on Ted Chiang's science fiction novella *Story of Your Life*, draws again on the resources of second sight, subjecting the future to the indeterminacies of language and interpretation to prevent global powers from hurtling towards self-destruction.

Authors' Foreword

ALTHOUGH THIS STORY is written in the form of fiction there are people who will recognise it as coming very close to fact. They will understand why names have been altered and incidents a little disguised and why the identity of one of the writers has been suppressed. They will realise, too, that we are writing, in the first place, for them.

During the confusions and distresses of that summer, things were done which, judged by ordinary standards, would seem unforgivable; and there were omissions which would appear almost criminal if they were only half understood.

For a full understanding, no brief explanation could be adequate, because the laws which generally govern human conduct do not apply, and because experiences outside the range of common credence are involved. To set out the entire sequence in detail seemed to us the one way open for the achievement of our purpose, which is the vindication of our friend.

What we are attempting, therefore, is, not to explain, but to show *the whole of what happened,* with the motives and emotions that were at work; with the doubts, the questionings and the fears that were conjured up by those dark events.

We are aware that in describing certain occasions of high nervous tension we have left our picture incomplete. That could not be helped. We have had to do our best with the evidence available, and it so happened that the person most intimately concerned in such a situation was rarely able to give a lucid account of it. Perhaps this particular sort of shock and agitation leaves the memory confused. Besides, there are natural reticences which we felt obliged to respect.

We know that our friends will excuse the element of fiction in this record, which in no way diminishes its psychological validity, and we trust that other readers will overlook the limitations imposed by the element of fact. Only the detailed and intimate form of writing permitted to a novelist seemed adequate to convey the truth. This paradox is our apology.

We were perplexed to know where our chronicle should begin: so many incidents, some apparently trivial, formed links in a fettering chain.

Some of those who shared in these events hold that free will played no part in them from first to last. With that idea the writers do not agree. It seems to us that on the narrow track of individual destiny there are forkings and crossroads where choice is free, and that the whole sequence of things would have been different if a different decision had been taken at this or that critical moment. We believe that Virgilia stood at such a point when, after months of solitary brooding that led nowhere, she took action, and went down from her mountain glen to consult a doctor who was an old friend.

That was on a warm and brilliant morning in thirty-eight: Tuesday, the seventh of June.

THE AUTHORS

Contents

The
UNFORESEEN

Chapter I

TUESDAY IN JUNE

DR STACK WAS AMUSED. Her stethoscope still suspended from her neck, she strapped a blood-pressure gauge to her patient's arm. When she had inflated, deflated and removed it and recorded the pressure she pricked Virgilia's left forefinger, sucked blood into a pipette and examined its colour. Virgilia, watching the square, honest face, felt that she was receiving good marks. She felt, also, that she had been foolish to come. All this was not going to help very much.

Next, the doctor tested her reflexes with smart taps from the edge of a firm hand. 'Plenty of kick in you still!' she remarked. With a satisfied grunt she completed the notes on her card.

'Everything normal?' Virgilia asked.

'Quite too beautifully normal, my dear,' Ada Stack replied drily. 'No jam to be earned on you.'

'Yes, I feel very fit,' her patient responded. 'I just thought I'd like you to give me an overhaul.'

'Just thought you'd show off, perhaps?' the doctor retorted. She turned her swivel chair to face Virgilia. It was a comfortable chair; her desk was massive; Ada had everything handsome about her. And why not? She had always been a worker and she had made for herself the solid reputation that she deserved.

'Well,' she went on, 'it's nice to see you, Virgilia. You don't often shed the light of your presence on your old friends. I thought, when England disgorged you, we'd see you occasionally but you've vanished into the blue. How's your mountain solitude suiting you?'

Virgilia smiled at her. 'Need you ask?'

'Not as far as health goes, and looks, anyhow! Not a grey hair! And look at mine!'

'It suits you, Ada: gives you authority – or, perhaps I should say,' Virgilia added, teasing, 'it supports the authority you always possessed.'

'Assumed, you mean! I was a natural-born boss.'

The doctor chuckled. She had no illusions about her manner or her appearance. She looked like Mrs Noah and dressed accordingly, but that did not inhibit her from appreciating the slender, long-limbed grace of her friend.

'Remember,' she asked, 'when I produced you as Desdemona in the Dramatic and tried to make you wear a wig? Your one rebellion! You were dead right. Desdemona was fair.'

'Nice of you to admit it.'

Virgilia was making no move to go. Her glance, wavering away from the doctor's scrutiny, rested on the roses that she had brought, now wilting on a chair. There was a nervous compression of her brows and sensitive lips; uneasiness in her smile. She said abruptly: 'Put them in water.'

Dumping the flowers in her hand-basin, the doctor waited for a clue. There was silence and she did not wait long. She turned to Virgilia, bracing and competent, asking, 'Well? What's up?'

'Nothing that I ought to bother you with, really,' was the apologetic reply. 'But odd things have been happening and I thought there might be a physical cause. And I've been to Cramb, and to an oculist: it isn't my ears or eyes.'

The doctor sat down again and turned alert dark eyes on her friend. 'What's the trouble?'

Virgilia hesitated, finding it difficult to frame her answer. She said, at last, 'My imagination is playing me tricks.'

'It was always lively,' Ada replied with a laugh.

'But it used not to get out of control.'

'Out of control?'

'Yes. I make mistakes, Ada. I imagine I've seen a thing and I haven't: it's not there.'

'Come to cases,' Ada demanded.

Virgilia moved her head distressfully.

'They seem so trivial. I remember them and forget them again. It's like trying to remember dreams. I thought there was snow on Knockree one day in April. It was so surprising I went up to look. There wasn't any. There couldn't have been.'

'What was it?' the doctor enquired. 'Sheep?'

'No. There was nothing white: nothing at all … And you know the feeling that what is happening has happened before?' Virgilia went on. 'I've had that overwhelmingly, lately, several times.'

'If everyone who had that ran to a doctor we'd do fine,' Ada responded. 'Any more instances?'

'Yes. I saw a coal-tit's nest, absolutely distinctly, in a hollow tree near the stream, and I hurried to the cottage for my camera. When I came back there was no nest there.'

Ada chuckled.

'I've always thought bird-watching a mug's occupation,' she remarked. 'You were barking up the wrong tree.'

Virgilia shook her head. Her face had lost some of the colour which had glowed pleasantly under the clear skin. She was taking all this rather seriously.

'Tell me, have you any particular worries just now?' the doctor asked, keeping her tone casual.

'I haven't, really,' her patient replied.

'And are these little mistakes all you have to complain of? I wish I may make no more serious ones!'

'No: I hear noises. I thought at first that the Doyles – they live on the nearest farm – had put up a wind-charger, but they hadn't. There's no other house anywhere near. And it isn't the stream.'

'What sort of a noise?'

'Humming: rhythmic humming that comes and goes.'

'*Tinnitus*, my dear! You're hearing your own circulation and pulses. Many people get it. I've had it myself. It will probably pass off. Don't go about without a hat in the sun.'

'It *is* in my head, then? I thought it was. But that doesn't help to account for the snow and the other things. I've seen shadows, impressions, rather – quick glimpses. It's difficult to put into words. It isn't so much that I see a thing as that I remember having seen it just a fraction of a second ago.'

'You're not, by any chance,' Ada enquired with a twinkle, 'brewing poteen up on your mountain? It's great stuff for making one see things, I believe.'

'It does sound intoxicated, doesn't it?'

Virgilia's laugh was forced. The doctor asked, a little impatiently, 'For how long has this been going on?'

'I began to notice it soon after Christmas,' Virgilia said nervously. 'But of course it may have been going on for a long time. How can I tell? You see, I probably don't always know when something I seem to see is a … is an illusion. That is what is so worrying. I could make such a fool of myself. It could make me do the craziest things.'

'Well, upon my soul!'

Ada leaned back in her chair and regarded her old friend incredulously.

'You, of all women, Virgilia, to come to me with a yarn like this!'

'Ridiculous, isn't it?'

There were patients in the waiting-room. The doctor had not time, really, for this sort of thing. Anyone else would have been sent packing; but Virgilia was no hysterical fool. She had seemed, at College, remarkably equable: had never wanted a fuss made of her, or worried too much, even over exams; even when rehearsing her own play. And now these notions! She was in excellent health; slept well; had a good digestion; her eyes were clear and candid; she moved youthfully, and was living an open-air life. What ailed her, in heaven's name?

'Look here, my dear,' Ada asked thoughtfully, 'how long is it since you planted yourself up there in the wilds of Wicklow?'

'About nine months.'

'H'm! Well, I could understand it as a reaction after Manchester, but I didn't suppose you would go to earth like this. No telephone, I take it?'

'No.'

'Nor a car?'

'That's still a dream.'

'So you're buried alive up there, with, I suppose, one servant?'

'I have Brigid Reenan. You remember her, don't you?'

'The little body who looked after your mother? She must be an antique!'

'She's a worker and a great dear.'

'H'm. And the beauteous daughter? Nan's become a Londoner, I suppose?'

A smile lit Virgilia's eyes.

'She loves London. She says Ireland's the ideal country to be home-sick for! She's doing well, Ada. She has just been given her first commission – illustrations for a new book. It's called *Puck and the Leprechauns*, and she says it's delicious. Puck comes to Ireland as a stowaway on a cattle boat! … She's delighted and so am I.'

Virgilia had relaxed and forgotten her troubles. The doctor reflected. This preoccupation with an only child often had its effect on a woman's nerves; but it was understandable. Ada had whole-heartedly disliked the handsome egoist whom Virgilia married, and had written the briefest possible note of condolence two years ago, when he died. It was a pity that the girl had elected to live in England. There would probably be none of these fancies if Nan were at home.

'How often has she been over since you marooned yourself up there?' Ada asked.

'Once, in October. At Christmas the roof was leaking and I couldn't let her come. I meant to go over in April but spent the money on the cottage instead.'

'She'll come for the summer, I suppose?'

'She's meant to – next month. That's the worry, Ada: I don't want her to come until I've got rid of this silly trouble. I can't have Nan thinking there's anything wrong with me.'

'So for nine months you've been living up there on your own!' There was grim disapprobation in Ada's voice. Virgilia said defensively:

'Yes, why not?'

'Why not!' the doctor repeated explosively. 'Good Lord, woman, what do you do with yourself? I can't see you sitting all day watching birds!'

'I've loads to do, with the cottage and the garden; and I walk and photograph birds and sketch them, and write ...'

'Don't tell me you've become a solemn ornithologist!'

'Goodness, no! I'm doing a bird book for children, that's all. Actually I enjoy the work very much.'

'Do you?'

It was almost a snort. Ada was angry. Virgilia, she thought, was merely putting up a front. She was economising, obviously, for the sake of Nan – living out of the world, going spooky from loneliness, laying an outrageous strain on her nerves. She'd need a neurologist soon if she went on like this. What she wanted was a straight talk from an old pal. She should have it.

'You enjoy it, do you?' she said sceptically. 'Let me tell you, my girl, you're fooling yourself. You liking solitude! You were always the centre of a swarm. A woman of your nervous energy studying birds! No: you are going to extremes, losing your balance – that's as plain as the nose on your face. You would, too! You over-did the dutiful daughter, marrying to please your papa; you over-did the faithful wife, those twenty mortal years in Manchester, and now it's the self-effacing mother stuff.'

Virgilia had flushed slightly and was looking abstracted. That meant she was angry: Ada remembered the signals and thought how much of her youthful looks and ways Virgilia had retained; and now, just as in Alexandra College days, her resentment was broken up by a thought that amused her. Her lips twitched in a one-sided smile.

'The Head Prefect still,' Virgilia retorted, and her friend laughed.

'Sorry, my dear,' Ada said then, 'but I don't see that there's anything I can do, as your doctor, to help you. There doesn't appear to be a thing wrong with your general health. My advice to you is, quit that cottage; join Nan in London or take a flat in Dublin and run around with your friends. In any case, let me see you again soon.'

'Thanks, Ada.'

Virgilia was standing up, her wide linen hat in her hand. She pulled it on absently. Lucky woman, the doctor thought: with her natural waves, she doesn't need to look in a glass. But why was she so strained and tense? After all, she had been given a clean bill ... She didn't seem to like it.

Virgilia turned, her blue eyes looking straight into her friend's.

'Do you think it can be mental?'

The doctor, on the point of rising, sat down again with an exasperated sigh.

'You doze, and have a dream; you mistake a dazzle of sunlight for snow; you see a bird's nest and can't find it again, and you go off the deep end. It's not like you, Virgilia!' She opened her telephone book. 'However, if you've got that notion into your head, you'd best go straight off and have it extracted. I'll give Franks a ring.'

'Franks?'

'BJ Franks. He's gone right to the top. There's no one in Dublin to touch him, nor in Britain either, in my opinion.'

'An alienist?' Virgilia's voice was thin.

'Psychiatrist.' Ada reached for her telephone.

'Wait, Ada! I'll think about it,' Virgilia said.

'Nonsense, my dear! That's exactly what I don't want you to do. A notion like that isn't good company. He probably won't be able to see you for a week or two; he's always full up; but we'll get an appointment.' She began to dial. Virgilia spoke sharply.

'Ada, don't, please!'

Ada paused, the instrument still in her hand.

'You'd like BJ, Virgilia, and I'd just as soon he saw you – unless you'd rather see a neurologist? Your nerves may be a bit more wonky than I imagined – must be, for you to get a notion like that.'

'I'll think about it,' Virgilia said again. She was pale. With a vexed gesture, Ada dropped the telephone back on its stand.

'Oh well, as you like. But in your place I'd think it worth a bit of trouble and expense to have BJ laugh at me for an ass! In case you change your mind – Fitzwilliam Square.'

She scribbled an address on a slip of paper and handed it to Virgilia, who put it carefully in her bag.

'Well,' Ada said, standing up, 'it's nice to see you so flourishing. Look in again the next day you're in town. Get Nan home and have a good time: I expect that's all the prescription you need. Goodbye, old thing, and keep that schoolgirl complexion. And may God give you sense!'

2

SHE HAD MEANT to have tea in town and do a lot of shopping, but the afternoon was too airless and hot. The trees in Merrion Square stood as stiff and still as the houses; Pearse Street smelled of petrol, and soot from the railway, and dust. She bought a Dutch hoe there and caught the four o'clock bus. In an hour and a half she would be home and the air of Glencree would blow these sticky, clinging cobwebs out of her mind. Ada had done nothing to banish them. Ada had too much common sense.

The bus became crowded and stuffy. At St Stephen's Green a group of students swung on, sparring in Irish. At Charlemont Bridge half a dozen small boys, carrying jam-pots on strings, rushed for the front seats, and Mrs Duggan of Enniskerry climbed on, carrying a heavy child. It was the boy who had been in St Ultan's Hospital for three months.

'He's better,' she told Virgilia. She was red and perspiring with excitement and thankfulness. 'Quite better, praise be to God! Look, Mrs Wilde, at the lovely flesh on his arms! He that was like a scaldeen in March.'

It was necessary to chatter, to make enquiries about the rest of the baker's long family and exchange expressions of commiseration over the drought, mixed with thankfulness that showers fell now and then in the hills.

Passing through Dundrum, Virgilia, from ineradicable habit, glanced out in the direction of Ballinteer. Her childhood home had been visible once between the sycamores, but new houses hid it now. It was a relief when at last Enniskerry showed up on its hill, spire and roofs ascending out of the trees. Virgilia called for her bicycle at The Powerscourt Arms, tied the hoe to it with the aid of two eagerly helpful men and a boy, and turned up the byroad that winds to Glencree. Walking up the long, steep hills and wheeling down the short declines, she came to the stretch of road that looks over the bay, and dismounted, as she always did, for love of the view. The flowing range of the hills sinks down, here; rises to the Sugar Loaf's shapely cone; dips and lifts and curves, to where Bray Head lies out on the water like a half-closed hand. That scene had been dazzling at noon; now it lay softly shining and warmly coloured, with hollows and contours appearing where none had shown, the sea and sky holding depth beyond depth of blue. Virgilia remembered those hills and those waters in winter, sombre and ominous. No wonder, she reflected, if Irish people are nervous and variable. Nothing we look at remains long the same. Colours and shapes have no solid existence: they shift and change with weather and wind; and so we look at life through our changing moods.

Her own mood cleared in this fresh and luminous air. It had been a mistake to consult Ada, she told herself as she walked on. There was really no need to consult anybody: these silly attacks of dreaminess probably arose from a lack of concentration on what one was doing at the moment, like those absent-minded habits that Brigid complained of – leaving gates open and doors unlocked. They could be dealt with. I have been confusing two worries, she thought, trying to be analytical and to apply a little knowledge of psychology to her own case. I have felt worried and apprehensive and pretended to myself that it was because of these illusions. It wasn't. It was because of Nan. I'm just an ordinary, fussy, possessive mother who doesn't like her child being out of her sight and imagines that she can't look after herself. There'll probably be a letter tomorrow.

This was Tuesday. Nan's regular Sunday letter had not come, and last week's, and the one before that, had been scrappy, much less gay and amusing than usual, and full of this sculptor who was modelling her head. Carlo. Sicilian, or half Sicilian, it seemed. He was a genius, it seemed. He had lived in Africa and Mexico and Peru and Paris and Rome. He was a poet. He said the most lyrical, flattering things with the detached air of a child. He looked powerful, yet had beautifully sensitive hands. *It's as well we didn't meet*, Nan had written, *when I was young and impressionable. I might have lost either my heart or my head – though not, I think, both at once.*

So Nan was young and impressionable no longer! Virgilia smiled, remembering that remark. Nan was twenty-two and younger than her age. She knew very little of the world, and men scarcely at all. Against that, she was an essentially reasoning creature who prided herself on being a realist. 'Somebody in this family has to be rational,' she had said teasingly to Virgilia when she was fifteen. Nan would do nothing rash and she would make no important decision without first coming home. It was mere weakness to feel anxious about her. But London must be a furnace and Nan had always begun to wilt in a city as soon as warm weather came. Their summers in Dundrum had been an absolute necessity. And it was nearly eight months since they had been together: too long; much, much too long; really absurd.

Shall I risk it? Virgilia asked her conscience. Shall I write and say how lovely the glen is and urge her to come? Perhaps nothing would happen that she would notice. Perhaps Ada was right and it is only that I'm too much alone … No, not yet, she decided: if the child did notice anything it would upset her too much. Because Nan is perceptive, imaginative; she'd understand. She would guess how it feels not to be able to trust one's own senses – the uneasiness; the sense of the world not being steady; the dread … No: not just yet.

Hers was an ailment, Virgilia decided, that she would have to cure for herself. She would keep busy: do manual jobs and keep her mind on them. There was plenty to do – hoeing and watering the garden; painting the bookshelves in the new room; making covers for the sofa and chairs. It might be wise, as soon as this book was finished, to give up bird-watching for a time, and there was only one more chapter to do: 'Lovers of Pools.' She wanted a photograph of a heron for that.

To have made a plan of action cheered her. She was nearly home now. Most of the cottages had been left behind, and there was not a soul on the road. It was curious, how this road suddenly dwindled, although, after passing Derreen Lane and crossing the river, it led out to the south road of Glencree.

This was Derreen Wood on her right; and these, now, were her own trees. Some day, she would have a path cut through the wood here, to save going more than half-way down the hill and then up and back again by the lane. There was a group of Scotch firs, and, between them, a glimpse of the back of her cottage: the chimneys, the tiled roof and ochre-stained walls, soon concealed again by trees. In another minute, Virgilia was pushing her bicycle up the lane that led crookedly to Derreen.

VIRGILIA STILL FELT a slight excitement whenever she turned the bend where her cottage came into view. It had been a cramped, half-derelict place a year ago, with mean little windows: one on either side of the porch and three above. Now it looked wide and ample: a home. She paused in the open gateway between the hollies, looking with pleasure at the new one-storey wing. Brigid called this new room 'the studio' and, since Nan would paint in it, the name would do. The old cottage faced south and the studio, projecting at a right angle to it, had a glass-panelled door and wide windows to take the afternoon light. They were glittering now. To her bedroom on the left of the old porch, Virgilia had added a big bay window, delightful to breakfast in. The window over it was Brigid's, and the two other upstairs windows belonged to Nan's room. The dining-room, on the right of the porch, was still dim and narrow, but that did not matter. The little place was lovely in summer, full of peace and life; the garden murmurous with bees. Virgilia listened. The stream, noisy in winter, made only a cool whispering now, scarcely audible through the calls of birds. The blackbird, king of the garden, was on his perch in the young ash on the lawn, improvising a sweet impudent tune, and a throstle was mimicking him. Virgilia's brown and white collie, who had been drowsing in the porch, suddenly roused himself and came bounding down the path. Shuiler was young, and vociferous in his affections. He charged her, barking and leaping, making it difficult to unfasten the hoe from her bicycle and put both in the shed. When that was done, he followed her through the glass-panelled door into the new room.

Virgilia was tired. She threw down her hat and gloves and pushed her fingers through her hair. An old sofa that had been her mother's stood against the wall opposite the windows. It was wide and inviting; she lay down. Shuiler's clamour would have told Brigid that she had come home. Lying there, she looked across the lawn to the row of larches that were rooted in the steep bank of the stream. They did not hide the slope of Knockree and the folds of the long valley beyond, shining green and gold, with grass and young wheat and furze. Presently, Brigid would come with tea.

There used to be sponge-cake fingers and milk. You soaked the finger in the milk and put it in your mouth quickly before the end dropped off, and swallowing them scarcely hurt a sore throat at all. The white kitten, Fairy, used to curl up under her chin, fluffy and warm and thrilling with joy. In England, childhood had seemed aeons away, a story out of a different world, to be forgotten because memory bred discontent, but here she was herself, the same person as that much-loved and happy child. She could remember without pain. Virgilia closed her eyes and lay quiet and allowed her thoughts to wander idly in time.

3

BRIGID HAD BEEN THERE. It was Brigid who watched her from the kitchen window while she climbed trees and rode the fat pony round the paddock and practised trick-cycling on the lawn. It was Brigid who bathed the cuts and told her there were no bones broken and that the stains on her pinny would wash out. She remembered Brigid grim, dark and silent for only a few weeks in all her life – the weeks before Virgilia's wedding. 'Some high-heeled London lady would suit *him* better,' had been her comment on Henry Wilde.

Brigid had been right. Within one desperate year Virgilia had found that out. Henry, engineer-in-chief to a prominent cotton concern in Manchester, was a man who made efficiency his god. His house had to run like a well-tended machine; to maintain it so was nearly the whole of his wife's duty, and her duty was supposed to be world enough for her. Virgilia had trained herself to do it and had given satisfaction, she believed. Two things had made life tolerable, after the first bitter, rebellious, incredulous year. There was Nan – Nan, with her boundless trust in her mother and her natural gaiety on which no shadow ever lay long. Nan was intelligent: as she grew older she observed her father's moods warily and learned to placate and elude him with childish tact. Virgilia sometimes suspected that Nan felt resentment against him for her sake, but it was never expressed. Then, every year, July brought release: a month of perfect happiness in Dundrum. Nan was the only grandchild and her grandmother gave her extravagant love.

When the child was twelve Virgilia began to talk about sending her to a boarding-school, but Nan refused to leave home. Her father, who expected a good many small services from a daughter, supported her. It was easy for Virgilia to yield: her heart had seemed to stop beating when she tried to think of life without Nan.

She faced the idea later, when Nan left school. She wanted her daughter to become independent of her father: to train for a career. Rather suddenly the girl proclaimed her own choice. 'It's absolutely irrevocable,' she declared. She had been studying at the School of Art and had discovered that painting mattered more to her than anything else – even than remaining with her mother. Her teachers encouraged her and Nan's ambition spread wings. She wanted, she told Virgilia, to work 'violently': to live the life of an art student with no thought or care for anything else. It was not possible, living at home.

'You are my Big Temptation, Mummie,' she confessed gracefully. 'I know how lost and lonely I'll feel without you, but to London I must go.'

Permission was categorically refused. It was then that Virgilia began to write some of the stories which Nan had revelled in as a child and to put the proceeds into a secret fund. She was projecting an act of open rebellion. It was never necessary. When Nan was nineteen her father fell ill. He refused to listen to the doctor who said that an operation was necessary, became more stubborn when his wife urged him to submit to it in good time, and died of peritonitis after an emergency operation in a nursing-home. That was in July 'thirty-six.

Virgilia had had to plan a new life, and there were financial problems to be faced. Her husband had earned a good income, but he had spent it. Nan was all eagerness to start work in London. There was enough to maintain her there as a student but not enough to give two women a London home and any sort of comfort at all. They went to London together, nevertheless. Virgilia told her daughter the truth: she said, 'We'll regard your training as an investment and spend capital on it for a few years. We'll have to be very careful. I'm sorry,' she added, with a little sigh:

'I wanted you to have fun.'

'I don't want fun; I want heavenly rapture; and that's what I'm going to have,' Nan replied.

London, with lodgings in Ebury Street, classes at Westminster, new friends, freedom and the longed-for prospect open before her, was Elysium to Nan. She was soon a busy and popular bachelor girl. Presently she was refusing invitations and curbing her adventurous spirit for fear of leaving her mother too much alone. Virgilia had just one function: to give advice. Nan wanted her mother's support and approval continually. It was time, Virgilia decided, for the fledgling to leave the nest. Besides, her own life was becoming narrow and sterile. She found writing in cramped lodgings impossible. If this went on she would lose her spirits and begin to depend on Nan.

Her decision was taken at Christmas, when they went to Dundrum. She realised then that her mother was a very lonely old woman with a weakening heart that could not last long. Soon after they returned to Ebury Street she said to her daughter, 'Darling, I have decided to let you stay in London without me. I'm going back to look after Gran.'

'I knew this would happen,' Nan said, her eyes stretched wide to keep tears away. She said, 'Dublin's an awfully long way off,' but immediately, reasonable as always, admitted: 'I do see that I can't expect to have things both ways. And Gran needs you. And it is your vocation, running a country home. Here you haven't any *real* things to do. You haven't been looking a bit well. And it won't be for always. And I've been a greedy egoistical pig – '

Nan arranged to share rooms with a fellow student, Freda Lennox; worked out a meticulous budget and assured her mother that, until she was earning, a quite small allowance would see her through. Before Virgilia left, Nan said something else. She told her, very gravely, one evening, that she realised that she would never be a great and famous artist.

'I'm not going to paint immortal masterpieces, Mummie. Do you mind?'

'Only as much as you do,' Virgilia replied.

'As long as I can paint well enough to feel justified in going on I don't mind anything much,' Nan assured her. 'But there's one thing definite,' she declared: 'I'm not going to spend my time "waiting for the spark from heaven to fall." I think I'll take up book illustration; would you approve?'

'I'd love it. We'd do a book together some day,' Virgilia said. She was feeling happy about Nan when, in February, she returned to her Irish home.

OLD MRS MORROW'S HEART had been slowly failing. She settled into a tranquil invalid life, was able to enjoy a visit from Nan at Easter and, one night in May, died in her sleep.

Virgilia had not imagined that she would feel so desolate. She was forty-two, full of unspent energy and vividly interested in life; this sense of having come to an end of things was absurd. Nan needed her, though not in London, and needed a home. They both needed a home in Ireland, however simple. Well, that could be managed. The house in Dundrum would have to be sold. It was too old and inconvenient to bring in much, but there would be enough to buy a cottage with a garden where one would be able to live on very little and grow vegetables and fruit.

There was another person who needed a home. Brigid was too old to seek a place with strangers and it scalded her heart to think of ending her days as a half-welcome guest in the house of her married niece in Ardee. 'What will I be,' she said to Virgilia idly, 'but a shadow beside their hearth?' Virgilia said, 'I want you with me: I want you always,' and saw contentment settle on Brigid's face.

There was one place where poverty would never be sordid; where no day or night would be without beauty – the hills. To discover a cottage, however, was difficult. It was only jerry-built bungalows or ruinous little hovels buried in nettles that were easy to find. Virgilia had explored Glendhu and Glencullen, Bohernabreena and nearly all the long five miles of Glencree when, one hot midsummer Sunday, Mrs Doyle, who lived on the south Glencree road, told her about Derreen.

She found a thick-walled cottage crouched under an oak wood on the southward slope of a hill. It had a room on either side of the door and three attics upstairs. There was a well from which water was pumped into a tank. The place was neglected, almost dilapidated, for the old couple who lived in it were past work, but the sum they asked for the freehold was so small that one would be able to have repairs done and add rooms.

Virgilia breathed the air, fresh and fragrant from sea and bog; looked over the sun-flooded valley and splendid hills; heard the birds and the bees. She smelled the honeysuckle that garlanded the hedges, and visited the stream that travelled in little cataracts to the river below.

It was necessary to be practical. With the cottage, one would own a portion of the woodland – such a wood as song-birds love best, with water, and tall trees, and thick undergrowth; and the "thistle field' between the stream and the farm-track below, and the tilled field beyond that, leased to Doyle now, and sown with oats. She wished Nan were with her, because it was important to be realistic about this and she was under a spell. She went back to talk to Brigid and think it over and came out within a week, with a lawyer, and bought Derreen.

The old couple left at once and, in September, when the house in Dundrum and most of its furniture had been sold, Virgilia and Brigid moved in and set to work. Nan wrote, protesting. Although she had delighted in the glen and the wood, seen in their midsummer beauty, she thought the place no cold-weather abode. 'You *can't* live there in the winter,' she wrote, '*please* don't try.'

'I'm not going to be a fair-weather country-woman,' was her mother's retort.

But the winter had been grim. There were times when Virgilia would have abandoned the place and fled to London had it not been for the impossibility of leaving the cottage shut up to moulder or of leaving Brigid in it alone. The incessant labour of both women was needed merely to keep up the supply of fuel, food and water and keep the house warm and dry. Virgilia did not mind that, but she wondered whether she could face, another year, the sense of vast surrounding solitude that came with the short days and the snow.

Courage returned with the spring; its enchantments were never-ending in the glen; and in March the builders started work. Upstairs, two rooms were knocked into one; downstairs, a bathroom was built out at the back and a bay added to Virgilia's room. Finally, the new wing was built. It included a square kitchen and a narrow dark-room, set against the east gable of the cottage, as well as the studio, which stood out like a small house on its own.

Nan had been told a good deal about the improvements, but the studio was to be a surprise.

She would like it, her mother thought. It was a good room to work in and good to rest in, like this, looking out at the changing sky.

Would Nan be happy and lucky at Derreen? Would she some-times stay the whole summer long? No place could be more peaceful. Now, in the late June afternoon, there were the hum of insects, the whisper of water and the lazy soliloquies of the birds; no other sound except one that Virgilia loved and listened to with deep contentment: that strange, half-heard, rhythmical pulsing which goes on and on in the earth and air and water, wherever nature is free and alive.

BRIGID HAD NOT EXPECTED her mistress for another hour. This, now, meant that she had come home without her tea.

Brigid filled the tin kettle and lit the oil stove under it. The iron kettle was steaming away on the crane over the fire, but Brigid knew better than to make tea with dead-boiled water, the way young Eileen would do.

Brigid was no more than sixty-five years of age, if as much, and she felt well able to run this little place. She would have liked to keep the work in her own hands, but rheumatism paid her out if she scrubbed or did too much washing, so she had had to give in to letting Eileen, the Doyles' eldest girl, come over to help most mornings and to wash on Tuesday afternoons. Eileen wasn't a bad little worker, though quick-tempered, like all red-heads, and a chatterer. She had the washing hung out now and was down at the stream pulling watercress.

Tired, the mistress should be, Brigid reflected while she beat up an egg with milk and put slices of bread to soak in it. There was a bit of nourishment in French toast. It should be dusty and hot down in the city. 'Twas a pity she'd had to go. She wasn't entirely herself, latterly: dreamy, sort of, and forgetful, and making mistakes.

Brigid fried the bread, sprinkled sugar on it, put it in a muffin dish, made the tea and carried the tray to the studio. Mrs Wilde was at the open door staring out; she did not look round or answer Brigid when she spoke. She was calling out in a startled voice, 'Who is it? Who's there?'

Brigid set the tray down carefully and then crossed to the door. The garden was empty; there was no one in sight.

'Ma'am, dear,' she asked quietly, 'what did you see?'

'A man,' was the answer. 'He must have been in the doorway – his shadow fell right across the floor.'

Brigid stepped out to the gate and looked down the lane. She closed the gate carefully and came back. 'There's not a soul in it,' she said. She added, under her breath, 'Not a living soul,' and made a quick movement with her right hand.

Virgilia sat on the sofa and lifted the teapot, but her hand was shaking and she put it down. Brigid came over, poured the tea out and put in the cream. For a moment neither spoke, then Virgilia asked, 'Brigid, why did you say that? And why did you make the sign of the cross?'

'Take your tea now: you need it,' Brigid said. 'It was only,' she went on tranquilly, 'that I was thinking there are more souls in it, maybe, than we see.'

Virgilia looked at her. There were scores of wrinkles on the old woman's face, but her brown eyes were quiet and clear. Virgilia asked her, 'Do you think I'm seeing ghosts?'

Uncovering the dish, Brigid answered, 'Well, now, I do be wondering, to tell you the truth.'

Virgilia shook her head.

'I'm certain that's not so.'

'Ah, well,' came the easy response, 'who knows?'

After a while, her mistress said in a low voice:

'Brigid, tell me honestly: does anything make you think that I may be? Anything besides the shadow just now?'

'Well, if you'll excuse me saying so, you have the look of it, time and again.'

'The look of it?'

'Aye: the wide blue look in your eyes. Three or four times I noticed you staring at what I couldn't see. And there's another thing ...'

Brigid hesitated. Her mistress was not eating and she looked in need of her food. I shouldn't have said it, Brigid thought, although you'd never expect her to be scared.

'Another thing?' Virgilia asked.

'Do you mind the time you told me you heard music below in the thistle field? Well,' Brigid said gently, ''tis my belief there was nobody there.' A vexatious thought crossed her mind. 'By the same token –' she began, but Virgilia interrupted:

'This place can't be haunted! Perhaps some places are – graveyards and ancient ruins: I've never known what to believe – but not this sunny hill!'

'And why wouldn't it be?' Brigid replied serenely.

'You think I ought not to mind if it is?'

'Why wouldn't it be?' Brigid repeated. She was gazing out at the cloudless, yellowing, western sky and the valley bathed in radiance under it. 'If I was in heaven itself, I think I'd be asking a day out, an odd time, to be visiting Glencree in June.'

'This place isn't haunted,' Virgilia said stubbornly. 'I'm not seeing ghosts.'

'What harm if you are? ... By the same token,' Brigid went on with displeasure, 'the tinkers are in Glencullen, I hear – the Vaughan lot that were here when we came. They'll be coming here next, I suppose; settling in for two or three weeks, with their mules and their asses and all, and no with-or by-your-leave.'

'That doesn't matter,' Virgilia said.

'Doesn't it? Faith, they'll do a sight more harm than the ghosts! Hacking wood from our trees and trampling the land and forever washing their things in the stream!'

'They're welcome as long as they don't scare the birds.'

'Och,' Brigid exclaimed resignedly, 'you'd give away the light out of your eyes!'

Leaving the room, she turned back to say, 'But as to seeing shadows or whatever they may be, I'd not let on to Eileen if I was you.'

She hurried to the kitchen to see that that same Eileen was not wasting her time.

Eileen was at the sink, washing the cress. Brigid began to make mayonnaise. Mayonnaise needed attention and she wished Eileen wouldn't chatter while the oil was going in drop by drop.

'There was no letter, this morning, was there? Isn't that queer? Miss Nan does be so regular writing. I wonder what is she taken up with? I bet you 'tis some young man. Wouldn't I give my two eyes to be at her wedding! Gorgeous, she'd look, with the airy way she does carry her head.'

Brigid ignored her nonsense, went to the studio for the tray and stopped to help her mistress cut a length from the stuff she was using to cover the chairs. Mrs Wilde looked all right again, and was measuring and cutting as carefully as if she had no other care in the world. A lovely tweed it was, the colour of strawberries when they're ripe. Brigid took the tray to the kitchen and stepped out to the back garden to pull chives, telling Eileen to wash up and go home.

She ought not to have trusted her. She should never have let that heedless gawm handle the Belleek cup. She let it slip from her fingers and smash to smithereens in the sink. Her excuse was the mistress had startled her, calling sharply. It was an angry call, like nothing heard in that cottage since they came there: 'Eileen, Eileen! What are you doing? Come here at once!'

Virgilia was standing in the little hall, the front door open behind her.

'Where is it?' she asked, astonished, when the girl appeared. 'What have you done with it? Don't you know a telegram ought to be brought at once?'

Bewilderment made the girl burst into tears and in a minute Brigid was on the scene, fragments of the cup in her hand. Her distress about the cup prevented her, at first, from comprehending of what Eileen was accused. Then she supported her. There had been no telegram. No boy had given Eileen anything. Eileen hadn't been out in the front at all. She hadn't put her things on.

Brigid stopped abruptly, looked hard at her mistress, then turned on the girl harshly, ordering her to put them on now, and stop bawling and go home.

Eileen ran back to the kitchen and Brigid shut the door after her.

'I saw it,' Virgilia said.

She went into her bedroom and sat on the bed. Brigid followed her.

'Ma'am, dear, what did you see?'

'They were there, in the gateway, between the hollies. Eileen took it out of his hand. It was Eileen: she had her red jacket and cap on. I saw the envelope in her hand.'

Brigid shook her head.

'None of that happened,' she said.

Staring out at the gate, Virgilia said under her breath, 'I was too close to make a mistake.'

'Look, ma'am,' Brigid suggested, 'you dreamed it: you fell asleep.'

'I was standing at the chair, pinning the stuff; I had pins between my lips.' Virgilia began to laugh. 'Whoever heard of the ghost of a telegram?'

The sound of her laughter was ugly. She stopped. Eileen ran past the window, her freckled face pink from crying. She wore her crimson jacket and scarlet tam. She was hurrying as though frightened; she fumbled at the latch before she got the gate open, banged it after her and ran out of sight down the lane. Virgilia asked, 'Who shut the gate?'

'I shut it,' Brigid answered, 'when you told me that … when I brought in your tea.'

'It was open,' Virgilia said. She was frowning. She said, 'The hollies don't look the same.'

A sick pallor had come to her face.

'What at all can I do for you?' Brigid murmured. 'What can I do?'

'Leave me alone for a little.'

Reluctantly, Brigid went out to the garden. She got secateurs from the shed and busied herself cutting dead-heads off the rose bushes. She did not want to be out of call. Presently, her mistress tapped at the studio window; she was writing inside. She said, when Brigid went in, 'I want this letter to go at once.'

No post left the glen, nor Enniskerry, either, so late. She surely knew that? She had a lost, helpless look.

'It's for Fitzwilliam Square,' she said.

Brigid searched her mind: What could they do?

'Look,' she said, 'I'll take it to Phil Doyle. I'll ask him to take the trap in to Enniskerry with it and give it to the busman to post in Dublin. Phil's always thankful for an excuse to go in. He's courting Annie Cullen.'

She took the letter. It twisted her heart to see the change in her mistress's face, to hear the shake in her voice and see her trying to smile.

'You're such a comfort to me, Brigid,' she said.

Chapter II

THURSDAY

NAN WAS GETTING a headache. The room was stuffy and smelly and hot. Carlo had shut the windows to keep out the clatter from the King's Road, but they did not keep it out and they kept in the heat, and the smoke of his poisonous cigarettes.

Nan wanted a cigarette herself, and a rest; also something to eat. She must have been sitting like this, looking serene and queenly, for hours. Carlo wouldn't notice. He was working obliviously. She waited for a chance to glance at her watch. Of course he had no clock in his room. What had Carlo to do with time? And if you mentioned the time, if you showed the slightest trace of restlessness, he would be thrown off his stroke, blaze into one of his wild, childish, tearful rages, and be good for nothing all day.

Past three! No wonder she felt hungry and stiff. She would give him ten more minutes and then strike. And she wouldn't come back again. It was senseless to keep this up. The head was finished: it had been finished last week. Billy had said so. He had said, 'For God's sake, Carlo, leave it alone. It's alive and you'll kill it.' Freda had agreed.

They were three to one, but Carlo could not or would not stop. As to his motive, two of the three were agreed.

Was Carlo in love with her? Was Carlo a genius? Were Carlo's yarns true? Had he really been born in Sicily and lived in Mexico and been made a member of an Indian tribe? Did he believe the outrageous witch-doctor stories that he told? Were those rages of his as uncontrollable as they seemed? Where had he been all April? ... It was absolutely ridiculous, the way Billy and Freda and their friends bothered and talked about Carlo. It was the tantalising mixture in him of a rather pathetic helplessness with real power. She herself had been the biggest fool of the lot. What a way to be spending these gorgeous June afternoons! Neglecting her own job; neglecting to write to her mother. She ought to have written on Sunday and this was Thursday. Fortunately, her mother never worried: she was too happy with her flowers and birds. It was pleasant to think about her in green, airy Glencree in weather like this.

'Hold that! Oh, go on smiling that soft, secret, dreaming smile!' Carlo pleaded, making her giggle.

He's getting me mixed up with Mona Lisa, she thought. He'll probably discover he's a reincarnation of Leonardo. He's quite daft, but very enjoyable.

'The youngest angel,' she heard him murmuring. '... fonder of earth than of heaven; loving us sinners better than the souls in bliss.'

What charming things he says, she reflected, and what hideous objects he keeps in his room. She looked at his devil masks and African carvings and the green geometrical faces that Carlo had done in Rome. 'Beauty repelled me,' he had said to her, 'until I met you.' He was always saying things that one remembered, and he always had clay under his nails.

'What is happening?' he said now, in a low tone, stepping back, and then, in mounting excitement, 'Nan, Nan, do you know who she is?'

He seized a little wooden tool and did something with a light, swift touch to the outer corner of each eye.

'I hope she is Anna Wilde,' his model replied.

'Come and look.'

Nan came down and stood frowning at the bust, perplexed.

'What have you done?'

'Don't you see?' Carlo went on. There was rapture in his voice, adoration in his gaze fixed on the head. 'The long throat, delicate as a child's; the lifted chin; the line of the jaw; the sweet, *thinking* lips; the just perceptible tilt of the nose! Everything! Everything except the eyes, and I'll get that lift …'

'You've done something queer with the eyes,' Nan said. 'They're not mine.'

'The new Nefertiti,' he murmured. 'Oh, don't you see?'

'Nefertiti!' Nan exclaimed. 'Yes, I do. How extraordinary!'

'She is Nefertiti,' he repeated. 'I adored her in ancient Egypt and she broke my heart.'

'That's a thrilling compliment, Carlo, but you can't put my name to it now.'

'Oh, yes, I will. It's you. It's you as I want you to be.'

'It's quite unlike me.' Nan was feeling angry.

'Is it, Nan?'

Relapsing from his infatuated mood suddenly, Carlo focused his eyes on her face. He had very dark eyes; the pupils looked very large; his dark hair was swept back from his forehead; his nervous lips and eyebrows and nostrils all expressed his excitable, vehement feelings: they revealed consternation, followed by remorse and despair.

'You're right,' he exclaimed desolately. 'I have ruined it. It was almost perfection. It was you and it will never be you again. Your soul has gone out of it.'

Nan was furious.

'Billy told you!' she cried. 'So did Freda and so did I. You ought to have let it alone. You've been fooling and messing it up and wasting my time. I gave you all these sittings because you said it was going to make your name for you, but you've made a fool me and yourself. This is the end of it, Carlo. I'm not coming again.'

'Oh, yes, you are.'

The words came quietly. One of his extraordinary transformations had come over Carlo: he was standing quite still, taut and muscular like a statue in bronze.

'I'm not,' Nan repeated. It was she who was strident and nervous now. She felt her own brittleness and his height. She understood now why Billy and Freda had been calling for her every afternoon.

'Go back to the throne!' There was implacable insistence in his voice.

'I won't, Carlo.'

'Go back.'

He had grown taller: quite definitely he had grown taller; but she was not afraid of him. If he thought he could frighten her he had made a mistake.

'Why do you think you can talk to me like that, Carlo? I think you must be out of your mind!'

'Yes? I've suspected that you thought that.'

He spoke slowly. His nostrils were flaring and pinching, out and in. 'That's what you and your clever friends say about me, is it?' he said tensely. 'I'm a crazy foreigner; a hysterical Latin? You probably call me a "wop".'

'That's insulting and absurd.'

'Insulting? It is you who insult me.'

'What are you talking about?'

'You come here, day after day …'

'Because you implored me to!'

'Because you liked me, you little hypocrite! Because you were bored with your Billies and Fredas! And what did you imagine? That you could have a nice game with me? Cat-and-mouse? A little, just a very little, bit of excitement and then, "thank you so much and good-bye"? Perhaps you imagined that I am made of wet clay?'

'What on earth do you mean?'

He began to tell her; he was telling her, quite elaborately, for some minutes. Nan became so angry that she could find no words to express her rage and contempt.

During that speechless moment Carlo snatched a rag from the table and tore it across. The rending sound brought Nan to her senses. She knew that she must use her wits. She looked round. Her hat and bag were on a chair in the far corner of the room; her white shawl hung over an arm of the throne; she would have to go without them. Billy would collect them for her afterwards.

'So you won't go back?' Carlo asked, coming towards her.

She managed to laugh.

'If you want me to sit again,' she said lightly, 'you'll have to give me something to eat.'

'Ah!'

It was an exclamation of triumph. Now he was satisfied. He moved with grace and swiftness to his cupboard, saying, 'We'll have a drink.'

The door was behind her; Carlo's cupboard was in the opposite wall. While he was selecting a bottle Nan slipped to the door, opened it and ran. She sped down three flights of uncarpeted stairs and out into the street. Dodging the traffic, while a taxi driver swore at her, she crossed the road. She thought she heard her name called but did not look back. Half laughing, but with her heart thumping uncomfortably, she walked towards Oakley Street.

2

SHE NEEDED A REST after that and thought gratefully of her bed-sitting-room, fragrant with white pinks which had come that morning from Derreen. With her own pictures and cushions and rugs in it, the room was nice. But she missed Freda. Freda, until her marriage at Easter, had rented a bedroom in the same house and Nan's had served as a sitting-room for them both. Freda had a key still and often came in, but always in a hurry to join Billy somewhere. London wasn't so much fun, Nan had discovered, when you lived alone.

She was pleased to find her door open and Freda sprawled on the divan, smoking and reading a magazine.

Freda regarded Nan with a quizzical grin.

'So you're all in one piece? I'm relieved. Are you aware that you said you'd meet us at The Blue Cockatoo for lunch?'

Nan sank into a chair.

'Oh, I'm sorry. I thought that was tomorrow!'

'Billy's gone on a bus to retrieve you. Our theory was that Carlo had done you in.'

'I'm through with Carlo.'

'So you think!'

'I definitely am.'

'What happened?'

Nan gave her a rather casual version of their clash. Freda, however, looked thoughtful, as if reading between the lines. She was older than Nan and rather wise in a light-hearted way.

'You came off lucky, considering,' was her comment.

She sat up and rubbed out her cigarette.

'My lamb, we'd decided it's time to warn you. Carlo's batty about you, in his own exorbitant way. We'd decided you were not to sit for him again. Sorry we left things a bit late.'

Nan replied soberly, 'You and Billy have been trumps.'

'It *would* happen the day we didn't turn up,' Freda said. 'For any sake, now, keep out of his way.'

'There's the Five Arts Dance.'

'And your breath-taking new dress? Cancel it.'

'They're copying the model for me; I had a fitting; I can't. Besides, I like it.'

'Cut the dance, my child; and Mac's party; and the life class. In fact, cut Carlo. To be frank, lass, if I were you, with a perfectly good mother and home to go to, I'd cut and run.'

'Away, vile temptress!'

'Why don't you?'

'My beloved job, Freda. Those illustrations.'

'How are they coming along?'

Nan looked at her, reluctant to confess the truth. Billy had secured this commission for Nan, who was, after all, a beginner. The publisher was a friend of his. On every account, she absolutely had to make good.

'Not so well,' she admitted. 'I've dried up. I can't get the leprechauns.'

'Funny. They're what Billy thought you'd do specially well.'

'They come out like those ghastly figures they sell for gardens.'

'What a blight!'

'Everything's a blight.'

Nan jerked impatiently in her student chair. She felt hot and sticky and tired and jarred. Her fastidious spirit was offended. It had been her own fault. She utterly despised the type of girl who lost her head – 'fell for a man' exactly and odiously expressed it – because he was 'attractive' and flattered her. It was so cheap. And it had very nearly happened to her. She had been led into doing an imbecile thing. She had relied on the poise and judgment she supposed herself to possess and had got into a grubby, common sort of jam, and been driven to extricate herself by a trick.

'It's the heat, partly,' Freda said.

'The heat,' Nan agreed with a sigh; 'and the King's Road; and the brown, mangy grass in the parks. Everything's so stale and orange-peely and fish-and-chippy! You think a person's a genius and he's bogus. You think you're helping and you find you're a fool. Life's a bargain basement, that's what it is. And there are no leprechauns in Battersea Park.'

Freda lit another cigarette.

'Why on earth hang on here, you mutt?' she demanded. 'You'd probably work much better at home.'

'I wouldn't. It's a dim little cottage. I'd be out in the sun all day. The glen's irresistible. Besides, I've got tied up with too many things.'

'What are they? Let's see!'

Enumerated, they did not seem so entangling. Freda would see to having the dress sent on; Billy's sister, who loathed the club she was in, would certainly take on the room for a month or two. The only thing of any importance was an interview with the publisher next week. And it was June. And you couldn't paint Irish colours from memory; and the hills would be heavenly; and she had been away from her mother much, much too long.

Having given way to temptation, Nan let her heart and mind fly off the course she had set. The wood and the running stream; wild flowers and mountain breezes; her mother – the world of love and sweetness that was her mother's – rapt her away. Nan's thoughts were far off when Billy came tearing upstairs and burst into the room.

He was carrying her hat and bag. He was hot and untidy; there was clay on the knees of his trousers and on his hands. 'What happened?' he asked, trying to conceal his relief.

Nan hesitated; Freda blew smoke into the air with a gesture and replied:

'The gentleman was rude; the lady, offended, gathered up her skirts and departed abruptly.'

Billy asked, 'Was there an accident while you were there?'

'No, why?' Nan asked, frightened. 'What's wrong?'

'I don't know. I didn't see Carlo. He's gone. The place was open and everything's messed about. And – I'm sorry, Nan; it's too bad: the bust is busted; it's smashed on the floor.'

Freda exclaimed in anger, Nan in distress.

'It looked,' he said soberly, 'as if it had been beaten up.' There was a silence such as might have followed the news of a death. Tears sprang to Nan's eyes. Carlo had put everything he had into that head. He had loved it. He would be heart-broken. Her trick had upset him too much.

'Poor Carlo,' she said shakily.

Freda, brisk and grim, said, 'It's as well you got away when you did.'

Billy, who was as kind as he was big and clumsy, said, 'You did your best for him, Nan. We've all done our best. He's the sort that's born to wreck everything round him; and it's just too bad, because there's a wiggly little streak of genius there. But fretting over Carlo's a waste of time … Look, Anna Wilde; it's past four o'clock. You let us down about lunch. Do you think you could give us some tea?'

3

DR FRANKS SAID QUIETLY, 'Try to relax now.'

Virgilia was in a deep chair, sitting forward, her hands poised on its arms, rather tense.

Two hours of being examined and questioned and cross-questioned! It had been tiring – and after two such nights. But it was all right: there had been weight and conviction in his voice as he said that her case was not one for a psychiatrist. Yes: it must be all right. For nearly two days and nights she had been in doubt.

The doctor offered her a cigarette, lit it for her and smoked one himself, while he formulated his letter to Dr Stack. The phrasing seemed to cause him a great deal of thought, but he sat in his armchair writing with a fountain pen, so much at ease that Virgilia's own muscles slackened and she sat back.

The sense of being held and crushed by a great heavy hand would be gone presently, she supposed, and she would be able to forget her heart, which, since Tuesday evening, had been obtrusive. What was Dr Franks writing? Not simply what he had told her: that would not require such scrupulous care. She was struck by the contrast of bodily ease and mental stress which Dr Franks presented. He was impressive. One felt his ability. The structure of his head suggested a powerful intellect, while the ridged brow, the taut cheeks with deep creases from nostril to mouth and the compressed lips told of will. There was a streak of grey in his hair. You would say he was a man in the middle fifties, she thought, but for the vigour of his movements and the force in his eyes … He glanced up at her, asking in a leisurely tone, 'What do you think of that chair?'

Relaxed against the cushioned back, she replied, 'It is the most sympathetic chair I have ever met.'

One felt fluid, like water arrived at its own level. The chair absorbed one into its own assurance, as did the pleasant room, which bore no sign of medical practice about it. The high window, with its curtains of fine net, framed a laburnum and a purple lilac and a red chestnut, all in bloom, behind the railings of the square.

The doctor looked up.

'You may like to hear what I have written.'

He read to her his account of the examination, with a remarkable summary of Virgilia's description of her visions. 'Hallucinations' was the word he used. She disliked it, although he had explained to her that it did not 'preclude a basis of actuality' for all that she had believed herself to have seen. He read his conclusions slowly:

'Apart from these experiences, of which I attempt no explanation, the mental condition appears wholly normal. I find no evidence of either functional disturbance or disease: no psychosis. The nervous system appears sound.'

Replacing his pen in his pocket, the doctor looked at her.

'Oh, thank you,' Virgilia exclaimed, and laughed. It was such a childish thing to say.

A slow smile came to his face.

'You know, Mrs Wilde,' he said thoughtfully, 'you are to be congratulated on an uncommonly equable temperament. These experiences would have made many people a little hysterical. You have not allowed that to happen, and I can see that you won't.'

He's warning me, she thought. He knows it *may* happen. So do I.

'It did for a moment,' she reminded him, 'the day before yesterday. I upset that girl. It might have been my daughter … She would have thought … It seems to me that, any day, I may make some really serious blunder. That is what worries me still – greatly though you have relieved my mind.'

'Naturally, you are worried.'

He was waiting. Virgilia went on:

'Where can they come from, these – hallucinations, if not out of my own brain? What am I to think of them?'

He shook his head slowly. 'That is where I must fail you. The whole thing is outside my province and beyond my experience. I can only repeat that, happily, yours is not a case for a psychiatrist. I have great pleasure in refusing to advise you, Mrs Wilde.'

Bleak disappointment fell on Virgilia. It had been such an effort to bring herself to the point of consulting doctors about this, and they had proved unable to help. She exclaimed involuntarily, 'Where *can* I go for advice?'

Dr Franks answered, 'I don't know.' He had an expressive voice. He sounded so baffled that Virgilia regretted her question and tried to speak lightly.

'Perhaps my old cook's diagnosis is the right one. She declares that I'm seeing ghosts!'

'Absurd.'

'You don't believe in them?'

'Of course not.'

It seemed that there was no more that Dr Franks could do. Virgilia supposed that she ought to go. There was no clock to be seen. She looked at her watch. It was half-past three.

'Don't hurry away. I have no other appointment just yet,' the doctor said.

She smiled at him.

'It was good of you to see me at such short notice. I can't express my relief.'

He gave her an answering smile.

'Your phrasing was very controlled, very far from being importunate, but your handwriting betrayed distress.'

'I am glad it did. Thank you.'

'No,' he said gravely, reverting to her question. 'I do not believe in ghosts, but I am becoming increasingly aware that there are forms of subjective experience that we do not as yet comprehend.'

'Subjective?' Virgilia echoed. 'I see a whole scene, with people and trees and things – and it isn't there. I see a man's shadow, and no one is casting it. And there is no cause outside my mind: yet ...'

The doctor checked her.

'Ah, no! That is begging the question. *Is* there some cause? In memory, for example; in subconscious memory, perhaps?'

'I never saw Eileen Doyle receiving a telegram.'

'You are sure of that?'

'Quite sure. And I never saw a nest in that tree. But I *had*, certainly, seen snow on Knockree in December; and the shadow ... I don't *remember* seeing one on that floor, and the room was only finished a week ago, but I *might* have seen it cast by one of the workmen, without consciously noticing it.'

'So, even if memory accounts for some of these hallucinations, it cannot account for all?'

'Not possibly.'

'I wonder whether ...'

The doctor checked himself and rose as if he had thrown off a weight: as if his responsibility in the matter had come to an end. He began to move about the room, half drawing books from the shelves and pushing them in again; asking her whether she had read much psychology; studied dreams at all. 'One is tempted to theorise,' he said, 'but I must not.' He smiled; his rather care-worn face became wreathed in smiles and he said, 'Though young Perry, my son, would have an elaborate explanation, no doubt! He maintains that we old stick-in-the-muds have a whole new science to learn.'

'Is your son in practice?'

'Not yet. He has just come back from a postgraduate course in the United States. He has brought back some astounding theories, I must say. I am glad he is taking up surgery, not my line! He'd scare his patients. But I begin to wonder whether there may be more in his ideas than I thought. Have you heard of Rhine's experiments in telepathy, Mrs Wilde?'

'Yes. I want to read his book. I wondered whether telepathy could account for all this. But how could it? … Could it, do you think?'

'I am afraid, you know, that I must not express an opinion on that.'

'I quite understand.'

She waited, hopeful, nevertheless.

The doctor stood frowning. 'There must be someone who could advise you,' he said.

Virgilia's mind was once more revolving the notion of telepathy as an explanation. She was trying to reflect in sequence on each remembered vision, recalling all the circumstances, but her mind was not clear enough: one memory merged into another. She was too comfortable in that armchair – so comfortable and so tired that she would have liked to fall asleep. There had sometimes been a slight dizziness, she remembered: a rhythmic humming sound in her head – almost, now and then, like a tune: an old half-forgotten tune …

The doctor crossed to the window quickly. Barrel organs are not allowed in the square. He had always rather liked them, but not when he was trying to concentrate. The organ-grinder looked a hundred years old. He was playing a very old, solemnly sentimental waltz. Dr Franks looked round, startled, as a light drowsy voice called his name.

'Oh, Barney, you *are* naughty. Miss Galbraith *told* you you mustn't run to the window like that for organs. She *will* be cross!'

It was his patient. She must have fallen asleep. But it was an odd coincidence. And now her blue eyes were open, wide with surprise. The music had stopped and the hall door had opened and shut. Mary had turned the old man away.

'Where were you?' he asked, amused.

'At a dancing class – untold ages ago.'

'In that mausoleum in Harcourt Street?'

'Why, yes! How did you know?'

'Did you fall asleep?'

'I must have. Forgive me. I never knew that I talked in my sleep! I suppose that tune recalled it all. There was a little boy called Barney who always used to dash to the window ... '

'I did: I remember.'

Virgilia sat up, startled; looked at him; flushed and laughed. *Dr Barnard J. Franks.* She had seen the brass plate.

'Do please believe that I hadn't recognised you!' she begged.

'Of course! And I can't remember you, I regret to say.'

'It was in another world.'

'Very curious; very interesting.'

He sat down in his armchair again.

'Tell me, Mrs Wilde, is your visual memory very strong?'

'Yes, it is. I can see a bird in flight and sketch it from memory, fairly accurately. I've been told that's unusual. Some old memories return, very acutely, too.'

What had happened was easily understood, they agreed. She had not been asleep for more than a minute or two. The old tune, to which they had probably danced in childhood – wasn't it 'The Choristers' Waltz'? – combining with something in him which her half-dreaming mind recognised, had produced the vivid dream of the small boy. Could there be a clue to her problem in this?

The doctor sat in silence, thinking. Having concluded that Mrs Wilde's hallucinations were due to some cause outside the range of his proper study, he had, from ingrained habit, forbidden his mind to speculate about them. Nevertheless, he felt strongly tempted to explore this unknown tract that lay dark before him. This was not like any ordinary case in which some other man's speciality was involved. There were no experts, no consultants, in the trouble from which this woman was suffering. He had as much right as any layman to open his mind to these questions. Indeed, it was not possible, having been brought in direct contact with so curious a problem concerning the human mind, to cease to cogitate on it. He could imagine Perry's wrath if he learned of such wilful self-blinding, and Perry would be right. He wanted to discuss this case with his son. How could he gain permission to do so? Besides, Mrs Wilde's situation was, actually, distressing: one would like to help. Was it possible? He looked up.

'I enjoyed those dancing lessons,' he said.

'Naturally you did!' she replied.

The atmosphere between them had been changed entirely by his genial remark. Virgilia felt a sudden reaction of gaiety. She had been depressed and depressing and she seized the chance to dispel the sense of disappointment that she must have created.

'You were our star performer,' she told him. 'You danced the Sailor's Hornpipe in a sailor suit.'

The smile deepened on the doctor's face. He whistled a snatch of the tune.

'And then,' Virgilia went on, 'half-a-dozen little girls in party frocks danced in a ring round you singing:

'He's my hero, he's my dear, O,
He's my beautiful sailor boy!'

'And to think,' he exclaimed ruefully, 'that I have forgotten that! Now, I envy you your flashes of memory!'

Amused, Virgilia chattered on:

'You waltzed with me. I couldn't reverse and you taught me – and I nearly had my hair pulled out by the roots afterwards by that jealous little wild-cat, Suzette … Suzette … ?'

She broke off, not only because she had forgotten the name but because that shocking memory sickened her: a dark little face, distorted with fury; narrowed eyes that glared like a cat's; hands like claws, threatening her, gripping her hair, shaking her head with terrifying violence, while the other children shrieked. Virgilia had screamed hysterically and afterwards had lain sobbing in her mother's arms, while the pounding of her mother's heart redoubled her fear. She had never gone to the class again. Until she was in the teens there had been nights when she woke screaming, and Suzette's face had come back to her in nightmares for years.

'Suzette?' she repeated. But the second name would not come.

'Suzette Perry,' the doctor said.

'You remember her?'

'She became my wife.'

Virgilia repressed an incredulous exclamation. To think of that nightmare child, so long a part of the past, as a living woman, here in this house, was disconcerting. She looked in distress and apology at the doctor. What had she said? He had spoken with a sort of gravity. Perhaps Suzette was dead. 'Your wife?' she murmured. 'Of course I didn't know.'

'She died five years ago,' Dr Franks said evenly. To put her at her ease, he went on: 'My son was named after her. I have two daughters also. They live abroad.' He smiled. 'They maintain that anyone who voluntarily lives in a damp northern island is 'wanting.' They run a teashop and library near Mentone and have a very good time.'

'How lovely in winter,' Virgilia responded as she rose, preparing to leave. 'Dr Franks,' she said warmly, 'I am very grateful. You have relieved me of a horrible fear.'

'I'm glad of that. I'm glad your case is not within my professional scope. All the same, I am sorry that I can do nothing to help you. These experiences must be quite distressing and, of course, some explanation, if not some remedy, exists.'

'If I came again?'

He shook his head regretfully.

'I must not set up as a consultant on matters beyond our range.'

'Of course!'

Virgilia was a little surprised by the degree of concern and frustration which had deepened all the lines on the doctor's face.

Did he not realise how much he had done for her? Instead of considering her abnormal, he had suggested that the boundary of what was accepted as normal ought probably to be widened to take in such a case. That meant a good deal, from a man with his trained, scientific brain.

'If only your son were in practice!' she said lightly.

To her surprise, his response was serious and deliberate.

'I wonder,' he said, 'what Perry would think.'

She smiled.

'I wish I were not so egoistically sensitive about wanting all this kept secret; otherwise I would suggest your telling him about me,' she said.

'He's a stranger to you,' the doctor replied.

She turned away, murmuring that she had left her hat in his waiting-room. He checked her movement, simply by standing where he was, stock-still. There was clearly something else that he wanted to say.

Dr Franks was in a dilemma. To attempt, now, to establish a non-professional relationship would be against the law and custom to which he had been faithful during twenty-four years of practice. But this case was unique. He was able to refer Mrs Wilde to no other source of help. Would he be yielding to mere curiosity, or to paternal self-interest, or would he genuinely act to Mrs Wilde's advantage if he brought her and Perry together? … No – he would never feel justified if there were no helpful result. He supposed that he ought to keep the rules.

He turned to her, saying, 'I am sorry: a notion occurred to me, but it must be dismissed.'

She had been looking at him with hope illuminating her face. He saw the light quenched. She said, again, 'I quite understand,' but so tonelessly that the depth of her disappointment and loneliness was betrayed. He realised that, for all her unusual courage, she was afraid.

'Mrs Wilde,' he said, smiling at her, 'we've known each other for quite a long time.'

She replied with a difficult little smile, 'So we have,' and added, 'Don't let us count how long.'

'Will you,' he suggested, 'allow me to presume on our having been introduced at a dance?'

She looked at him, surprised. His voice was light and warm and his eyes were twinkling.

'Why not?' she replied. 'I am sure Miss Galbraith's introduction was supremely correct.' The affected drawl of the dancing mistress was clear in her memory. She mimicked her elocutionary style: 'Mees Morrow, may I present Master Barnard Franks? He hopes that you will give him the pleeshah!'

'How do you do?' Barnard Franks said, with a stiff little bow. Virgilia inclined her head. She could almost feel the weight of the ribbon on top of it.

'How do you do?'

'Will you,' the doctor said, with small-boy directness, 'come and have lunch in our house and I'll give you ice-cream?'

'Strawberry ice?' she enquired.

'Yes, if you like.'

'Then I will, thank you. When?'

'Next Sunday? One o'clock?'

'I have to think about buses; one-fifteen?'

'One-fifteen, then. You really will? Mrs Wilde, that's very nice of you. Perry will be in. He seems to have concluded to give me Sunday afternoons. When you have made his acquaintance you will be able to decide whether or not you wish to talk about all this again. You may, of course, find him much too young.'

WHILE VIRGILIA WENT into the waiting-room to collect her things the doctor stood in the hall. Perry must be told, merely, that they had renewed their acquaintance through Ada Stack. When she had met the boy she would probably feel like confiding in him. And Perry would be discreet unless pure interest carried him away: that must be guarded against ...

A cry from the waiting-room sent him striding to the door. Mary appeared at the head of the kitchen stairs and retired quickly, seeing him there. He called, 'Mrs Wilde,' sharply, and, hearing only a gasping breath in answer, went in. She was alone in the room. She was leaning on the table, staring across it; the pupils of her eyes were dilated and her face pale. He spoke quietly.

'What was it this time?'

'My daughter.'

'A shadow?'

'No: I thought she was sitting there in that chair.'

She pointed to the chair at the foot of the table.

The doctor made her sit down. This was his dining-room and there was brandy in the sideboard. He found it and poured some out, but her hand shook and she did not lift the glass to her lips.

He sat down on the chair at which she was staring. 'Tell me, was it just as you recall her?' he asked.

She shook her head. 'She was different. Her hair was done on the top of her head. She doesn't wear it like that.'

'Did you see how she was dressed?'

'There was colour: a lot of bright colour. She doesn't wear colours like that ... I must cross tonight. She's in trouble,' Virgilia said.

The doctor thought for a moment and then he spoke quietly. 'Mrs Wilde, you haven't found any trace of a telepathic origin for these hallucinations of yours, have you? Not in a single instance? Don't let yourself imagine one now. Remember, you have been under a great weight of anxiety and you are tired. These long examinations are a strain. Try not to let this affect you more than it ought.'

'But what can it mean?'

'Did she look happy?'

'Why, yes: yes, she did!'

'Well, then?'

'I must go, all the same.'

'Try to drink that brandy.' Virgilia sipped it. After a moment the doctor said: 'You do see, don't you, that you might upset your daughter very much, and quite wear your own nerves out, if every time this sort of thing happens you at once rush to some tragic conclusion?'

Virgilia's voice shook as she answered.

'Oh, I do see that! That is what has worried me so much. I might become a terrible burden. She mustn't know; mustn't suspect. It would be devastating for Nan … Dr Franks, what am I to do?'

'Is she on the telephone?'

'No.'

'I suggest that you should send a telegram then. It's just four o'clock and the mail-boat doesn't go till a quarter to nine. I suggest you should send a wire. Go home and wait for a reply. As a precaution, if there is no local car or trap, you could order one on the way home to call for you in case you decide to go. But I think you'll get an answer and find all's well.'

Virgilia nodded and drank the brandy. She felt weak and shaken, and it was helpful to have a course of action laid down with decision like this. Regaining some self-control, she rose.

'Yes, yes. I'll do that. I'm sorry, Dr Franks. You are right: I'll have to learn not to panic. Thank you. You've been kind.'

He went with her to the hall door and opened it, saying cheerfully, 'We'll see you on Sunday, then.'

'Sunday? Oh, yes: to lunch! Yes: if all's well … I have taken too much of your time, I'm afraid,' she added before she went down the steps.

It was seven minutes past four.

4

DR FRANKS MADE a brief entry in his case-book and a much longer one in a private journal, then locked his desk. A colleague was coming to see him at five. He was free until then. He went thoughtfully upstairs, paused at the door of his study but did not go in. He went on to a room which he seldom visited – his son's room on the second floor. Perry was out – at a tennis tournament, the doctor remembered – he would return victorious, as usual, no doubt.

Did Mary never tidy this room? Forbidden to, probably. The apparent disorder was orderly in its own way. Papers and periodicals lay on chairs and the floor, but the books were usefully grouped. Dr Franks examined the shelves by the fireplace, pulled out half a dozen volumes, most of them new and with American imprints, and settled himself in the hollow armchair. He lit his pipe and began to turn over the leaves.

He had read a good deal that surprised and puzzled him before Perry dashed in, looking browner than an Indian in his white things.

'Hello, Dad! Why the honour?' he exclaimed. 'Wish you had this idea oftener. A spot of idleness would do you a whole lot of good.'

'Idleness,' his father protested. 'Digesting this stuff you collect is very like work.'

Perry took a look at the books and whistled.

'Well, bless us and save us if the old man isn't trying to improve his mind!'

'Young Ingram writes well,' the doctor commented. 'Extraordinary to find a barrister, and an ambitious one, taking so much interest in all this.'

'Interest! He's becoming a recognised authority. His mind snaps back automatically to haunted houses whenever the law lets it go. He collected his wife in one.'

Perry took a shirt from a drawer and disappeared into the bathroom across the landing where he washed vigorously while he talked.

'Are they back from their honeymoon?' Dr Franks enquired.

'Should be.'

'We ought to entertain them, I suppose.'

'Bright idea.'

'Well, did you beat O'Malley?'

'I did, in the last game. Those courts are in great condition.' Perry reappeared, drying his face. 'I say, Dad,' he suggested, 'if you really are coming alive to these questions you should read the last *Proceedings* – I have it somewhere – and there's an article in the *Digest ...*' He began a strenuous search.

'By the way, Perry, I hope you're lunching at home on Sunday?' his father remarked.

'Righto! Is someone coming?'

'Yes: a lady whom I'd like you to meet. She's an old acquaintance whom I've lost sight of for some time. Ada Stack made her look me up. They were at Alexandra College together.'

'At college with Noah's wife? What sort of age?'

The doctor very nearly said 'forty-three.' Such precision would have suggested a case-card to Perry. The boy was quick in the up-take.

'A very charming age,' he replied. 'By the way,' he added, 'you might convey a tactful hint to Mrs McCruskie. Mrs Wilde particularly requests a strawberry ice-cream.'

'Sounds a bit frivolous for your visiting list! Good, I'll be there.'

5

SHE HAD PEDALLED too fast and exhausted herself and was forced to dismount and walk. The boy who had been pelting along on his bicycle in front of her had disappeared over the top of the hill. He was a telegraph boy; she felt sure of it, and the load of her anxiety began to lighten. I've lost caste now, she thought, smiling a little; my reputation as an unfussy parent will be ruined. The wire she had sent would seem quite foolish.

UNEASY FOR NO REASON ARE YOU ALL RIGHT
DARLING SHALL I COME

Reaching the top of the hill, she saw him again. He was turning up the lane to Derreen. In a few minutes she was walking up the lane herself. She passed his bicycle which he had left propped against a gate-post. Virgilia hurried and turned the bend. Eileen and the boy were both there between the hollies. Eileen had her outdoor things on – her red jacket and cap. The boy spoke to her and she gaped at him, then snatched the telegram from his hand and dashed back to the house with it.

As Virgilia, hurrying after her, passed the messenger, he said something, but she did not wait to hear what it was. She left her bicycle leaning against the gate and hurried to the back door. Something had lurched and settled again in her brain. The hollies: the tall one on her right, next to Eileen: she had seen them like that on Tuesday: exactly like that, and Eileen's gesture, and everything …

Brigid was at the kitchen door, the envelope in her hand.

Eileen was tearing away round the other side of the house. Virgilia opened the envelope and read Nan's message:

WHY THE FUSSATION DARLING AM ALL RIGHT BUT
LONELY FOR YOU AND COMING HOME

The two women sat down at the kitchen table.

'She's coming home. Nan's coming home. She's coming, Brigid,' Virgilia said. She added, in a bewildered tone, 'I saw this telegram arriving, didn't I? On Tuesday afternoon. Two days ago. That's what I saw.'

'That's what you saw, sure enough,' Brigid said happily. 'Joy on the way. I've been praying for this. This is what'll do you good. You'll be all right now.'

Chapter III

SUNDAY AFTERNOON

'I HOPE THE ice-cream will materialise,' Perry said anxiously. 'You never know, with McCruskie. This mayn't be the day.'

'I did my best to create the right psychological atmosphere,' his father returned gravely.

'For four years,' Perry explained to Virgilia, 'Mrs McCruskie has been boring my father to dyspepsia with her good plain cooking. But whenever I have him screwed to the point of giving her the boot she produces either mince pies or ice-cream ... '

'According to the season,' his father interpolated.

'And,' Perry concluded, 'we subside.'

The subject was dexterously changed because the austere parlour maid had re-appeared conveying the *bombe*. It was excellent.

'Don't lose Mrs McCruskie,' Virgilia advised, when the maid had withdrawn. 'An artist must be allowed to be a dictator in her own sphere.'

Perry grinned at her. He was in high spirits. He had received a letter from America offering him hospital work for a year under a man whose research interested him enormously. The soup and cutlets had been accompanied by a disquisition on saline baths and the plaster treatment for burns.

'We grow out of it,' his father had said, in apology, to Virgilia. 'As a symptom in youth it is not unfavourable.'

Perry asked now: 'What's your own sphere, Mrs Wilde? Dad hasn't told me a thing except that you live in the hills. My first bet is, you paint. My second, that you keep bees – or rabbits – the sort you only clip and don't kill.'

'A near hit,' Virgilia said, entertained. 'I am planning to keep bees next year, and I sketch, in a utilitarian sort of way.' She was surprised at the genuine interest with which both men listened to her trivial tale of the improving of her cottage, the redeeming of her garden, and days spent among birds and books.

'There used to be a great variety of song-birds in those glens,' Dr Franks said. 'Some kinds are disappearing, I've heard.'

'Almost,' she told him. 'Goldcrests and goldfinches, especially. Wretched boys trap them and pack them off alive in the coal-boats to Wales – a dozen birds in one tiny cage; half of them die. But I have both kinds in my little wood, and, by dint of getting the local boys to help me with setting up nesting boxes and food-tables, I have made a good many of them pro-bird. We have a surprising number of species at Derreen. It's the kind of wood birds like best – sunny, with thick undergrowth; and there is a stream that never freezes, it runs so swiftly.'

'Just where is this Arcadia of yours?' the doctor asked enviously. 'Perry and I used to know those hills fairly well.'

She explained without difficulty. They knew her mountain byroad of old. They told her how, during Perry's school holidays, he and his father used to take a bus to Rathfarnham, walk up through the Pine Forest and over the Featherbed Mountain, and then eastward along Glencree and home by that road. They remembered Doyle's farm, where Doyles had lived at that time also, and where they had once been invited to take a cup of tea.

'Those were the days,' Perry said, and his father nodded.

'I wonder,' he mused, aloud, 'just how much damage we are doing to our finer perceptive faculties by living in towns.'

'Ruining them,' Perry responded, with a grin. 'Mrs Wilde, Dad has been talking since I was a kid about building a fishing hut up at Loch Dan, and he hasn't bought the site yet.'

'It has grown to a fine cottage since those days,' his father asserted.

'It has, in the air! You'll never build it!' Perry was half mocking, half serious. 'You'll wind yourself round and round in a cocoon of work until you can't hear a sound from the outside world. You'll forget that a world exists.'

His father said speculatively, 'I wonder if silk-worms do.' Virgilia was amused by all this; but how, she wondered, was she to find an opportunity to tell Dr Franks about the arrival of the telegram? She knew that he would be extremely interested. It was difficult to believe that his son concerned himself about such matters. He looked as if riding and rowing were more in his line. He is a nice boy, really, Virgilia thought. The faint resistance to him which she had felt at first sight was absurd. It was only in profile that he resembled his mother – he was fundamentally quite unlike her. His easy movements, ready smile and the friendly regard of his hazel eyes were pleasant, and made him seem rather young for a qualified medical man. Virgilia did not believe that he would be able to help her, but she would tell him about her experiences, she decided, if the chance came. Upstairs, in the elegantly furnished and quite impersonal drawing-room, their talk ranged over the Dublin of twenty years ago: 'So much more dirty and poverty-stricken,' Dr Franks commented; 'so much more full of genius and wit and eccentricity than the prosperous, puritanical city we have today.'

'Puritanical, is it?' Perry said ironically. 'That's all you know!'

The robot parlour-maid brought coffee. The tray, with the percolator bubbling, was set on a low table beside Virgilia, who was asked to pour out and warned that she would be kept busy.

'We are not permitted to use large cups as we should like to,' the doctor explained. In casual tone he asked his son whether Garrett Ingram was coming in.

'Why, no, I told you,' Perry answered, surprised. He added with a chuckle, 'He's taking his wife to Avoca to visit his mother. I wonder how they'll get on! The old lady always said he'd pick up a wife on one of his ghost-hunting stunts, and, sure enough, it's just what he's done.'

'A ghost-hunter!' Virgilia exclaimed.

'*And* a barrister, and an alpinist and a writer,' Perry informed her, clearly proud of his friend.

The doctor said, 'He has written a rather interesting book: a study of certain types of paranormal phenomena.'

'Paranormal?'

Filling his pipe with care and deliberation, Dr Franks explained: 'Phenomena that lie outside the area of our accepted knowledge of cause and effect.'

'What folks call "supernatural"', Perry said.

'Perry and Garrett Ingram run a sort of all-male club for studying such questions,' the doctor told her. 'I suppose Mrs Ingram will have to be admitted now.'

'I hope she will: we need some women; Garrett's a bit too logical,' Perry responded seriously. Virgilia was amused at the implied comment on women's mental processes; she observed, however, that although Perry seemed ready to be jocular about many things he was very much in earnest about his surgical studies and about all this. He was sitting beside her, adjusting the wick under the percolator. The doctor passed his cup back and Virgilia refilled it. Perry, she thought, has good hands, sensitive and strong, like his father's; he has his father's voice, too – a reassuring voice. Her hesitation lasted only another moment. She said, 'I wonder what you would think of an experience that I had the other day.'

'An experience?' Perry's eyes, stretched wide, were turned on hers with an expression of avid interest. The doctor smoked in silence, leaning back in his armchair. It was to his son that Virgilia turned, describing her vision of the delivery of a telegram.

'Then, on Thursday, when I was in town,' she went on, 'something entirely unexpected made me send a reply-paid wire. I sent it soon after four and went home.'

Whilst she recounted what had happened then, Perry sat listening, immobile, as though something of extreme importance were happening to him. She was aware of the doctor gazing at her, amazed.

'But this is stupendous!' Perry exclaimed, when the story was told.

'The oddest part of it is,' she went on, 'that in my vision on Tuesday the background was wrong. I realised that just afterwards. On Thursday, I understood. What had happened was that, looking from my window the first time, I had seen the two hollies reversed. I had seen them from the other side.'

Perry said, his eyes never leaving her face: 'You saw what you were going to see.'

'Exactly,' she replied.

'Paranormal precognition,' Perry said.

'Precognition?'

'"Prevision" to be exact.'

'Brigid called it "a plain, ordinary case of second sight."'

'Good. I must meet Brigid.'

'Her grandmother was a "terror with it," it seems.'

'Oh, the thing happens, but the difficulty is to get first-hand, witnessed, watertight, fool-proof instances from subjects whose integrity can't be questioned. This is superb!'

'You make me feel as if I had performed a public service,' Virgilia told him ruefully. His enthusiasm made her uneasy.

'You're going to,' he declared.

She looked across at the doctor, who was leaning forward, his pipe forgotten, a frown of concentration cutting a deep trench between his brows.

'I can accept hyperaesthesia,' he said slowly; 'many forms of clairvoyance; telepathy, even; but this – this requires a revolution in our ideas of causation.'

'It does,' Perry said bluntly.

'It requires,' the doctor continued, 'a new concept of time.'

'Dunne has worked that out.'

'Has he?'

Virgilia said, 'I've rather avoided books on these subjects; I should read them, I suppose.'

They began to ask her questions, listening with absorbed interest to her answers.

'Do you actually see those holly trees from that window?' the doctor enquired.

'Yes, if you look sideways, as I happened to do. The taller is on my left. But in my vision – my prevision – it was on my right. I saw the gate standing open, too, while actually it was closed.' He asked, 'Did the whole scene take place, as it appeared to you, in the appropriate part of your garden?'

'Yes.'

'Superimposed, as it were, on your closed gateway?'

'Yes.'

'Were the colours just as usual?'

'They were: even to Eileen's dreadful magenta jacket and scarlet cap.'

'How much movement did you see?'

'Only her gesture, snatching the envelope. I left the window then.'

Perry asked whether she had heard any sound.

'No,' she told him. 'I don't think I did. I think, actually, all sound stopped – the birds, and the stream, and trees. I may be imagining it, but it seems to me now that a sort of humming, and then a strange kind of stillness, came. But I'm very likely imagining that.'

'Very, very curious,' Dr Franks said. 'I suppose you have no notion how much time was occupied by all this?'

'I have no idea,' she replied.

'The element of place is peculiar, isn't it?' he suggested. 'It is as if the actual spot merely provided a link or associative stimulus.'

'Good for you, Dad!' Perry exclaimed. 'I was just wondering about that: more or less the same place and an interval of two days! Mrs Wilde,' he asked eagerly, 'there have been other things, haven't there?'

She answered him carefully.

'I have been wondering. I have seen what were apparently phantasms – snow, a bird's nest, a shadow, which were not there. Perhaps memory had something to do with them. I don't know. Perhaps I'm going to see them, next winter, next spring. How can I tell? I can't know how many of the things I am seeing are really there.'

'It's terrifically interesting,' Perry said.

Virgilia was not able to respond; she was becoming more and more appalled by the thought of all that this power of hers might involve. She remembered something. She exclaimed, rather bewildered, 'There was a book. I didn't understand. I had forgotten,' she told them, 'until now.'

They waited.

'It was soon after Christmas. I had a book-token to exchange. I was in Combridge's shop, looking at books about birds. They brought me a pile and I turned them over. You know that deadly depression that comes when you look at dozens of books that are not what you want! I felt that, until I saw one, small and squarish, with a glazed yellow jacket. There was a photograph on it – a heron alighting near a pool. The title was *Neighbours with Wings*. I glanced at the other books and then looked for that one again, but it wasn't there.'

'You made quite sure?' the doctor asked.

'Yes, I wanted it. I don't quite know why. I gave no end of trouble. They told me there was no such book in the shop. They had never heard of it. It was not in the catalogue.'

'Has it been published yet?' Perry asked.

'I hope not, because I'm using the title! I liked it.'

'You're using the title?' Perry exclaimed.

'Yes,' she said, smiling. 'If that was a case of prevision it will be awkward for me. You can't imagine how hard it is …'

She stopped short, holding her breath.

'You are *making* it a case of prevision,' Perry said.

His father rose and walked up and down the room.

'This is incredible!' he exclaimed. 'Wheels within wheels. What is cause and what is effect?'

'Have you got a snap of a heron?' Perry enquired.

'Not yet, but I … I see what you mean.'

Perry said excitedly, 'Will you put a wagtail on the cover instead? Or any old bird, only not a heron – just to please me?'

Virgilia protested: 'There's nothing so decorative as a heron. I've set my heart on getting a photograph of one for my last chapter. And, you see, many local farmers think they're unlucky. They'll be killed off in Wicklow if that goes on. And fishermen complain that they eat eels and I want to show that eels eat the spawn of the trout ...'

Perry interrupted her, 'Don't put the heron on the cover.'

'I'll promise this,' she said. 'I'll leave the choice of the picture for the cover to the publisher. If I send him a photograph of a heron it will be interesting, won't it, to see what he does?'

Perry was satisfied.

'And do this, won't you?' he begged. 'Write down all these things that you've told us, with dates, and get the signature of witnesses. Do that with every case, Mrs Wilde. Then, when the precognised event occurs, describe that in the same way. You simply can't imagine how valuable such a record will be. You're the answer to a psychic researcher's prayer. Ingram will shoot out of his hat.'

Virgilia listened with dismay. Dr Franks spoke before she did.

'Does it occur to you, Perry, that Mrs Wilde may not want her faculty publicised?'

'Please,' she said, 'nobody must know.'

Perry had started up. He swung round on her angrily, saying, 'You can't possibly refuse!'

'But I do.' She felt herself shrink and flush. 'I can't tell you how I should hate my daughter to guess anything about this. It's not normal. It's rather horrible. I don't want the edge of the shadow of it to touch Nan.'

Dr Franks said, 'That is absolutely understood, Mrs Wilde.'

Perry's eyes looked dark and his face hard with frustration. Virgilia saw the likeness to Suzette now. It made her nervous. He was going to say something, but his father's glance, stern, yet lightened with a slight smile of understanding, silenced him. Laying an easy hand on his son's shoulder, the doctor said, 'What about lending Mrs Wilde Ingram's book?'

Perry left the room.

The doctor said to Virgilia quietly, 'His passion for research carries him away sometimes, but I can answer for his discretion. May I tell him you consulted me?'

'As you think best,' she said.

'Please have no anxiety about our respecting your confidence.'

She replied with sincerity, 'I have none.'

'I am afraid this discovery has increased your worry rather than relieved it.'

She hesitated, then admitted it. 'One feels so helpless. It's like driving a car that's gone out of control. I seem to be skidding about in time.'

'I'm afraid that expresses it only too well.'

'I wish I could learn how to hold the road.'

'That may come,' the doctor said gently. 'First the diagnosis, you know, and afterwards, we must hope, the cure. You may find that your daughter's companionship helps a great deal ...By the way!' He began to smile. 'If it's really the future you are seeing I'm going to have a great pleasure: your daughter is coming to lunch or dine with us here.'

Virgilia laughed. 'I thought of that.'

'When do you expect her?'

'Next Thursday afternoon.'

Perry came in, bringing a number of books. While he talked about them he recovered his good humour. Virgilia said to herself, he thinks I'll change my mind. His manner was kind and gentle, as if he wanted to make up for his bad behaviour. He's a nice lad, really, she decided again. When she was leaving he asked whether, if he could borrow his father's car on Thursday, he might drive her to Dun Laoghaire to meet the boat.

'Thursday evening?' the doctor said reflectively. 'I wonder whether I might be able to come myself. I would enjoy it. I would like to see that view of the bay again.' He calculated that he could come and be home for his engagement at half-past six.

'That would be very pleasant,' Virgilia answered. 'I shall probably be shopping in town all the afternoon. I'll come here, shall I, at about five?'

Perry gave her a shy, grateful smile. He took her consent as a sign of forgiveness and confidence, which was what she had meant it to be.

'You know,' she said lightly, on the door-step, 'I am very grateful for your diagnosis. You have made it all sound more than respectable! I had been wondering whether I was just a plain, ordinary witch.'

Perry laughed.

'A witch, certainly: but not so ordinary! Nor ...' he began cheekily, but was checked by a glance from his father.

They would have burnt me in the Middle Ages, Virgilia reflected as she walked away. And that is because witches are a nuisance. Because they are dangerous.

Virgilia wanted to think. As a very small child she had been taken to a fair by a young uncle and he had lifted her into one of the cars of a merry-go-round. She had not screamed, but she had been awfully frightened. She had been carried round and round in the whirligig, unable to stop it and unable to escape. She had not enjoyed it at all. And she did not like her situation now. The important thing was not to panic: not to let anyone know.

Baggot Street was a furnace. She had a quarter of an hour to wait. Gratefully, she left the sun-baked pavement and turned into the shady walks beside the duck-thronged water of St Stephen's Green.

Chapter IV

SEA BREEZE

IN PINK ICING, **Brigid traced** *Céad Mile Fáilte* on the cake. It was an orange cake, the same as Mrs Morrow had ordered every summer for a welcome to Nan. It told no lie, then nor now: a hundred thousand welcomes awaited the girl. Why wouldn't she stay in a place where so much was made of her? If she'd stay in it now, her mother's troubles would be at an end ... A fine rush they'd had this week past, since the telegram came, with that omadhaun, Eileen, taking fright and staying away. Did she never hear of anyone dreaming sharp? And why wouldn't a person do it awake as easily as asleep? ... Mrs Wilde sounded busy still, running up and down stairs. Brigid looked at the clock. In twenty minutes the mistress ought to be starting for the bus. That's a terrible creak Nan's wardrobe door has, Brigid remarked to herself. It needs oil.

Nan's wardrobe was built into the wall, a great and capacious press. No piece of furniture of those dimensions could have been carried up the steep, narrow stairs. Virgilia slung a dozen dress hangers on the brass rod. She had padded them and covered them with silk and made a lavender sachet for each. Nan would tease her about her luxurious ideas and enjoy them.

Nan would like this room. Knocking the two into one had been a success. The shape was charming, with the ceiling sloping on two sides to the walls, and the little built-out windows. The primrose tint of the walls and of the cretonne, patterned with tiny posies, which Virgilia had made into bedspread and curtains, was gay and fresh. She had given them flounces – a self-indulgent nursery touch. How Nurse had disapproved of the cradle, with its frilly cover of muslin! And how deliciously pretty it looked, with the baby asleep in it, her long lashes dark on her cheeks! Virgilia stood smiling into the cradle, knowing well that it was only a memory, yet humming a lullaby; then looked across to the bed, smiling at herself, filled with delight because Nan would be lying asleep in this room tonight … The room suited Nan. It was easy to visualise her in it, asleep in the bed or sitting in the little chair by the window, her chin on her fists, or turning in front of the mirror to admire a new dress … a white dress, gleaming like moonlight, stately, with its sheath-like bodice and long skirt that swirled and swayed … It was gone: it had not been there.

Virgilia stepped back to a window and steadied herself with a hand on the sill. Her head hummed and her heart had quickened a little, but she was not frightened; not upset. I knew this time, she told herself with elation; I knew the difference; scarcely for one second was I confused. And I know what it means, – now only that I'm going to see Nan trying on a new dress! Not illness nor accident; nothing wrong; nothing whatever to worry about. I can be calm about it: perfectly calm.

She was calm and busy again by the time Brigid came up with the yellow porcelain lamp polished and filled. She was even able to smile at Brigid and say lightly, 'I've just seen something: I saw Nan in a new evening dress.'

'Did you, now?' Brigid responded, interested. 'I'm sure 'twas a beauty. She has great taste.'

'Listen, Brigid,' Virgilia said gravely: 'there is something you must promise me faithfully. I don't want Nan to know that this ever happens. Promise me that you'll try not to let her know.'

Brigid chuckled.

"Faith, I'll never forget the way my grannie had me moidhered and tormented with her dreams and foretellings. Don't worry: I'll not say a word. You should be starting now,' she said warningly. 'And take your coat. There's a nice breeze getting up: it should be powerful down by the sea. I hope Nan won't be sea-sick.'

'Not she!' Virgilia answered gaily. 'Nan loves wind and waves.'

2

NAN HAD ENJOYED the brief voyage and the best moment was coming now. She stood on the deck bare-headed, hugging her white coat round her against the wind, waiting for the thing that had been a myth and a dream and a memory to become real again – the line of the Wicklow hills. First it was a haze, then a mirage, then it was the long arm of the bay reaching out and drawing her in. She saw the Dublin mountains: the Sugar Loaf, like a young eagle waking and spreading his wings; Bray Head with its trees and white houses; then Dalkey, and the terraced cottages climbing up. Westward, in the curl of the arm, lay the city's shadow and glitter, with steeples pricking the sky.

The boat was turning. She lifted her suitcase. The harbour was crowded with yachts and small painted boats. People were walking and running along the pier and waving from the base of the light-house. The boat slid to rest at the quay-side. Her mother was there.

Nan laughed. Her mother had obeyed orders: she was wearing a dress of gentian blue. She looked sunburnt and well and young.

It was unexpected to discover that her mother had not come alone but had two good-looking men in attendance with a resplendent car.

'I like surprises,' Nan said as the younger man took the driver's seat.

He glanced at her sideways as he let the clutch in, and responded, 'So do I.'

Smoothly the car wound its way up the coast road and with a low, self-satisfied purr gathered speed. The driver's hands lay easily on the wheel.

Nan laughed. She said, 'The old crock that met me last time groaned and panted till you felt that you ought to get out and walk up the hills.'

He began to talk. He described his two-seater, bought a few weeks ago for twenty-five pounds and able to take the Devil's Elbow in second. He talked about the bay: Did she swim? Had she ever crossed to Howth in a yacht? Had she dived from the cliffs?

'I can't dive. I don't swim very well. I live in London,' she replied.

'And you confess that without a blush?'

The young driver's eyes left the road to range from the dazzling sea to the green hills.

'And I'm going to Pittsburgh. Which of us is the crazier?' he said.

'Pittsburgh: yawning black caverns and blast furnaces and slag heaps and huge chimneys belching black smoke?' she suggested.

'Cobbled hills,' he responded, 'and all the cars shrieking in first gear. The snow comes down black. That's down-town, of course. But none of that matters to me.'

He took the Vico Hill at high speed and idled a little at the summit.

'How's that?' he demanded, waving his arm as if he had created the radiant scene. He turned to his passengers in the back. 'Do we have to take the shortest way? What about running out by the Rocky Valley and Glencree?'

Virgilia said, 'I would enjoy it,' and his father agreed, provided they could be back at Fitzwilliam Square in an hour.

Perry interpreted that as a permit to speed. He opened the throttle on the wide Wicklow road, and would have torn through the Rocky Valley but that he was brought to a halt by a straggle of sheep and had to nose his way slowly along. Sheep butted the bumper and huddled against the wings and blundered among the wheels, baa-ing in a quavering bass and bleating in a high, frightened treble while the herd, following on a bicycle, devoted his whole attention to keeping his balance at the slowest possible pace.

'Infuriating idiot,' Perry muttered as he shot past the lad at last.

'Moon-faced moron,' Nan said, and he grinned.

'Sheep are such asinine goats, aren't they?'

'Elephantine mules,' she agreed, and they burst into peals of childish hilarity.

The road was rough and Perry drove fast, but Nan loved it. She felt what Brigid called 'aeriated' and needed speed. So, it appeared, did he: he nearly ran over a magpie and Nan called, 'Look out!' He raced on, saying that he would spare the beasts of the field but the birds of the air must look after themselves.

The flanks of the great Sugar Loaf Mountain and Carrigoona, rising up on either side of the road, were glorious with masses of furze pouring their scent out on the hot air.

'Have you been to the top of the Sugar Loaf?' Perry asked

'Only in dreams. When I was a child I thought there were silver thrones on the top. I don't know who put that into my head: Brigid, probably: she has all the myths and superstitions there are.'

'Beware how you dismiss them as superstitions,' Perry warned her. 'There *are* silver thrones and we're going up there some day to sit on them.'

'I do want to go.'

They were turning into Glencree now, at its wooded eastern end. On their left Maulin and the Tonduff Mountains towered up. Perry, accelerating, swerved neatly to avoid two hens who seemed to be playing 'last across' on the road. Nan chuckled, saying, 'Birds of the earth, I suppose.' He's a good driver, she thought.

In the back of the car their parents had been quiet for some time, their silence deepening as Perry's speed increased.

'Are you enjoying this?' Dr Franks asked Virgilia now.

'They are,' she replied.

'Well,' he said ruefully, 'I can't protest if you won't!'

'I hate slowing people down.'

'Lesson One in the art of being a parent, I dare say,' the doctor observed.

'It's a long lesson book, isn't it?' she responded. 'I have no hope of ever mastering it.'

'I doubt if there's any way of learning this job, except by making mistakes ... The eldest, I suppose, comes off worst.'

Perry is his eldest, probably, Virgilia thought. She said, with a laugh, 'My unfortunate only child!'

He smiled at her. 'I'm sure some women are born knowing the job ... Perry's a good driver, though you might not think so,' he said reassuringly as the car smoothly surmounted a humpy bridge.

Virgilia was not convinced. Perry seemed to her to be taking risks. You never knew what might happen on these roads; a crash now would be frightful; even a twisted ankle would spoil Nan's holiday. A cut face could be a tragedy for a girl. But young people must be allowed to take risks, she reminded herself. She had been faithful to that principle, leaving Nan in London alone. She was not going to break down now. She said nothing and tried to distract her mind. She recalled the quick, vivid image of Nan in her new dress. She had not mentioned it. Should she tell Dr Franks about it now? He would be pleased to know how quickly she had recognised the phantasy for what it was, and curious, as she felt, to know whether Nan possessed such a dress. No, she would wait: she would tell him afterwards, if it proved true. It would seem so foolish if she began to take every flash of visual thinking seriously. It had been so very brief: only a kind of dream, perhaps, after all. She could almost recall ...

'Take care!' she cried suddenly. 'Oh, stop!'

'What on earth's wrong?'

Perry spoke sharply. He had braked and stopped with a jolt. Virgilia was leaning out, looking up the road, saying, 'Did you hit it?'

'Hit what?' Perry asked.

'The dog; the collie.'

'There wasn't a dog.'

Nan supported Perry.

'There wasn't; the road was clear.'

'He jumped out on the left.'

'But, Mummie, where from?'

'Where from? From the ... I don't know.'

'Anyway, it's okay now,' Perry said, and started the car again.

Virgilia had put her hands over her eyes; she lowered them as the noise and confusion cleared. She was cold and her heart dragged. She whispered, 'Was there a hedge on my left?'

'No,' Dr Franks answered quietly: 'there was a low stone wall.'

'Was there a dog?'

'No.'

He was watching her anxiously. The car was picking up speed.

'Oh, don't let him!' she pleaded. 'Don't let him go so fast.'

'Perry, keep down to thirty, please,' the doctor ordered at once.

Perry, obeying, protested: 'Thirty! This isn't a funeral.'

'Sorry, but it's to be thirty,' his father insisted, and added, more lightly, 'You're not driving the Bouncer now.'

Virgilia was leaning out on her side, staring into the hedges ahead, but she said nothing. Desperately she wanted to stop the car and make Nan get out and walk, but you have to risk your life, risk your child's life, she thought, rather than keep upsetting people. That was what she had to remember. She had to learn to live like this. She could not have kept quiet now but for Dr Franks's steadying presence at her side.

'Perry's a first-class driver,' he said.

Perry was annoyed. And no wonder, Nan thought: there'd been no dog. It was too bad. He had been enjoying it all so tremendously. The speedometer hand was quivering at the thirty mark, never leaving it.

'It's a pity your mother's nervous,' he said in a low tone. 'I didn't know. Why didn't you warn me?'

'Because she isn't,' Nan answered, perplexed. 'I simply can't understand it. I've never known anything make her nervous before … You turn to the right in a moment, just when you come in sight of Doyle's.'

But he had stopped. He glanced back with a look of astonishment, then took the turn with such extreme caution that Nan said, with a reproachful little smile, 'Now you're being rude to my mother.'

'I'm not, honestly,' he replied, his eyes ranging the road, 'though,' he admitted, 'going slow did get me all screwed up.'

'Me too.'

'My driving doesn't scare *you* then?'

'Goodness, no.'

'Will you come out with me in the Bouncer?'

'I would like to.'

'May I come tomorrow? We'll go up the Sugar Loaf.'

'Tomorrow?' Nan hesitated.

'Say, two o'clock.'

'Mother may have plans. I'll ask her.'

'Not now: she wouldn't feel like letting you. I'll come on the chance.'

'If you don't mind doing that … Now, across the bridge: our lane turns off to the left. You can hardly see it. It's about half-way up that hill. The cottage is up among those trees.'

She could not see the cottage; the June foliage was too thick. She saw, coasting down the hill straight towards them, a cyclist who did not seem to be in very good control of his machine. She said nothing because Perry was watching him, but her mother cried sharply, 'Look out to the left!' and Perry swerved to his right. He was just in time to avoid hitting the collie, who had dashed from the lane as if trying to charge the car, and he just left room for the cyclist to pass. It was nicely done. The cyclist, however, was less quick. He wobbled, bumped into the off front wing of the car and hopped off his machine. He stood on one leg, contemplating a bent mudguard and rubbing his shin.

In a moment they were all out of the car. Nan was looking across the bonnet at the grimacing youth. Perry stood over him, blazing. 'Either you're incompetent,' he said furiously, 'or your machine isn't fit to ride.'

Nan heard her mother gasp and turned to her. Virgilia's face was white and her eyes were fixed on Perry with an expression of something very like fear. Shuiler was gazing up at her, panting for forgiveness in vain. The doctor was standing close to her, his hand on her arm.

'Don't talk for a moment,' he was saying. 'It's all over now and no harm's done.'

'It wasn't his fault, Mummie: he coped splendidly!' Nan declared, and the doctor said, 'Really, Perry did very well.'

Nan felt worried about her mother. She had never seen her look like this. She's had a shock, she thought. What a shame, spoiling all the fun of my coming home.

'We'll walk up the lane, shall we, Mummie?' she said.

When she turned she saw that Perry was staring at her mother, quite still and silent. Nan smiled at him across the car, saying again, 'It wasn't your fault.'

He didn't respond. He was looking almost stupid. The cyclist was trying to straighten his mudguard and free his wheel. Nan went round to him and asked whether he wanted iodine or anything for his leg. He shook his head and muttered something about his bicycle. There was a dent in the wing of the car. 'What a pity,' she said to Perry. 'Your father's beautiful car!'

Perry stood looking at her as if he had not seen her before. He seemed to have nothing to say, but his eyes were very serious. Had there been real danger? Nan wondered. They all seemed very much shaken up by a harmless little collision. Her mother was murmuring something about sherry, but the doctor said no. They would run the car straight up with the luggage. He mustn't be late. Perry roused himself and came round the car.

'Mighty lucky you stopped me speeding, Mrs Wilde; otherwise … ' He stopped, glanced at his father, then swung round and went back to the boy. He examined the bicycle and gave the boy money, telling him to get his brakes seen to. The boy rode off and Perry and his father got into the car.

Nan and her mother walked up the lane, letting the car pass them. For a few minutes they did not talk. Then Virgilia said weakly, 'That was a lucky coincidence, wasn't it?'

Nan replied thoughtfully, 'I don't know. I was just thinking about it. If you hadn't thought you saw the dog and made Dr Franks slow down we would have been at that spot earlier and the cyclist wouldn't have arrived, and Shuiler mightn't have dashed out … You were wonderfully quick to see him … Feeling better?'

'I'm all right; there's nothing wrong with me.'

Nan smiled at her, taking her arm.

'You put the heart across me, turning as white as a ghost, so you did.'

'Am I a disgrace to the family?'

'That's what you are.'

They walked slowly, and before they had reached the bend in the lane the car came down again. Perry barely paused for good-byes and then it was gone. Nan turned the bend and stopped, laughing, enchanted.

'Why, Mummie! You witch! What a transformation scene! The cottage has grown!'

Virgilia laughed. She had forgotten all about the new room.

3

PERRY SEEMED CONTENT to drive home at a sober pace. His father was relieved. He did not want to pull him up again. The boy enjoyed driving this powerful car.

Dr Franks disliked driving himself: he found that a car's motion induced a useful mental process, a half-conscious imaginative brooding in which, often, obscure tracts of some difficult case became clear, and attending to gears and signals checked this. His chauffeur drove always in silence and at a moderate pace; being driven by Perry was an entirely different experience, enjoyable, too; for, usually, Perry, whether speeding or not, talked. Some recent Sundays had been spent with an old friend, now, unhappily, a patient, in Armagh, and Perry had replaced Quin at the wheel. While driving he had released a spate of questions, propositions and problems, accumulated during his American year, on which he had demanded, and then, for the most part, rebutted, his father's views. It had been a return to something like the companionship of their long-gone Sunday walks. Perry's silence this evening was the more remarkable. He was lost in specula-tion, his father supposed.

The experience had certainly been extraordinary – trying, also a strain, waiting for the thing to happen; wondering whether it would; then a shock when it did. One felt disoriented by the astounding subversion of all preconceived ideas of cause and effect. For Mrs Wilde, of course, there had been a really serious shock: severe suspense, remarkably well endured; then a bad moment. Also, no doubt, there was dismay at the recrudescence tendency in herself. It affected her as the recurrence of a disease. It was indeed a misfortune: a menace to the peaceful life she had tried to create for herself and her daughter ... Very charming, that low, wide cottage under the trees. These glens, he thought, have great beauty, and this view of the bay, in the mellow light, is superb.

Perry had not spoken a word; the ebullience of his early mood was quite gone; he looked white and tense. There was none of the triumphant excitement over this nice case of prevision that might have been expected. He was surely not blaming himself for the little mishap?

'I suppose,' Dr Franks asked him, 'you are quite certain that there was no dog?'

There was a line of cars ahead in Enniskerry. Perry accelerated and overtook them.

'Definitely, there was not,' he replied with emphasis. 'The road was dead empty except for a crow.'

His father told him that Mrs Wilde had imagined she saw a hedge where there was actually only a wall.

'She did?' Perry exclaimed. 'And it was out of a thick hedge that the dog came! So her backgrounds can show up, too, in a completely different spot! Sakes, this is interesting! It's a flat-out case – the rarest sort, too, where the prevision serves a purpose. There'd be tremendous interest in it because of that. And three perfectly good witnesses – you with your standing, for one. Look, Dad, Mrs Wilde has got to give in about this! Not to publish it would be a crime. You've got to persuade her, Dad.'

He broke off, halted by the stem look his father turned on him.

'I will use no such persuasion, Perry, and neither will you.'

'But, look, Dad! She's a reasonable woman – rather exceptionally reasonable, I imagine. She could be made to see.'

'Listen, my son.' There was authority, now, in his father's voice. Perry slowed down, attentive. 'Listen: Mrs Wilde told me about her hallucinations in the strictest confidence. I broke a rule in inviting her to meet you. I did it solely because I believed that you might be willing and able to help her to overcome this very distressing tendency. I didn't do it to aid research, or to provide subject matter for discussion between Ingram and you – that would have been wholly unjustifiable. The situation precludes, absolutely, any reference to the matter which she does not herself introduce, and any attempt at pressing her to dwell on this unfortunate faculty. Now, is that understood?'

Perry whistled, then his face became grave. He looked acutely disappointed.

'So that's the way of it, is it? Poor woman! That puts the lid on it, of course … Thanks, Dad. Nice that you let me in on this. I don't know how I'd bring myself to help her to get rid of the power, even if I'd the remotest notion how that could be done, which I haven't … There's no harm, is there, in lending her books?'

'You may when she asks for them.'

'I'll "burst in ignorance".'

'If you can't trust yourself you must keep out of her way.'

Perry did not reply to that. He relapsed into brooding, a single deep furrow between his brows. This conflict was going to torment him, his father feared. In an effort to distract him, he talked about Mrs Wilde's home.

'It may do a great deal for her having her daughter there. I imagine there has been a good deal of repression of the natural wish for the child's companionship. Mothers often carry self-sacrifice to a harmful extreme. She seems a sensible type of girl. Rather charming, I thought, didn't you?'

'"Sensible!"' The word was an explosion of irritation. '"Rather charming!"' I dare say you thought her "pretty" – or didn't you?'

Dr Franks smiled to himself, thinking how far out one could be when presuming to guess at a young man's thoughts. He had supposed the boy's preoccupation to be metaphysical. He said, 'Mind that bus.'

NAN RAN UPSTAIRS and down again, excited.

'It's like something out of a fairy-tale,' she declared. 'The dark little cottage, with the leaky roof and nettles up to the windows and rooms you could hardly turn round in, magicked into this gem of a place. Why, Mummie, what a home we possess!'

Virgilia was sitting by the fire in the kitchen. She felt cold. The chill was leaving her now; she sat smiling, looking at Nan, reaping the reward of all her labours, released from the last of her doubts.

Brigid said, 'You haven't seen my new window,' and led Nan upstairs once more.

Brigid's room had a casement window over the valley now, as well as the one that looked south. Under it was her old rocking-chair. 'There I sit and I knit and I watch the sun going down in glory,' she said.

Nan began to explore all over again. The hallway, which had led out straight into the yard, opened into a sea-green bathroom, with a tank and taps. The little dining-room was unchanged except that there were doors on each side of the fireplace now. The one on the left opened into the new kitchen; the other into the studio.

For the studio, Nan found no words. She could not have said why the room seemed to her so enchanting. It was long and barn-like in shape with the ceiling sloped on two sides. The wall of the south gable-end was nearly all taken up by the red brick hearth and the narrow windows on either side of it. That fireplace had its own tall chimney which gave the room an important look from outside. In the wall opposite was the big kitchen dresser from Dundrum, painted light grey like the walls, its shelves full of books; beside it, the door of the dark-room. Against the long wall there were low shelves and the old sofa and the radiogram. The west wall was half glass. Under each of its windows a square table was set; her mother's, nearer the fireplace, was piled with notebooks and bird-maps, but the other was bare. Her mother, coming in smiling, said, 'That's for you.'

Nan stood there, bathed in light, looking out. The western sky was a limitless space of brilliance; the folds of the hills, flowing gently down to the river, held shadowy blues and luminous greens; the room was filled with a topaz glow. Virgilia was not looking at these; she was looking at her daughter's face, seeing in it that serious joy which rarely outlives childhood.

'It's an enchanted room. It's a room to do good work in. I should think nothing disagreeable could ever happen in it,' Nan said.

NAN WONDERED a little at her mother's quietness. While they sipped the ceremonial sherry of welcome and ate the ritual cake it was Brigid who laughed and chattered, telling stories about the builder, Larry Fazackerly, and the carpenter, Mick Walsh, and the tribe of the Doyles who had swarmed around pretending to help. In return, Nan gave her a dramatised account of the drive home and the odd coincidence about the dog. Brigid, the imperturbable, seemed rather upset by the thought of their having so narrowly escaped an accident. She looked with quick solicitude at her mistress and poured more sherry into her glass. She said, quite gravely, ''Twas your guardian angel gave you the warning, so you wouldn't go racing on to your deaths.' She turned to Nan then, her eyes twinkling.

'Two fine handsome gentlemen brought you home this time, and I hope 'tis for luck. Up the stairs with your trunk between them as if 'twas my basket! That's a grand laughing young man.'

Nan had a splash in the new bath, and then, huddled in her mother's wrapper, lingered in the studio again.

'I love it, I love it. It makes you want to work and sing. But my bedroom is your masterpiece, darling. Come up and help me unpack.'

When the wardrobe door was opened fragrance flowed out. 'Your old shot-silk petticoat! You *are* a mummie!' Nan exclaimed. She chattered, but she was worried. What could be done? Even a glass and a half of sherry had not brought the colour back to her mother's face and her hands were all nervous and fluttery, turning over the things in the trunk. She gave a little gasp of astonishment as she handed up the Harlequin dress.

'Don't you like it?' Nan enquired. 'I made it myself out of a remnant. I bought it when I couldn't come for Christmas, to comfort myself. It's a bit skimpy, but amusing, don't you think?' The question was not answered.

'Have you no dance dress?' her mother asked.

'Ah-ha, have I not? It's being finished and sent after me. The beading for the neck, modom, has to be sent for to Paris, modom. I bought it instead of a new summer coat and now I've cut out the dance it was meant for, but I'm not sorry … Mummie, you're awfully white still; come and lie down on the bed.' Nan drew down the cover, put a cushion under the pillows, and Virgilia lay and rested, while her daughter, wandering about the room in her slip, unpacked and put things away. When Nan took a portfolio from the bottom of her trunk, Virgilia held out her hand.

'Your illustrations! Let me see.'

'After supper I will.'

'How are they coming?'

'I'm not sure. I want to know what you think. But I'm enjoying them. The book's fun. In the bit I'm at now Puck is politely asking the young leprechauns to teach him "Ers", and their pulling his leg. The trouble is, I can't keep Puck English: he's really a Celt; and I can't get the leprechauns. The set has to be in the middle of August. I must work quite a lot.'

'Here?'

'Yes, please.'

'Darling, how lovely! Two whole months!'

'It seems too good to be true, having a home where you can work and have a holiday at the same time. I hope I'm not dreaming.'

Virgilia closed her eyes and saw long, lovely years unfold.

'Tell me things,' Nan demanded. She was setting out her little boxes and pots on the dressing-table.

'Where shall I begin?'

'Where did you meet the Frankses? You said in your letter "an old acquaintance," that's all.'

'Through Ada Stack.'

Nan turned and regarded her mother with puckered brows. 'Has she been doctoring you?'

'Certainly not. I don't need doctoring. What put such a notion into your head?'

'Doctors, I suppose, and dogs, and telegrams, and you going so shaky about the car. I've never seen you like that before.'

'You've put two and two together and made thirteen.'

Nan was not satisfied. She frowned, asking, 'Mummie, what *did* make you wire like that?'

'Wasn't I a mutt? Perhaps I got worried about your Carlo.'

'Oh, dear! I'm sorry. The odd thing was, it came just when I was trying to decide whether to come. Freda said it was telepathy. We got quite captious.'

'Did you? Why?'

'Because she's too intelligent to go in for all that unscientific irrational stuff.'

'I see.'

Virgilia had a little smile on her face. It made Nan feel young.

'You look a bit better,' she said.

'I'm all right … You tell me things, now.'

'Where shall I begin?'

'With Carlo.'

'Carlo?' There was a pause, then a drawer was shut emphatically. 'Carlo's a squib.'

'A squib?' Virgilia laughed. 'Oh, darling, and I nearly took him seriously. I was all worried up.'

'My flapperish letters?' Remorseful, Nan sat on the foot of the bed. 'Sorry, dearest. Actually, for three weeks I *was* in a bit of a spin. Do you have to have that sort of an attack once, like mumps and measles? Do you suppose I'm immunised now?'

'Against just what?'

'Against going all romantic about a person you don't know a thing about.'

' I can't imagine you doing that.'

'Neither could I. Anyhow, never again. It makes you feel shrunk.'

'Did you part amicably?'

'I walked out on him, and he lost his temper and smashed my beautiful head.'

'The bust?'

'Yes. Billy found it pulped. Carlo's vanished. The real catastrophe is, his landlady packed his things off to store, because he's done this vanishing trick once too often; and with them she's sent my white shawl. I used to wear it over my jumper at the sittings and I left it behind.'

'Naneen, you'll have to get that back.'

'Of course, I must. I adore it. I remember the lovely way Gran used to cuddle it round me.'

She went to the dressing-table and touched her cheeks with rouge. Virgilia preferred the ardent, clear little face without any. Nan's eyes, large and of the deepest blue, under dark eyebrows and lashes, and her shell-tinted lips had colour enough. Her brown, burnished curls spread wide, framing her face. She brushed her hair upwards now, bunched it on the crown of her head and fixed it with a comb, then turned to her mother and asked if she liked it worn so. Virgilia sat up and narrowed her eyes.

'It's nice. When did you wear it like that before?'

'Never, that I remember.'

'You did, darling; you certainly did.'

Nan shook her head, loosened her curls again and pulled on a yellow dress.

'You dreamed it.'

'You're thin, darling; you stayed in London too long; you must live in the sun.'

'Live in the sun.' Nan moved to the window and stood in the little recess looking out. From here she could see her work-table, washed with light.

'It's all rather perfect, isn't it, Mummie?' she said in a low voice. 'And, you know, I love London, too. And I am getting on. They've half promised to let me do *Peer Gynt* next. Imagine! Åse and the Trolls. And soon, when I'm paying my way, you'll come over often, and, here, you'll have a car. Every summer, this delicious place. You'll write books and I'll illustrate them. I'll draw and paint and paint and draw and not bother about anybody except you.'

Virgilia rose. She stood behind Nan at the mirror and tidied her hair. Not much danger of that, she thought to herself.

'Yes?' she said teasingly. 'That programme begins at once, I suppose? What are your plans for tomorrow?'

Nan laughed as she buckled her sandals.

'Tomorrow? Dr Franks, junior, is taking me for a drive.'

Brigid's bell was ringing for supper and they went down.

Chapter V

HIGH SUMMER

WHEN NAN WOKE, she thought she was in her grandmother's house; then she remembered. That had gone into the past, but something new and lovely had come. It was early; the room was dim but the windows showed sky palely tinted and the open curtains were stirred by a light breeze.

She had been wakened by an Alleluia chorus – the bird population in joyous song. She lay listening, glad to have come before the midsummer hush fell on the woods. Through all the jubilation she could hear a blackbird beneath her window singing a wistful little *aubade* of his own. 'Lady, sweet, arise!' he was saying. 'Lady, sweet, arise!' Nan waited to let her thoughts wander out over the wide, wild acres spreading around her and home again to her mother; then she got up.

The air had colour in it. Everything was giving out light – that diffused watery Irish light that seemed to shine out of the hills, not on to them – that she would never in this world be able to paint, though she would never cease to try. There were no clouds, only wreaths of mist slowly lifting from the summits of the Tonduff Mountains and Maulin.

She pulled on her grey jumper and slacks. She wanted to run up Knockree and watch the sunrise; she wanted to walk through the bracken and splash in the stream, but, not being a horse she reflected, I can't 'gallop off in all directions at once.' Carrying a towel and sandals, she crept downstairs, through the dining-room and the kitchen, and out by the back door.

She was in the kitchen garden now. It was neat. Much more work had been done here than on the flower-border in front. Beds of vegetables and herbs and rows of raspberry canes were laid out under the old apple and pear trees. This was the only part of the garden that was fenced; the rest was bounded by the stream and a rough hedge. The fence was well made. Beyond it, tall oak and ash trees climbed the rise that sheltered Derreen from north winds. On the east side, the wood stretched a thick arm of pine and Scotch fir between the road and the cottage; to the west, a thin row of larches bordered the stream. The light boughs of the larches were swaying gently, but the oaks were still. The rapture of the birds had quieted into a soft, busy calling; an anxious clucking rose from the hen-house; white butterflies with orange tips to their wings – 'poached-egg butterflies' Gran had called them – were hovering over the straggling buddleia; a cabbage-rose tree, heavy with overblown roses, grew near the fence. In everything, colour was coming to life.

The wooden gate was locked. That must be a precaution of Brigid's, Nan thought. Her mother never locked anything. However, it was quite easy, by climbing an apple tree, to drop over the fence. In a moment Nan was running under the trees, through the dew-dropping bracken, down to the stream.

It was shallow, but very rapid and busy: a mountain torrent in miniature. It frothed over boulders and eddied in pools. A short distance upstream, sheltered by a group of rowans and hazels, was a smooth little fall. There Nan stripped and bathed, shivering and laughing to herself and wishing she were a water nymph. After that she was hungry and walked up through the wood again. It will be more difficult to cross the fence from this side, she was thinking, when she saw a piece of sawn log leaning, conveniently against it. Standing on it, looking over the fence, she realised that someone or something was in the garden. Perhaps it was an animal. It was shaking the roses. Nan watched. It was not an animal: she saw a bright blade and a rose was cut off; then another was cut; then a third. The knife was held in a small brown hand. Nan decided on an ambush and slipped behind the thick trunk of an oak. Presently she saw the thief in the apple tree: she saw a shock of red hair, ears that stuck out and two round brown eyes in a small face. He dropped down and was lifting his log when she pounced. The two rolled over together, Nan breathless with laughter, and presently she was kneeling astride the child, who lay, as still as a captured bird, on his back. His face was a triangle, his mouth a down-turned crescent; freckles were spattered all over his short nose. Keeping a grip of his wrist, Nan let him sit up. 'Now,' she commanded, 'show me the crock of gold!'

The thin wrist twisted and he was gone. Agile as a squirrel, he darted and dodged, but Nan could run fast and soon she had him again. The roses were gripped in his fist all the time.

The child was not laughing; he was frightened. 'Let me go!' he cried. 'I done no harm, I done nothing; let me go!'

'You're a good boy,' Nan said quickly. 'You may have the roses, but don't run away.'

'I didn't steal them; she said I could have them,' he stammered.

'Mrs Wilde did?'

'Aye.'

'If she said you may why did you creep like a thief?'

'The old one hunts me.'

'Brigid hunts you?'

'She said she'd set the dog on me.'

'Nobody's going to set the dog on you. Do you like apples?'

He looked at her doubtfully; the crescent turned up suddenly and he nodded.

'I do.'

'Will you wait here while I fetch some?'

'Where's th' old one?'

'Asleep upstairs.'

'Where's the dog?'

'Asleep in the front porch. They're big, juicy apples.'

She ran in, collected her sketch-book, pencils and four apples. He was there, sitting on his log. He chewed the apples contentedly while she sketched. She heard a repeated metallic tapping from the direction of the thistle field and saw slender columns of blue smoke going up. So he belonged to the tinkers! And Brigid had said they would be staying a couple of weeks. What luck!

'Who are you?' she asked.

'I'm Sal's Timeen.'

'You're one of the Vaughans?'

'Bat Vaughan's me da.'

She worked rapidly, sketching the limbs and thin body clad in ragged jacket and shorts, and then concentrated patiently on the face. There was an innocent boldness, a frank wariness in it, not easy to catch. She bent over her paper, absorbed, for a moment, and when she looked up again he was gone. It didn't matter; her leprechaun peered at her from the paper, shy, daring and alert. She went in.

The sunlit kitchen looked cheerful with its butter-coloured walls and blue delph. Brigid was blowing up the fire. Among the white ashes a few vermilion sparks winked. Nan took the bellows and woke the smouldering turf to a golden glow, then set dry sods over it standing on end. The sweet reek that rose was the very smell of childhood to Nan.

She told Brigid, 'I caught a leprechaun.'

'He'll lep if I catch him,' Brigid retorted.

'He was picking roses; he said Mother said he might.'

'She did, I believe. Some bargain she has with him; but if I see him I'll hunt him, sure as he's born.'

Nan laughed. She enjoyed catching the placid Brigid in one of her cross early-morning moods.

'You will,' she said teasingly, 'the way you used to hunt me: with a tea-cosy on your head and a toasting fork! I adored it.'

'It's with the bristle-brush I'll chase that ladeen!'

'Was he with the tinkers last year?'

'No. Shut up in a reformatory, the police had him. He's after breaking out and finding his way to the Vaughans, the devil knows how. He got a warm welcome, I can tell you. Bat gave him such a skelping he roared the birds out of the trees … Drat that Eileen, reneging on us just when she's wanted! Like a good child, bring me in some turf and see did the hens lay any eggs.'

Nan found the two-handled basket; went out and collected a load of sods from the clamp; found three new-laid eggs and carried them in. She pumped water into the tank, then cut bread and butter while Brigid made the tea and set breakfast for two on the big tray.

She found her mother sitting at a table in the bay-window wearing the blue house-gown Nan had sent her at Christmas. The light shone full on her face. She looked as if she had not slept very well, but she spoke gaily.

'Where do you come from so early with the dew on your hair?'

Nan sat in a cane chair and the sun warmed her back. While they drank tea and ate bread and honey she related her adventure and showed her sketches.

'Good!' Virgilia said. 'You've caught Timeen's nervousness. It's an animal nervousness, like a hare's: a hare that's been trapped.'

'That child in a reform school! Would they stick him in again if he's caught?'

'I'm afraid they would, and he lives in terror of it, poor mite.'

'Brigid says Bat Vaughan beats him.'

'He does; but Timeen would rather be beaten than caged.'

Nan frowned. 'What a life for a child.'

Virgilia nodded. She had never kept a bird in a cage. Her widowed canary, Tweedledee, was at the moment flitting in and out of the small window at the other side of the bed.

'Tweedledee's a very valuable ally,' she said. 'The wild birds see him sitting on my shoulder and then they are not afraid of me. He apparently informs them that I'm not dangerous and don't keep a cat.'

Nan could not detach her mind from the boy. She asked whether he had been put in for theft.

'I shouldn't think so,' her mother answered: 'probably just as a waif. There are pious ladies who'll give a child money in order to get him committed for begging, because they think the school is good for his soul … The Vaughans don't steal.'

'Did you say he might pick the roses?'

'No, but I said he might *cut* them, with a knife.'

'Then why do you let Brigid chase him?'

'That makes it more fun for him.'

Nan laughed. 'Your ethics!'

'Sound psychology! I'm diverting his predatory instincts into a harmless channel.'

'Your logic, Mummie!'

'Logic is wisdom in youth but folly in age.'

Nan reflected, but there seemed to be no answer to that. 'Aren't they a worry,' she asked, 'camping beside your land?'

'Not a bit. They don't scare the birds. And the music they play on their gramophone is very good. And they mend pans very well. Sal's a picture! We must go down and visit Sal. She has hair as black as a raven's wing, a queenly carriage and flashing eyes.'

Nan looked at her mother's serious face. 'Is that a troof or a story?' she asked.

This formula, invented by Nan at the age of five, was still useful in conversation with her mother.

'It's a troof.'

'I must paint Sal; there are tinkers in the book, you know. What incredible luck! Mummie, I want to start on these leprechauns. Please may I start this minute? Promise you or Brigid won't make my bed? I'll do it immediately after lunch.'

'I promise.'

Virgilia heard Nan run upstairs and down again. From her chair in the bay she saw her in the studio window setting out her things on the table. The girl's movements were delicate and precise. Lovely, that young energy and ardour, Virgilia thought; that impatience to be at work. It was one of the secrets of happiness, surely. Nan was heartwhole and care-free, her universe singing in tune. Nothing and no one, Virgilia resolved, should spoil this summer for Nan.

PERRY ARRIVED at the stroke of two. His red two-seater choked and spluttered as he turned in and brought it to rest inside the gate. Virgilia was sewing in the shade of the ash on the lawn. Nan looked out from a window upstairs; she called to Perry, 'Shall I bring something to eat?'

'Good idea!' he replied, and Nan disappeared again.

'I didn't dare ask McCruskie,' he said to Virgilia, and talked amusingly about his father's awe-inspiring domestic staff. He's making conversation, she thought. He asked whether she felt all right and was assured that she did. He was standing against the tree, uneasily. She wondered when the torrent of questions was coming.

'Lovely weather we're having,' he said with a crooked grin.

Virgilia answered gravely, 'I'm afraid if the drought continues it will be bad for the crops.'

'There's often thunder towards the end of June.'

Virgilia laughed. 'How discreet you are being, Dr Franks!'

'Could I be "Perry," please, Mrs Wilde? I like having a separate identity.'

'Certainly, Perry. Isn't all this etiquette very hard work?'

'Very.' He became serious. 'But, Mrs Wilde, I want to apologise for badgering you. It was awful of me. But you see, I didn't know that my father knew.'

'I understood that.' She flushed slightly. 'I imagined this was due to some sort of illness, at first.'

'I'm sorry – honestly, I am – that I can't give you the help you want. I can understand, after yesterday, that it's a bit nerve-racking for you.'

'Do people ever lose this wretched faculty once they've developed it?' she asked.

'I think it fades out quite often,' he told her. 'I'll ask Garrett Ingram; he'll know. I won't let him guess it's a case.'

'I know you won't, Perry. Please tell me what he says.'

He hesitated. There were amused crinkles at the corners of his eyes. He said, 'Look, I'm threatened with disgrace, disinheritance and excommunication if I ever mention this subject to you.'

'I see,' Virgilia responded. 'That's kind and considerate, really. I want to forget all about it when I can. I'll consult you if I'm in trouble, Perry … Where are you going to take Nan?'

Nan was coming out in a dress as blue as the delphiniums in the border. Neither dress nor flowers were as blue as her eyes. Virgilia, looking at Perry, could scarcely believe that his young, pleasant face was the face she had seen, ugly with anger, confronting that cyclist yesterday. She observed the gentle care with which he made Nan comfortable in his car and tucked her dress in before closing the door. He was getting in when he changed his mind on an impulse, and moved back to Virgilia for a minute to say, 'Look, Mrs Wilde, you won't be anxious, will you? I won't take risks, I promise. Yesterday was a lesson. She'll be all right.'

'I trust you, Perry,' Virgilia said.

THEY DROVE SO FAST and talked so fast that they were up on the windy levels of Calary Bog and heading for the mountain before Perry came to his senses and pulled up.

'I'm a complete eejit!' he exclaimed. 'You're not in training for the Sugar Loaf climb. I clean forgot you're a Londoner. Why didn't you remind me?'

'You seemed to consider it such a shady thing to be.'

'But not incurable.'

'I walk quite a lot there, as a matter of fact.'

'It isn't rock-climbing. There's quite a scramble when you get to the cone.'

'I want to try it.'

'You shall, but not in heat like this, and you'll have to train gradually. I think Carrigoona will do nicely for today.'

Feeling demoted, Nan made no protest beyond the lifting of an eyebrow – the one on his side – while he thought aloud, assessing gradients and reviewing obstacles. By the time they were climbing the rough road that zig-zags up Carrigoona he had worked out a graduated programme culminating in Lugnaquillia. He appears to be organising my summer, Nan thought.

'That would be fine if this were a holiday, but it isn't, exactly,' she told him.

'What are you busy about? Painting? Can't that wait? This weather won't last forever, you know.'

Nan tried to adjust her mind without either smiling or frowning. She was not used to that kind of remark. She told him about her commission and that the work had to be finished within a few weeks. 'And, you see, this gorgeous weather is one of the things that I want to try to paint,' she said. 'It's the most fascinating problem you can imagine. For instance, just what colour *is* that blazing furze?' Gamboge wouldn't be rich enough, she was thinking, perhaps cadmium ...

'Yellow, I would have thought: or isn't it?' Perry said doubtfully. 'But I don't know the first thing about art.'

He looked depressed. Nan felt that she had been clumsy – that she had probably sounded affected or snobbish.

'It's the particular tint of yellow that I was puzzling about,' she said. 'There are so many. Look at that bush of broom. What a place this is!' she exclaimed as they came out over a wide view. 'I've never been here before. That's the Deer Park, isn't it? And the Scalp! The sea's like stretched silk.'

They walked across the sheep-tracks and round the slab of rock on top of the hill. Her companion was rather silent, but he was a person with whom you could be silent without uneasiness for a long time. He was, altogether, Nan thought, a man to whom nothing appeared to give any trouble. Tall and well made, he moved as if he enjoyed movement, and he talked as if he liked using his mind. With his lively hazel eyes and brown hair that seemed disinclined to lie down on his head, he gave the impression of being in command of a great deal more energy than he was finding it necessary to use. Pittsburgh didn't seem the right place for him.

'Does the snow really come down black there?' Nan asked.

He laughed. 'I don't know and don't care. Maybe Washington would be more in your line – white buildings, clean air, magnolias and cherry-trees and all that … You'd like America,' he affirmed.

'I thought it was usually to Germany or Austria that doctors went for special study,' she said.

'So it used to be: they had great teachers. But those are the sort of men the Nazis have scattered.'

He told her about Abraham Landauer, under whom he was going to work – a famous surgeon, a German Jew. When he went as a refugee to the United States Dr Franks's brother in Baltimore sponsored him. Now, with the help of a Carnegie grant, he was to continue his treatments and researches in Pittsburgh.

'We hadn't half-a-dozen talks,' Perry said. 'It's the most amazing luck that he should have remembered me, and gone to all this trouble to fix me up. He's doing it out of gratitude to my uncle, of course: they worked it out between them. The thing about it is, if there's a world war these treatments may make quite a difference. So you see!'

'I see,' Nan replied. She wanted to know whether he thought war was coming, but that was not a question to ask a man in the pride of his life on a hilltop in June. She said, 'So you know what you want to do.'

He smiled at her. 'So do you, I take it?'

'Thank heaven, yes. Isn't it extraordinary? Some people don't!'

'And some know but will never have the chance to do it.'

'To spend all your days at work that means nothing at all to you,' Nan said. The thought, as always, left her aghast. 'It's sickening to think about.'

He gave her a quizzical look. 'Do you think about it?'

'Not *think* exactly,' she answered with honesty. 'It just jabs at me now and then.'

His smile deepened. 'Something will have to be done about this.'

They found a grassy hollow, unpacked the rucksack and had their tea there under the scrutiny of two solemn bearded goats.

'How wise they look,' Nan remarked, lazily returning their gaze.

'This won't make a mountaineer of you,' Perry said.

They walked down the hill and round and up again to the rock. While Perry sprawled in the sun Nan sat in the shade. She watched the mail-boat glide over the bay and come smoothly to harbour. Nan felt as if a great deal had happened since she had landed: as if a new phase of life had not only begun but had grown familiar. Could it possibly be only twenty-four hours ago? A lark, invisible in the hazy heights of the air, was spilling out his exuberant music. Nan lifted her face, watching for him, in vain. She said, 'He sounds a bit delirious, doesn't he?'

'I wouldn't blame him,' Perry replied.

VIRGILIA DECIDED to call upon Mrs Doyle. Eileen must be persuaded to return to her job or Nan would be spending too much time in housework. As soon as the heat was a little diminished, she called Shuiler and set out on the fifteen minutes' walk. She went by the lane and the byroad. There was a shorter way; she could have turned to the right just below her own gate and followed the farm-track and the field-paths. The track was a rough road which split up to serve the farm-houses scattered about the hillside and the turf-banks up on the bog. At this end, the land on both sides was Virgilia's. The poor and neglected fields beyond belonged to Greg Cox, an old miser as sour as his land, which produced more poppies than grain. Secretly, Virgilia forgave him his bad farming for delight in the scarlet flare on the side of the hill. She would have taken that way but for the tinkers camped there. She would have been obliged to linger and converse with them and their dogs would probably have engaged Shuiler in controversy. He was over-excited as always when taken out. When Virgilia went on her bird walks poor Shuiler had to be left at home.

The birds were still, this afternoon; the tinkering of the Vaughans and the barking and whinnying of their animals were the only sounds to be heard. The Glencree River ran quietly under the bridge. The byroad was deep in dust; the hollies in the hedges had lost their sparkle and the wild roses their sheen. In the Doyles' meadow the hay looked ready for cutting; in a few days the mowers would be at work. The rich smell of meadowsweet hung in the air. It was replaced by the smell of dung, as Virgilia, to cut off the corner, went through the wicket and up through the Doyles' backyard.

Mrs Doyle was there, sweeping vigorously. She was a spare, active woman with straw-coloured, wispy hair. She ruled her family of six, from Phil, already courting, to the twins, aged eight, with a brisk manner and a caustic tongue, but the household was a cheerful one; her husband, a man notable for his silent but easy ways, prospered and her reputation stood high in the glen. If from any house in the neighbourhood there came news of sickness or accident, before the sun set Mrs Doyle would be there. The worst that the bitter-tongued Miss Clancy could find to say of her was, 'You do that one a kindness by falling ill.'

She guessed Mrs Wilde's errand and led her indoors at once. The usual chatter and clatter could be heard from the big kitchen. Virgilia was conducted into the parlour, a neat, seldom-used room. It contained a piece of furniture whose secret Virgilia had been interested to learn, as old perhaps as Goldsmith's *Deserted Village* – 'A bed by night, a chest of drawers by day.' Brigid had slept on it in December when the roof of Derreen cottage had sprung a leak.

'The little fool's sorry already,' Mrs Doyle said severely. 'You should have seen her face this morning when I made her take money out of her savings to pay her share and she saving up for shoes and her soles the way they are slapping off her feet. ''Tis all play-acting that she's scared. Lazy, that's what she is. Sure, who in their senses would be frightened of you? You had a dream, it seems, and it came true after; and isn't there many a one done the same? She'll go back to you, Mrs Wilde: I give you my word.'

'You see, my daughter has come,' Virgilia explained.

'Sure, don't I know. I was up the road and she waved to me from the little car. You'll have gay old times up there now, with young men flocking round. Pretty she is as the thorn in May.'

'She has a red jumper she thought might fit Eileen.'

'Eileen fancies red.'

Virgilia was aware of that deplorable fact. The idea of the jumper had come as pure inspiration. She would have to compound with Nan with one of her own.

'I'll expect her tomorrow, then?'

'You may, Mrs Wilde; she'll come.'

Turning homeward, Virgilia smiled to herself. If you had to have paranormal experiences this was a good place to have them in.

Under the hedge two school satchels lay on the grass. Three heads, one red and two tow-coloured, were bent together over some grave employment. High-pitched voices called to her excitedly and three sunburnt faces were turned up to hers: Timeen with the Doyle twins. He was showing them how the tinkers make the frames for their tarpaulin tents, with sally rods pushed into rows of holes on either side of a stick, their free ends bent and stuck in the ground.

'Will we make some tents for the birds for you?' Denny suggested.

'No; but do you think you could make a roof for a food-table?' Virgilia asked, and the youngsters promised with delight. Timeen looked supremely happy. For some reason that made her sorry for him.

3

JUNE GREW in splendour. In the mornings nothing could lure Nan from her work, but there were few afternoons on which the blast of a strident horn was not heard from the end of the lane, to be followed by the arrival of Perry in his car. Often, he and Nan would be out until nearly seven, when Perry, having delivered her at the garden gate, would turn by backing into the track and race off, probably late for dinner again. On Midsummer's Eve he borrowed his father's car and drove Virgilia as well as Nan round and about the glens until all hours, looking at the bonfires that blazed, as in pagan times, on the hills, lit in honour, now, of St John.

Virgilia's days were full. She cut sandwiches, made patties, mended and laundered summer frocks, devised suppers for a daughter hungry from climbing or swimming or riding. Perry had friends near Roundwood who mounted them both – two young bachelors, Nigel and Malachy Redmond, who were running a rather isolated farm and delighted in visits from him and Nan. Virgilia had few friends left in Ireland other than contemporaries of her mother, and had feared that

Nan might lack companionship. She was relieved to find her so well entertained and refused to attend to the faint misgivings that visited her without any rational cause.

Nan talked about Perry surprisingly little; in the evenings she drew or read or sewed, listened to the radio, went through Virgilia's manuscript with interest and talked a good deal about her own work. It was going better. Nan's palette was distinctive and lovely, Virgilia thought: she used very pure tints, contrasting them in a way that gave liveliness and brilliance to the whole. She painted the world as seen through rather young eyes; her background had an airy wildness and her creatures were quick with intention and vitality. Her anatomy was weak, still, and her pookas and leprechauns were more convincing than her humans, but she was working and learning.

'Timeen's better than a life class,' Nan declared. 'If only you could ever see the whole of him at one time! He looks down from a tree or up out of the bracken and seems to think that as long as half of him is invisible he's safe from the police.'

Virgilia's book might have been neglected but for Nan's insistence on her finishing it. When she was able to give a long afternoon to it she found herself working with unusual ease. The last chapter, 'Lovers of Pools,' was planned and the sketches and photographs for the rest of the book chosen and put in order.

The principal illustrations were all photographic; her sketches were mere head-and tail-pieces, and in these the birds – their arrogance, their belligerence and their flirtatious ways – were slightly and gaily caricatured. It would be a nice little book, she believed. Every story in it was realistic, recounting such things as could and did happen to birds, and she had scrupulously tried not to attribute to them any kind of intelligence but their own. Trying to comprehend the workings of their minds, their sense of direction, their responses and understandings with one another, fascinated her. It was a subject she wanted to study much more deeply. She would keep homing-pigeons later on. She wondered whether they could be taught to return to a mobile home moved to a different spot from that where they had left it.

Her mind was at peace. Day after busy day went by and she was unvisited by hallucinations. She slept well and woke free from the memory of dream. Perhaps that strange ailment was passing away; perhaps all she had needed was to be less inactive, less solitary. Her fears dwindled to the size of the light little summer clouds that feathered the sky.

Tom Cullen gave it as his opinion that the weather was too bright to last. He added, 'Thanks be to God,' either because he was tired of hoeing and watering, or because any continuing brightness was an offence to his pessimistic philosophy of life. Of all the gardens he worked in, Mrs Wilde's gave him the finest scope for grumbling. At Derreen on Saturday afternoons he was able to luxuriate in complaints. No doubt about it, the mistress was a queer one; given his own way, Tom could have had the garden in front of the house a picture, with nice patterned beds on the bit of lawn. But would he be let? Not for the land of Ireland! Long, the grass had to be left, with the daisies in it, and bulbs abroad and astray every place in no order at all. 'Twas a wonder she'd let you root out the dandelions; as for the foxgloves, they had to be left seed themselves everywhere. And 'twas as much as your place was worth to root the fool's-parsley up. When the weeds and flowers get the same treatment, was it any wonder for weeds to thrive? As for fruit – it was for birds and not for Christians they grew fruit at Derreen; if you left the nets off the raspberries for five minutes the blackbirds would be feasting; they had the gooseberries stripped; thrushes pecked the pears and devil a cherry escaped the tits. It was a heart-scald to see them at it, and not be supposed as much as to fling a stone.

For a time Virgilia had laboured for Tom's conversion, telling him how the starlings eat the wire-worms that spoil the grass; how the blue tits gorge on caterpillars and grubs, and woodpeckers operate on diseased trees. She called him to watch the goldfinches eating the seeds of the thistles which were his bane. Timeen, anxiously collaborating, had led Tom to a thrush's killing stone and shown him the smashed shells of the slaughtered snails. She had lent him books. It was useless, so she laid down the law and left his opinions alone.

Philosophic pessimism was Tom's element and he was deep in it this afternoon. The fruit was not swelling; the crops needed rain; everything was perishing, and some people seemed to be dancing with pleasure over the drought.

He started to water and Virgilia joined him. Since the well yielded only what was required for the house, bucketfuls had to be carried up from the stream. Timeen appeared at this point: this was the one useful job he would do. He would sprawl across a bit of rock, filling his bucket with the maximum of splashing and getting as wet as a fish.

There was something Virgilia wanted to ask Tom. She waited until he was going in to his tea and in a more mellow mood.

'I want to sketch a heron,' she told him. 'Have you any idea where I would be likely to see one?'

'Is it a *corr éisc*? You'll not get a *corr éisc* now nearer than Loch Dan. Left this glen they have, and a good thing too.'

'I seen one,' Timeen's high voice called. 'I seen one back at Loch Bray, when I was young; and he speared a fish – a big fat fish it was, and he swalleyed it. An' me da let a shout and he spit it back, and he flew off and left it laying on the rock and I got it and we ate it for breakfast.'

Virgilia was pleased. She would enjoy the walk to Loch Bray, westward, along almost the whole length of Glencree and a steep stretch of the Sally Gap road. The craggy hollow where the water lay was a lost, unvisited place. Very probably, the heron still came there. She felt a sudden eagerness to have a long quiet day of bird-watching.

THAT EVENING – it was the twenty-fifth of June and Nan had been home ten days – the girl returned from a ride with Perry in an abstracted mood. Her mother asked no questions except about small matters: what dress was Nan going to wear the next evening when they were to dine with Dr Franks? Would Mr and Mrs Ingram be there?

'My Harlequin dress,' Nan answered, and said that she must write to Freda again about the white dress and her shawl because Perry was talking about taking her somewhere some evening to dance. Yes, the Ingrams were to be there.

'I want to see you in the Harlequin dress,' Virgilia said with a smile. What a curious interest, she thought, my subconscious seems to take in Nan's clothes! How foolish I was to become so agitated over foreseeing such simple and such pleasant things!

Nan laid down the book she was reading. She was lying on the sofa, a little tired after her ride. Virgilia was at her table, filling in one of her own bird-maps.

'I'm not sure that I ought to,' Nan said.

Virgilia marked the site of the goldcrest's nest.

'It's difficult to know,' Nan went on. 'You see, he used to talk so eagerly about going to America, but now he doesn't any more. It would be a shame, wouldn't it, to take the pleasure out of it for him when he's not getting a thing in return?'

Virgilia, still working carefully, answered, 'He's getting the pleasure of your companionship, darling, just as you are of his. Isn't that understood?'

'I don't know. I'm getting worried. He's so considerate, and, sort of, controlled.'

Virgilia exclaimed involuntarily, 'I'm glad he keeps his temper under control.'

Nan's eyes opened wide.

'Perry's temper? His temper's the flick of a wing. What on earth are you thinking about?'

'That cyclist, I suppose. Perry looked as if he could have murdered him.'

There was a moment's silence. Then Nan said, 'I thought you liked him. I thought you and he were rather good friends.'

'So we are; so I do,' Virgilia said hastily. 'You know, Naneen, how I dread a violent temper. But apart from that I like Perry very much. He's intelligent, loyal and kind.'

'He gets cross for a second, and then laughs. His temper is *not* violent; he knows all about it; he's on his guard.'

'His father helps him, I expect.'

91

'Yes. His mother ruined his temper,' Nan went on; 'he told me. He says they fought like fiends. His father sent him away to school, poor kid, when he was seven. Perry had a rotten childhood. If anyone loathes tempers, he does.'

'Poor boy! Didn't his sisters stand up for him?'

'No. They and his mother teamed up; they teamed up on the Riviera finally, and didn't come home. She died there: food poisoning: it was awful. Perry was at Trinity College by then. He and Dr Franks tore out to Menton, but they weren't in time … Dr Franks hasn't had a whole lot of fun.'

Virgilia was silent. To marry a girl, clever, vivacious; to give her profound devotion, as such a man would, and then to discover an ineradicable vixen in her; to find himself inextricably attached, perhaps, to a woman whose nature ruined the peace of his home, strained his own nerves and tormented his little son … Nan looked at her mother, wishing that she would sometimes offer advice, but no advice was forthcoming except, 'Think very carefully, darling; think with your heart, as the Indians do. Then you won't go wrong.'

Nan went to bed early and so did Virgilia; but Virgilia did not sleep well. The old nightmare revisited her – the burning eyes and threatening hands of Suzette. She woke and saw the beginning of dawn – a grey triangle of sky at the top of her window-bay where she had left the curtains apart. When a woman wants to make a man suffer … she thought.

She fell asleep but woke again, and then she saw him sitting in a chair between her bed and the window, very still. She saw the whiteness of his face and hands. He looked old. He looked as if he had received a blow: a physical blow on the heart or in the face; his eyes were half closed and his mouth was distorted; the sense of grief that came from him appalled her. She shut her eyes and slept once more.

When next she woke there was blue sky outside. The memory of the doctor's face chilled her, but that, she told herself, had been a dream; a sharp-edged dream, it was true; she would never forget it. But then, she had been thinking of the doctor, and feeling a keen pity for him. That was why she had dreamed. Such cases were mentioned in Perry's books. What she had seen was no more than an externalisation of her own emotion; a projection from her subconscious mind perceived between waking and sleep. It was no portent for the future. She must not waste another thought on it. All the same, she would not tell Dr Franks … She and Nan were dining with him tonight. She would wear a spray of sweet-pea with that old grey dress.

Chapter VI

THE INGRAMS

THE VAUGHANS would soon be leaving the glen. There was a tradition governing these visitations: for a fortnight a neighbourhood would tolerate the tinkers kindly enough, let them ply their trade and call at back doors peddling their wares and collecting pots and pans for mending. They would even be given contributions of milk, butter and eggs. For just two weeks they might dig their dinner out of the potato fields and lift their cabbages from the different farms in rotation. If they snared a few hares and rabbits no one minded. To grudge the creatures their living would be uncharitable; moreover, the tinker's ill-will was well known to bring bad luck. The Vaughans were a well-behaved lot, and if, what with the mare foaling on them and an accident to one of their carts, they stayed a few days beyond their time, as looked likely, nobody except Greg Cox would complain. As for Greg, whose soul and body were as crooked, in Mrs Doyle's opinion, as the hovel he lived in, the tinkers made less call on him than on anyone else in the glen. They'd pass a mile wide of his place sooner than face his vicious terrier bitch. No question, but he had her trained to go for them.

Brigid's relations with the Vaughans were something of a puzzle. For her, the making of jams and jellies crowned the year, and she insisted on Shuiler's being put to sleep at the back, in the wood-shed, so that he might guard the fruit. Nan teased her –

'Aren't you every bit as mean as Greg Cox?' – only to learn that Brigid was sending Sal a daily supply of vegetables by Timeen and had presented the boy to Shuiler as a friend.

'I don't mind giving,' she stated, 'but to be robbed makes a fool of me. Moreover, I wouldn't like that one to be putting a bad wish on me. 'Tis plain to the eye that Sal has gypsy blood.' Nan, repeating this conversation to her mother, asked, bewildered, 'How can anyone be such a mixture of wisdom and crass, ignorant superstition as Brigid is?'

Virgilia said, 'Aren't you rather intolerant, darling?'

'I *am* intolerant of superstition and I always will be,' was the reply.

NAN HOPED that the tinkers would lengthen their stay. Timeen was the perfect model for her young leprechauns, with his bright, startled glances and his movements that were like a squirrel's – sudden and supple and smooth. Fortunately he had a quite human greed for sweets; she made pounds of toffee and it proved a useful bribe. There was a bagful ready for him on Sunday afternoon and she took it, with her sketching block, to the wood after lunch.

The day had grown sultry and thunderous. Virgilia did not know whether it was the heat that made her uneasy in her own company, or a sense of oppression left by her dream. The house felt empty. Brigid was in her own room and probably asleep, and Shuiler had disappeared. The weather was changing; a great cloud loomed over Maulin; it was a thunder-cloud, the colour of black grapes, its foamy edges dazzling white. She thought of taking a photograph of it but lacked the energy. Well, she decided, if I'm going to idle I may as well idle in the wood, and she followed Nan. Nan's whistle, answering hers, came from the hazel copse. There the girl was standing, amusement and compassion playing on her face. What she was contemplating was a patch of soil which had been dug, weeded, watered and raked. There were flowers in it – roses, each stuck in the ground up to its calyx and all except one dead.

'Timeen's garden,' Virgilia murmured. 'I remember he told me he's going to be a gardener. I wonder if a tinker's child ever does.'

Nan walked with her mother down to the water. She quoted Brigid: 'You wouldn't know whether to laugh or to cry.'

It was useless to search for her young model; he would either find her or keep out of her way. They chose a nook near a little fall and waited. Presently larch-cones began to pelt the ground round them, and a throaty *Cuckoo* sounded from a tree.

'Stay there!' Nan called up, and sketched the child riding a branch. He swung for her, then, like a monkey; landed and turned catherine wheels; stood on his hands. Virgilia was entertained but she protested: 'You're making him earn his toffee too hard.'

'Pull your shirt off and have a splash in the water,' Nan suggested, and Timeen sat in the stream, squealing with glee, while the water spilled over him, silvery and cold.

'I wish I could buy him,' Nan murmured, sketching rapidly; 'but look at his ribs: it's wicked.' Every bone in the little body showed.

When he had taken himself off to some hide-out of his own, Nan sat on filling in her sketches and Virgilia rested, watching for the dipper that she could hear, somewhere upstream, uttering his beady ripples of song. Most of the birds were quiet, drowsed with the heat. The tinkers were playing Grieg on their gramophone; the music stopped presently, deepening the sense of peace; then the dipper appeared, his white breast and throat flashing, and took his perch on a stone in the stream. He called three or four times on the same note, threw out a bright little jet of song, then curtsied solemnly several times – a performer acknowledging applause. Nan saw him and laughed and he began darting about, upstream and down again, until he dived and went walking under the water searching for food. Virgilia borrowed pencil and paper and drew his postures from memory, pleased to have seen the bird's pretty antics so close.

Her restlessness had left her; she felt soothed by the green shade, the quiet, the gentle swaying motion of the light boughs of the rowan against the sky, the pattern that its leaves, interweaving, made. It was strange, she reflected. This sense of beneficence in nature came to her only in Ireland; never in even the loveliest places elsewhere. Nowhere else did one feel like this – soothed and mothered and caressed. Did each country, she wondered, have this charm only for its own? As though there were local gods …

She sat erect suddenly, turning sharply to Nan. She wanted Nan to move, to say something quickly. In another moment she would have cried, 'Listen! Look!' Now she had forgotten what it was that she had almost, for a moment, heard and seen. Nan would have thought … What was she thinking now?

'Headache, Mummie?' Nan asked, concerned but calm. 'Shall I get you a hat? I didn't think you'd need one under the trees.'

Virgilia sighed. Things were in place again.

'It's nothing,' she said.

'You look funny.'

'Electricity in the air.' Virgilia rose. 'But I don't want to be head-achy at the party. I'll go and lie down.'

VIRGILIA CHANGED into the dress she was going to wear at dinner. It was of silver-grey lace and Nan did not approve.

'It's too fortyish and widowish,' she pronounced.

'I am forty and a widow,' her mother replied.

'You are also a very enjoying and young-minded person,' her daughter said firmly. 'And you look it. And that's how you ought to dress.'

Nan was in high spirits. She ran off and could be heard singing while she bathed:

'My mother said
I never should
Play with the gypsies
In the wood.'

Brigid, coming in with a glass of sherry, her own prescription for Virgilia's pallor, listened with a contented smile.

'That's a lucky young gentleman Dr Perry is; he'll have the light of springtime in his home. They'll be living in some fine house in Merrion Square, I suppose?'

'Brigid, dear, what are you talking about?' Virgilia protested. 'They are just friends. Nan won't think about marriage for a long time. And she'll marry a painter. She's not ready.'

Now why am I protesting like this? she asked herself. Nan's old enough to marry. I'd be bitterly disappointed if she didn't, and before very long. What have I against Perry? Nothing! Not a thing …

Brigid was telling some tale of his friendly ways: '… and didn't he come round and work like a navvy at that pump!'

'He's kind. He's a fine boy. I like him. But Nan's so young.'

'She's older than you were,' Brigid was saying as she left the room. A horn was hooting loudly. It was Perry's. In two minutes he was at the gate.

Nan had heard his horn. She ran down.

'Gaudy night!' he exclaimed when he came in and saw her. 'Why wasn't I warned?'

She was certainly a brilliant vision in her Harlequin dress. It was a slim sheath of diamond-patterned, many-coloured silk with a round frill at the neck, out of which her head rose like a flower. Her opal ear-rings sparkled blue.

She gave Perry an affectionate smile and immediately his cheeks tightened; his gay mood became brittle and forced. Yes; Nan should be careful, Virgilia thought.

He took the long way to the city, passing Doyle's and driving westward. The sun was in his eyes for a time, but great billows of cumulus were waiting for it and before long it was engulfed.

Now trees and hedges were left behind. The westward league of the glen is nearly all pasture and bog. The flank of Kippure on the left was already a cavern of shadow. Loch Bray, hidden under it, must look black now, Virgilia thought. A bright little torrent that rushed down on that side ran under the road, crossed by a stone-walled bridge. Down on the right, stark and ugly, stood the old reformatory. It looked what it was – a barracks. Built to keep insurgents in awe, its subsequent history, as a boys' reformatory, was grim. Perry said, 'Dev did a good day's work when he came up and closed it down.' Tilled fields surrounded it now.

The drive was refreshing. By the time they arrived at Fitzwilliam Square, Virgilia felt keyed to enjoy the evening. So, evidently, was Dr Franks. His clean-shaven face with its strong lines looked less tired than usual, and so different from the face in her dream that the grey image which had oppressed Virgilia's memory dissolved.

Golden lads and girls, she thought as she looked at the four young people around the table. Mrs Ingram sat on the doctor's right, because the dinner was in her honour as a bride. Virgilia's impression was of an active-looking girl with friendly, direct grey eyes and dark curls worn in a boyish crop. Her husband's face, aquiline, critical and alert, with hints of dry humour at the mouth and eyes, was less like the face of a person interested in psychic faculties than anything Virgilia could have conceived. He was swift-moving and compact as befitted an insatiable alpinist. During the meal, which suggested that Mrs McCruskie had for once submitted to dictation, the talk was all about places – about travel, and hills and inns, with a purple passage or two from Garrett Ingram on wines. Nan was thoughtful and talked rather less than the rest; in spite of her carnival colours she looked, to her mother's eyes, more mature than usual, sitting at the foot of the table, between Perry and Ingram, her hair brushed up and fixed on the top of her head. It was when Perry rose and refilled her glass and she looked up at him, smiling, that the dizzy sense of a double experience seized Virgilia. It had been exactly like that. But she had been prepared and only Dr Franks noticed that she caught her breath. He turned to her, saying, 'That's an old hair-style come back, isn't it?'

'Yes,' she replied. 'This is my daughter's first experiment with it as far as I know.'

'Very charming – and very interesting,' he murmured, and turned his attention to Pamela Ingram, who was talking about the house in Donnybrook that she and her husband had found.

It had a walled garden and a vine. Pamela, who had been trying to grow flowers on the rock and sand of the coast of Devon, looked forward to working on proper soil. She said that her husband's mother, an 'almost famous' horticulturist, was going to give her rock-plants from her garden in Avoca, and her own cousin, who had a nursery-garden in Templeogue, had promised seeds and advice. 'The difficulty is to find time to see everybody and collect things,' she said.

'*My* difficulty,' Garrett interjected, 'is to find time to be a married man.'

They all went upstairs together and he enlarged on his grievances. He wanted to take his wife everywhere – to meet his friends and relations, to visit the places she remembered from childhood holidays, to play tennis and swim; but his play was in rehearsal; the law-term had begun; he had to spend his days in the Four Courts, and weekends were the only time he had for his own legal work.

Nan smiled at Pamela.

'Come swimming with me!'

Perry gave Nan a baffled glance. Virgilia felt sorry for him but relieved: Nan had found a graceful way out of her little dilemma. Virgilia found herself and Perry being included in plans for drives in the Ingrams' four-seater car. She issued a general invitation for supper at the cottage on Sunday in return.

'I'm afraid I may prove a spoil-sport on Sunday,' Dr Franks said regretfully. 'I may want Perry to drive me. My chauffeur is a married man and he holds that the Sabbath was made for women. But perhaps, for once, I could drive myself.'

'Sure, I'll drive you, Dad,' Perry said cheerfully. 'Perhaps we'll get back in time,' and Virgilia promised that a cold supper would be waiting, however late they might turn up.

'If I might come some other time, instead,' the doctor suggested, 'after a less strenuous day?'

'No good inviting Dad,' Perry remarked, sitting down beside her. 'When he isn't working he's conserving his energies for his work. An evening like this is a terrific dissipation for him.'

The Ingrams accepted. Garrett thought that if he could get some clients to settle their case he might be able to take the day off for visits to Avoca and Glendaloch and come to Derreen Cottage on the way home. Dr Franks asked him about his play, saying, 'From the rumours I've heard, you've taken about an equal amount of skin off every party in the Dáil!'

'I've tried to be impartial,' Ingram replied drily.

'Who or what are the "Sleeping Dogs"? It's a very pretty title for a political comedy.'

Perry protested: 'That would be telling.'

'Who wakes them up?' Nan enquired.

'A certain lady – of course having no resemblance to any living person,' Ingram told her, 'becomes a member for Rathmines and proceeds to demand straight answers to straight questions.'

The doctor chuckled. 'I hope they'll make the most of it.'

'The company's doing me proud,' the author declared. 'Hilton's being the juiciest auld scallywag, and MacLiammoir's done a nice back-cloth – Leinster House gone slightly cock-eyed from shock and the statue of Queen Victoria casting an eye at it sideways, more in sorrow than in anger.'

Nan, enthralled by all aspects of stage-design, a field in which she had ambitions, listened eagerly to the discussion which sprang up. She described a setting that she had seen in London – the interior set of a new play.

'The woman is supposed,' she expounded, 'to be all sophisticated and modern, but she's a primitive savage underneath. Her rooms were grand: they might *almost* have come straight out of a posh shop, yet every shape and colour was just wrong. Not easy to look at, but it did make your nerves crawl. Peter Carey did the sets. He's exciting … Isn't it awful about writers?' she said, with an apologetic glance at Ingram. 'I can't remember the author's name.'

Pamela was smiling at her. 'Roderick Fitzgerald,' she said.

'He's her brother,' Garrett informed them.

'God help her,' Perry exclaimed. 'What a den of dramatists! Out of the frying-pan into the fire!'

Dr Franks rose, smiling. His young guests needed no more attention from him. He crossed the room, turned Perry off the chesterfield and took his place by Virgilia. 'I'm congratulating myself,' he said, pleasure and satisfaction in his voice. 'I did prescribe companionship, didn't I? I can see that a miracle has been worked.'

Perry had opened a book of stage-designs and the girls were immersed in it. Garrett was talking to him about the curious origin of Roderick's play. Virgilia's quiet voice reached no one but the doctor while she reported progress. He listened intently. The fact that she had found herself able to break off a mood of brooding in which a hallucination seemed imminent appeared to him extremely promising. He said, 'It begins to look as if you were learning, in your own phrase, "to hold the road". That disturbing sequence of sharp and detailed hallucinations may simply have shown that the strain of solitude had increased to breaking-point,' he said.

'It was disturbing,' she admitted, 'four times in nine days – five if that white dress comes along! I have never heard of anything like it, have you?'

'No – and I never shall again, I hope,' he answered with sympathy, 'for if you have identified the predisposing cause …'

'I believe we have.'

She told him about the small, cheerful activities with which she was filling her days and how a new sense of purpose had come into everything. The news gave him so much pleasure that it was easy to talk to him. 'In fact,' she concluded, 'I feel like a jigsaw puzzle when the missing bits have been found and put in! You see,' she explained, 'my daughter is much, much happier than the day is long.'

There was a pause while the doctor refilled his pipe. Then he said, 'Perry isn't being a nuisance, I hope?'

She responded warmly: 'He's giving Nan a wonderful time, and he is being very good and considerate: he never asks me a question.' She smiled.

'I think his passionate concern with the paranormal has ebbed somewhat,' was the deliberate reply. 'I think he has a more normal preoccupation now.'

Virgilia said candidly, 'I think he has.'

'I found him studying advertisements in *The Lancet*,' the doctor said. His tone had become flat.

'Advertisements of posts vacant?' She was puzzled.

'Yes.'

'But he is to go to Pittsburgh, isn't he, in August?'

'He doesn't talk about that any more.'

'Surely it would be disastrous for him to lose that chance?'

'Disastrous, yes!' The doctor spoke with strong feeling. 'Some men go through life dragging a load of regret – regret for the sort of work they most wished to do. They can bring a single mind and a whole heart to nothing. They don't go far. I don't want that to happen to him.'

Virgilia understood. His son was all this man had left of his personal life. His own disappointments and loneliness would no longer spell failure for him if Perry achieved success. But, she thought, Nan's world is the world of painting. No man who is not an artist will ever understand her, ever appreciate the subtleties of her elusive, sensitive mind. Nan's reasonableness would mislead any other type of man. He wouldn't understand that it is cultivated and sustained deliberately – brittle armour over a too vulnerable heart. It is hard to see Nan as a doctor's wife. And Perry ... Perry is the son of Suzette.

Virgilia's silence perturbed the doctor; she saw that with remorse. She said, 'What can I do?'

'I am trespassing,' he said in a low tone, 'but I think you will forgive me. I believe that the boy would go if he were sure of her, and that he would go if he knew that there was no chance for him – though very unhappily.'

'But I don't think that is the case. She has no attachment,' Virgilia said. She thought, what an old-fashioned conversation this is!

'I imagine he knows that,' Dr Franks answered. 'I imagine he thinks it worthwhile to stay near her, working in London, perhaps, and fight his own cause against all comers as best he can.'

'And you believe he would go if they could be engaged?'

'I am convinced he would. It would mean a year of waiting. His American programme has no place in it for a wife. But a young man is prepared for that.'

Her unresponsiveness was disturbing him and she knew it. He looked almost resentful. He was probably thinking that she did not appreciate Perry and was holding Nan back. This was all rather unfair and absurd. The children had known each other for less than two weeks. She said, 'I didn't think young people were so precipitate nowadays.'

He replied, 'One thing about human nature which never ceases to surprise me is the way it does *not* change.'

'Nan is a rather deliberating person,' Virgilia told him. 'She likes to test, and reason, and analyse. She gives her affection slowly and very completely. In your son's place I would go, and write to her very often and try my luck again in a year's time.'

He shook his head and smiled, rather sadly, looking at Nan.

'There are too many men in the world, and far too many artists; and her charm and beauty will unfold and increase. No,' he confessed, 'in his place, I'm very much afraid, I would stay. But I am being selfish: I have worried you, and that is the last thing I wish to do.'

HE HAD WORRIED Virgilia a good deal. She felt a little abstracted for the rest of the evening and acquiesced, without paying much attention, in the intricate plans that were being made. There were to be drives to Greystones and Athgreany and Avoca and Glendaloch. Nan was invited to the final rehearsal of the play. 'Monday week. Six o'clock, until all hours,' Garrett gave warning. Perry announced that he was giving a first-night dinner party at the Gresham on the Tuesday and invited his father and their guests, who accepted. Pamela talked of a house-warming party at Donnybrook for which she expected to be ready in about a month. Her husband, giving her a quizzical grin, said he hoped she would have no uninvited guests. At this point Virgilia decided that it was time to leave. She did not want Nan to become involved in a discussion about psychic things. Perry brought his father's car round and drove them home.

He had a case of records in the back of the car – Mexican and Indian music, dances and cowboy songs, which he had promised to lend Nan. He talked a good deal about them and obviously wanted an invitation to come in and play one or two, but none was forthcoming. He stood in the garden looking rather unhappy when they got out of the car.

'It was a quite perfect evening,' Nan said.

He replied, 'Not quite. Never mind. The silver thrones tomorrow!' and said good-night and drove away.

'He's in a bad humour,' Nan said, distressed.

A LAMP WAS BURNING in Virgilia's room. Presently, mother and daughter, both in dressing-gowns, were sipping orange drinks in the window-bay. The curtains were drawn back and the windows open; still the room felt airless. The ceiling was rather low. In the distance, thunder was rumbling among the hills; now and then their summits sprang into visibility for the time of a lightning flash, then the night was more obscure than before. Nan heaved a deep, grievous sigh.

'What is it?' her mother asked with smiling sympathy. '"The burthen of the mystery … Of all this unintelligible world?"'

'Just Perry,' Nan confessed.

'You seem to have crowded him out, rather, for the rest of the week.'

'Yes, and he's hurt.'

'It won't hurt him to be hurt a little like that.'

'But it seems mean; I played with him until there was somebody else.'

'He'll know it's not that.'

'Yes, but he won't know my real reason: he won't understand.'

Virgilia waited.

'You see, Mummie, how can I know? How can I tell whether it's Perry who is making these days the most perfect ever, or just everything combined? The trouble is, I'm having too good a time.'

'That *is* deceptive. You are quite right.'

'And, you see, for our generation, life is not going to be a summer holiday. What we've got to find out is whether we shall want one another when things are frightening and terrible.'

'"Frightening and terrible," darling?'

'Yes, Mummie, we *must* face that.'

Virgilia sighed. 'Dearest, I sometimes wish you were not quite so far-seeing,' she said.

'I'm not far-seeing! The very opposite! I try to look into the future and it is blinder than the night outside: never a flash! I try to see myself as – as a doctor's wife, and I can't. I've always thought I'd marry a painter. Then I try to see life without Perry and I – I don't like it … If I let him go away without knowing, how will he feel? Will it mess up this year for him? Would it be decenter to say "no?"'

Virgilia was silent. She was wondering whether to repeat any part of what Dr Franks had said. The thought of interfering was repugnant to her, as always. Life was so infinitely complex; such tenuous feelings, such imponderable factors might count for so much. The heart of another is a dark forest, indeed, she thought – even the heart of one's own child.

'Mummie,' Nan said pleadingly. She wore that childish look of worry and trustfulness with which she had always brought her problems to her mother. 'What ought I to do?'

Virgilia shook her head slowly.

'Perhaps you'll know when Perry speaks about it,' she answered. 'You must be guided by nothing except your own feelings in this.'

Nan beat her hand on the bed-rail impatiently.

'I want advice! You carry this non-intervention stuff too far! What are you *for* if not to tell me about things I can't understand? I want to know how he'll feel if I say that I simply can't decide for a long time.'

'I think that's what you *must* say, Nan, no matter how he's going to feel. You can't be rushed about this.' She spoke firmly now: 'After all, why should Perry expect …'

Nan broke in: 'He expects nothing; he's perfectly aware that it's all a ridiculous rush; he's sort of patient and careful … It makes me sorry for him.'

'Don't let that weaken you, darling. It is all too important.' The thought of her own marriage had shaken Virgilia. 'Tell him he must go to America and leave you to find out; leave you free.'

'But then, if I find out that it is "yes", Nan demurred, 'we'll both have a whole empty, wasted year.'

The bleak note in her voice made Virgilia's heart sink again.

AND WHY SHOULD my heart sink? she asked herself once more when Nan had gone to bed. This would probably end with an engagement very soon. Something had been said about dancing. Virgilia sat on in her chair, watching the summer lightning playing in the east now, making the studio roof and chimney appear and vanish again. Nan danced beautifully and loved it. I ought to give a dance here for her, Virgilia thought. I *would* if I wanted to help. But do I? But why not? ... Nan is happy as she is: she likes her life in London and loves this place ... How weak and vacillating I am being about this!

The lightning had ceased now and the thunder seemed to be drawing farther away; she heard it continually, swelling and fading, like a sea on a far-off shore, or like music about the sea. Her eyes were growing accustomed to the darkness. She could see the studio, softly lit from within, and the motion of the two who passed, and came again, and passed again, gliding, circling, as smoothly as ghosts. She saw the ice-white shimmer of Nan's dress, the twinkling at the shoulder-line and the wide swirl of the skirt as she danced. Perry was looking down at her, smiling, his profile clear. Nan's hair, drawn up to a top-knot, made the delicate outline of her head and cheek and the neck, thin as a child's, exquisite. It was the prettiest picture imaginable, and as distinct as one of those old silhouettes. When lightning flashed again it vanished. Virgilia sat still. She felt a little faint and her heart dragged, but she knew that these discomforts would pass. There had been nothing to be afraid of. Whether the vision had been a creation of her own thought or a true foreshadowing, there was nothing but beauty and happiness here. That had been a moment of flawless harmony.

Am I being foolish and cowardly about Perry? she wondered. Nan is not only an artist: she is a woman – very feminine in her nature, really, and vivid, and young. It isn't for his profession you choose your mate. Suppose Perry *is* the right man for her? Nan doesn't know: she is like someone struggling to wake out of sleep. And I haven't helped her. I ought to help. My response matters to her a good deal. I could either chill her spirit and spoil her confidence, or I could redouble her courage and joy. I mustn't show reluctance: there's no valid reason for it. I must act as though all were well. I will. I will give a dance.

Chapter VII

MACKEREL SKY

THE SHREDDED CLOUDS of a mackerel sky protected them from the sun and they climbed with ease until they came to the rock. Perry was right, Nan thought: you need to be in training for this. She was equal to it, and he did not help her too much. Proud of her prowess, he watched her feats of balancing and her work with hands and knees. She wore her old jumper and slacks and the freedom of her young, supple muscles gave her delight. She was filled with well-being and aware that Perry's frank admiration made a part of it – just how much, she was not sure.

He was on the peak before her and came back to pull her up. Green woods and blue water lay below; soft valleys and the tumbled summits of hills. A fresh, lively breeze tossed and teased them, delicious after the scorching rock. Perry held her arm, steadying her against the wind, while they looked down at the cloud-dappled sea and land, then he drew her round to show her where the great seats waited, hewn in the quartzite by the weather of centuries. They sat there on the silver thrones.

What was Perry thinking about? Nan wondered. Sometimes he had an arrogant look. Was he imagining himself the King of Ireland's Son, sitting there? You might think so from the smile on his face and the light in his eyes. Up here you could feel the earth going round: you were riding it: it turned at your will. That was the air he wore.

Well, this was the culmination of a plan of his, patiently carried out. He had trained her and brought her up here. What else had he been preparing at the same time? Had his brotherly casualness, only tensing at moments into acute care for her safety, been part of the same plan? She did not want anything to change that casualness. She liked things just as they were. She wanted him to say nothing that would create a crisis. She began to chatter. She recalled her childish ideas about this place and said thoughtlessly, 'I used to imagine that if a person sat here, and wished, their wish would come true.'

Perry turned and looked at her, laughing, his eyes very bright. The wind buffeted his sunburnt face, flipping his hair and the collar of his shirt. He looked untamed. He belongs a lot more to the hills than to hospitals, Nan thought. He answered her seriously.

'If two people wish the same thing it happens, Nan.'

So her remark had not been a non-conductor! Thinking quickly, she said, 'But they mustn't tell each other, you know.'

'Mustn't they?' he asked in a challenging tone.

'No,' she insisted. 'No, Perry: they mustn't! If you talk about wishes too soon the magic doesn't happen.'

'If you never talk about them nothing happens,' he retorted. The wind whistled in her ears and brought tears to her eyes. This wasn't the best place in which to keep your wits about you. He had known what he was doing when he brought her up here. She did not want to make things sound hopeless. She said:

'Something might, in time.'

He said, 'Something will, in time, because I ...'

He broke off. He had been going to say, 'because I will make it,' Nan thought. An overweening confidence was written in every inch of him. He might try to conceal it, but it was there – as if he believed that the force of his own feeling was invincible. And, yes, it was powerful. Its pressure was tremendous. It almost lifted you off your feet, like the wind. One had to dig one's heels in. But would it last? She said weakly, 'It has been such a short time. How can you be so sure?'

'It doesn't take very long to be struck by lightning,' he replied, almost angrily. 'You're jolly well sure when you're blazed at and burnt up.'

'Blazed at and burnt up': it sounded rather wonderful. But she did not feel like that. And it is not what you want for marriage, she thought. Something steadfast and lasting is needed for that. Perry was so much of a boy still, and for marriage, in the sort of times that might be ahead, a woman would need a man.

She checked these thoughts. I'm not being honest. I'm looking for an alibi, she thought. It is myself, not Perry, who might not be able to stay the course. Perry's grand, and he loves me and wants me for always. It's my own mind that isn't made up. Perhaps I'll never marry.

Perry's eyes had urgent light in them, turned to hers. Summoning all her resistance, she looked at him squarely and said, 'I'm sorry. Truly I am.'

'I see,' he said. The fire died out in him; his jaw became hard and set; then he gave her a difficult little smile and said: 'So, it's a question of time.'

'I didn't say that,' she protested.

He said, as if to himself, 'But that's what it is. All right, then,' he declared, 'I know what to do.' He stood up. 'We can't talk here with the wind in our teeth.'

He led her down to a sheltered patch of bog-myrtle and heather and stood braced against the rock. She sat on the heather and stripped the flowers of their buds, feeling, alternately, ashamed and exhilarated, depressed and happy. He gave her his old comradely grin.

'Cheer up! I haven't told you anything you didn't know. You can forget it for a while if you like. I was trying to have things both ways, and I can't – and why should I? Why should I expect to get the two best things in life? Anyhow, I'm not such a fool as to hunt two hares at once. When do you go back to London?'

'About the middle of August.' She was not quite sure what all this was about until he said: 'I'll be there.'

Then she protested urgently, vehemently. His work mattered. He mustn't give up his big chance of doing the work he wanted to do. She could have cried, and not only for the pity of it, and for Perry's sake, but because of the flat, dead disappointment she felt. His single-minded passion for his work was the thing she understood best and liked best about him. He would not be Perry if he let that go. He would become ordinary. Besides, if he married her at that price he would hate her for it in some secret part of him.

He took no notice. 'I'll wangle into the same researches in London. It's going on there, too,' he said.

'It won't be the same! You'd be so happy with Dr Landauer.'

'The snag is,' Perry said, more or less to himself, 'letting Landauer down. But he'll have time to get someone else if I cable at once.'

Nan repeated, 'This is your big chance!'

He looked at her and said quietly:

'But if, to take it, I have to risk losing the biggest chance of all? You see, Nan – you won't understand this, because you are still three-quarters asleep – but nothing else that could happen would be much use to me without you.'

Her throat worked and when she said, 'I wish I could help,' her voice trembled. She was tempted – greatly tempted – to agree to an engagement just in order to let him go to America happily and work well. But then, she thought, if, when he comes back, I break it, everything will be worse. You can't give a man a jolt like that. So she hardened her heart, though she could not make her voice steady, and repeated, 'I wish I could.'

Perry was tugging at a clump of bog-myrtle anchored by tough roots against mountain storms. His face and neck were red. He could not pull it up and he wrenched and broke the stems. He has fine hands strong hands, Nan thought. Not an artist's – a surgeon's, I suppose.

'Don't do that: you should take care of your hands, Perry,' she said.

He stared at her, started up and began striding down the mountain without her. She ran and caught him up and strode on beside him. She had all that she could do to keep up.

It was earlier than usual when they arrived back at Derreen. Perry would not come in. He asked her:

'Well, how are you fixed for the rest of the week? Being monopolised by Pamela, I rather gathered.'

When she told him – a day at home to receive her aged godmother; shopping for the dance and an exhibition of pictures with her mother; a swim and a sketching expedition with Pamela – she found that Perry did not want to share any of these. He was not, as he expressed it, 'feeling all that sociable.'

'I'll fill in the time catching up on my reading with Dad and watching some operations,' he said, trying to sound reasonable. 'What about Saturday?'

'Yes, Perry, I'm quite free on Saturday,' she said. 'Come on Saturday afternoon! Then there'll be our supper on Sunday and the rehearsal on Monday. You're coming, aren't you? And on Tuesday your dinner.'

'Lots and lots of nice things,' he responded drily, 'if I'm a good boy. Okay. So long, Nan.'

He sped away down the lane and did not look round to wave to her from the bend.

2

'SO WE'RE LETTING the world in on us,' was Brigid's comment when she was told about the supper-party and dance. ''Tis time for ye,' she added incisively. 'Birds is all very well.'

The shopping-list she presented was formidable. With this to be attended to and rugs and other things still to be bought for the studio, and the exhibition to be visited, Virgilia and Nan had to make an early start for Dublin. Nan borrowed a bicycle from Julia Doyle and they were on the road by ten o'clock. She was glad of this distraction. A good deal of remorse could be eased by a day in town.

She liked Grafton Street, narrow but sun-lit, with its crowd of lively, leisurely people, with colour in their faces and light in their eyes, all looking as if they shopped for pleasure and whether they obtained what they asked for or not really did not matter at all. She liked the well-cut tweeds and good handmade shoes of the women up from the country and the cotton dresses and coloured jackets of the city girls with a day off from their work. There were few men to be seen other than students in noisy groups round the bookshops and cafes. Nan had an ice while her mother drank coffee at Mitchell's, where the subaqueous atmosphere demanded the manners of a more formal epoch and the faces of staff and patrons alike bore the stamp of a bygone regime.

Then, the groceries were ordered, to be sent with the weekly delivery. Brigid had demanded unconscionable quantities of icing sugar and gelatine. Next, kapok and cushion squares were bought: the hereditary cushions were rather lumpy and thin. They found tints of green and rich blue and amber to give warmth to the grey-painted room. In a shop in an area basement they found rugs, hand-woven in greys and browns and reds by an old man living in a two-roomed cottage in Connemara who made up his patterns as he went along and made them well. They had budgeted for two rugs and bought three. 'This settles one matter,' Virgilia remarked; 'I have now *got* to finish my book!' At the exhibition, Virgilia found eight or nine landscapes and seascapes that delighted her and spent her time with these, losing sight of Nan. Nan was standing, bemused and enthralled, most of the time, before an abstract painting in which three god-like and tranquil figures could be discerned, less with the eye than the imagination, among strange harmonies of jewel-like colour and form. Rain was falling by the time they started for home.

THE NEXT DAY was wet. Nan's formidable godmother did not come. In the afternoon, the studio was given up to sewing and before dusk all the cushions were done. When the oil-lamps were lit and placed on their brackets they lit up a colourful room. No scheme of decoration had been followed and nothing in it, except the two Jack Yeats pictures, had cost very much. The colours of cushions and rugs were jumbled, but all of them were good and, with the reddish tweed of the sofa and chairs, they made up a pleasant harmony. On the top of the bookshelves Virgilia's lustre kept company with Nan's green witch-ball and Russian toys. The only curtains were of thin white silk.

'It's chancy, but I like it ... Winter curtains will cost you a fortune,' Nan said.

'They'll cost me nothing,' her mother retorted. 'I'm going to cut old blankets in strips and dye them and sew them up.'

'That will cost you new blankets.'

'We'll have the blankets.'

'You win.'

By Thursday Nan was conscious of missing Perry quite definitely. Saturday seemed a long time away, but she enjoyed swimming at Greystones with her mother and Pamela – or, rather, learning to swim, for they were very proficient and she had not yet learnt to manage her breathing. They had a picnic tea and made plans for the next day, when pleasure and profit were to be combined.

Nan wanted to draw a Stone Circle. Puck, having transgressed the Brehon Code, still the law of the leprechauns, had to stand trial, and it was in such a place, they agreed, that the court should be held. Garrett had advised them to go to the Druidic Circle in Athgreany, known as 'The Piper Stones.' In that place, it appeared, godless people had danced on a Sunday and the devil had been permitted to petrify them. There they stood in a ring forever with the piper outside. Pamela had arranged to call on her cousin, Nesta Fitzgerald, at Templeogue, on the way, to collect plants and have lunch. Virgilia was invited but could not go.

'I'm afraid I really must go heron-hunting tomorrow,' she said. She would not want the bicycle; Nan could ride it to Enniskerry. Pamela said she would meet the bus in Harcourt Street with her car.

'I invited Perry,' she told them, laughing, 'but he said, "You can be all girls together; I've got much prettier business on hand; I'm going to see a man build a nose." He sounded annoyed.'

There had been heavy rain in the glen. The trees in Derreen Wood glistened. 'Come down to the stream,' Nan said to her mother, 'and tell me how to paint wet woods. Puck hates rain. The leprechauns love it, of course, because they like rainbows. I have to paint sunny wetness and I don't know how.'

'I wish I did,' Virgilia said.

They made their way by the narrow path, parting the dripping bracken with their hands. Small birds were flitting and singing exultantly for joy in the moisture. A spangle of honeysuckle, swayed by Nan's passing, splashed fragrant raindrops in Virgilia's face. Virgilia began to talk about the old Irish poem praising the woodbine as the monarch who can hug all the tough trees and must not be destroyed. 'The pliant woodbine if thou burn, wailings for misfortune will abound ...'

Nan laughed – they had broken in so appropriately, the shouts and cries from the field, but when she heard a child's scream she ran. Virgilia hesitated, seized with dizziness for a moment, doubtful that this was more than a repetition of something imagined; then, recovering, she hastened, crossed the stream by the foot-plank and followed Nan down the thistle field.

It was Timeen. He was in flight to the wood, like a fox with the pack after him. Roaring men, with women screaming and pulling at them, pursued the terrified child. Bat led the hunt, a thick stick in his hand, and Sal, wresting a bigger one from another man, tore after him. Timeen caught sight of his friends and swerved towards them. Nan had almost reached him when he fell.

Three women now stood between the boy and the mob. Sal was the most effective, being armed with a long spiky blackthorn. 'Come on, ye slob!' she yelled at her husband, whirling the stick round her head. Bat wavered, looking doubtfully from her to Nan, who stood, a firebrand of anger, beside Sal.

Nan advanced on him. 'Go back!' she said fiercely. 'Go back and settle your quarrels your own way, but leave the child out of it!'

The crowd grumbled, seethed and split into small groups. The hunt was over. Virgilia murmured to Sal, 'Come up for him by and by.'

Nan watched with amusement the thrawn, wizened Bat cringe away from his towering mate and retire with his sulky cohorts back to their tents. Then she joined her mother and they led Timeen between them back to the house.

Timeen was not hurt, but he was silent from fright until they were in the kitchen. There he quickly recovered and began to relate, with lively gestures and grimaces, how Mr Doyle had come complaining about the tinkers' animals and how the row had begun.

'Sure enough, the grey mare and the jennet was in his field of oats, and they had the *braird* destroyed on him, and he says to me da, "Ye done it a-purpose," and me da says 'twas me, and he'd kick the guts out o' me; and me ma says 'twasn't – nor *'twasn't* – 'twas that Greg Cox; he put the animals in for to start a row betwixt us and the Doyles so's we'd get sent away. And me da says ...'

Not anxious to hear any more of Bat's language repeated by Timeen, they delivered him to Brigid, who clucked over the bedraggled child and soothed him with milk and cake.

Half an hour later, when Virgilia and Nan were having their tea, Sal presented herself at the back door to retrieve Timeen. She was entertained with a glass of cider in the dining-room. Big and handsome, with her black eyes and weathered face, Sal sat there like an empress. She was washed, brushed and dressed in her best, and adorned with bangles, long ear-rings, a thick silver chain and a coral brooch. She apologised for the bad behaviour of the men in general terms, implying that Mrs Wilde knew as well as herself that men could be expected to know no better. She expressed with eloquence her admiration of the comfort and beauty of the house; she was anxious to placate Virgilia, and Virgilia thought the occasion ought to be improved. She had been revolving a proposition for some days. This seemed the moment to advance it, and amicable relations were to be desired. There was a coral necklace in the back of a drawer in her room. She sent Nan to find it and when it lay on the table she said to Sal, 'I would like you to have this; it would go so well with your brooch.'

Sal's nostrils dilated and she breathed deeply. As she clasped it round her neck a rich colour rose in her face. She had her strong emotions under control, however, to be loosed only when there was a purpose to be served. She said, 'I thank you, ma'am,' with a great casualness, as though used to receiving such tributes. She began to talk freely about Timeen, asserting that he had done nothing, that he was a kind, biddable child, and a cut above the Vaughans; 'as he should be,' she added without shame, indeed, with a flash of pride.

'Bat,' she said earnestly, 'has it in for him. Out to murder the child he is, or to leave him be grabbed by the police – to get shut of him any old way. He swears when we go on now to Rathdrum he'll hand him over to the first Garda we'll meet. There does be a good few of them cycling the Calary Bog road.'

'When are you going to Rathdrum?' Virgilia asked.

'Och, any day now, I suppose,' Sal answered, 'and the sooner the better, for we're going to have rain.'

Virgilia asked diffidently, 'Supposing, Sal, that I could find a family where there was a kind, sensible woman who would take Timeen, would you let him stay? I would pay his board; he could go to school. He's a bright little boy: I think he would get on.' She spoke nervously; it seemed outrageous to ask a mother to part with her child, yet something had to be done. But Sal only hesitated for a moment.

'I'd miss the spalpeen,' she murmured; then stood up and said gratefully, 'Do that, and I'll be thankful to you, Mrs Wilde. I believe, on my soul, you'll be saving the child's life.'

She took herself off with a swaying of hips and skirts.

Nan regarded her mother with an amused, affectionate smile. 'Mrs Doyle, is it?'

Virgilia nodded. 'Yes. She had a boarded-out boy once, she told me, and was as sorry when he left as if he'd been one of her own. Timeen's perfectly happy with her twins. I believe he'd even go to school with them. He's not the real tinker type. Look at his garden! I believe he could settle down on a farm. She'd only want a few shillings a week. It's important really.'

Nan shook her head, laughing.

'You'll never possess a car.'

'I will: a second-hand one, perhaps. You'll see ... But this *is* important, Nan. Bat's a vile-tempered man. And a child like that could easily disappear ... Nan,' she asked on an impulse, 'did you ever hear Timeen scream?'

'Never before today. Did you?'

'I don't think so. I think it was only ... It was a curlew, perhaps.'

'*You* mistaking Timeen for a bird!' Nan's tone was half-laughing and half-worried. 'You know, Mummie,' she said, 'sometimes you don't look so well; are you working in the garden too much? Do come tomorrow; the drive would do you good.'

'No, no,' Virgilia said quickly. She wanted to escape from the probing of those clear young eyes. 'I really must look for that heron. I can't come.'

'Oh, please, Mummie! We're doing so few things together.'

'I must see Mrs Doyle. That's urgent. And if I'm to earn Timeen's living *and* buy a car *and* a Leica with a telephoto thing, *and* a cine-kodak, I must finish that book.'

Virgilia smiled, but her daughter regarded her with pained surprise. To want her mother's company and be refused it was a new experience.

'You're a disappointment to me,' she said.

Chapter VIII

THE WATERFALL

NAN WAS JUST STARTING when the postman arrived.

'Your trousseau, Miss Wilde,' he said gravely.

She seized the dress-box with an exclamation of gratitude so emphatic that he grinned; then, leaving her bicycle on his hands, she dashed indoors. Virgilia dropped her hoe and followed her as far as the foot of the stairs. In a minute, she thought, she will call me. She'll be looking at herself in the long glass.

That did not happen. What seemed a considerable time went by and then Nan ran down again in her blue linen suit, tying a scarf round her head as she came.

'It's a dream!' she said excitedly. 'Just wait till you see your gorgeous daughter! But, my grief, no shawl! Read that.'

She tossed a letter to Virgilia and calling back, 'Good hunting, Mummie!' mounted her bicycle and wheeled down the lane.

Freda had sent a fly-away pencilled scrawl:

Sorry, no shawl, no Carlo, no news! He has vanished without trace. I posted your impassioned demand on to a bank address

Leslie had, but L. doesn't believe there's no such place. What would Carlo want with a bank? Landlady opines he's at that 'ome again. Query, 'ome for 'oom? My guess is dipsos, but Billy doesn't agree: says he never saw C. under the influence. He thinks mental but I don't. Carlo's crackers of course but not nuts. What's your bet? Good luck for the dance.

Thankfully, Virgilia put the letter away in the drawer of the table in Nan's room. Nan might have become involved with a drunkard or drug-addict, and she had escaped with only the loss of her shawl. It was a pity to lose that shawl, all the same …

The dress-box lay on the floor, empty, its tissue paper flung far and wide. Virgilia tidied it. Very likely, she told herself, the dress is that love-in-the-mist colour that Nan likes. She felt sure, all the same, that it was white: white, with a long-waisted, close-fitting bodice and something at the shoulder-line that twinkled, and a wide, flared skirt. Acute as was her eagerness to see it, there was a certain pleasure in waiting – pleasure in knowing that Nan was still the child who so loved giving surprises and who knew so securely that her mother would never pry.

SHUILER, HELD BACK from escorting the bicycle, was rampaging for a walk. 'No, poor old chap, no!' Virgilia said, shutting him into the kitchen in Brigid's charge.

'Take your mackintosh,' Brigid warned her. 'It will be raining before you're back,' but Virgilia preferred the risk of a wetting to carrying anything more. Slung round with camera, field-glasses, sketch-book and notebook, she set out. She had sandwiches and coffee in her rucksack. If her vigil was long she would ask Mrs McGuirk to give her some tea. She was half-way to Doyle's when she spied a small brown creature dodging after her on the far side of the hedge. She called and Timeen crept out.

'You'll be going to look for the heron,' he said delightedly, skipping along by her side. 'Will I come and show you? Sure, there doesn't be no police on the glen road? And if I was with you, sure they'd be thinking I was your own little boy and they'd leave me be.'

'I wouldn't let them lay a finger on you, Timeen.'

'To be sure you wouldn't ... Look, there's a yellow-hammer, same as the one you showed me, only smaller. Maybe 'tis his wife.'

Timeen was darting round and about just as Shuiler always did and, like Shuiler, would have to be left behind. He came back and looked up at her.

'They do be on the big roads though.'

'Yes, they are.'

'I do be afeared of the big roads and the towns ... Do you know,' he went on, with a sly, sidelong glance and a tightening of his voice; 'do you know what I'll do if they take me and shut me up? I'll steal the cook's big butcher-knife and I'll hide it in me bed, and when they're asleep I'll kill them, so I will. I'll kill them dead.'

'Then you'd be shut up for your whole life long in a big dark jail.'

'I'll kill everybody,' Timeen replied.

She looked at the child. What age was he? Eight? Ten? Young enough still to be civilised, or already past help? He answered her regard with a wide smile that made him look like a candid and trustful child.

'D'you know what me ma's after telling me?' he said in a low thrilled voice. 'She told me when they go off on the big road, I'll not be going with them at all. She told me you'll keep me by you some place, and I'll be learning how to make flowers grow, and the police won't never be after me no more.'

Dismayed, Virgilia exclaimed, 'Oh, Timeen, suppose I can't?'

It was cruel of Sal to have told him this.

'Me ma says ye surely will.'

'I'll try.' To change the subject she remarked, 'That's a fine pair of britches you're wearing today.' They bore large patches, but he had been in tatters before.

'Mrs Doyle give me those,' he announced proudly.

Virgilia was pleased: the omens were good for her mission. They looked better still when Timeen caught sight of the twins, excused from school, no doubt, for the haymaking, in a corner of the meadow. Without a word he was away to join them. He could run like a hare.

The boy was overcharged with vitality; anything might come out of him – achievement or crime.

The smell of the hay was good. In the meadow the horse-mower was at work. Virgilia crossed the Doyles' backyard.

Mrs Doyle was busy peeling potatoes by the dozen to put in the stew. The never-dying fire of turf burned under the skillet and the kitchen was fearfully hot. Virgilia received an easy welcome and was given a chair by the table while the work went on.

'Some do say put them in, jackets and all, but I could never feel satisfied that scrubbing cleans them enough.'

Virgilia agreed. Conversation was general for a while as manners required. Then, by way of Timeen's britches, she came to her request.

Mrs Doyle laid down her knife. Shocked amazement appeared in her blue eyes. She spoke with a quietness which gave emphasis to her words.

'How can you ask such a thing, Mrs Wilde? To put Bat Vaughan's young varmint in with my own well-reared childer!' Virgilia saw that persistence would be futile, yet could not at once give way. She said, 'He's different from the other youngsters, isn't he? I doubt if Bat is his father, you know.'

'Aye, and I know well the name they'd put on him,' was the grim retort: '"Sal's brat", and worse: a word I wouldn't wish mine to hear.'

'He's a bright little fellow. The example of nice children is all he needs. He's devoted to your twins.'

'He is, faith, and I'm after getting the edge of Miss Clancy's tongue for allowing them to be consorting with him. I wouldn't go that far myself, for I think on my soul he's honest, and there's something you can't help liking about the child, but across this door he doesn't come.'

'Bat's cruel to him, Mrs Doyle: dangerous. And if the police take Timeen again ...'

'Look, Mrs Wilde, they say there's a big improvement in those industrial schools. They're not like the old reformatories at all. He'd no call to run away. They give the boys fine food and teach them a trade. The best thing could happen him, maybe, would be to go back.'

'The child needs a home.'

'I'm sorry, but it won't be my home he'll get!'

The thought of Timeen's disappointment and of what would become of the boy, driven wild by confinement or left to Bat's mercy, made Virgilia tenacious. With Nan at home, she could not take the child, even temporarily, herself, and to do so would be unfair to Brigid, at any time. No – her own home was not suitable and she couldn't think of one that might be. 'Perhaps,' she said, 'if I asked the priest?'

'He'll tell you the industrial school is the place for him,' was the reply. 'No, Mrs Wilde – you may spare yourself seeking, for 'tis the one answer you'd get everywhere. And, believe me, you needn't worry your head about that boyo; he'll come to no harm. He's as tough as a whippet … No, ma'am. You're a good neighbour and a kind mistress to Eileen; nor I'm not forgetting, nor I won't forget, all you did for us the time Phil broke his leg, but I have to say "no" to you about this.'

AND MRS DOYLE is the best mother and the kindest woman in the glen, Virgilia reminded herself as she went away defeated and sore at heart. She decided to ask Mr Ingram whether there was any legal resort. But the Vaughans would be gone to Rathdrum any day now and out of reach. Would it be possible to keep track of Sal? Would any offer she might secure come too late?

Phil Doyle overtook her, driving a truck. His leg was not strong enough yet for work on the farm and he had a temporary job, hauling turf and gravel to Rathfarnham several times a week. He was a big awkward lad, taciturn like his father, and as good-natured. He offered her a lift, but she thanked him and let him go on without her. Every yard of this glen road was interesting and she wanted to walk.

The small loch, hidden away in its hollow and often dark, was shining blue in the noon light when she reached it. She settled herself on the rough grassy margin, a boulder at her back, her camera on its tripod near at hand and her sketch-book beside her, and let her problems slide away from her mind. A few willow warblers flickered about, dipping their wings in the water. They were the only living creatures in sight, for the larks were lost in the light of the sky. On the far side of the water the Eagle Rock was in shadow and Kippure Mountain loomed up. A shining castle of cloud was being slowly piled up on its summit. There was movement, apparently, in the upper air, but in this sheltered and secret place no wind stirred.

Virgilia sat quiescent, knowing that soon there would come to her the blissful sense of release and extension of being that timeless and solitary places gave. One lost one's separateness at those moments and individual troubles were no more. To be alive was to be filled with a sweet elation. Nothing was necessary for happiness except health.

A water wagtail visited the loch for a while and flew away. Among the pines, magpies went in and out. Once, a stark silence fell; the small birds disappeared; the very air seemed immobile; a kestrel was circling overhead. He flew off and the small stir of life was renewed.

Now she felt hungry and ate her lunch and scattered crumbs for the birds. She sat so relaxed and idle that soon they were pecking from the palm of her hand.

She saw the shining castle change to a giant's anvil, darken, and drift. A ragged cavalcade of clouds began to travel low over the sky. There would be rain over the Sally Gap. Virgilia waited, care-free and content. The heat ebbed from the air as the sun declined and the shadow of Kippure crawled towards her over the water. A grouse started up crying harshly, 'Go back! Go back!' She waited. The loch was half in shade when the heron came. He rose, beating his great wings, out of the gap, then sank, to sail smoothly close to the water; he held his neck curved proudly, his long legs streaming out straight behind him; his black plume swung; his wings were a drooping mantle, richly fringed. Virgilia's finger and thumb were on the bulb of her camera when he flapped across her view-finder, his image trailing under him in the loch. She caught him then, and, again, as with slow beats he landed on the shore.

He strode on his stilt-like legs into the shallows where the water rippled, sunlit still. Standing there, he hunched his head down between his shoulders and became as lifeless an object as any weathered old stone.

Virgilia took her last photograph, made a few notes and sketches, glanced at the marching clouds and began to pack up. At least two of the pictures ought to be beautiful, she believed – the stately bird defined sharply between the glinting water and the dark cliff. She was amused in her mind at the buoyancy that so small an adventure could produce.

She was soon on the road again and, turning into the glen, found it still unshadowed, the river glimmering in its bed. The clouds would not close over for a while yet, she thought. Presently, ahead, at the end of the long valley, she would see the Sugar Loaf rise, aspiring and shapely, taking the sunset glow. There was a primrose softness in the light already; even the old reformatory was mellowed by it. She walked lightly for a mile or so, then paused on the little stone-walled bridge. The small torrent that fell down a craggy bank and ran under the bridge had gold in its shallows and diamonds in its foam.

There was not much water falling, but it made a great jubilation, leaping down the steep zig-zagging cleft. I must have been an Irish bard in my past life, Virgilia was thinking frivolously as she leaned on the parapet, entranced by the whorls and arches of water, ever dissolving, ever renewed. They had lived by running water; it was their rule. One could understand how the sound woke the lyric mood. The rhythm of it entered one's senses; your pulses seemed to beat in time. Had there been a great torrent here once? Big boulders, worn smooth as pebbles, some green with moss, crowded the bed and the sides of the stream.

Always there had been this continuing murmur here ... It was a droning, ominous sound; it was like a wicked whispering, now, in the dark. Under the arches the darkness was very deep. The rain was blinding. Giddiness overcame her, and deathly weakness, as she peered down. She could only see where the white disc of light fell ... What she saw made her run down, scrambling frantically over boulders and slipping on mossy stones. She discarded her rucksack and camera as she ran. It was Timeen down there.

It startled her, it made her dizzy, when she stood under the archway, to see him no longer. The water ran shallow and clear. She clambered up and down, peering and calling, until at last she was convinced that no child lay in the water, stunned or dead.

He's alive, was her first thought. I was mistaken. Timeen's all right.

She sat on a stone and hung her head down and splashed water on her face and neck. If one fainted here one might not be found.

She was shivering as she made her way up to the road again and collected her things. The road was dry still. There was no cloud over the sun. It had all been a hallucination: the darkness and the rain and everything. It had been a prevision. It was something that she was going to see. Timeen would be there, under the arch, his body twisted, his limbs limp in the flow. How long would he lie there, drowned or dying? It would happen, and she knew that it would happen, and no one else did or could know, and what could she do?

I prevented an accident with the car, she told herself, trying to control her shuddering, as she strode on into a mountain shower. A thin drizzle was driving against her face, now. There was not a soul to be seen on the long road. She had certainly prevented a collision that time, but then she hadn't seen an accident: she had seen only the cause of danger, the dog; and so it had been possible to prepare. But there was nothing to be done about this … warn Timeen? He would immediately want to look at the place. Warn Sal? Sal could not keep him beside her; she never knew where the child was. Besides, that was not possible: anything except that. Sal could keep nothing to herself; the story would be told at every door in the glen and Nan would hear it. Nan would have to live with this misery, this load of useless knowledge on her heart. Not for anything or anyone should Nan be dragged under the shadow of this appalling abnormality.

The rain blurred everything. Virgilia struggled on through it, wondering how far she still had to go. She had lost all sense of time.

And telling Sal wouldn't help, she told herself. This is predestined; otherwise it couldn't be foreseen. But perhaps not – dreams can be meaningless; why not these visions also, sometimes? That shadow hasn't appeared on the floor … Nan's dress may not be the same … She tried to hurry; she wanted to see the dress; but she was walking slowly now, growing tired, and her efforts to reassure herself were in vain. There had been a shock with this vision – actually *with* it, not only after it – such as had not come with any previous one. While she looked down into the water she had felt horror and fear; and she had heard the torrent and felt the rain. Compared to this, the other hallucinations had been fleeting and dream-like. Yes: this tragedy would happen, and there was nothing she could do.

2

WHEN PHIL DOYLE, driving back from Rathfarnham, overtook Virgilia he did not recognise her at first. When he did, he looked startled and asked whether she had had a fall. She let him think that had happened. His strong hands gave her comfort, lifting her up. He settled her on the seat beside him and put his tarpaulin over her, head and all.

When she stood on her doorstep at last she could not find her key at the bottom of her rucksack. It didn't matter: the door was open and Brigid was there, exclaiming over her and telling her that Nan was not in yet. Timeen was sitting on Brigid's footstool, half stripped, eating a baked apple, his face rosy from the heat, while his jacket steamed on the back of a chair. He had got himself half drowned, Brigid told her, putting out buckets for her, to catch the rain. Virgilia sat down by the table, struggling to hold back an outburst of tears.

'Would ye eat a bite of it, Mrs Wilde?' the child said, thrusting his plate at her. ''Twill save ye catching a cold.'

Virgilia rose and ran out by the back door, heedless of Brigid's protesting call. Sal must be warned. I have to warn Sal: it's my duty, she was telling herself in desperation as she stumbled through the drenched woods to the foot-bridge. In the middle of the plank she stood still. This was hysteria and nothing else. She was seeing, on her right, Nan's happiness and, on her left, Timeen's life, as if they lay in her hands to choose – as if she had to save one and throw the other away. It is not real, she told herself. It is not true. She felt the plank swaying; that was not true either, the plank was steady. Her heart was knocking like a wild suppliant at her breast. The premonition of danger to Nan was overwhelming. If this thing touched Nan it meant wreckage ... Besides, the danger wasn't immediate. They would go soon, the opposite way ... Virgilia stepped back into the wood, began to move up towards the cottage, stopped, turned and ran across the plank into the field. She *had* to tell Sal; there was no way out.

Her eyes searched the rain-swept field where the tinkers' beasts stood in misery, heads hanging, under the trees. The carts and tents stood in a row. Not a human being was to be seen. Which was Sal's tent? Virgilia began calling in a voice so wild and shrill that she scarcely knew it for her own: 'Sal Vaughan! Sal!'

A man's voice close beside her made her start violently. There was malice in it. He was sheltering there under a larch.

'And what might you be wanting with Sal Vaughan, calling her out in the storm?' he asked, with narrowed bright eyes. 'Since when is she your ladyship's servant?' It was Bat.

Virgilia shrank back as the man came and planted himself in her path. Bat mustn't know; Bat would make mischief – all the mischief he could. A lie came quickly to her lips.

'I wanted to tell her Timeen's safe in the house.'

'In your house, is he?' She had seen a dog snarl like that, but never a man. 'Let you send him out of it so! Send him back where he belongs! ... I'll thank you, Mrs Wilde,' Bat went on hoarsely, 'I'll thank you to leave my wife and her brat alone. Whoever owns Timeen, it's not you. Feeding the birds you have him, instead of snaring them! But I'll learn him and I'll learn him my own way. You and your bangles! You and your promises!'

Virgilia tried to explain about Mrs Doyle, but she was incoherent and blundering, repelled by the man, undecided how much to say. 'I can't help you; I can't help him,' she said. 'There's nothing anyone can do – only go quickly: you must go away from this glen.'

Bat thrust his face close to hers; it was squeezed into a small mask of hate.

'So that's the way of it? Bidding us out on the roads in a storm? Hunting us out to the long hill and the bog where there isn't enough shelter for a rat! We'll see then, my kind Christian lady; we'll see!

We'll see the name that'll be left on you in this glen. 'Tis not long you'll be here behind us if we go.'

'Go tomorrow; you must all go,' she said again.

'We'll go when it suits us,' he shouted, and spat on the ground at her feet. Then he turned and went loping down to the tents.

Virgilia walked home slowly. She was exhausted. I can't make a decision in this state, she thought; it would be a foolish one. They won't be gone till mid-day tomorrow at the earliest ... She stood still: an idea had come to her. I will let them go, she thought: wait until they are well on the Calary Bog road, away from the glen, not likely ever to meet Nan again; then I will bicycle after them and overtake Sal and tell her ... That was the solution. That was the thing to do. With a deep sigh of relief she walked on.

She expected voluble protests from Brigid, but there were none. There was an egg-flip waiting and a warm bath, and a hot-water bottle in her bed. Virgilia bathed and dried herself hastily, threw her wrap on and ran upstairs. She went straight across Nan's room to the wardrobe, threw the door open, took the dress out and spread it on the bed: white silk and ninon; fitted bodice; crystal beading on the shoulders; flared skirt that would shimmer and whirl. It was the dress of her vision. She left it there and went down. She let Brigid put her to bed and bring her soup and sandwiches on a tray.

She told Brigid. There was no resisting the question in the eyes of the gentle old woman who sat, her hands folded, quiet as a child's nanny, beside the bed. Virgilia told all that she had seen and what she had said to Bat and what she had made up her mind to do. Brigid listened and sat in thought for a time, murmuring, 'The poor little child! ... Tell me,' she asked, 'did he look to be dead?'

'He did.'

'Och, *Mhuire*, 'tis a pity.'

'Perhaps it won't happen,' Virgilia said weakly.

Brigid shook her head.

'That vision wasn't sent you for nothing. It is to come. As for telling Sal, I'd say nothing if I was you. It will make no difference and Sal could do harm.'

Brigid rose, hearing the sound of a car. She tucked the blankets in around Virgilia's shoulders, stood lingering and then said: 'Timeen hasn't made his First Communion yet. You might say a word to Sal about that. We might give her something towards a suit for him. No doubt his clothes is the cause of her delay. She's no pagan. I never knew the tinkers miss Mass. Please God, now, if 'tis death you saw, the poor child will die in a state of grace.'

Virgilia lay gazing at her. Brigid turned back at the door and added, ''Twas maybe for that the vision was sent you … That will be Nan coming home. Her supper's ready. I'll just go and heat the soup. She'd best eat in the kitchen and get dry.'

The Austin stopped at the gate for a few minutes and then was driven away. Nan crossed to the shed with her bicycle, bags and a basket, then walked round the house to the back door.

There was a brief exchange with Brigid and then Nan came into her mother's bedroom, saying, 'Wise old lady, to go to bed.'

'Brigid's wisdom and my weakness,' Virgilia said with a smile. 'I think we'd better keep you there for a day or two. You're the colour of a peeled onion, my beautiful. You got the father and mother of a wetting, Brigid says.'

'I like walking in rain.'

'Oh, I know your shady habits. What luck with Mrs Doyle?'

Nan found Mrs Doyle's refusal hard to understand; was angry with Sal for raising false hopes in Timeen and sorry about the child's disappointment, but she did not dwell on this. She said, 'Well, you did your best, Mummie,' and asked, 'Did the heron oblige?'

'The heron was an angel,' her mother told her. 'Did you sketch the stones?'

'I did. They're queer, suggestive, just what I wanted. Pamela drove me home because of the rain. We fixed the bike on the wing. We had a grand day. I wish you had come. Her cousin's nice – Miss Fitzgerald. She sent you some rock-roses and stuff. She and her partner are coming to the dance. Her partner paints, unfortunately. She's probably a good gardener. Pamela's tremendously pleased with life; she has acquired a nephew. "Rory by name and by nature," her brother's telegram said. Do they yell when they're all that new?'

'They usually enter their protest.'

Nan, sitting on the bed, pursued the topic.

'What is it like for the mother? When the baby's safely there, I mean? Do you really sort of hear the morning stars?'

'I did.'

'But then you're maternal by nature, and I'm afraid I don't seem to be.'

'How do you know?'

'Well, I've never thought about that end of things much.'

'You'd be a very successful mother, Nan.'

'Do you honestly think I would?'

'Yes, provided you were a happy wife.'

Nan became thoughtful. She said:

'They needn't go together. A woman can have a difficult life and give her child a gorgeous one. I've seen it done.' Nan smiled and did a thing she did seldom, gave her mother an impulsive kiss. 'Take care of yourself, precious,' she said softly. 'I'm famished, but I'd better change.'

It was only when she heard Nan running upstairs that Virgilia remembered where she had left the dress.

SHE HEARD NAN come down and go to the kitchen and shut the door. She listened, but no sound reached her. Soon, restlessness seized her. She could not lie here any longer. The shivering was over. She was not ill. She got up and dressed and went to her work-table in the studio. Nan, when she came in, found her there.

Saying nothing except, 'You ought to have stayed in bed,' Nan took wood from the basket and lit a fire. She went to her table then and sat in her usual place, with her back to her mother; but she did not begin working; she sat and stared out. There was nothing to see. Rain blanketed the landscape, slaughtered the flowers and streamed down the window-panes. Dusk and silence closed gradually over the room. Virgilia waited. She said at last, 'You haven't shown me your Piper Stones.'

'I know I haven't.'

Nan turned and sat with her hands on the back of her chair, looking straight at Virgilia. She said, 'You looked at my dress.'

'Sorry, darling!' Virgilia tried to keep her voice light. 'I couldn't resist.'

Nan's eyes remained fixed on hers; they looked dark, in the half-light, and large.

'It was awfully unlike you,' she said.

'To be inquisitive?'

'To break a promise.'

'Had I promised?'

'I thought you had. In any case, you knew perfectly well ... And not to say anything about it ... But perhaps ...' A pained high note came into her voice. 'Perhaps you think I'm childish about all this?'

'Dearest, about what?'

'Promises, and our pact to tell each other if we're ill and ... and the things that go with all that.'

Virgilia said softly, 'If caring for those things, my darling, is childish, don't grow up. I don't want you to change.'

'But *you* have changed, Mummie!'

'Not really, Nan. I've been a bit – preoccupied lately ... I've found myself doing things without stopping to think – like running up to look at your dress.'

'But, why? What are you worried about?'

'I didn't say "worried".'

'Preoccupied, then.'

'Well, I suppose, *you*.'

'Me and Perry? Have you anything against Perry?'

'Not one single thing.'

'Then you have nothing to worry about. And it's so *unlike* you to make mountains. You always used to dwindle worries to molehills. And you used to be such a darling to all my friends.'

Nan's voice broke.

Virgilia said: 'I'll be good, *acushla*. I'm sorry. I'll never do it again. Please show me your stones.'

It was nearly ten when the rain ceased at last. The silk curtains had been drawn and a lamp lit and set on a table near the fire. Shuiler dozed on the hearth-rug, his nose to the blaze. In low chairs, Virgilia was sewing and Nan working at her sketch of the stones. They did not talk much. Virgilia was exceedingly tired and Nan was troubled and subdued. Brigid came, bringing a bedtime drink of hot chocolate, instead of the usual orange or lemonade, and told them they should go to bed. They heard her going up herself. Her steps sounded slower than usual: an old woman's laborious tread.

'There'll be no Brigid for you and your children,' Virgilia said to her daughter. 'One doesn't meet her kind any more. The mould is broken, I'm afraid.'

'She has peace like a light inside her,' Nan responded.

'Are you thinking of Joseph Campbell's poem?' her mother asked. 'No.'

Virgilia recalled the lines and began to repeat them:

'As a white candle
In a holy place,
So is the beauty
Of an aged face.

'As the spent radiance
Of the winter sun,
So is a woman
With her travail done.'

The tapping at the window had been going on for a time, but neither of them had noticed it. It was Shuiler who, cocking an ear, observed it first. Virgilia put down her sewing. Nan crossed to the window and pulled a curtain aside. A small blotched face was there pressed to the glass. She opened the door and let Timeen in.

He was crying. He could do nothing but cry. He stood on the rug between them, oblivious to the dog's friendly nuzzling and their words, gulping his tears down only to weep again. He was a sorry little object, his clothes soaked, his legs scratched and bruised and his feet bare. They thought he had been beaten, but he denied it, shaking his head violently. After many questions they got an answer from him.

'It's what me da's after saying.'

'What did he say, Timeen?' Virgilia's voice shook. To see this child living and breathing shrivelled her heart. She was tempted to keep him and guard him but knew that her watchfulness would fail some day and then … No: he must go away from this place, so that, at least, what was to happen should not happen yet.

'He says you are chasing us,' Timeen answered, and choked on the words. 'He says you said they're to quit and me with them. He says you're going to put the police on us and he's going to hand me over to them and they'll shut me up in a reform'ry for me whole life. Sure you wouldn't let him, Mrs Wilde? Sure you'll hide me? Won't you hide me from them? I'll water the flowers for you. I'll be no trouble at all.'

'It isn't true, Timeen.' Nan had fetched a towel and was rubbing him; half laughing, shaking him gently, she said, 'Don't you know, you little silly, it isn't true?'

Timeen blinked at her, then looked up at Virgilia. She tried not to meet his eyes or Nan's. He mustn't hide in the glen. He mustn't stay here. What could she say to make him willing to go?

'The police are coming here, Timeen,' she said quickly. 'That's why I told Bat to take you away. You must all go away to Rathdrum as soon as you can.'

His face became stupid from fright. He whispered, shivering, 'Will they not get me if I go?'

'I don't think they will. Bat doesn't mean it, Timeen. He won't give you up. Tell your mother. Tell her to come and see me and say good-bye. Tell her … '

But Timeen had slipped from Nan's ministering hands and run out into the darkness. Virgilia's cry was shrill and Nan was after him in a minute. She ran to the front gate, found it shut and sped round the west gable-end while Virgilia with the dog ran the other way. Timeen eluded them, doubled back and was making for the lane when Nan wheeled and overtook him. He stood struggling with her. They could hear a girl in the field calling his name roughly and Virgilia called in reply until she came to them – a strong slatternly tinker lass who seized Timeen angrily by the arm. He surrendered to her and was led away, not resisting any more.

Back in the lighted room again, Nan turned a bewildered face to her mother. 'When did all that happen? The police! You would have told me … *Did* it happen?' she demanded.

Virgilia moved her head slowly, confused. She said, 'Don't question me, Nan.'

Slowly and incredulously, Nan said, 'It didn't happen. You told a lie.'

Her mother was silent; Nan went on, her voice thin and edged with distress: 'How can I know? You are hiding things from me. You terrified Timeen. You were brutal to him. *You*, Mummie! I can't understand.'

'And I can't explain.'

'But you must! Don't you see that you must?'

Virgilia looked at her daughter. She was so tired that she could not trust herself any longer. If this went on she might break down and pour out her hideous story as she had done to Brigid. No more evasions came to her; no more inspired lies, so she said merely, 'I'm going to bed.'

In a low voice Nan said, 'Mummie, you frighten me.'

Virgilia stood up. 'My darling, don't be frightened,' she pleaded. 'There's nothing to be frightened about. It's only that they mustn't stay.'

Nan hesitated and then said, 'I do know about things, you know. About things, I mean, that go wrong – that some people do.'

Virgilia looked at her quickly. Why not let Nan suspect the tinkers of some iniquity? It would do no harm. She repeated, 'They must leave the glen.'

'I should have thought, if it was that, you'd keep Timeen, at least until we could find a home for him. *Couldn't* you? I'd look after him.'

'Oh, Naneen, don't you know I would if I dared? … Bat,' she said, 'won't hear of it. I can't kidnap the boy.'

Nan shook her head, sceptical, puzzled, hurt. 'There's something you won't tell me,' she said.

'Don't ask me any more questions,' Virgilia repeated; 'I'm tired, darling; tired to death.'

Nan drew her breath sharply.

And now, Virgilia thought helplessly, she believes I'm ill. But there were no more questions. Nan became quiet and practical, covering the fire, turning out the lamps, fastening the windows and door.

'Give me one promise, and keep it,' she begged. 'Don't get up in the morning until I've seen you.'

Virgilia agreed. 'Very well; but I'm not ill.'

She thought, Brigid can keep a watch on the field and warn me in time. It will take them a long time to get under way. I'll call Brigid when she comes down.

She went to her room, leaving Nan to spend the first sleepless and fear-ridden night of her life.

Chapter IX

THE TINKER'S CURSE

NAN'S TORMENTED EFFORTS, between waking and sleeping, to find an explanation of her mother's behaviour led her to one conclusion: She is ill.

By the time she was dressing she felt convinced of it. A fit of inquisitiveness might account for her mother's looking at the dress but not for her forgetting to say anything about it afterwards. Some awful conduct on the part of the tinkers might have made her decide to get rid of them, but it would never have made her speak so to Timeen. It had been horrible. There must be some kind of illness that made a person do things without altogether realising …

Lacking courage to think along that line any farther, Nan ran down to the kitchen. Brigid would have noticed. Brigid probably understood what was wrong. She would have something wise and steadying to say.

Brigid was not there. She had evidently been out already: bundles of wet sticks had been set round the fire to dry. The sods burnt brightly and the kettle was on the boil. Nan began to put cups and plates on the tray. Brigid came in from Virgilia's room and said, 'Not that tray, alannah – the little one. She's tired and she'll take her breakfast alone.'

'Brigid, is she ill?'

'She is not, thanks be to God. I was afraid she'd take a terrible chill.'

When Nan carried the tea and toast into the half-darkened room her distress increased. Her mother, who, as a rule, looked lush and wide-awake in the morning, lay pallid and limp against her pillows as if she had been a long time ill. There were shadows under her eyes. Her smile wavered. She said, 'Sorry to be unsociable, darling. Don't open the curtains: I'll doze again.'

The shred of resentment which had clung to Nan's mind melted away. She kissed her mother and put a cushion behind her pillows, trying to conceal her dismay. She had seen her mother look exhausted before, but never before had she seen defeat and helplessness in her face.

Brigid had spread a blue and yellow cloth on the kitchen table and had baked the eggs in Nan's favourite way. Nan tried to eat. Presently she realised that the silence settling between them had heaviness in it, not peace. She said, 'You were out early: are the Vaughans packing up?'

'Not a sign of it,' Brigid replied.

'Did Mother tell you about Timeen?'

'She did.'

'I'm afraid she didn't sleep well.'

'Mrs Doyle disappointed her; she had her heart set on fixing him up; but the great thing is she got no cold or chill. All the same, she'd best stay where she is for lunch.'

'She's strong, isn't she?' Nan said.

'She has great health, thank God, in this place.'

'But she has been a bit run down lately, don't you think?' Brigid gave her a sharp glance. Nan was conscience-smitten. If her mother was trying to keep a secret from her she ought not to be asking questions like this. But she *had* to know. Brigid answered: 'Not a day in bed since we came to the glen – in a good hour be it spoken.' She rose. 'I think the fire will make toast now,' she said, and, turning her back to Nan, began arranging the red sods with the tongs. Nan remained at the table. She was silent for a while, then said in a low voice, 'There's something wrong.'

'There now, I nearly burnt it!' Brigid exclaimed, and handed Nan a piece of toast. 'Here's Eileen, early for once, just because we're not ready for her! She can be washing up the mistress's things while you finish. I'll get the tray.'

Eileen came in with more energy than usual. She put the milk and cream in the larder and hung her cardigan up by the neck, talking all the time.

'How's Mrs Wilde? Phil said she looked terrible when he picked her up – shivering and shaking and wandering criss-cross on the road as if she didn't know where she was; and me mother says she looked grand in the morning.' As soon as Brigid had gone the girl lowered her voice: 'Isn't it queer, Miss Nan, how sudden-like an upset can come over a person? The day Mrs Wilde flew at me about the telegram – did they tell you? Now that morning I saw her starting for town …' Brigid had come back hastily without the tray and was looking at her.

'Stop your jabberation,' Brigid said, 'and get the table cleared.'

'What was it about a telegram?' Nan asked.

Brigid, in her turn, became voluble.

'The mistress called Eileen suddenly about taking it from the boy and Eileen smashed a lovely Belleek cup – dashed it in smithereens in the sink; one of the set; treating valuable china as if 'twas tin! … Like a good child, Nan, get your room done before I go up to sweep the stairs. I've a mountain of baking before me. I have a pie planned out for tomorrow that will give Dr Perry something to talk about to that McCruskie one.'

Nan was defeated. Brigid – the direct, honest, simple Brigid – was evading her questions, covering things up. But she could not question Eileen Doyle. She took the brushes and dustpan and went upstairs.

PERRY WAS in a sober frame of mind as he drove to Derreen. Four days and nights spent in a featureless void had taught him what to expect if he lost Nan. A man was all right before he had found the girl he wanted – he assumed that he'd meet her some day and meanwhile he gave his heart to his work. But to have found her and know that however long you lived nobody else would ever do, and then to be left without hope – that would make a desert of life.

I made a mistake, he thought, talking on Monday. It stiffened her. If I'd waited till today I might have had a better chance. After all, you can't commandeer a girl who has everything already – friends with all sorts of talents and a perfect home and a job she loves and a mother like Mrs Wilde ... Nan really cares a lot about her painting and I keep forgetting that she does anything. Well – a woman can surely be married and paint. I'll have to swot up something about art.

I bet she hasn't missed me for a minute, he was thinking as he turned into the lane. It was just two o'clock.

He could scarcely believe it when he saw her coming to meet him. She had never done that before. And she had never before looked quite so lovely and lovable. He stopped the car to watch her walking along. She wore a cream dress and her head was bare and her face rather tense and pale. Of the challenging little smile with which she usually greeted him, as if armed to match him in a battle of wits, there was not a sign; forgotten, too, were the crisp little ways by means of which she had seemed to measure the distance and settle the level of their companionship. The smile that she gave him had a plea in it. His heart leaped. She has missed me, he told himself; she has!

'Please,' she said, 'will you drive me down the track?'

She explained, as she took her place beside him and he drove on, that the tinkers were leaving; that she wanted to see Timeen without having to talk to the others. She wanted to make Timeen promise to come back some day; to convince him that she and her mother were his friends. Perry could not make out what it was all about, except that Timeen was the kid she had been sketching, but he drove down the rutted road as far as the tinkers' camp.

There were no signs of preparation for leaving. The din of their work rang and clanged; the air was full of the smells of wood-smoke and tar; the spring-carts stood in a row with their shafts up; beside each was a hump-backed, tarpaulin-covered tent. Two men were greasing the axles of their carts; a large woman, strung round with gleaming pans and cans, was crossing the field to Doyle's; a sandy lad came towards the car leading two piebalds. Perry stopped and surveyed the picturesque scene. He asked, 'Haven't you painted this?'

'It's an early Jack Yeats subject,' Nan answered. 'If I paint for twenty years I might begin to be equal to it. All those animals!'

Ponies, jennets, mules, a melancholy donkey and a lean-ribbed, wild-eyed mare with a foal at foot were grazing, some on long tethers, some free. Greyhounds lay elongated in the sun, their eyes and noses turned to the cooking-fires. Strong-armed women were hanging iron pots on tripods and yelling at the children, who were running up to the wood and down again with bundles of sticks. The fires smoked a great deal and the women swore. Timeen was at the far end of the field with some girls. At first, Nan could not identify Sal; then she saw her flinging a kettle down suddenly and starting to stride up the hill.

It was Perry who saw Virgilia under the oak at the edge of the wood. She seemed to be coming down to meet Sal. A lot of the Vaughan women, and then some of the men, turned to stare at her, left their work, uttered oaths and exclamations and followed Sal. Soon the whole mob was moving. Perry and Nan left the car and dashed up the field.

Virgilia was trying to speak, but the tinkers would not let her. They seemed all to be shouting at her at once. Nan, when she stood beside her mother, clutching her arm, felt a thick ring of hate pressing round them. Somebody flung handfuls of earth.

At first no one came very close. They seemed to be competing in terms of abuse. They allowed Sal to go forward alone: she was the leader of the chorus with the first right to a grievance and the most powerful tongue.

Sal's fury and hatred were real. The stately matron had changed to a scald-crow. She accompanied her voice with violent gestures, as if she were flinging stones instead of a volley of poisonous words.

'That your lying tongue may be blistered!' she screamed. 'That your heart may shrivel! That your false smile may be struck from your face! That you may bring ...' Dramatically, she paused and gathered her strength before she said, slowly and heavily: 'That you may bring tears and terror to your own child as you have brought them to mine!'

Perry ended it. In a single swift gesture, he had the woman's face pressed down against his shoulder with his left hand and her arms confined behind her back with his right. He was laughing, and suddenly a cackle of laughter broke out. It was from Bat. This was the first time, probably, that he had seen his redoubtable woman put down. Another man echoed his glee, then another; some of the women joined in, while others rushed against Perry with claw-like hands, but when, after swinging Sal round, he released her, the whole rabble went laughing and quarrelling down the field.

Virgilia, her back to the tree, was gazing at Perry as if he and not Sal had given her a shock. She said, 'You're strong! You are terribly strong,' again and again. She said: 'I only came to make sure they were going to Rathdrum today. I expect, after this, they will. Thank you, Perry; you were a great help.'

Perry looked at her, puzzled. Her reaction to the episode seemed to him odd. She had been on very good terms with the tinkers, he understood. She appeared scarcely surprised by their fury, and yet she looked white and shocked.

'Come on; we'll see you home,' he said.

'I think I'll stay at home, Perry,' Nan began as they walked, one on each side of Virgilia, between the trees.

Virgilia shook her head. 'No, no. I'll be busy: I'm going to develop my photographs. I'd rather you went for your drive. You're going to deliver those invitations, aren't you, at Roundwood?'

'Good!' Perry exclaimed. 'Does that mean that Nigel and Malachy are being invited to the dance? They don't get a dance twice in a year. They'll go up in smoke.'

'That will be five couples, won't it?' Virgilia said, and began to count up. 'I wonder if your father will come, Perry? Ada has accepted.

Ada Stack, I mean. I wish he would. This is Saturday, isn't it? The second of July, isn't it? Yes. We have ten days.'

She was talking very fast and shakily. Nan noticed, against her pallor, a spot of colour in each cheek and realised that her mother had put on rouge. She hasn't got any, Nan reflected. She has used mine. Why did she, suddenly? What a queer thing to do. It's all wrong. It doesn't suit her at all.

Perry was chattering about gramophone records.

'Dad's not only coming; he's pestering me about the music,' he said with a grin. When they were in the kitchen he started to tease Brigid, asking what she was going to give them for supper tomorrow. 'I'll be hungry,' he warned her, 'after driving all the way from the Black North.'

'I'll keep a sardine sandwich for you,' she promised with a chuckle.

Virgilia sat crouching over the kitchen fire. Perry turned to Nan, saying, 'We might go on to Loch Dan for tea and borrow a boat. Perhaps you'd better bring a coat, hadn't you?'

Virgilia said, 'You'll have to change your dress, I'm afraid, Nan. There's mud on the skirt.'

Brigid said, 'Let you sit by the fire now, ma'am, and be aisy. I'll ready your room before I start on the cakes.'

As Nan went upstairs Brigid was going into Virgilia's room.

Perry sat by the kitchen table.

'I'm afraid, ma'am, the weather is broken,' he said in country conversational style. He was smiling at her. She wanted to respond. She *had* to tell Perry. And he could be trusted. He was a fine boy, too, in his light, funny way. But that gesture of his – it had been the gesture of an apache: uncivilised, too sudden, too strong.

'Perry,' she said, 'it is Timeen. It was yesterday. You know the stone bridge on the glen road, about four miles from here? A little torrent flows under it … I saw him lying there, in the water. I ran down. It was the clearest vision I've ever had.'

'Is he all right?' Perry asked sharply.

'Yes: he's all right; and now they are going off the opposite way – to Rathdrum, over Calary Bog.'

'I see! So that's why you're trying to hurry them off? And they don't want to go?'

'They resent being asked to.'

'They would. I suppose you didn't say why?'

'No, Perry: I only said they must go.'

'Yes, of course!'

'But, you see,' she went on, 'some time – next spring, very likely – they'll pass over that bridge.'

Perry nodded. He was frowning. He said, 'This is absolutely foul for you.'

He has changed, she thought. His interest was no longer impersonal and detached. She said, 'I don't know what to do.'

He asked thoughtfully: 'Did he seem to be dead?'

'Yes,' she replied, 'but I'm not sure.'

'I suppose, then, his father ought to be told,' Perry said reluctantly, 'or his mother. But, right enough, they could make trouble for you.'

Perry was baffled and Virgilia felt keen disappointment. She had imagined that he might say something that would make it all seem less serious – less inevitable. She talked hurriedly. In a moment Nan would come down.

'*Must* it happen, Perry? May it not have been just a sort of dream or projection? I had been worrying about him, and had sort of suppressed the worry. I was alone, bird-watching ... Couldn't it be a mix-up in my own mind?'

'A clear mind like yours? No!' Perry responded emphatically, 'I'd work on the hypothesis that it is a plain case of prevision, Mrs Wilde. It's hard to know what you should do.'

Rapidly, she told him about her plan to tell Sal. He approved warmly.

'I think that's a first-rate idea,' he said.

'Do you, Perry?'

'I'm sure you can't do better than that.'

His certitude was a relief. It was a relief to have told him. She said, 'You've been very good, Perry. Try to keep Nan distracted. Try not to let her worry about me.'

They heard Nan coming downstairs.

'I think you should tell her,' Perry said quickly. 'Sooner or later she's got to know. Let me explain to her, now, or while we are out. She *will* worry. You don't look well.'

Virgilia shook her head.

Nan came in, wearing her yellow frock. She said, 'I don't think your dark-room's the place for you, Mummie, after all that. Do you, Perry?'

'I'd prescribe anything that will keep the lady amused,' he said airily, and went with Nan to the car.

3

HE ASKED NAN no questions. She told him: 'Mother wanted to get Timeen boarded at Doyle's and Sal agreed, but his father was furious and some mischief seems to have been worked up. I don't understand it.'

'The ways of tinkers are past understanding,' he answered cheerfully, and began to talk about a post in London which he had been offered and had refused. 'Too cushy,' he said, 'no research. I'll get something nearer to it than that.'

She said, 'You ought to go to Pittsburgh; you know you ought.' But there was much less conviction in her tone than there had been on Monday – so much less that Perry turned on her a quick, bright glance.

She told him hastily that her own plans were a bit unsettled. She might return to London for only a few weeks and spend the autumn with her mother.

'At least,' he said quietly, 'you wouldn't be three thousand miles away.' Then he asked her whether a lazy afternoon would suit her.

'Quite perfectly,' she agreed.

They called at the Redmonds', found the young farmers in the hayfield and delivered the invitation, which was accepted with whoops of enthusiasm.

'I'll have to get my dicky back from Uncle,' Nigel said, his blue eyes twinkling.

Malachy boasted, 'I'm all right. I've got a pal at the Abbey who plays gents.'

'As we hope to provide a full moon, a garden and a wood complete with running water, I think it had better be flannels,' Nan told them.

'I like girls in flowing robes, though,' Malachy protested, and Nan promised that she and her female friends would sacrifice themselves and dress up.

'Just you stick to that!' Perry ordered as they drove away to Loch Dan.

They had tea at the inn and borrowed the innkeeper's boat. The small mountain lake, with grassy hillsides sloping away from it, glimmered softly under the veiled sky. Trout were leaping and two fishermen sat on the bank. Perry pulled the heavy boat, its rowlocks creaking, to a nook among tall sedges and shipped the oars. He felt exhilarated, yet anxious. Nan, he believed, was going to confide in him. Except for the moments of gaiety with the Redmonds she had been very quiet the whole afternoon. There was trouble in the depths of her eyes. It was not all because he was going to London instead of to America. He believed, and the thought was sweet to his heart, that today she was half glad of that. He believed he could make her entirely glad if she would tell him her trouble and he could comfort her. Her worry could be cleared up. She wasn't a nervy girl: she wouldn't take things as hard as her mother did, especially if he could explain it all in his own way. But *could* he? Was he going to be able to reassure her, tied up with promises as he was? He said gently, 'What is it, Nan?'

She was trailing her hand in the water and watching it. She looked up and her eyes rested on his face.

'I'm worried about Mother,' she said.

'She'll be all right.'

'Perry, she's not herself: she's not well.'

He had foreseen this. Nan had been kept guessing. She had realised that something was wrong. Now, for the first time, her eyes were fixed on his in appeal. He thought, she is remembering that I'm a medical man.

'People have ups and downs; I wouldn't worry,' he said.

'But Mother doesn't; she never used to, and I've seen her in some very difficult times. She has always been so *equal* to things. She never fusses or makes complications. She never made mysteries, even when I was a child. She's the *clearest* person. And now, quite suddenly, she's shut away in some dark place of her own. All I know is, something is eating her up with worry, so that she's doing things and saying things utterly unlike her. And she's pushing me out.'

Nan bent her head down. She was frightened. Perry had seen fear darken her eyes. Something in the way Nan bent her head made him want to throw promises, loyalties, everything, overboard. He said helplessly, 'Perhaps it will be over soon.'

Nan looked at him, puzzled.

'What will be over? What do you mean?'

He did not answer that question; he said instead, 'Look, Nan, people having no secrets from one another is all very well, but it can't go on always, can it? What I mean is, refusing to let her keep anything to herself could become a bit of a tyranny, couldn't it?'

'I ought to know ...' She hesitated, and looked into the water again before saying in a low voice, 'She has no one else now. I ought to know if she is ill. Yet she swears she's not and I mustn't nag her. I do see that.'

He played for time. 'What makes you think she is ill?'

'You saw,' Nan replied. 'That wasn't a natural reaction – all that chatter about the dance, and then shivering. It wasn't *her* – and there have been other things.'

Perry searched his mind desperately for something to say. Before he could devise anything Nan confronted him with the question he had feared must come. It took all her courage to ask it, he knew.

'Tell me, Perry, how did she meet your father again?'

He said gently, 'She was never his patient, Nan.'

Her face lit up.

'You are sure?'

'Quite sure.'

'Then how *did* they meet?'

'You must ask *her* about that.'

Nan sat staring at him. She said slowly, 'You know and you won't tell me. There *is* something. You and your father know about this. And Brigid. And Eileen Doyle. You do know; you were talking to Mother after you got rid of me. You are not on my side.'

She was looking away from him, shrinking a little, as if he were an enemy. She looked frozen. Perry felt his own face burning. This is hell, he was thinking. She had got to be told. He would have it out with his father the moment he got home. No. That would be worse than useless ... He'd have it out with Mrs Wilde ... But he hadn't the right. It was a deadlock. Nan must make her mother explain. Yet he couldn't very well put her up to insisting. There was nothing for it but to wait. He said imploringly, 'Nan, listen! You wouldn't be angry with me if you understood.'

She sat still, a stricken and desolate figure. He leaned forward and caught her hands. With a violent movement she tore them away. She turned with a mute, closed face, then groped for the steering ropes and said, 'It's time to go home.'

Perry decided on silence. He realised that anything short of the truth would make his offence blacker and her misery more complete. A rage of frustration filled him, but he said nothing. He pushed off and rowed back to the inn.

Nan's anger lasted all the way home. Their efforts to talk about other things failed. When they came to the bottom of Derreen Lane she told him she wanted to walk up; made him stop there and let her out. He asked her whether she was going with the Ingrams to Avoca and Glendaloch the next morning and whether the supper invitation still held.

'There's no change that I know of,' she said.

'I'll be latish,' he told her, 'but I'll come.' Leaning from the driver's seat, he said, 'Listen, Nan: you've got to trust me. I'll get this put straight somehow. I'll do everything I can for you. There's nothing I wouldn't do. Nothing matters to me except you. Nothing, Nan. Get that?'

She gave him a bleak look, said, 'I'm sorry if I'm being unreasonable,' and turned and walked away from him up the lane.

I AM OLDER than she was when she was married, Nan said to herself; and yet none of them think I can stand being told that she's ill. They tell me clever lies: 'Not a day in bed ...' You can have a nervous breakdown without going to bed ... What kind of illness is there that can change a gay, sweet, adventurous person into one who gets up scares about nothing, and bullies people, and terrifies a child, and tells wild lies? I could stand anything, she thought bitterly, if she'd tell me the truth.

Then she began to wonder, Why doesn't she? Am I not the sort of daughter you turn to in trouble? Do they all think I'm a weak creature who must be spared – who would be hysterical and no use? Am I nothing, after all, but a spoilt child? I suppose Perry thinks that about me. Well, I'm glad I haven't promised to marry him. I'm not looking for anybody to cling to.

Anger and love and dread and pity were churning in her all at once.

Her mother gave her a surprised glance from her bay-window and, when Nan came in, asked quickly, 'Is anything wrong with the car?'

'No. I made Perry drop me,' Nan replied.

Virgilia glanced keenly at her daughter and said, 'He's been worrying you.'

'Everybody's worrying me,' Nan said.

Virgilia sighed: 'We are, dearest; I know we are ... I'm sorry about Perry,' she added, very unhappily.

Nan was standing, rather rigid, in the middle of the room.

'I asked him a question and he wouldn't answer,' she said.

Virgilia looked at her and said nothing. Nan told her:

'I asked him how you had met his father.'

For a moment her mother was silent, then she sighed and said, 'I can't have you fretting like this, darling: I'll tell you. Ada Stack sent me to consult him. I was nervy and worried: not really ill ...'

Nan caught her breath sharply.

'It's all right! He refused me as a patient. He said I wasn't a case for him. You see, he's a psychiatrist.' She smiled. 'And all I really needed was "pastime and good company".'

Nan had dropped into the chair on the other side of the table; she sighed with relief.

'Perry told me that you were "never his patient." For an awful moment I thought you *had* been, and that he ... that you ... Ada is a blasted old ass.'

Nan flushed and tears sprang to her eyes. Her mother was laughing. She said, 'You and Ada never did get on ... Perry wasn't free to answer your question,' she explained. 'Don't be angry with him.'

'I dare say I'll get over that part of it,' Nan answered. Then she asked, 'You feel nervy still, don't you?'

'Sometimes. I'm sleeping badly for some reason ... What a solemn little face! Truly, sweetheart, I'm not ill. Insomnia makes a woman of my age look awful, I know, and "'tis the folks out in front get the jar." But don't look *quite* so jarred! It isn't polite.'

Nan stared out of the window. This disarming frivolity of her mother's: you could do nothing against it. But it rang false. And sleeplessness wouldn't explain things. Nan wanted to drag the truth from her, but her mother gave her a look so wistful, so pleading – as if imploring her to accept or doubt or reject, but to leave things alone, not to nag or question – that Nan could not say any more.

'Did you develop your photographs?' she asked.

'No, I went out on the bicycle instead.'

'Weren't you too tired? Did you go far?'

'Only about four miles.' Then she said: 'Run along to Brigid, darling. There's some serious matter on which she wants to go into conference with you. I think it's about the trifle. I believe she wants to know whether Perry prefers sherry or rum.'

Nan started up indignantly. Trifle! she thought. That's what I *am* allowed to know about. Trifles!

Hysterical laughter was shaking her heart and rising into her throat. She fought it down and went to the kitchen, discussed Brigid's problem, and decided in favour of rum.

Chapter X

THUNDER

THE INGRAMS ARRIVED in their Austin at eleven. Because the excursion was to include lunch with the elder Mrs Ingram at Avoca, Nan was very correctly attired in her blue suit. She was glad when, after a consultation in the garden, they decided to take down the hood of the car.

'It cuts off the tops of the hills,' Pamela said.

Her husband declared that it would rain very hard very soon. There were at least three layers of spreading clouds in the sky, but he did as she wished.

Virgilia was not coming. She said that she had too many small things to do, and wanted to be fresh to enjoy her party. She had slept a little better, Nan thought. She had been up early and had cleaned her bicycle. It was leaning against the porch.

The tinkers had gone; about half an hour ago the last of the long cavalcade had disappeared, with abusive shouts and whistling, round the bend of the lane.

'Will you be overtaking them? Are you going by Calary Bog?' Virgilia asked.

No, they told her. They were going the opposite way. Pamela wanted to visit Loch Bray and Laragh and they were going by the Sally Gap.

'My tyres will pay for it and they're new,' Garrett complained.

'So is your wife,' Pamela reminded him.

Virgilia said, 'You should start off at once before the showers come, so I won't offer you coffee.'

Nan, who had prepared coffee, said, 'Oh,' in a rather disappointed tone. Ingram noticed it and turned to his wife. 'Coffee would be awfully nice, Pamela, don't you think?' He explained that he had had to breakfast early and do some work.

Nan brought the tray out and they drank the coffee standing on the lawn. Her mother was not in her most hospitable mood, Nan thought.

She got into the back of the car; obviously Mr Ingram wanted to have his wife with him in front. Presently they were on the glen road, going west.

The road was populous this morning. When they approached Doyle's they encountered the family, all in their best clothes, setting out for Mass – two on bicycles; the twins, the parents and Phil in the trap. Eileen looked terrible in three different shades of red; five, Nan observed, if you counted her face and hair. They gave Nan their best Sunday bows and smiles, looking with interest at her friends. As soon as that group was out of sight, another was to be seen ahead. This was not a church-going family.

'It's like a circus,' Pamela exclaimed, greatly intrigued.

'It's the Vaughans, the tinkers,' Nan told her. 'They've changed their minds.'

Garrett slowed down to pass that straggle of travellers meandering all over the road. Pamela wanted to see everything, but Nan would have preferred to hurry past. She murmured, 'There's a "black and midnight hag" among this lot that I don't specially want to be seen by.' Garrett, in whom curiosity of a certain kind was a potent passion, said, 'Oh, which one?' and did not quicken the pace.

A pony followed the procession, its reins held by a boy who sat with bare legs dangling on the tail of the last cart. He gave Nan a wink and a grin; two of the girls with him spat. The carts were piled with women and babies, bundles and gramophones. On one, a litter of puppies peered over the rim of a basket; from another looked out the satanic faces of goats. Lean dogs were running between the wheels. Horses, mules and donkeys were led. Men and boys walked with long easy strides. Among a cluster of youngsters who were running along a precarious path on the bank, Nan saw Timeen. She had drawn the child until she knew him by heart and felt a little pang of distress because he did not see her and she would probably never see him again.

As he overtook the foremost cart, Garrett put on speed, but a yell from it made them look back. A woman was standing erect at the front of the cart, making violent gestures with clenched fists over her head, face distorted, mouth stretched, screeching abuse. Garrett, accelerating, said to Nan with a chuckle, 'Who's your girlfriend?'

'That's Sal, the queen of the tinkers,' Nan replied. Her depression was lifting a little. She *had* to get rid of it. For the Ingrams this was a real day out, and they were terribly nice to take her along.

'The perfect Shakespearean witch. I'm sorry I couldn't hear her curses. I bet they were eloquent,' Garrett remarked, and Nan said, 'You're telling me.'

He was interested. 'Have you been a recipient? What's your crime?'

'They were camped by our land, and we made friends with one of the little boys and there was a mix-up about him and when their usual time was up my mother asked them to go and ... I honestly haven't made out what's behind it all.'

'So she cursed the tribe of you, root and branch, did she?' Garrett said with a grin. 'Wish I'd been there.'

'She looks the sort that would have been burnt in the Middle Ages,' Pamela observed.

'And would have deserved it,' her husband said.

His wife shook her head. 'No one deserved that.'

'Perhaps not, but a genuine witch would be a highly unpleasant party to have as a neighbour.'

He spoke seriously and Nan's eyes stretched wide.

'"A genuine witch?"'

'He believes in them,' his wife explained, looking round at her with a smile.

Nan laughed, incredulous.

'A barrister, believing in witchcraft? Mr Ingram, you can't!'

Pamela was beginning to recognise places seen on excursions years ago. 'I remember this little waterfall, and that awful old reformatory,' she said. 'We're coming to the Loch Bray turn, aren't we?'

Very soon the car was parked on the grassy margin of the Sally Gap road and they walked to the shore of the little lake. Garrett began to tackle Nan about her scepticism.

'You see,' he said, 'we have got to admit the powers of witchdoctors in Africa and Polynesia and Haiti, haven't we? How can we assume that the western countries were always immune, or even that they're quite immune now? We just mustn't make these assumptions; it's unscientific. Hasn't Perry convinced you of that?'

'Unscientific!' Nan exclaimed, amazed. She contended with Garrett rather angrily, irritated to find such beliefs surviving in a rational man.

Pamela said: 'I'm afraid, you know, that he knows what he's talking about. He's done no end of research about this. He's working on his third book on it now.'

'Does he? Are you?' Nan stood looking from one to the other. They were both perfectly serious. She asked, 'What, exactly, is this book about?'

'Witchcraft, cursing and prophecy,' Garrett replied.

'Cursing? Do you mean to say you believe in cursing, too?'

He answered, 'I haven't reached a definite conclusion, but I imagine we can't rule it out.'

Nan was silent as they drove on over the Sally Gap and through Glenmacnaas. It didn't matter: Garrett and Pamela had plenty to talk about. They were in tremendous spirits. They paid a call on an old woman in a cottage in Laragh who welcomed Pamela with cries and tears of delight, then drove through the Vale of Avoca without stopping at the Meeting of the Waters and arrived at Mrs Ingram's house

– a neat square house in a very large and perfectly kept garden – in time for an early lunch.

Garrett's mother was an amusing person with a very straight spine, an alert, expressive face like her son's, a witty tongue and shrewd dark eyes. She talked about an aunt of Pamela's who had died six months ago, saying, 'She was a bonny fighter. I miss our controversies over natural composting. She was a bit of a fanatic about that.' She had a great deal to ask Garrett and his wife about. The play, the new house, plans for furnishing and for the garden were discussed with lively, inquisitive interest. The house was searched for possessions which Garrett wanted, including some beautiful Waterford glass, and the garden explored for plants and shrubs to be moved in due season. A package of alpines was made up and put in the car. Nan had only to show a polite interest, like a well-behaved child. She was jerked to attention, however – she could hardly believe her senses – when the old lady began to ask Pamela serious, detailed questions about the haunting of her Devonshire home. These are Perry's friends – clever, sensible people, Nan reflected, amazed, and they believe the sort of stuff I'm always teasing and scolding Brigid about! ... But Perry doesn't. He can't, or he'd have talked about it. But they spoke as if he does. Has he been hiding all this from me, too? How many things has Perry been hiding from me? And why? Why?

Between the bewilderment caused by the Ingrams' conversation and her dragging anxiety about her mother and these doubts about Perry, Nan felt as if darkness were closing her mind in as thickly as clouds were lowering in the sky.

While they were in Avoca, a slate-coloured canopy unrolled overhead. They put up the hood of the car before driving on. Nan was searching her mind for something to talk about when Pamela, eyeing the cloud-bank with interest, said to her husband:

'Max would like that, wouldn't he?'

'He would,' Garrett agreed, and asked her, 'How soon do you think we can invite them to stay?'

'March, for clouds,' Pamela said.

'Clouds!' Nan exclaimed. 'Is it Max Hilliard you are talking about?'

She had an intense admiration for his work and curiosity about his technique.

'How *does* he get that watery light? He breaks the light up, doesn't he? Yet it isn't *pointillism*. I've wished he would paint in Ireland. Have you seen "Cotswold Weather", and one of rocks and sand called "The Ghouls"?'

'He gave me "The Ghouls" for a wedding present,' Pamela told her, charmed by this appreciation of her friend.

For a while, Nan's problems ceased to oppress her, but her mood became heavy again in the deep cup of Glendaloch, closed in by its wooded hills.

'Every time I've come to this place,' Garrett commented, 'this loch has been as black as sin. I wonder whether St Kevin's gallant deed was effect or cause? … Kevin wished to save his soul,' he explained, 'so he lived over there in a cave in a rock; but one Kathleen brought him food every day, and Kathleen was so pretty that there was nothing for it but to drown her. He threw her in.'

While they were wandering among the ruins of the seven churches, rain began splashing down in great drops. A heavy pall of cloud hung low and the summits showed darkly against a dull sulphur edge of sky. They hurried to a house at the lakeside and asked for tea. The place was half shut up and no one was about except an old woman who looked at them doubtfully, but brought tea. The room in which they sat was low-ceilinged and smelt of tobacco smoke. Pamela would have opened a window but for the driving rain.

'It would be a pity to let the smoke out: it's historical,' Garrett remarked. 'Pipes of peace that turned into fumes of war. No end of underground meetings were held here in the troubled times.'

'It's easy to imagine them,' Pamela said.

The thick walls of the low, wide house, the small windows, the enclosing mountains gave the place a sombre atmosphere. The depression and sense of disorientation against which Nan had been struggling closed down on her now. But, she reflected, the ideas that appalled her did not worry the Ingrams at all and so they could be talked about. Talking about them might take some of this nervousness away. They had the little room to themselves. She asked, 'Just how much *do* you believe in curses, Mr Ingram?'

He smiled at her. His clever eyes were nice when he smiled. He answered her carefully while he spread butter and damson jam very thick on a slice of hot soda-bread.

'As I told you, I haven't formed a firm opinion, but it seems to me that the power exists. There are curious instances here in Ireland, you know. How the thing works, I cannot conceive.'

'Do you mean,' she asked, 'that a person can really start bad luck working – illness, or harm of some sort, against another, just by willing it? Just by words?'

'The thing seems to happen,' he declared.

Pamela was smiling at Nan; she said, 'We may be thankful that your tinkers don't seem to possess it, otherwise we would have had a puncture, at least.'

'Oh, of course,' her husband agreed quickly, 'that's not the type.'

But isn't she? Nan was wondering. Power had seemed to pour out of Sal yesterday under the oak, and her mother had looked withered, grey. Nan's heart shrank and sickened within her. That would explain things, as nothing else did. It would. If Sal had the power of cursing; if Sal were a witch, and her mother, somehow, had found it out … If foolishly, crazily, she had offended Sal. She would be afraid for my sake and forget about guarding herself, Nan's thoughts ran on jerkily, like her heart. 'Tears and terror … Tears and terror …'

'Do you dislike thunder?' Pamela was asking her. Thunder was drumming among the hills, echoing tremendously in that shut-in glen. As a rule, Nan enjoyed thunder, but she was not enjoying this. The low house was besieged by a deluge of rain. The Ingrams were talking to her. They talked in a cool, analytical way about telepathy and clairvoyance: 'second sight.'

'I thought all that was Dark Ages, blind superstition,' Nan managed to say.

'That remains also,' Garrett replied. 'That is what obstructs and confuses the research. You see, ninety-nine cases out of a hundred that one hears of are at third- or fourth-hand, and when you track them down you find there's such an agglomeration of superstitious rubbish and marvel-mongering attached to them that there's no evidential value left. The difficulty is to find a rational person with a trained mind who has had first-hand psychic experience. When I found one,' he added, chuckling, 'I stuck to her.'

Pamela answered his glance at her, laughing. Husband and wife chattered, enjoying their tea, enjoying the rain and everything, and Nan did her best to be responsive, but cold horror was seeping into her mind. She was thankful when Pamela looked at her watch and said, 'It will be a slow drive back through the rain and Mrs Wilde expects us about seven. There's no point in waiting, is there? It isn't going to stop.'

2

IT WAS a very slow drive, with water sluicing down upon the hood and windscreen and splashing up from pools on the road. Nan nearly failed to see the turn into Derreen Lane.

Doyle's cart was there, backed into the track, the horse standing dismally patient with drenched sacks over his flanks. The garden gate was open and Garrett drove in.

There were people in the studio. A woman, her back to the window, was talking excitedly. Phil Doyle was there. He pulled the door open. Nan, with the Ingrams after her, hurried in. It was Sal who was there, hysterical and dishevelled, and Virgilia and Brigid were listening to her, trying to make sense of her wild laments.

'What'll I do? Och, what'll I do?' She turned as Nan came in. 'Miss, darling, did you see e'er a sight of the child?'

'Timeen? Not since we passed you,' Nan answered. She shrank from Sal, and stood beside her mother, gripping her hand. Her mother was tense and trembling a little. She locked her fingers in Nan's. She took no notice of the Ingrams and for the moment seemed to have forgotten Sal in the effort to remember something. She was staring out into the rain, her forehead contracted in a frown. Sal was quiet, at last, waiting; everything became quiet except the rain. Brigid whispered, 'They're after losing the child.' Sal threw herself into a chair and sat rocking her body and swinging her head, moaning, 'Killed by the lightning he is, or drowned in a ditch! In a ditch or a bog-hole, they'll find him, like a dead lamb.'

'His head's not in the water,' Virgilia said.

Sal stopped her outcry and stared, then whispered, 'What's that you say?' They were all staring at Virgilia now. Virgilia took a quick breath and shook her head, as if to rid herself of a dream. Her eyes focused on Garrett and lit up.

'Mr Ingram! You've come. You'll drive me, won't you?' she said.

'Of course, anywhere.'

'It's the bridge: the stone bridge over the fall. About a mile on this side of the turn to Loch Bray.'

'I know it.' He looked interested.

A deep sigh broke from Virgilia. Nan felt her arm, which had been rigid, relax. Her mother looked at her and said, 'Don't worry; we know what to do, but be quick. There's no time to lose.'

Nobody asked questions. Like Garrett and Pamela, Nan waited, watching Virgilia's eyes.

'Hot coffee will be best, won't it?' Virgilia asked.

'For shock and exposure?' Garrett responded at once. 'Yes, very sweet and strong.'

'I've lashings made,' Brigid said.

Virgilia gave quick and precise directions now. Hot-water bottles were filled, brandy and the first-aid box collected, and blankets and rugs. Garrett said, 'A stretcher may be needed,' but, immediately, Virgilia said, 'No.'

Through all their hurried preparations, Sal went on repeating her questions and lamentations: 'Who seen him? Are ye telling me he's hurted? Is it see the child and leave him lying they did? Och, the murderers! Och, the heathen beasts! Take me to him,' she demanded; 'take me to the child!' Garrett refused to have her with him in the car, saying she was hysterical. Phil murmured soothingly but he was scared of the woman and did not know what to do. It was Brigid, returning with thermos flasks, who turned on Sal in a fury and subdued her with language as violent as her own.

'Shut your mouth, ye old blackguard! Who but yourself is to blame? You and your lies and abuse! Wasn't it you told her you were taking the bog road? And when she went twice to make sure, what thanks did she get from you? Mud and curses and stones! Chasing and searching for you she was since morning, up the long hill and the old road and back as far as Kilmacanogue and round the mountain again. Came back to me half dead, she did, after traipsing hills and bogs and hollows in the rain and storm. Ye thankless vagabond!'

Nan was dumbfounded. What was all this? Virgilia's sharp rebuke stopped the old woman and then Sal began again, protesting loudly that she had told no lie, that the storm coming up had made them change their plans. There wasn't shelter enough for a crow on the bog road, and there was a grand empty barn in Glendhu ... Virgilia cut in. She was pulling on a waterproof, Nan helping her. Garrett was stowing the rugs and other things in the car.

'Get my bed ready for him, Brigid. Have the blankets warm. Light a fire,' Virgilia said, but Phil Doyle intervened. 'Wouldn't you bring him to our house?' he said. "Tis nearer and my mother's a wonder with a sick child.'

Virgilia shook her head. 'She wouldn't take Timeen.'

'Ah, ma'am, you're wronging her,' he protested; 'she'd take any child that's hurted or sick.'

Brigid, looking anxiously at her mistress, said, "Twould be better. You're not fit. 'Tis you I'll have to be nursing after this. I'll send Dr Perry after you when he comes.'

'Tell him, the bridge,' Nan whispered, and Brigid promised with a nod.

'I'll warn me mother be ready so,' Phil said. 'Sal can come down with me now.'

Sal had grown quiet. Her lively, defiant face had fallen into sagging lines of stupefaction. She stood bemused while the Ingrams, Virgilia and Nan got into the car.

Garrett drove fast through the splashing puddles and thrashing rain. He sat silent, leaning over the wheel, brows drawn and lips compressed. Nan and Virgilia, in the back seat, were equally silent until Pamela turned to them and, seeing their white, strained faces, suggested that a nip of brandy might be a good precaution against chills. Virgilia said, 'There isn't enough,' and then Nan asked, 'What happened? What can have happened?' in a taut voice.

'I couldn't quite make out: Sal is so incoherent,' Virgilia replied. 'Bat frightened him, I suppose. When they came in sight of the old reformatory Bat began talking about it and pretending that he was going to leave Timeen there. Timeen hasn't been seen since. They've camped in an old barn in Glendhu. When he didn't turn up for dinner or supper Sal took fright and started back. She got it into her head that he'd run to Derreen. She wanted to search the wood.'

'Did you search it?' Nan asked.

'No.'

Pamela had turned and was listening. Fast though Garrett was driving, he listened too. Virgilia did not go on. It was Nan who asked her, 'But how do you know where he is?'

'I think it's a likely place,' Virgilia replied.

'But,' Nan persisted, 'you said – I heard you – you said, "His head isn't in the water."'

'Did I?' Virgilia looked greatly surprised.

'Of course you did. It was as if you were remembering.'

'How could I be remembering?' her mother asked weakly.

Nan's eyes met Pamela's, very troubled and dark in her pale face. Virgilia looked desperate.

'You've had an awful day, Mrs Wilde, haven't you?' Pamela said.

'I have, and I can't answer any more questions. I won't be questioned.'

Virgilia's voice was sharp-edged and harsh. Nan turned away and looked out at a blurred world from which every known landmark had disappeared.

Perry will come after us, she told herself; Perry will come.

She turned and watched through the little window in the back of the car. There was nothing but streaming rain to be seen.

THERE WAS A TORCH in the glove-hole of the car. When they leaned over the parapet of the bridge they looked down into shadowed water. The rain beat on them, and the noise of the torrent roared in their ears. Pamela played the disc of light over the stream below. In a moment it found pale limbs sprawling, legs under the water, arms lying across a stone; it shone on a small white face. Virgilia drooped, moaning, and Nan held her while Garrett and Pamela ran down. Swift and sure-footed, Garrett was under the arch in a moment, lifting the cold little body with the utmost care. Pamela, at the water's edge, directed him with the torch-light as he climbed up. He almost slipped once on a stone slimed with a coating of moss.

Nan and Virgilia spread a rug on the grass margin. They knelt there on either side of the child, making a shelter for him by means of stretching another rug over their own heads. While Garrett listened for heartbeats Virgilia held Timeen's wrist. Timeen's face was like the face of a wax doll from which all colour has been washed away, but his forehead was stained with a great bruise. Virgilia and Garrett looked up at the same moment. 'Yes, but very faint,' Garrett said. He began to feel the ribs, spine and limbs. 'Shoulder damaged,' he said.

Pamela went for the brandy and tried to pour some between the white lips. All the time Virgilia was rubbing the child's legs.

'He's so cold,' she murmured; 'so fearfully cold.' Nothing brought a flicker of the closed eyelids or a quickening of the almost imperceptible breath.

'I'm afraid he's almost gone,' Garrett said. 'We'd best hurry him in as he is. I hope to God Perry will come.'

He turned the car, lifted the child and, when Virgilia was in the back seat, laid him on her lap. Nan ran up, meanwhile, to the top of the bank. The world that she saw was dark, and ghastly with the threat of death. Then it was alight and alive.

'Lights! Perry's coming,' she called down, and in a few minutes Perry was there.

HIS EXAMINATION in that cramped space was brief.

'You're right, Garrett: the left shoulder is dislocated,' he said. 'There's concussion, of course, but exposure's the serious thing. He's in a bad enough way.'

Perry, whose car had no hood, was drenched. He drove back alone, going in front, his powerful headlamps piloting Garrett's car. It was a rough road. If Timeen had recovered consciousness the jolting would have caused him great pain. Nan, with her hand under the rug that wrapped him, rubbed his stone-cold feet all the time. His legs lay heavy across her knees. For a moment she thought his breathing had stopped, then she felt it on her cheek. It was faint and uneven, but it went on. Virgilia's head was bent, listening. The three heads were close.

'His pulse is much better,' Virgilia declared. 'He's warmer and he's breathing better.' Garrett slowed down and she managed to put a little brandy between the boy's lips. He seemed to swallow it. 'I believe he will recover,' she said as they went on. She was weeping. She cried softly, as if with relief. 'It's over already. It's over,' she said, 'and I thought it might be years.'

'You knew this would happen,' Nan whispered. She felt that her mother's secretiveness was over too. She asked gently, 'How did you know?'

'I didn't want you to know, but after this you have to,' her mother replied. 'Yes: I knew this was going to happen but I didn't know when. I saw it, Nan – last Friday, when I was coming home over that bridge. It is what Brigid calls "second sight".'

Nan could not answer. Thoughts were colliding in her, knocking one another to bits. Perry – the scientific mind; Garrett Ingram – a legal one; her mother – wise and truth-loving, and always steady-minded through everything. It must be true. It fitted. It was on Friday that all this queerness began. And now she knew that her mother was telling the truth.

'Second sight! You?' was all she could say.

'Yes,' her mother answered. 'It isn't at all rare, you know.'

It wasn't rare. And after all, it was much, much less dreadful than the things that Nan had imagined.

'You're not ill, then,' she sighed.

'No, I'm not ill.'

'And Sal didn't ... It wasn't Sal?'

'You know just how much Sal had to do with it all.'

'I can't tell you what horrible things I've been imagining. I thought you were bewitched.'

Virgilia smiled. 'It is I who am the witch, I'm afraid.'

'You could have told me,' Nan said under her breath. 'Why didn't you tell me the truth?'

'Because that sort of knowledge is unendurable,' her mother replied.

TIMEEN WAS STILL unconscious when Perry had finished his work. He lay, clean, flushed and firmly bandaged, in the feather bed, breathing evenly through his half-open mouth. Mrs Doyle smoothed the white counterpane and stood looking down compassionately at the bandaged head.

'He's going to need a lot of care,' Perry told her.

'He'll get it,' she responded, and, turning to Virgilia, said earnestly: 'May God forgive me for refusing the poor child. To tell you the truth, Mrs Wilde, I haven't felt right since! 'Tis heavenly mercy that gives me a second chance. I'll make it up to him. He'll be minded like one of my own. I'll sleep on the floor beside him tonight.'

Nan saw the look by which her mother answered Mrs Doyle. There was fellow-feeling in it as well as relief. 'Perhaps in the end,' she said, 'we'll find that what happened was the best thing for him. Perhaps neither of us will feel so greatly to blame.' Perry gave his instructions. 'Unless the boy develops pneumonia it should be a straightforward case,' he said.

Then they went into the kitchen where nine heads were turned to Perry at once. Sal, a steaming cup before her, was sitting at the table between Eileen and Julia. Phil and his father rose, with the stiffness of bone-weary men, from their wooden armchairs, and Garrett and Pamela got up from the settle by the fire. The twins, quiet as mice on their creepy-stools in the corner, peered up out of round, scared eyes.

Perry went and stood with his back to the fire, his clothes steaming. He explained to the Doyles how quiet they would have to be: not a voice must be raised, not a door banged. With good nursing Timeen should soon be all right.

He had at once to quell an outburst from Sal. She rose in her place and blessings poured from her, as eloquent as her curses had been.

'May God bless and reward you for all eternity, Doctor, and give you a string of the finest sons in Ireland, for you are after saving my son's life.'

Perry said curtly, 'Mrs Wilde saved his life.'

Sal came to Virgilia, her eyes black and deep with wonder. 'Mrs Wilde, I wronged you,' she said in her strong voice. 'Stone-blind I was. Since what Eileen here has told me I understand. I ought to have known it for myself. I ought to have seen what I see now in your eyes. You meant only good to me and we treated you bad. I ask your forgiveness. My prayers and blessings will be before your feet and above your head every step of your road from this out, as many as the Christmas stars. I'll be praying for yourself and your lovely girl.'

Garrett looked at Nan, his eyes twinkling. 'At any rate,' he whispered, 'the curses are reversed.'

Sal, her oration ended, turned to John Doyle, asking him to let her sleep in his haggard that night. 'I'll stay only till I see the light of his eyes.' Doyle, a man of few words, who preferred to leave all such arrangements to the women, replied with a sideways nod of the head and led her outside.

Virgilia was smiling a little. She looked at Pamela and Garrett; at Perry and Nan. 'Do you know,' she said, 'it's half-past nine? Do you feel ready for that supper Brigid has been fussing over all day?'

4

BRIGID HAD DECIDED that, no matter what you did with it, the dining-room couldn't be made cosy, and there had been gloom enough for one day, so she had lit a fire in the studio, put the tables together and laid the meal in there. With the lamps burning, the Spanish cloth on the table, her glazed pie and salad, bowl of raspberries and posy of mixed flowers, all looked as pretty as you could wish. If they had rescued the poor child in time, they'd feel like enjoying themselves. And if he was past help, well, good food and warmth would do no harm.

She had never had a better moment than when they came in, wet, muddy and hungry, elated and content, and began to exclaim with pleasure at the sight of the food. She would never forget the way her mistress said, 'We were in time, Brigid. He's hurt, but not very badly … How nicely you've done everything! This is just what we all need.'

When Pamela had put on borrowed stockings and slippers; when they were all washed and warm and sat down to supper, there was an outburst of chatter at first. Later, when Brigid had left them, there fell a silence so charged with unspoken words that Pamela began to laugh. She said, 'I'm afraid we're making an awful noise with our thoughts.'

'It's Garrett,' Perry said. Garrett had scarcely been able for one instant to take his alert, probing eyes from his hostess's face.

Virgilia smiled at their lively, questioning faces and said, 'You've all been models of patience. Perry has exercised quite heroic discretion.'

This was too much for Garrett. He cried explosively, 'Do you mean to say that Perry has been in on all this?'

'I've been holding out on you,' Perry admitted with a wide grin.

Words failed Garrett, but not for long. 'Well, of all the double-crossing, two-faced twisters …'

But Virgilia defended Perry: 'You don't know how terrifically he was pledged and sworn and committed.'

Perry smiled at Nan, who flushed.

All the time, Perry had been attending to her, waiting on her, trying to talk to her without words. They had not had a moment alone together, and he thought there was a good deal to say. But Nan wanted to avoid that conversation with Perry. For the first time she felt shy of him. She felt that she scarcely knew this young doctor who had been her mother's confidant through such stresses, who understood so much, who had so loyally kept the promises that she had herself tried to make him break.

When they had finished their meal he helped to carry dishes to the kitchen and, returning through the candle-lit dining-room, put a hand on Nan's shoulder to draw her back. She stiffened a little but stayed. In the flickering light she could not make out the expression on Perry's face. The eyes looked deep-set, the features strong. Now he looked vexed; then tender; now serious; then amused.

'Anything to say to me?' he asked.

'Only that I'm sorry,' she said. 'That I understand.'

'You're not so worried now, are you?'

'No, why should I be?'

'Grand! Then you don't take your mother's view of all this?'

'I don't know what her view is.'

'It scares her.'

'I won't be scared.'

'Splendid; that's great ... Nan ...'

She did not want to talk to him yet; and not here, with the light and the chatter from the studio coming through the half-open door. She shook her head and they went in.

The sofa had been pulled over to the fire. Virgilia was lying on it and the Ingrams were in armchairs. Perry pulled a chair over for Nan, but she chose a stool and he sat down and threw his head back, tired and content.

Nan leaned against the sofa where her mother's hand could rest on her shoulder. She felt that she wanted never to let her mother out of her sight again. She felt young and ignorant, like a child surrounded by grown-up people who move in a universe of their own, at whose nature she can only guess; and they were all being gentle and kind to her, as grown-up people are to a child; but underneath her diffidence a great excitement was accumulating – excitement about the boundless horizons that were opening and her mother's unfathomed powers. She listened, enthralled, while Garrett asked keen, exact questions and her mother answered them with precision and care. Virgilia looked physically exhausted, but her mind seemed lively and clear. 'Go on,' she said, 'I want to tell you. You'll help Nan to understand.'

Virgilia tried to recount the whole history of her hallucinations, but her memory, vivid about so many things, was vague and faulty about these. Perry remembered many that she forgot. He had made notes of all that she had told him, he confessed, and won from Garrett an approving nod.

The sound of the rain eased to a drizzle. Brigid was heard going upstairs. Virgilia and Perry built up the chronicle between them and Garrett interposed questions. Neither Pamela nor Nan said a word.

'The dog, Mrs Wilde: did you think it was Shuiler?' Garrett wanted to know.

'I did for an instant; then I thought it couldn't have been, so far from home. I thought, Brown and white collies are much alike. And it had been a mere flash. It remains in my mind like a picture, with the dog in the air.'

'And the background?'

'A hedge.'

'Actually,' Perry said, 'there were walls there on both sides of the road.'

When she told of the dancing couple, Perry laughed. 'Your subconscious has bright ideas,' he said.

Virgilia smiled at her daughter. 'My subconscious is greatly concerned about your clothes.'

'I realise now,' Nan said, 'why you looked at my dress.'

'You see, I wanted so much to think that a vision need have no meaning at all,' her mother explained. 'If the dress had been different it would have given me hope. It was just after I'd seen Timeen.'

To her account of that vision they listened avidly; no more questions were asked until the whole story was told.

'Magnificent!' Garrett exclaimed then. 'Touch and hearing; movement; the rain; the darkness; I never heard anything so complete. It's perfection.'

Perry said, 'And useful. It saved a life.'

'But knowing it was to happen,' Pamela murmured; 'waiting for it! Wondering what to do! Terrible!'

'What is terrible,' Virgilia said, 'is that I didn't warn Sal.'

'Why ever didn't you?' Nan asked.

'I was afraid of your hearing the story.'

'That wouldn't have mattered in comparison … And, anyhow, guessing was a thousand times worse. But it doesn't matter now; you've saved his life.'

'I caused his danger and his injury,' Virgilia said. 'I was utterly wrong. I was cowardly and weak and confused. I thought I would tell her when they were leaving the glen, and I cycled about crazily, trying to find her, all day. People told me tinkers had gone towards Kilmacanogue. It was another lot. It never occurred to me until hours after I came home that they might have gone the opposite way; I was going to set off again when Sal came. It was a piece of blank stupidity that I can't understand.'

'You can't live in two worlds at once,' Pamela said. Her husband gave her a flicker of a smile.

'Mrs Wilde,' he said emphatically, 'I doubt very much whether you *could* have told Sal.'

'But why? I saw the tinkers leaving this morning. If I hadn't waited until you were gone … '

'If you had warned her, it wouldn't have happened; but it *had* to happen; you only foresaw it because it was going to happen.'

'It's such a crazy circle!' Virgilia exclaimed. 'It was only because I foresaw it that I forced them to hurry away; and because they had to go without waiting for good weather they changed their plans and took that road. And because they took that road I couldn't warn Sal! It's a whirligig.'

'And because you didn't tell her, it happened?' Garrett smiled. 'Aren't you assuming free will, Mrs Wilde? I think we mustn't do that.'

'Not to assume it would,' Virgilia said hesitantly, 'make one's responsibility seem less.'

'You had no responsibility,' Garrett declared.

'Do you mean,' she asked slowly, 'that what one sees in this way is *bound* to happen? That nothing one could do would prevent it?'

'I'd say, rather, that one cannot do any of the things that would prevent it,' Garrett replied.

Perry quoted flippantly, '"In fact, not a bus but a tram"', and added, 'Kindly register protest as per usual.'

Garrett said, 'Objection noted.'

Pamela glanced at Perry, saying, 'I'm on your side about this.' She smiled at Virgilia. 'I think I should warn you that if you let my husband begin on these questions he'll talk for as long, and almost as eloquently, as the fallen angels,' she said.

Virgilia gave her a half-smile in return, murmuring:

'and reason'd high
Of providence, foreknowledge, will, and fate,
Fix'd fate, free will, foreknowledge absolute,
And found no end, in wand'ring mazes lost.'

'All right,' Garrett gave in. 'We'll leave all that; the facts are what I want to get; I want to understand your state of mind – for instance, at the moment of prevision about Timeen and the corresponding actual moment.'

'There was a split second,' Virgilia answered with concentration, 'in which they were exactly the same. I thought: It's Timeen and he's dead. I felt extreme pity and then guilt. I thought: It's my fault. Both times, a kind of sickness and dizziness came over me. All the rest, before and after, were quite different; but for that second there was no difference at all. But looking back, now, I see that moment as static. Have you ever been watching a film when a still photograph was suddenly shown? It's like that in my memory; as if even the torrent had ceased to move. But I may be imagining this. I certainly didn't *remark* it at the time.'

Garrett was insatiably interested. He said, 'That stillness is a frequent sign and that exact correspondence is enthralling. And what a good witness you are, Mrs Wilde!' He turned an excited face to Perry, saying, 'Boy, if this had happened in the Antipodes we'd have had to go after it.'

'The great brain agrees with me, you see,' Perry said to her, smiling. 'It is your own experience that is displaced in time, and you not only see what you are going to see, but you think what you are going to think about it, and feel what you are going to feel.'

Virgilia sighed.

'We're being rather tiring, aren't we?' Pamela asked her. It was growing late.

'Wait, please,' Virgilia said. 'There are things I want to ask Mr Ingram: three questions.'

'It sure is your turn,' Perry observed.

'Are there any time-limits about these things? Any limit to the possible interval?' Virgilia asked.

'None that I've ever heard of,' was Garrett's careful reply.

'So one could wait nearly all one's life?'

'It appears so.'

Virgilia was silent for a moment, then went on:

'The second is: Do other things – memories, or fears, or expectations – sometimes get mixed up with the visions, so that one would misinterpret them?'

Pamela nodded, but her husband replied very firmly, 'Not in your case, I should say, Mrs Wilde. From what you have told us, you appear to me to be an almost flawless metagnome.'

'Metagnome?'

'Simply a person with a strong psi function – psychic faculty. It seems probable,' he went on, 'that your visions are examples of absolute paranormal precognition. I should say they form a more complete and perfect sequence than any on record so far.'

'So I can't hope to escape or avert what I see? … Perry,' Virgilia asked unhappily, turning to him, 'do you agree with that?'

'I hate to agree with Garrett,' Perry said, 'but I'm afraid he's right this time.'

'But, Mummie,' Nan broke in, 'what does that matter when you can stop the *consequences?* Look what you've done already – prevented a crash that might have killed five people and, quite definitely, saved Timeen's life. I think it's tremendous. I think it's the most marvellous power anybody could have. Of course it would be frightful if a selfish, unscrupulous person had it – but a person like you!'

'Good for you, Nan!' Perry exclaimed, immensely pleased. Nan flashed him a smile.

Pamela interjected, 'But the strain!'

'Yes,' Nan agreed. 'You would have to pay that price. There would be awful times, like these few days – but if it shows you what to do; if it saves life!'

Virgilia looked at her daughter with astonishment.

'Is that really how you feel about it, Nan? It doesn't repel you at all?'

'No, Mummie. I think you're the right person to have such powers, absolutely.'

Virgilia shook her head, wondering but relieved; then she turned to Garrett.

'My third question,' she said, 'is this: Have you ever heard of a case of a person who had these powers and who got rid of them?'

'I never heard of anyone wishing to get rid of them,' he replied. 'But they can be brought under control. I know a woman in London who has a remarkable psi function and who can turn it on and off at will, like a tap. She says it's very much like focusing your eyes. There are, of course, cases,' he went on, 'in which the power diminishes as the percipient grows older. But,' he said earnestly, 'I hope yours won't, Mrs Wilde. I honestly believe you can make an immensely valuable contribution to this research – even if you wish your name suppressed, as, of course, would be understandable.'

Virgilia shook her head. 'I want to rid myself of this faculty absolutely,' she declared. 'To me, it's a disease.'

'But, Mummie, it's been such a *help*,' Nan said protestingly.

Pamela did not join her husband in his ardent plea that Virgilia would cultivate her psychic power, join his research group, keep exact records, and allow him to publish them. Perry's eagerness was evident in his face, but he said little. Nan exclaimed now and then in urgent agreement with Garrett. Pamela felt the strength of Virgilia's resistance and could guess how she must have suffered and how she might suffer by the repetition of such experiences. Finally she intervened, saying that it was past eleven o'clock and Mrs Wilde's day had surely been long enough.

WHEN THEY WERE in Nan's room together, Nan asked Pamela: 'What do *you* think about free will?'

'I'm convinced we have it,' Pamela said. 'Garrett and I argue endlessly about this.'

'I *feel* we have it,' Nan said; 'but how can that be so if what is to happen tomorrow has been decided already today?'

'The decision could still be your own, couldn't it? If, for instance, your mother looks into the future and sees you as the wife of a certain man, can't it simply mean that he will have decided to ask you and you will have decided to accept him?'

'I see; oh, I understand!' Nan said, immensely relieved. 'But, then, if she sees other things – for instance, what sort of place he'll be working in, or what I will be doing?'

Pamela had put her things on quickly. She was ready to go down. She paused, however, to answer Nan's question as best she could.

'Well,' she said, 'I suppose those things are settled in a way by factors that exist already – your disposition and the man's, and the sort of work you've begun, and your interests and friends. It's as if you'd sown the seeds and the only question is which will grow – "which grain will grow and which will not."'

'I see!' Nan responded. 'That sounds very convincing and rather comforting. And it makes no practical difference at all.'

They hurried down.

'Do you think you'll feel like the rehearsal?' Garrett asked Nan as they stood sorting waterproofs in the narrow hall.

Nan began doubtfully, 'I don't know that I want to leave Mother ...' But Virgilia heard her.

'If that sort of thing begins!' she threatened. She was serious about this, Nan knew very well.

'All right, I'll come; I'd love to,' she said.

Perry promised to call for her at six. There had been a smile behind Perry's eyes the whole evening.

'I'll be at Doyle's in the morning, to see the youngster,' he said.

She did not respond. She had never in her life wanted to do so much thinking in such a short time or felt so incapable of rational thought.

WHEN SHE WAS ALONE with her mother again in the studio, Nan began mechanically to empty ash-trays out of the window and plump up cushions. Her mother, seated on the sofa, was watching her. Some of the pallor and tension had left Virgilia's face. She was smiling, but it was a rather worried smile. She said remorsefully, 'I wish you need never have known about all this.'

Nan came and stood opposite her. She spoke firmly: 'You made a mistake about me, Mummie; you forgot I'm grown up. You thought I'd be frightened, so you shut me out and went through your private hell by yourself. And so I was in a separate hell. If, another time, it could be the same one, please.'

'I was such a fool, darling,' her mother responded. 'I imagined you'd worry furiously.'

Nan looked down into her mother's clear, delicate face; into the blue eyes so full of trouble and love; she saw the lips tremble a little, trying to smile. She sat down beside her and said: 'I think you've been simply too courageous and wise and unselfish for words, Mummie; but I don't want it to happen again. It was ghastly. You can't imagine. Seeing you completely changed; knowing you were in some awful trouble … Listen: I'm not going to be – tyrannical, and say you mustn't ever have any secrets, and I won't nag, but please promise just this – promise that you'll remember' – her voice shook – 'you'll remember I'm not a child.'

Tears choked Nan and overflowed. Her mother caught her in her arms and sat hugging and rocking her, half laughing, almost weeping, promising, 'Child, child, of course I will.'

Chapter XI

LANDSCAPE WITH RAINBOW

'I WOULDN'T GO DOWN for a while yet if I were you: you'd not be welcome,' Brigid advised. 'And you'll find Timeen's all right,' she added confidently. 'The tinkers don't take cold, and didn't Dr Perry tell you he would be? That young man knows what he's talking about. He's a lad that knows his own mind – and has one that's worth knowing, what's more.'

Nan listened and worked, smiling. She had taken her breakfast with Brigid because her mother was sleeping late. Eileen had been told to stay at home and help with Timeen and the hay, and there was a great pile of plates and dishes from the supper-party to be washed up. Nan dried while Brigid washed. Brigid was quick but, without having to think about it, Nan kept pace. They had done this together in summer holidays since Nan was twelve.

'You're always right about people, aren't you, Brigid?' she said. She was thinking how dense she had been – dense about her mother, and Perry, and herself, and about Brigid too. Brigid, whom she had thought a dear, funny, superstitious old thing, was the one who had understood and been able to help. Nan's proud tower of reason and logic lay overthrown and wisdom had to be sought for in old wives' tales.

'You don't believe in curses, do you, Brigid?' she asked.

Brigid was drying the Belleek cups herself. She would not trust even Nan with those. She narrowed her eyes against the sunlight that showed crow's-foot wrinkles all over her soft old face.

'Don't forget to bring the milk back with you from Doyle's,' she said: 'every drop in the place turned on me in the night, only what I scalded with the coffee for breakfast.'

'Scones for tea,' Nan said gaily; but she wanted her question answered. '*Do* you, Brigid?'

'Curses? Och, they work an odd time. But not the sort given out by the like of Sal. That sort goes home to roost.'

Nan laughed. That had certainly happened.

'What about blessings?' she asked. 'You should have heard Sal pouring out blessings last night!'

'A blessing is good, no matter from where it comes ... She did, I suppose?'

Brigid was greedy for every detail of the evening's story. She listened with thoughtful interest, but without surprise.

''Twill be a far-told tale,' she commented, 'but no harm will come of it. If she wasn't liked they'd be making a witch of her, maybe, and if she was a Catholic there's some would be setting her up for a saint, but, the way it is, she'll always be just Mrs Wilde.'

'Do many people have second sight?' Nan asked.

'There's many get warnings now and again, but not like the mistress's,' was Brigid's reply. 'With her 'tis different. 'Tis what I'm thinking, her visions are sent.'

'I wish she wasn't afraid of them.'

'Well, I suppose they would make you uneasy. I'm thankful my grannie's gift didn't come down to me.'

'I wish I had inherited Mother's!' Nan declared. 'I wish I could see ahead. One could be so much more *wise*.'

Brigid looked at her warningly.

'Now don't you go asking for trouble, acushla,' she advised. 'When all's said, we're better the way we are. That'll do now: I'll finish. Tell Mrs Doyle to send up if she wants anything. And remember the milk.'

THE SKY WAS CLEAR. Nan set out without coat or hat. Her mother was in her bedroom brushing her hair. After the wet night the stocks and pinks in the border were giving out a rich spicy scent. Nan picked a few and handed them in at the open window. There was colour in her mother's cheeks.

'It isn't rouge today, is it?' Nan asked.

'No,' Virgilia assured her. 'It's a gorgeous night's sleep. I wish,' she said, 'that stocks had a nicer name. Come back and tell me how Timeen is before you go climbing mountains, won't you?'

'I will.'

Regardless of puddles, Nan ran all the way down the lane. She felt as fresh as the rain-washed morning, light-footed, lighthearted, almost light-headed, the chill fog of doubts and fears stripped away from her heart and mind. How she could ever have been so blind and slow and stupid she could not conceive. Why had she wasted time putting up such a fight? Ever since that day on Carrigoona she had known – at least, with *nearly* the whole of herself. What an idiot she had been, theorising about artists marrying artists; accusing herself of wanting just a flirtation; letting her cold, conceited chit of an intellect take charge! What that chit had needed was a thoroughly good shaking! Well, the shaking had been provided, thanks be, in good time! I might have lost Perry, she thought. To be without Perry for the rest of her life! She did not know how she was going to let him go away for a year. Anything might happen in a year. It was really an impossible thought.

She paused for a minute to look down into the Glencree River. The water had risen a little. Though golden-brown, it was clear: she could see blades of grass waving underneath the flow – fascinating to watch, as Monet had said. He had said, too, that trying to paint them was enough to drive one insane. It *would* he a problem. It was the sort of thing you wanted to talk about … No good talking about it to Perry. Perry probably didn't know Monet from Manet. He wouldn't, when he looked at green-shadowed weedy water, think of 'The Lily Pool.' He would just be in tearing spirits because of being in a grand place on a grand day with her, and knowing what he wanted to do and knowing that he would do it. There was something purposeful in him, even when he was deliberately idling. Well, you couldn't have everything. But can I ever, she asked herself as she went on her way again, can I ever turn myself into a good doctor's wife?

There was great activity in the hayfield; men, boys and girls, the twins even, were hard at work turning over the hay. Some of them shouted to her cheerfully. Shuiler wasn't following her: that was a good thing. The Doyles' dogs, when they saw him, always started to bark. She walked round to the front of the house. Perry's car was there.

Mrs Doyle was making bread-and-milk in the kitchen. Timeen had wakened and cried a good deal, she said. 'I was thankful indeed when the doctor arrived,' she chattered. 'God pity the child; there's no more on his ribs than a rake! Yet he's wiry: fancy, he seems to have taken no cold! I could make a fine child of him in six months, and Sal says she'll leave him with me. I'm glad. You know how it is when you nurse a child through a sickness: you don't want to let him go.'

Nan was watching the door across the passage. Presently it opened. Perry stood there looking at her for a moment before he beckoned her in. She took the bowl of sweet bread-and-milk with her and sat down and fed Timeen with a spoon. His face was flushed and tear-stained and the eye that peeped up at her from under the bandage was swollen. The smells of bread-and-milk and iodine brought back her childhood illnesses to Nan. Her mother had told her stories and fed her and sung to her. You had to sit up all night with a sick child. Her mother had sat up alone. Some fathers would watch too.

'One more spoonful! Just a little one, all full of sugar! That's a good boy.'

Perry looked very tall standing over the bed. He was looking at the boy, not at Nan.

'He should do fine; there's no fracture, no bronchial symptoms, and the concussion doesn't seem to be much,' he said. 'He must be tougher than he looks.' His stethoscope was on the table. He put it away in his bag.

Timeen began whispering fretfully: 'They'll not come here for me, will they? Sure they couldn't take me, and me in the bed?'

Nan glanced in distress at Perry.

'It's all right,' Perry told her. 'I asked Garrett. The order can be rescinded. It can be fixed with the magistrate who committed him. The thing is to get it into the kid's head.'

He sat down by the bed, saying, 'Listen to me.' The boy lay still, taking in every careful word. 'The head policeman's a great friend of mine,' Perry said. 'And do you know what I'm going to tell him? I'm going to tell him you're a good boy and he's to let you alone.'

'And so will he?'

'And so he will.'

Nan took up the story:

'You're going to live here with the Doyles, Timeen. Every morning, Denny and Joey will take you with them to school.' Nan stroked his arm while she talked. 'You'll help with the hay and the turf and the chickens. You'll have lovely pies and jellies to eat.'

'And toffee?' a dreamy voice enquired.

'Lots of toffee; I'll make it for you myself.'

'And will I be watering Mrs Wilde's garden?'

'Yes, and you'll be learning how to make roses grow. You'll have a little garden of your own.'

She saw his eye close and felt the thin arm and hand relax.

She sat still, looking into the bowl on her knees. She thought of all the women down all the centuries who had sat like this, putting a child to sleep, and of all who would do it before the world came to an end. This was the first time, for her, and it had come to her as naturally as if she had done it always. It gave her a strange, restful sense of being carried on the main stream of life. She felt Perry's eyes on her. Very gently, he took the bowl and spoon from her and set them on the table at the foot of the bed. Nan said, 'He's asleep.'

The house and the fields around it were quiet. She listened to the child's breathing and Perry's and her own. Her head was bent.

Perry came and stood over her and said, 'Look at me, Nan.'

She tried to straighten her lips, but they were still curved, betraying all her secrets, when she looked up.

THEY FOUND MRS DOYLE in the yard and told her that she need not have much anxiety about her patient. She gave them a glance from her shrewd eyes.

Sal was out on the road with Phil, who was helping her to mount his truck. She sat in front, her pride and poise restored, and started to shower a largesse of blessings on all below. Nan and Perry escaped, turning into the byroad and walking past the hayfield to the stretch near the river where not a soul was in sight.

'I've got something to show you,' Perry said, and took a telegraph form from his pocket. It was a cable signed 'Landauer.'

URGE YOU RECONSIDER STOP CAN POSTPONE
DECISION ONE WEEK

'So you did cable!' Nan exclaimed. 'What did you say?'

'I told you I was going to. Did you think I was bluffing? I sent miles of a cable, asking him whether it would put him or the hospital out awfully if I cancelled. I gave no reason. It's frightfully decent of him to take it like this.'

'Well,' Nan said in a voice that did not sound nearly as cheerful and bracing as she intended it to, 'it won't be gambling, now, so of course you'll go.'

Perry stood still, then turned. They walked back towards Doyle's.

'I just don't know how to,' he said.

'And I don't know how to let you, but you must.'

'It seems crazy.'

'It would be crazy not to, you know.'

'Does it matter that much?'

'You're the sort of person whose work matters a lot.'

Perry groaned. 'Do you honestly think that?'

'I'm quite certain of it.'

'Well, aren't you the cold-blooded, heartless girl! ... It means sailing in six weeks, you know.'

'I know, Perry.'

'Three thousand miles, for nearly a year.'

'Don't.'

They walked as far as the corner in silence, then turned again. It was Nan who said at last: 'Couldn't I go with you? Couldn't we be married at once?'

'Married at once?'

The elation in his voice as he echoed her and his sudden gesture, pulling her towards him, made Nan believe, for a moment, that Perry's resistance was quite overcome; but presently he released her, half laughing, frowning, and declaring that that would be neither work nor marriage and could only end in his muffing both.

'No, honey,' he said obstinately. 'Either I marry and take a job here or in London and support my wife, or I go to Pittsburgh and we wait a year.'

'Then we wait a year,' Nan said with a sigh ... 'Anyway,' she added, 'it would be unkind to go all that distance from Mother just now. She's shaken up. I think,' she went on diffidently, 'if you don't mind waiting to tell your father I'd rather not tell her just yet.'

Perry looked disappointed.

'Dad's going to be enormously pleased, you know.'

Nan wanted to respond, 'So is Mother,' but could not. There was a reservation in her mother's mind about Perry. If they went and surprised her now with their news, he might notice it, and that would be a pity. Perry admired her mother so much, was ready to give her no end of attentiveness and affection – everything his own mother had never wanted from him. She said, 'This doesn't seem just the day to talk to her about leaving her.'

'As you say!' Perry responded and asked, 'Is she all right?'

'She's splendid this morning. Perry, how incredible it seems – foreseeing things and all that – in daylight, with the sun shining! I believe I don't believe it, quite.'

'Get used to the idea of it, Nan,' Perry said warningly. 'It is true. And now,' he complained, 'do you know how I have to spend the morning? Instead of climbing Djouce with you or driving you to Tir-na-nOge, I'm going to watch a man having a bit of his shin-bone grafted into his hip.' He glanced at his watch. 'I'll have to rush, too.' He gave her his wide, amused, affectionate smile. 'My timetable didn't allow for all this.'

He took her in the car as far as the bottom of the lane. She stood there, watching, while he drove up the hill, paused at the crest, looked round and waved to her. Not until he was out of sight did she turn up to Derreen.

She had to walk the whole way back to Doyle's then; she had forgotten the milk.

WHEN SHE RETURNED, her mother was not to be seen. She could be heard, however, in her dark-room and they talked through the door which divided it from the studio. Nan gave a brief report about Timeen and Mrs Doyle's decision, then retrieved her own things from the lower shelf of the cupboard where Brigid had stowed them with excellent care. She laid them out on her table and sat down to work, and did not stop to talk when Virgilia came out of the dark-room and settled at her own table to write.

'The Trial of Puck' was half done. Nan put it aside. Today, overcharged as she felt with power and excitement, she wanted to begin something new. The next picture was going to be fun.

Puck, denounced as an undesirable alien, had been extradited and outlawed by the Conclave of Elder Leprechauns. They tried to deport him, but there were difficulties: none of the sea-captains would have him on board, and, during the negotiations, Puck contrived to escape. He was anxious, by this time, to be back in his own country, but he intended, before he left Ireland, to have his revenge. He meant to remove the crock of gold. Stonehenge was the proper place for it, he thought. It was common knowledge that the leprechauns kept it buried at the foot of the rainbow, so to reach that spot was Puck's problem now.

In the course of his rainbow-chasing he had a number of mishaps, not all accidental. His worst enemy was the Pooka, who was furious because of a confusion that had arisen between his own name and that of this Sassenach. Disguised, sometimes as a goat, sometimes as a pony, he led Puck into bog-holes and quagmires and finally on to a large patch of 'hungry-grass.'

Straight ahead of Puck, shining and perfect, the rainbow sprang from the mountain and spanned the sky, but there Puck stood helpless, doubled up in an agony of hunger and as weak as a famine-child. He staggered and stumbled this way and that, his famished eyes seeking food, his arms clutched across his starved, shrinking middle. Suddenly, he beheld a blackberry bush weighed down with masses of berries – multiple, purple-black, iridescent berries, swollen with juice. He made for it, grabbed the berries by handfuls and stuffed them into his mouth, looking at the same time over his shoulder, only to see the rainbow fading away.

Nan found that her picture composed delightfully – the rainbow on the left, the bush on the right, and Puck, with arms stretched out one way and neck the other, straddling between. It called for strong colours – the purple of the berries, the emerald of the grass; but the fading rainbow would not be easy to do.

'If you see a rainbow, tell me,' she murmured to Brigid, who came in to place a cup of coffee on each table and departed again without a word. A chuckle at the sketch of Puck's face was all she allowed herself. Brigid was a great respecter of what she called, indiscriminately, 'literary work.'

Nan worked undistracted except by the alluring play of light and shadow over the valley. Puffed clouds were drifting up. There would be more rain. She drew the silk casement-curtains over her window to shut out temptation and soften the light. Her mother was writing steadily on. This is convenient, Nan thought, sitting with my back to her. She believed that her secret must be laughing out of her eyes. I'll never get through the day without telling her, she thought.

Yet she wished to, seriously, because she knew that the faintest lack of response, the least hint of unwillingness from her mother would shadow the magical happiness of this time. She wants me to marry an artist: she thinks if I don't I'll never do good work and that I'll miss it too desperately. Artists ought to marry one another, obviously. They need so much encouragement all the time. Well, it just hasn't happened like that. I have just got to make myself into a good wife for a doctor and keep up my own work too. It can be done, and I'm going to do it. I only wish mother could *see* that ... I wish she'd look into our future and see! But perhaps that will happen, Nan thought with sudden excitement; perhaps she will!

Her mother was at her elbow. Lunch was ready.

'Why, Nan, that's charming!' she exclaimed. 'What lovely rhythms! And Puck is sparkling with life. It's much, much the best thing you've done. How famished he looks!'

'It should be nice,' Nan agreed. 'Doing it has made me violently hungry,' she said. 'Come on.'

A shower fell while they were at lunch. They did not talk much; neither felt inclined to, as a rule, in the middle of a spell of work. Nan asked her mother whether she was going to visit Timeen.

'No,' Virgilia replied; 'I'll leave him to you and Perry until Mrs Doyle invites me. If I go she may feel that she is being supervised, then she couldn't take quite so much interest in him. What I *am* going to do is make some nightshirts for him. I've an old blouse and night-gown that can be cut up.' Nan said she wanted to try her hand at pyjamas and would cut up an old pair of her own.

Later in the afternoon the garments were spread on the dining room table and the re-making was begun. Nan's experiment was the cause of a good deal of laughter before she abandoned it, defeated, and decided that nightshirts would have to do.

'Isn't it perfectly extraordinary,' Nan said, thinking aloud, 'how ordinary everything is?'

'Is it?' her mother said, sounding pleased.

'Why, yes! Everything is just the same as it was before. All the ideas I ever had about free will and cause and effect and time have been turned upside down and inside out. I'm wondering if the world is really round. And yet it seems to make no difference.'

'Never let it make any difference,' her mother advised her earnestly. 'Normality is the precious thing.'

Nan ran up a seam on the sewing-machine before she spoke again. Then she asked how the photographs had turned out.

'See what you think of them,' Virgilia replied.

Nan found the negatives and held them up to the light. They were striking and beautiful pictures with strong shadows and sharply defined highlights on the bird's head and wings. She thought them the most successful bird photographs her mother had ever taken.

'You can't imagine how I funked developing them,' Virgilia told her. 'I thought there might have been no bird there.'

'I see!' Nan exclaimed soberly. 'That must be uncomfortable – not being sure. I suppose,' she went on, 'this *is* the one you saw on that book-jacket?'

'I'm afraid it is.'

'Then the publisher will choose it, of course.'

'I suppose he will.'

Nan thought she sounded depressed. The cutting-out and machining were finished and they carried their work to the studio, opening the door to the garden and sitting just inside it in armchairs. The sun had come out again. She is a little morbid about this power of hers, Nan was thinking. She is letting it make her unhappy. It's the only thing I have ever known her to lack courage about. She said quietly, 'I don't believe you realise that if you hadn't had that vision on Friday, Timeen would be dead.'

Virgilia was working at a buttonhole. Her hands became still. She said, 'It was I who made them go.'

'But it was past their proper time to go, in any case. You may have had nothing to do with when they started or where they went.'

'Perhaps. But don't let us begin running round these mazes again.'

Nan decided to be a little persistent about this. She said:

'Brigid believes your visions are "sent".'

'I wish I could think that.'

'Well, Mummie, wherever they come from, it's just staggering to think of all the good you may be able to do with them.'

'I can imagine doing nothing but harm.'

'But think!' Nan spoke eagerly. 'Suppose there is a ship that's going to be wrecked, or a train that will be in a collision, or a house that is going to be burnt down and you are able to warn people not to be there! I do see that there would be bad times of anxiety. All the same, if I had your power, I'd work it for all I was worth.'

Virgilia gave her a troubled smile.

'And if people refused to take my advice? If *you* refused? That would end in my going out of my mind.'

Nan looked at her thoughtfully.

'But one would *have* to take it, wouldn't one? I mean, after yesterday, and everything, if you got your knowledge in *that* way how could one dare to refuse?'

'Don't you see what a tyrant I could be?'

'Yes, but you wouldn't. You couldn't be tyrannical. You haven't a grain of the love of power in you, I do believe.'

'I certainly don't want *this* power, Nan.'

'Mummie, you're inhuman! Haven't you even plain curiosity? Wouldn't you like to see *my* future, for instance? I wish ...' Nan paused.

'What do you wish, Nan? That I could?'

'Of course; of course I do.'

'Why?'

'Why?' Nan repeated. She did not want to explain her real reason – her desire to be able to visualise herself as Perry's wife; to be sure that she would not fail him in any way, and her wish that her mother should be satisfied about their marriage. She said: 'One would know what to expect. One could prepare oneself.' She stopped and lowered her head over her work.

Her mother knew that this was a plea. She felt Nan's diffident happiness reaching out, needing only her own encouragement to be perfect. She had seen the quiet light in her daughter's face and the grave little smile that curved her thoughtful lips. Her doubts are all over, Virgilia was thinking as she looked out at the garden and listened to the rejoicing birds. She was thankful to be spared temptation: thankful that it was not within her power to look into the future at will. She said: 'Even if I were able to induce visions, Nan, I would never have the courage to try.'

'You're afraid of something,' Nan murmured uneasily.

She changed the subject, talking about the dance, now eight days away, and about Dr Franks. She said, 'His ambitions for Perry have always been exactly the same as Perry's ambitions for himself. That makes a grand relationship, doesn't it?'

Her mother gave her a little smile, saying, 'They are still, you know.'

Brigid opened the door.

'Your rainbow, Nan.'

It was time to change. Perry would probably come as early as he could. Nan bundled up her sewing and ran upstairs. The rainbow was only a fragment, but vivid. She stood at the landing window looking at it. The rain-washed, sunlit evening was going to be lovely – the loveliest she had ever known.

2

VIRGILIA SAT SEWING ALONE. She wondered whether Nan meant to keep her secret long. She was glad not to have been told it in words. She wanted to be ready when that happened to respond with her whole heart. She did not want to dim the child's happiness with the least shadow of reluctance or doubt.

For her doubts, and her reluctance, had no rational origin. Of that Virgilia was acutely aware. It was true that Perry had shown little interest in Nan's work, but probably the interest would come. When he discovered that Nan really cared about it; that it was seriously regarded by other people, and gave her a standing – as it would – he would be proud of it. He would want to understand it then. And Nan was so reasonable. She knew that a price had to be paid for everything. She would know how to wait.

There is nothing really to account for my anxiety except a vague premonition, Virgilia told herself. A premonition: that was the word.

It was similar to the forewarning she had felt that her clairvoyant power would bring grief to Nan – and had it not done so, for two wretched days? That had come true. This feeling was equally formless and equally strong. It was, simply, that when she thought of Nan and Perry a painful constriction came at her heart. It was like the sensation one had from the shock of seeing an accident or from receiving very bad news. There was nothing to be done about it. To speak of it to Nan or Perry would be cruel. There was nothing to be done except thrust it down into the limbo of one's mind.

Perhaps, she thought, attempting another approach to the question, it is just that I'm apprehensive about marriage in general. Her own was not the only disastrous marriage with which she had come into contact. Dr Franks's marriage had half crushed him. He had not recovered from it. It must have been a long, nerve-racking torment. Suzette, of course, ought never to have married, and ought never to have had a child … Nan was not the sort of person to recover easily from a broken marriage. There were women who did, but she was not made like that. Nan would give her husband a profound, intense and very sensitive love.

And perhaps, Virgilia reflected, there was a good deal of plain, selfish possessiveness at the back of all this. Perry was going to America. He would qualify to practise there; it was quite possible that he and Nan would live there. And loneliness was a dreadful thing. Trying to deny that was useless. Long, fading days with nobody coming home. Long, fading years …

She stitched carefully, attaching the cuff to the sleeve. She wished that Nan were not going out. She did not want to spend this evening alone. It was a beautiful evening. Now, clear sunshine was streaming across the floor and a song-thrush was experimenting with delicious improvisations in the hedge. Such peace and beauty intensified loneliness.

A common, contemptible egoist is all I am, she told herself; that's what I am in my black Freudian depths. She decided that she would ask Brigid to sit with her and help with the shirts. But Brigid liked to go early to bed.

She put her sewing aside, went to her table and began working there. The book was practically finished. On the back of each sketch and photograph she had to write the number of the page of the manuscript to which it belonged. She was engrossed in this when she heard the drone of the car, heard it pull in and stop outside. Afraid of losing the thread of her work, she continued and did not glance up until she became aware that someone was standing still in the doorway, while his shadow lay long and straight across the floor. It was Dr Franks.

PERRY, COMING IN behind his father, was saying, 'This house is the answer to a burglar's prayer'; then he stood still and laughed.

'I say, it's the famous shadow, isn't it?' he exclaimed, and Virgilia, going to meet them, answered, 'It is.'

'Is it really?' the doctor asked, looking down at his shadow as if it were something of which he were rather ashamed. 'I hope this doesn't make me unwelcome?' he said.

'You couldn't,' she told him, 'have come at a better time, especially if you have the evening to spare.'

'Thank you; it happens that I have,' he said diffidently. 'I wondered whether I might share your scrambled egg?'

Nan, coming in, greeted him with the little challenging air which she wore to cover shyness sometimes. 'Why,' she asked him, 'should you think it's a scrambled egg?'

'Isn't that ritualistic for deserted mothers?'

'She isn't the scrambled egg sort of mother, I'm glad to say.' She gave her mother a very sweet little smile as she went out with Perry.

'That is the sort of remark,' Dr Franks said, 'that turns parents' heads.'

Nan wore a white coat with a fluffy angora cap on her dark curls. She and Perry stood for a moment, looking over the valley with its gilded river, themselves the most radiant things the sun shone on.

Dr Franks turned from the window.

'Enviable fellow,' he said.

'They think the world is theirs,' Virgilia murmured; 'and I wonder whether God, on the seventh day of creation, was quite as certain as they are that it is good?'

They watched the car start away.

'It *is* good, really,' Dr Franks responded. 'The potentialities of the natural law are admirable. And it is always new. I think that is pleasant: to realise that never, actually, for any human consciousness, is this earth, for all its burden of antiquity, more than eighty or ninety years old.'

'But we are so old when we are born,' Virgilia protested, 'with our ancestral memories and our atavistic instincts and all that lumber we are supposed to be loaded with.'

The doctor smiled at her.

'Yes,' he said. 'But, happily, each conscious mind comes fresh to life – that is,' he added, 'if the old folks don't burden youth with the weight of their own experience. Some do.'

'Our two don't appear overburdened, at any rate,' Virgilia said gaily.

'No.' He chuckled. 'Young Perry has been a little above himself all day. And indeed I can't blame him.' Smiles wreathed his face. 'I brought wrath on my head the first day we met your daughter by observing that she was "charming." He was right. It was inadequate. Her beauty is almost luminous, isn't it?'

'She is intensely happy,' Virgilia said.

The doctor's glance at her face was brief but keen.

'And you, Mrs Wilde?'

'I'm greatly pleased, naturally. By the way, I'm supposed not to know.'

'So am I. We mustn't forget that. And now, will you tell me about this delightful house?'

They went into the garden and walked round the cottage. Dr Franks wanted to know just what was the original structure and how the additions had been planned; his interest was so lively that Virgilia allowed him to look into the kitchen where Brigid was being very efficient with sweetcorn, tomatoes and ham and was producing a most delectable smell.

'I realise how wrong I was,' the doctor said, 'about that scrambled egg.'

''Tis not the remains of the party you'll be getting, either,' Brigid said with a chuckle; 'for they had every dish licked clean.'

The meal that she served was excellent, as was the sherry that Virgilia opened, saying, 'We know that today is an occasion, even if we know it illicitly.'

She felt relaxed and happy, her misgivings forgotten, she did not know why.

Afterwards they sat by the open door of the studio watching the sun go down over Glencree. The evening was cool and fragrant with a light breeze. Curds of cloud, afloat in the sea-green air, flushed and thinned into vermilion plumes. The evening star appeared, very white and large. They talked about Virgilia's vision and its sequel. Perry had told his father about it in detail.

'It must have been an atrocious experience,' the doctor said. 'It was dreadful for everybody,' Virgilia replied. 'I gave Nan a very bad time, and Perry, too.'

He smiled.

'Yes: I heard all about that. On Saturday evening, Perry and I came near to having our first serious clash.'

Virgilia sighed. 'I'm sorry. He's been such a brick about the whole thing.'

'There's bed-rock in Perry,' his father said. He went on quickly: 'I have been reading a good deal about these faculties, Mrs Wilde, and I am astounded. I am rather humiliated, to tell you the truth, to think of the complacent ignorance in which I have existed for so long.'

His cigarette was finished and he threw it outside.

'You agree with Perry?' Virgilia asked him. She closed the door. The evening was growing cold.

'I do,' he replied. 'It has been culpable ignorance. The data has been within reach; clues have lain under our eyes and we have blinded ourselves; there is a vast reservoir of inherited knowledge in all corners of the world: we have dismissed far too much of it as mere superstition. At least, that is the conclusion to which I find myself being led.'

Virgilia asked: 'Does it all make any practical difference? Nan said to me today, "It is extraordinary how ordinary things are." It seems to me that to live as if these – these *accidents* of knowledge did not happen, is the sanest course.'

'For a layman, yes. For you, yes: I agree.'

Virgilia rose and lit the lamps and the fire. They drew their chairs to the hearth and the doctor smoked his pipe, still absorbed in his theme.

'But not for practising psychologists and psychiatrists,' he went on. 'Perry and Garrett are right about that. We *have* a whole new science to learn – or, rather, to accept. Freud, you know, after stiff resistance to the idea of telepathy, has accepted it.'

'Has he?' Virgilia exclaimed, surprised.

'Yes, he goes so far as to suggest that it may have been the original, archaic means of communication between human beings – as it still appears to be between animals and insects – bees and termites, for example.'

'And birds,' Virgilia said.

'Is that your belief, Mrs Wilde?'

Virgilia frowned. She was puzzled. She realised that she did not entirely believe this, yet did not know what to believe.

'I don't know. Isn't it accepted?' she asked. 'Isn't it supposed to work by electro-magnetic waves?'

'There is this difficulty, you see,' the doctor explained, 'that the strength of the message should decrease with the distance, but that doesn't appear to happen in telepathy. Do you think it happens in the case of birds?'

'I have often wondered; there's such instantaneous concerted movement … But you see, I'm not an ornithologist,' Virgilia said. She recalled something that she had read: 'Isn't it suggested that homing birds follow magnetic currents that are somehow perceptible to them in the atmosphere? But then,' she went on thoughtfully, 'what about cats who walk over miles of country that they have covered only by train, and ants that bore their way to water lying deep underground? And water-diviners, for that matter.'

'Yes: there appear to be radiations.'

'And Fabre's peacock moths,' Virgilia went on, 'who flew through storm and darkness, through a screen of trees, to the sleeping place of a newly born female. Sight didn't guide them – and he scattered scent about: it didn't distract them; apparently, it wasn't smell. And the "banded minim" … I have puzzled a great deal over these things but I have met very few people who are interested in them except as animal anecdotes.'

Dr Franks had been following intently.

'Specialisation is the trouble,' he said. 'A psychologist ought to be a zoologist also, but the span of man's working life is too short.'

Virgilia, recalling the theories of Edmund Selous, found his book about birds. The doctor had read but forgotten it. Interested, now, he discussed the conceptions of thought-transfusion and subliminal unity, then adventured beyond them:

'Can there be some reservoir of knowledge, planetary, perhaps, with which individual minds come into touch?'

Their talk ranged lightly, probed deeply, produced question after question, but no answer, while the dusk closed in. Brigid came and left a tray with a tea-caddy on the table and a kettle near the fire, then went up to bed. Dr Franks talked about strange faculties of primitive peoples, their priests and medicine-men, and about some of the so-called delusions of the insane which, he had begun to suspect, were perhaps not wholly without a basis in fact.

He smiled at Virgilia, saying, 'I don't know to whom else, except Perry and Ingram, I would dare to talk this way.'

For a time he became so silent that Virgilia took up her sewing and went on with it. She remembered that she had had a dream about Dr Franks – a bad dream. It did not trouble her. She had accounted for it, she thought.

After a while, he said, 'I am thinking about your own strange faculty, Mrs Wilde.'

'So am I,' she said. 'I am wondering whether those other powers have any connection with mine.'

He replied reflectively, 'I should say that the *origin* of your visions must have a quite separate explanation – possibly, in the nature of time; but your receptive faculty – your peculiar sensitivity – may be akin to that of a telepathic percipient, or that, say, of birds.'

'And the white ant?' she suggested.

Dr Franks laughed. 'And the white ant!'

He glanced at her clock; it was half-past ten. He said, 'I gave Perry the strictest injunctions … Am I tiring you, Mrs Wilde?'

'On the contrary! This is refreshing.'

'Actually,' he confessed, 'I had a particular reason for coming this evening, in addition to sheer self-indulgence. I felt uneasy when Perry told me about your latest experience. I wondered whether you would think me intrusive … whether you would allow me to give you a wholly non-professional piece of advice.'

Virgilia said warmly, 'You don't know how grateful I should be.'

'It amounts to this, Mrs Wilde: I feel most strongly that you ought to remove yourself from the conditions which conduce to such experiences. I don't imagine that there is any one set of circumstances which is associated with all of them, but I think it likely that a certain proportion of your visions have been due to some condition over which you have control – that is, that your abnormal degree of sensitivity may have such a cause. I thought we might try to go into the question of what those conditions seem to be. Solitude – your life in this charming place, possibly. No matter at what sacrifice, I would urge you most earnestly to make whatever change may be necessary.'

Virgilia was silent. He thinks I may get my nerves destroyed, or perhaps my reason, she said to herself. To alter her whole plan of life at this stage was more easily said than done. She asked: 'You think that surroundings could make a difference, then?'

'I can't, of course, be sure of it,' he answered. 'I understand that many psychic mediums live in cities and lead active lives, but I wish you could try what a change, say, to Dublin or London would do.'

'I'd have less occupation,' Virgilia said, 'and that wouldn't help, would it? Besides, Dr Franks, my own conviction is that this is a psychological battle that I have to fight out inside myself. Perhaps there are *moods* I ought to avoid, and states of mind.'

'And physical conditions, such as weariness,' he suggested.

'That afternoon in my waiting-room, for example; you must have been very tired ... By the way ...' He sat erect, suddenly. 'This has only just occurred to me. It may be significant. Had you been looking into the mirror in my dining-room just before that hallucination came?'

'Why, yes,' Virgilia answered, surprised at the extraordinary interest in his face. The moment came back to her vividly. She said, 'Your mirror happens to reflect the window in a rather intriguing way. I moved sideways, looking into it and thinking about the angle ... Yes, yes!' She looked at the doctor with startled eyes. 'And the mirror in Nan's room! When I thought I saw her there I was looking at that.'

'And on Friday?' the doctor asked. 'What were you looking at on Friday afternoon?'

'Water,' she answered. 'I had been looking at water nearly all day.'

'Go on.' His voice was tense, his eyes, under drawn brows, very bright.

'I'd been alone for hours,' she said, 'by Loch Bray, watching for a heron. There is a sort of quiescence that comes at such times. I ... I like to let it come. You feel at one with the whole life of the earth when it happens. And birds come to your hand, unafraid. I was there for some hours; then the heron came. I photographed him and left. I walked about a mile, I suppose; I was still full of peace when I came to the waterfall. I stood looking at it. The foam in the sunshine was dazzling and the eddies were weaving patterns like those in old Celtic ornaments. It was then that it happened.'

'It was then that you looked down and saw the child?'

'Yes ... Oh, and again,' Virgilia exclaimed, 'that Sunday! The Sunday before last, in the wood. I had been watching a dipper playing along the stream and I just *began* to hear the outcry that, actually, I did hear a few days later when the tinkers tried to beat Timeen. But Nan was with me and I was somehow able to free myself: to cut it off in time ... The dance vision, too ... Lightning was flashing – the flashes were reflected from these windows and I was watching from mine.'

With a gesture of relief and astonishment, the doctor sank back in his chair and looked at her.

'Mrs Wilde, do you realise what you have just told me?' he said. 'Do you not know how hypnosis is induced?'

'Hypnosis? By the eyes, isn't it? And movements of the hands?'

'Yes, or by keeping the eyes fixed on a point of light – rhythmically moving light, perhaps. Mirrors.' He spoke slowly. 'Mirrors; a pool; a waterfall in sunlight; glass – you have been inducing auto-hypnosis by the most approved means.'

Virgilia stood up; the doctor's eyes followed her.

'That ornament, yes!' he exclaimed.

'Nan's witch-ball,' she said.

'Witch-ball?'

'That's what they are called – a little too appropriately ... I remember, now: I was looking at it; I was thinking how prettily it caught the light from the garden, just before I turned and saw – *thought* I saw – that shadow – your shadow – on the floor.'

She took the ball, opened the door of her dark-room and put it away in there, saying, 'That, at least, is something I can do.' The doctor said drily, 'You haven't been crystal-gazing, also, by any chance?'

She turned to him, excited.

'Suppose you've found the cause of it all! Suppose I've only to take precautions as simple as that – to avoid staring at mirrors, and moving water, and reflections of light! I do stare at them; it's a habit: it's a habit I can easily break.'

'Break it, Mrs Wilde!' The doctor, too, was elated. 'We shall see how much difference that will make. Don't expect too much, but we may find that your previsions decrease both in number and intensity; and how splendid that would be!'

Virgilia turned sharply away. Her throat was working. This sudden uprush of hope had shaken her self-control.

Dr Franks walked to the window and opened it, murmuring, 'I believe I hear my car.'

'I'll make tea, then,' Virgilia said.

HE HAD NOT HEARD his car; it was another ten minutes before the Chrysler drew up outside. The kettle was steaming on the hob, the tray was on a low table by the hearth and their parents were in deep chairs on either side of it, drinking tea, when Nan and Perry came in. Nobody said anything for a moment while eyes challenged laughing eyes. Then Perry helped Nan out of her coat.

'I think,' he said in a stage-whisper, 'the signs are propitious.'

In a whisper still more audible she said, 'Let's pretend we don't know that they know.'

They advanced, hand in hand, Perry saying politely, 'We have something to tell you, Mrs Wilde.'

Virgilia rose. She stood with her left hand clutching the back of her chair and held out her right to Nan. Nan, who had been prepared to speak lightly, changed her mind. She put her arms round her mother and murmured to her: 'You are pleased, aren't you, Mummie? Oh, Mummie, please be pleased!'

'Of course, of course I am, my darling,' Virgilia repeated vehemently.

Perry was standing there awkwardly, colour mounting in his face. His father stood beside him.

'My dear boy,' Virgilia said warmly.

'You can trust me with her: you can, honestly, Mrs Wilde,' he promised, just as he had done when he was taking Nan out for the first time in his own car.

'I know I can, Perry.'

Nan turned to the doctor and gave him both her hands. He stood looking down at her, a smile spreading over his whole face.

'What nice things can happen! What very, *very* nice things can happen,' he said.

Chapter XII

DARK WINDOWS

THE INGRAMS WERE talkative. Pamela was frankly nervous and Garrett, for all his pretence of detachment, keyed up. He wanted this play to be a success. That is, he wanted it to be attacked with the ferocity proper to Dublin; championed in the Press by the judicious; received, later, in London, with somewhat puzzled respect, and awarded the Critics' Circle prize in New York. The dress rehearsal had been so prodigiously rich in accidents that by all the traditions of the theatre the first performance ought to go well.

'And if it is a success, I'm sunk,' the author declared. 'They'll never make me a judge.'

The Minister of Justice was coming and the Opposition was to be present in force.

'"Learned judge and distinguished dramatist,"' Dr Franks said reflectively. 'I don't think they're quite incompatible.'

'"Learned judge, distinguished dramatist and world-famous ghost-hunter" sounds a bit unlikely, however,' Perry remarked. 'One of the three will have to go overboard.'

'The judge,' Pamela prophesied.

'The ghost-hunter,' Virgilia suggested. 'That's a pursuit one would tire of rather quickly, I would think.'

'The dramatist probably commits suicide at 11pm this evening,' Garrett remarked.

Nan shook her head. 'No. He'll be too curious about the Press notices; he'll wait to read them and then he'll decide to live to have his revenge.'

'Press notices!' Garrett shuddered noisily. The most acidulous critic in England had come to Dublin. He would enjoy the play hugely, in the wrong way, being an Orangeman.

'I'll read the *Dictator* and feel a traitor,' Garrett rhymed lugubriously.

Pamela, studiously noting the excellence of Dublin Bay prawns in aspic, said, without perceptible hesitation, 'In the *Independent* you'll shine resplendent.'

Her success was so resounding that other diners turned to smile at the hilarious group in the corner, and some who recognised Garrett lifted their glasses to wish him luck. Perry's '*The Irish Press* will like you less' was agreed to as opinion but voted unenterprising as verse.

Nan did not compete. She was too happy to be clever this evening. All the afternoon she and Perry had bathed and swum and lain on warm sands. She was saturated with sunlight. How many times, she was thinking, we shall have dinners like this, just the six of us, sitting just the same way! She was at the foot of the table, Dr Franks on her right, with Pamela Ingram beside him; on Nan's other side Garrett sat, with Virgilia on his left. Perry was being a very attentive host, especially to her mother. Why wasn't her mother as gay and amusing as she usually was on social occasions?

Virgilia felt her own depression to be quite inexcusable. This was a very enjoyable party. Perry was a charming host. How well he looked in evening clothes! The Ingrams were in high spirits; Dr Franks was looking younger than usual and deeply contented; as for Nan, her sense of well-being, her love for Perry and faith in life were radiating from her like light. Virgilia received that radiance and caught joyous, confiding glances from Nan's eyes, and yet could not relax. She had all she could do to force herself to eat, talk and laugh.

A bad night's sleep was responsible, probably. She had gone to sleep early but had repeatedly waked to a sense of something urgent that ought to be done. The sensation reminded her of the time when she had nursed Nan through pneumonia, when the child's life had depended from second to second on her mother's vigilance. That shock of guilt and remorse was such as might remain if one had neglected some duty at such a time. Virgilia could find no such failure or neglect in her past, and yet the sense of it had persisted all day. Is it in the future, she asked herself, or is it in the present? Am I failing to do something which I ought to do, for Nan's sake, now?

She was thankful for Mrs Ingram's vivacity, which made it unnecessary for her to exert herself much. Pamela was recounting some tragi-comedy of the production of her brother's play in London and the others were listening to it, very much entertained. Garrett, sitting at Virgilia's right, turned his attention to her, saying, 'You know, this is a Tantalus feast for me! It's agony for me not to ask you all sorts of questions, but I suppose they are taboo?'

'No,' Virgilia said quickly in a low voice. 'In fact, there is something I have been wanting to ask you. You spoke about controlling this power. Tell me, if one learned how to induce it, would one be learning how to suppress it at the same time?'

'I would think so,' he answered eagerly. 'I would say it's like learning to adjust the focus of your eyes … If you would only try, Mrs Wilde!' he went on persuasively. 'Try to look into the future, perhaps at night, when you are sleepy! You might learn something about how your own psi function works, and, you know, it wouldn't alarm you so much once you had it under control.'

'I see.' Virgilia sighed. 'I expect you are right. I'm sure that would be the sensible and courageous thing to do.'

She relapsed into silence, crumbling the bread on her plate.

Garrett smiled at her, his eyes alight.

'Besides,' he murmured, 'if I'm not mistaken, you might see something rather pleasant.'

He glanced across her at Perry. 'I believe young Perry is holding out on me again. Tell him, if he does, it will be the end. Tell him he's got to come clean!'

'What's this?'

Dr Franks was looking from Garrett to Perry, amused, and now the others wanted to know what the charge was. Virgilia relayed the message, but she did not want Perry to respond; she did not want the engagement announced now. Perry, however, looked round the table, then questioned Nan with an eyebrow, and Nan, after a moment's hesitation, consented with a smile.

Perry could not find words. He flushed. Virgilia thought he looked very young: much too young to marry, she thought. The smiles on his guests' faces broadened; nobody helped him. At last he said bluntly, 'Nan has promised to marry me.'

He allowed his father to order champagne.

NAN BELIEVED that she would remember every minute of that evening to the end of her days. She could imagine talking about it to her children and grandchildren; describing her own Harlequin frock, and Pamela's dark red ninon, and her mother, looking so fair and sweet and dreamy in grey. Everything had been perfect – Perry such a good host; the Ingrams so pleased over the reception of the play; Dr Franks making her feel, in his dry, half-humorous way, that he liked and admired her and that in consenting to marry Perry she had made him happier than he had been for years. When they left him at his door and Perry drove on again, she said, 'I'm going to get awfully fond of my father-in-law.'

'You bet your life,' Perry said.

The night was very still; there were heavy clouds lying close to the tops of the mountains, but they did not move. Now and then, clouds and summits flared into brief stark clarity, when summer lightning fired the sky. The half-moon hung low. Nan thought of the dance, of a full moon lighting the garden, of how her dress would shine, and her lovely shawl. Her shawl was coming in time. Carlo had sworn it to

Freda by all his gods. The letter had arrived that morning. Recalling it, Nan realised that it might have worried her if London and Carlo had not gone such worlds away. Carlo had reappeared, Freda wrote: 'gnawed and gnashing with remorse and hell-bent on doing your head again.' He was prowling and growling, doing the sick tiger act, refusing commissions, not eating, not sleeping, pestering everyone to know when Nan would be back. 'Not until the autumn,' Freda had told him, lying to him for his soul's sake. 'And if I were you,' she had concluded, 'I'd stay put. For the present, leave London for Carlo to bustle in.'

He can have London! Nan thought, amused at her own progress in callousness. Perry glanced sideways at her face, asking, 'What – or who – are you smiling about?' To tease him, she answered, 'One Carlo.' He said, 'Oh!' with so poorly acted an air of indifference that she laughed and related the tragi-comedy of the shawl.

'I'm so thankful it's coming,' her mother said.

Perry was not driving very fast. He took them the longer way home, through Rathfarnham. In Glendhu he stopped the car and they looked down on the city, twinkling through the blue summer night; at the lamps festooning the pier and outlining the bay; at the eyes of the lighthouses opening in white brilliance and closing and opening again.

'Could you paint that?' Perry asked.

Nan said: 'I wouldn't be so daft as to try! But I'll remember it; won't you?'

He drove on over the Featherbed Mountain and into Glencree and slowed down again on the bridge by the waterfall. Nan looked at the little torrent throwing its silver foam into the moonlight, singing aloud to itself in the night. It was up there, on the bank, while she peered desperately into the darkness, when she, at last, saw the lights of Perry's car – it was there, at that moment, that she had first known the whole force of her love for Perry and her need of him. It had been like the sudden, fierce visibility in that lightning flash, but it had remained.

'Next summer,' Perry said, 'we'll go to all our places again.'

Every place and every incident, great or little, that had led them to the magical world in which they were together seemed part of some blessed mysterious scheme. If it had not been for this or for that Perry might not have dared, Nan might not have been sure … And yet, Nan thought, it had *had* to happen, their coming together. If anything in life was predestined that must have been.

'Is Mother asleep, I wonder?' she murmured. Virgilia was sitting with her eyes closed, rather pale, in the back of the car. As if she had heard the whisper, she opened her eyes.

'I'm just deliciously sleepy,' she said.

The Chrysler glided into the garden so quietly that Shuiler was undisturbed in his shed at the back. The flowers of the ash-tree were creamy curds in the moonlight; its shadow lay on the lawn, delicate and still. Moonlight glinted on the studio windows. A lamp burned in Virgilia's room. In the black and silver-white world nothing seemed to be moving except the stream and nothing else made a sound.

'There ought to be nightingales. You're no good of a bird-woman, Mummie, if you can't breed them in Ireland,' Nan said.

'I'll try,' Virgilia promised, smiling. 'But you know, darling,' she said, looking around at the tranquil scene, 'I think everything's pretty complete! … Perry, what a really delightful party you gave us! Thank you very, very much.'

Perry said 'good-night,' moved towards the stream and waited under the larches for Nan. Nan put an arm round her mother.

'If only you were perfectly happy, everything would be perfect,' she said.

'Perhaps I shall be very soon,' her mother replied gently and kissed her, and then shivered as if suddenly cold. She opened the door with her key and went in. Nan ran in with her, changed her slippers for sandals and then joined Perry under the trees. He was looking at the cottage. 'It is pretty,' he said.

It had an enchanted look, lying, moonlit, under the tall oaks. Virgilia, standing still in her open window, looking towards the studio, lamplight behind her, made part of a picture that seemed to Nan as if it belonged to some unwritten fairy-tale. Virgilia moved, turned out her lamp, and stood there again, a still grey figure dimly lit by the moon. The white summer lightning came and went.

2

'THE WATER IS TALKING about us,' Nan whispered. Perry caught her hand and they stood for a while, listening. The quietude of the night seemed only deepened by the gossiping of the stream. Lightning played beyond the trees three or four times, then ceased. They made their way up through the wood slowly and came out on the moonlit fields of Knockree.

'Nobody was meant ever to see this,' Nan breathed, overawed by the silence of the empty valley, the void of the sky, the stark midnight dignity of the hills. Creation lay vacant except for themselves and the moon and stars – a vast bowl with nothing to fill it but human happiness and love. It filled, brimmed and overflowed.

They stood there for only a moment, then Nan shivered and presently they were under the trees again, searching, chattering, finding and losing again the elusive little fern-hidden path. A dog barked below. They paused; heard the barking grow frantic, and then heard a high, tearing cry.

Nan began to run. Perry gripped her arm and guided her. The barking went on, coming nearer, and then the cry came again, desperate: 'Nan! Oh, Nan, Nan!'

'I'm coming, Mummie!' Nan called; and Perry shouted, 'We're coming!'

'Where are you?' Virgilia's voice came from among the larches, where they had been. The dog's barking drowned their reply. In a minute Shuiler had found them and was running backwards and forwards excitedly.

'She's gone down to the water and hurt herself,' Nan gasped; but when they saw Virgilia she was running towards them, stumbling in her long dress along the edge of the stream. Nan caught her in her arms.

Perry's first thought had been that something was on fire, but there was no sign of fire anywhere. Brigid was standing in the front garden, a coat over her shoulders, her hair a white halo round her head. She sped to her mistress and, between her and Nan, Virgilia was led up to the house. Nan signed to him not to come. Nobody told him what was wrong. He stood there, quieting the dog.

In the porch, Virgilia seemed to recover her strength. She said, 'Go in, Brigid,' pushed Nan behind her and then stood there, clinging to the timbers of the porch with both hands. Her face was ghastly. She said in a high quavering voice, 'Please go away; please, please go away!' Perry thought that she looked and sounded mad. Nan tried to come to him, but her mother held her; without handling Virgilia violently no one could have passed.

It was not a fire and it was not an accident; nobody was hurt. Burglary wouldn't upset her like this. If something were wrong in the house she would call him in. Perry could think of nothing except that Virgilia had suddenly gone out of her mind.

'Nan!' he called. 'For God's sake, come out to me, Nan!' Virgilia was gripping Nan's wrist. Nan did not struggle and her mother drew her inside. She has had some frightful shock, Perry thought: some perfectly hideous shock. It was one of her visions. There was nothing else it could be. His skin turned cold.

The front door had been slammed shut. Every window in the house was dark. Perry waited, his heart pounding. A flickering light appeared in Virgilia's room. The windows were closed. For a moment, he could look in. Brigid, with a lighted candle in her shaking hand, was trying to put a match to the lamp. Nan's face was as white as her mother's. Brigid moved to the window and drew the curtains across.

Light fell from the gable-end at his left. Perry ran round the angle of the house and looked in at the small window in that wall. Brigid saw him and waved him away as if he were an object of fear. Nan turned to the little window, but her mother cried out and held her back. Brigid, shaking her head at him sadly and helplessly, pulled a curtain over that window, too.

The dog was quiet now. For a time everything seemed quiet to Perry, except his own thudding heart. Nan must be got out of that house; he had no other thought. How could it be done, without a scene which might drive her mother to violence? He decided simply to wait there, no matter for how long, until something happened. He stood close to the small window, waiting and listening. Voices were discernible, Nan's and her mother's, but not words. The curtains were not stirred. After what seemed a long time, he heard a low growl from the dog and heard Brigid's footsteps padding round from the back of the house. Stepping as silently as he could, he went to her. She drew him down the kitchen garden, saying under her breath, 'Don't let her know you're here.'

They whispered.

'What happened, Brigid?'

'Nothing happened. It must be something she's after seeing. God help us, Dr Perry, she's in a fearful state. She won't loosen her hands off Nan.'

'What did she see?'

'That's what we can't get her to tell.'

'Is she dangerous, Brigid?'

'Heaven pity her, no. She's in shivering misery. I think she thought Nan was lost in the woods.'

'We only walked up the hill.'

'To be sure. I told her that.'

'She's in a state of shock, isn't she?'

'She is, indeed. All she's waiting for is to hear your car going off. I think she'll be better then.'

'How can I go and leave Nan?'

'You'll have to go, Dr Perry; and she'll have to know you're gone, or no one will get rest or sleep this night.'

'I'll leave the car at Doyle's and walk back.'

'You wouldn't let the Doyles know about this?'

'Can't Nan come to me?'

Brigid shook her head. There were tears in her voice.

'Dr Perry, dear, whatever she's after seeing, you're in it. 'Tis of you she's afraid. Have pity on her. Have pity on us all now and go away.'

Perry stood still, trying to think. It was necessary to be steady. This was a case of illness: simply of illness ... At last he said, 'Very well, Brigid, I'll go. Give Mrs Wilde something to make her sleep. Tell Nan not to question her or upset her. Tell Nan to wait in the lane in the morning. I'll come with my father. How early do you think we can come?'

'Come at half-past eight. If she won't let Nan go, I'll be looking out for you then.'

'Very well. Brigid … Give her … give her my love.' Perry went to the window and listened again. He heard weeping – shuddering, exhausted sobs. There is no danger now, he thought; she is worn out. He tapped as lightly as he could with his finger-tips on the window. For a while nothing happened, then a corner of the curtain was lifted and dropped again. He waited. The weeping went on. Then, again, the curtain was moved and against the light he saw a hand. It was Nan's hand; she made her 'goodbye' signal with fingers spread. He tapped once again and then went to his car. He started it, turned it, taking time, as he always had to in that narrow driveway, then drove away from the dark unanswering cottage, his horn sounding ruthlessly through the night.

3

WHEN THE CAR had gone, Virgilia became less rigid. Her eyes still followed Nan's every movement, but the clutching fingers relaxed and let go. A kind of smile came on her face; her face was extremely pale and looked crooked; her lips were compressed but kept twitching.

'Sleep is what she needs,' Brigid said.

Nan's knees were trembling; she could not help it. She whispered to Brigid, 'Do you think it's a stroke?'

Brigid said, 'No,' emphatically. Then, loud enough for Virgilia to hear, she said: ''Tis some dream or vision she's after having. She'll tell us in her own time what it was, and then we'll know what to do. But first she should sleep.'

'I can't sleep. Nan, don't leave me,' Virgilia implored.

'If you go to bed I'll bring my mattress down here,' Nan managed to say.

As if eager to comply, Virgilia began to take off her dress. She stammered a little, calling them to leave the door open, as Brigid went upstairs with Nan.

'It must have been a dream,' Nan whispered. 'Perhaps she lay down and fell asleep. She was tired; she nearly fell asleep in the car.'

'Maybe 'twas a dream,' Brigid replied.

Nan believed that her mother had seen her dead – had seen her and Perry dead. Nothing else would account for the wild pity and fear in her eyes and her voice and her hands, and her desperate haste to send Perry away. It had been all that Nan could do not to scream and rage and force her mother to say what she had seen. Fear kept surging up from her heart to her throat. It was Brigid's reiterated 'Be quiet, child; wait,' that had made her keep her terror under control.

'Don't upset her,' Brigid whispered now, while they stripped the mattress. 'Dr Perry says to ask her no questions but get her asleep. He's coming with his father in the morning. You're to go down the lane if you can at half-past eight. If she won't let you out of her sight, I'll go.'

'I'll go, Brigid; I must talk to Perry, I must.'

'I'll see will she take a cup of sedebrand now.'

Virgilia refused to take anything. She lay in bed, her eyes strained and bright-looking, as if she would never sleep again. Nan's bed was made up on the floor beside hers. Nan undressed and burrowed in under the blankets. Her mother would not put out the light.

Brigid left them. For a long time Nan lay huddled there, fighting against her fear; telling herself, We are all being scared by a dream. That's the worst of her gift: she's going to think that every nightmare means something; we're never going to have any peace. Oh, why did I ask her to use it? Why were we all such fools? We were so happy …

A sob broke from her and her mother said, 'Naneen, can't you sleep?'

Nan lifted her head. The lamp was alight still, and her mother's face was turned to hers, looking down from the side of her bed.

'I'll keep you safe, darling,' Virgilia said.

Nan knelt up on her mattress and caught at her mother's hand. She could not bear this any longer. She said, 'Mummie, can't you understand that guessing and guessing is simply unbearable? Anything would be better than guessing. There's no horror that isn't coming into my mind. Tell me. Oh, Mummie, you must tell me.'

'I can't tell you. I can never tell anyone.'

Virgilia said that so quietly that Nan was appalled. That voice, steady and calm at last, left her no hope. It had not been a nightmare: it had been a vision, and a vision of something too awful to be told.

'Mummie!' she cried imploringly.

'Don't, Nan. If you knew, you would tell him, and that would *make* it happen. I've enough sense now to see that. I mustn't lose my judgment. I mustn't forget. Don't wear me out with questions, or something will go wrong. I have got to keep my head. I can prevent this. If you obey me I *can*. But I must keep my mind quite clear and cool. You promised,' she reminded her daughter. 'You said that if I looked into the future and then told you what you should do, you would take my advice.'

'So I would, if I knew why.'

'That's what I can't tell you, Nan. You've got to trust me.'

'But there's nothing you couldn't tell. There's nothing that I couldn't guard against better if I knew.'

Virgilia shook her head slowly; her eyes grew almost expressionless.

'Go to sleep, Nan,' she said. 'We won't talk any more. We'll try … We'll both try to sleep.'

She turned out the light. Nan lay in the dark and listened to her mother's breathing. For a time it would be very even, then she would hear convulsive gasping, then it would become even again. Nan tried to calm herself by thinking about the things in the room. The moon must have set or have gone down behind clouds, because not a glimmer of light came in. The little window was over her head; the small brick fireplace across the comer at her left hand, with a jar of sweet-peas on top. There were the old oak tall-boy and a wardrobe, and, opposite her mother's bed, the door. There was the old ottoman with a pattern of blue poppies, and the dressing-table across the corner by the bay-window; in the window, Nan's cane chair and the table, and her mother's old wing chair, covered in blue; bookshelves at the right of her mother's bed ...

Nan slept, to be wakened again by her mother's hand moving gropingly over her.

'I'm here, Mummie,' she said, and heard the distressed answer:

'Did I wake you? I didn't mean to. I was asleep.'

She slept again, and a second time was wakened in the same way. Once she woke to hear her mother moving about the room. It was stuffy. There seemed to be no air to breathe. Her mother opened the casement windows, opened the long curtains and drew them together again at the bottom, leaving the upper part open; then she went back to bed. Nan lay awake, visited by thoughts of one dreadful fate after another falling on Perry and herself until, at the top of the window, a triangular space of light showed grey and faint. She thought, then, It is morning. Perry is coming. Perry will know that it's simply not true. A soft unreality fell over everything and she slept.

Chapter XII

LOCKED DOORS

NAN LEFT HER MOTHER asleep in the half-dark room. Moving about stealthily, she was dressed by a quarter past eight. Now, she thought, if I go out and she wakes and finds me gone, what will happen? Will it throw her into a state of terror again? She crept down to the kitchen where Brigid was going about her work noiselessly.

'Don't leave the house,' Brigid advised. 'At any cost at all we must keep her mind quiet. I'll go. You can say I've gone down to stop Eileen. We don't want Eileen here today.'

Nan could scarcely bear it but she knew that Brigid was right and went back to her mother's room. She was just in time. Her mother's eyes opened and fixed her, first with an incredulous, then with an anguished gaze.

'Don't go away,' Virgilia said under her breath.

'I won't go,' Nan promised, so wrung with pity that for a moment fear was overcome. How could one night change anyone so? She is like Gran – like Gran when she was old and ill, Nan thought. She lay there as if she could scarcely find strength to move, then suddenly sprang out of bed and set to work hurriedly, washing in the bathroom and dressing in the half-light of the curtained bedroom, with the air of having something urgent to do.

Nan had never felt so desolate. Always there had been her mother to run to in any trouble, but her mother had no comfort to give her now. There ought to have been Perry to hold her and steady her, but Perry was shut out. She was alone. It's my turn, she thought; it's my turn to be alone with things and to take care of her, but I've never taken care of anybody; I don't know how. I can't stop thinking about myself. If nobody helps Mummie, she'll go mad. She said: 'I won't worry you, Mummie. I'm not going out of the house; don't be afraid. Sit down and let me brush your hair.'

She had always liked brushing her mother's hair. It had honey-coloured lights in it, and it sprang from her forehead and clung round her head in soft, lively waves. Virgilia sat down to let her do it, but could not keep still.

'I don't hear Brigid. Where's Brigid?' she asked.

'She doesn't want Eileen to come,' Nan replied quickly. 'She's gone down to send her home.' She would have looked out, but Virgilia, as if the curtains gave her a sense of safety, said, 'Don't touch them. Come away from the window, Nan.' In silence they made the bed. Nan did not hear the Chrysler, but she heard footsteps outside – Brigid's steps and a man's. Virgilia drew her breath sharply and Nan said at once, 'It's not Perry. It's Dr Franks.'

'Dr Franks!'

There was relief – almost longing – in Virgilia's voice. She will see him! Nan thought exultantly. But her mother's face changed.

'He is the last person – the last person …' she said. 'I can't see him; I can never see him again. Don't look out, Nan. He's not to come in.'

But Nan had looked out. Perry was not there. Her eyes had met the doctor's, sending him one glance of appeal, before her mother pulled her back, drew the curtains across again, and stood holding them together behind her. There was no ring or knock, but presently Brigid came into the room, saying, as if a call at that hour were nothing out of the ordinary, 'Here's Dr Franks wanting to have a chat with you, ma'am.'

Virgilia stood rigid. She said:

'Tell Dr Franks that I can't see him. Tell him I'm sorry, and thank him for calling. Say that I will write later on, and that, meanwhile, I would rather that neither he nor Dr Perry came here.'

It was an order. Virgilia rarely spoke in that imperative tone. Her phrases were so deliberate and her voice so hard that Brigid stood helpless, not venturing to expostulate although reluctant to obey.

'Don't keep the doctor waiting,' Virgilia said.

Nan moved to the door.

'I'm going, Mummie: I have to talk to him.'

Her mother sprang forward and caught her arm.

'Brigid!' Virgilia said sharply, and the old woman went sadly out of the room, shutting the door.

The pallor of her mother's face and the blue fire in her eyes alarmed Nan.

'All right,' she said quietly. 'Don't worry! I'll stay with you; I won't go.'

Virgilia sank into the armchair and buried her face in her hands. Brigid could be heard opening the front door, going down to the gate with the doctor, talking and shutting the gate after him. She returned slowly and came into the room.

'He's mortal disappointed,' she said. 'He says, surely you'll let him know if there's anything he can do.'

'I'll never send for him,' Virgilia said.

Brigid went away and after a while came with breakfast. The curtains were still drawn. Virgilia rose and opened them. She sat in her chair by the table and Nan sat opposite her. Brigid put the tray down and poured out the tea; then she left the room with a sigh. Sunlight was playing over the table, sparkling on the blue ware. They ate and drank until Nan, overcome with misery, put her cup down and leaned her head on her hand.

'What are you doing, Mummie?' she asked. 'What are you trying to do?'

Virgilia answered in a low voice, 'I'm trying to save you, my darling, and I'm trying to work out some way in which we can live.'

'What about Perry?' Nan said.

Virgilia rose. She crossed the room to the little window and stood there looking out with her back to Nan. She said, 'You must never see Perry again.'

Nan ran up to her own room and looked out of the windows. The trees in their July leafage entirely hid the lane and the road. The landing window was the only one in the back of the house. From it, looking to the right, one could still see a few yards of the Enniskerry road, half-way up the hill. She stood there, listening and watching, and presently heard the hum of a car. She saw it shoot by. In a moment it was backed again to stop at the gap. She leaned out and waved. Perry stood up and waved to her, and his father turned and waved also. Then Perry drove on.

Nan's brain began to work again. She decided to leave her mother alone for a while, and try to think this out for herself. She sat by the window, hunched in her low chair, her chin on her fists. She could hear her mother and Brigid in the dining-room underneath. Presently her mother came upstairs and paused on the landing. Nan called, 'I'm here, Mummie; resting,' and Virgilia went down again and passed through the dining-room into the studio. Nan glanced out and saw her at the studio window. She returned to her brooding. Gradually, what seemed a feasible explanation began building itself in her mind.

Brigid knocked and came in quietly with a big cup of coffee. 'Alannah,' she pleaded, 'don't sit here breaking your heart. We'll come out of this before long with the help of God ... Drink this now. You took no breakfast at all.'

Nan took the cup. 'Please sit down, Brigid,' she said.

Brigid drew over the stool and sat there. There was deep trouble in her face.

'Brigid,' Nan said, 'I believe I know what it was Mother saw. Because, obviously, I'm in it – killed or hurt; and Perry's in it. It's the car, I think: I think she saw a smash with his car.'

'Do you know,' Brigid said, 'I was wondering if it was that ... God between you and harm!'

'You thought of this, too?'

215

'When she wouldn't see the doctor, I thought of it. She wouldn't wish to tell him the like of that.'

'Exactly! … We could give up motoring.'

'To be sure you could.'

'But why won't she tell me? Why on earth won't she tell me? Then we'd know what not to do. She said that if Perry knew, that would *make* it come on. I suppose she imagined he'd want just to defy it and – and elope with me. I suppose that must be it.'

'I think, Nan, 'tis confused-like her mind is, from the shock. She'll surely talk to you later on.'

'That's what I think.'

'Dr Perry sent you a message by his father. You are to be sure to remember that a person who'd had a shock might think the case was worse than it is.'

'Yes, yes, I know,' Nan exclaimed. 'Is that what he says? He's probably right about that.'

'And what Dr Franks says,' Brigid went on, 'is that what we should think of first is her peace of mind. When she's better, he thinks she'll tell her trouble and maybe then it can all be cleared up.'

Nan said gravely, 'I'm sure he's afraid of her mind giving way. At one minute I think it's going to, and the next she seems quite clear-headed again. But I'll try not to ask her questions yet.'

'That's a wise child.'

Nan finished her coffee. She was feeling much, much calmer now. She asked, 'Can things be prevented when they've been seen?'

'And why not?' Brigid responded. 'There are dreams and fancies, and visions and dreams, and who's to say which is true? 'Tis maybe a sort of nightmare she had, only. Or 'tis maybe a warning like the others, sent to protect you. There's no call to be thinking the worst.'

'It *would* give her a shock to see me in an accident.'

'It would, 'faith. 'Twould be enough to put the wits astray on her for a while, and you the only light of her life.'

'She's so *sane*, Brigid.' Nan's voice trembled.

'She is, and please God she'll soon be herself again. She'll see the good doctor and he'll put her right.'

'Perry and I are going to be married, no matter what it is.'

'To be sure you are!'

Nan began to smile. 'You wanted me to say "yes," didn't you?'

Brigid said simply, 'I was praying for it, asthore.'

Nan rose and kissed her. 'Oh, Brigid,' she said, 'you are such a dear!'

'I'm an old woman,' Brigid said, getting slowly up, 'and there's many a saying I doubted when I was young that I know the truth of now, and one is: "The grace of God is nearer than the door."'

Nan heard unfamiliar noises downstairs. She asked, 'What's Mother doing now?'

'Och, you'd never guess,' Brigid answered unwillingly. 'We are locked in the house; front door and back doors she's after locking on us and she's hid the keys. She's at work on the windows with a screwdriver now.'

NAN WENT DOWN. It was true. With screws and strips of wood, the windows of the ground-floor rooms had been fixed so that nothing could be opened except, in the studio, the small panes at the top. Virgilia was at work in her own room now.

The sheer incongruity of such behaviour, at once needless and useless, in her mother, who slept with her windows open in all weathers, who could never remember to lock anything up, first made Nan angry, then afraid, and then gave her hope. That her mother was unbalanced was the least terrible of the ideas that were crowding into her imagination. A temporary, curable nervous upset – that was the thought to hold on to now; that thought made Nan able to pity her mother instead of being distractedly angry with her. It made her able to go to her now and say evenly and quietly: 'All this isn't necessary, you know.'

Virgilia leaned her head against the window-glass as if it ached. She said desolately, 'You'll never forgive me, will you?'

Nan replied, 'This doesn't matter much except that it will be horribly stuffy tonight.'

'Tonight?'

Virgilia sighed and looked at her.

'You look so white and tired, darling,' she said. 'I kept on waking you all night. I shall have to let you sleep in your own room.'

Thankfully, Nan carried her bedclothes and mattress upstairs. If I really wanted to I could let myself down from this window, she thought. What her mother was doing came from a sick mind ... It was shock that had made her think 'so brain-sickly of things.' ... Macbeth; I seem to be haunted, she thought, by Macbeth. The little red volume was among the set on her chest of drawers. She opened it.

Presently she heard her mother come upstairs and stop at the landing window. Nan wanted to be able to lean out there. She went to her mother and said lightly, 'I'll give you my parole for twenty-four hours, but do leave that window alone.'

Virgilia shook her head. She said sadly, 'That's no good, now.'

'Have I ever broken a promise I gave you?' Nan asked.

'No; but now it's different: now you're thinking I'm out of my mind. That's why you're being so patient, and with a mad person anything would seem justified.'

Shocked by the reasonableness with which her mother said this, and because it was nearly true, Nan began to cry like a child. She dashed back to her own room and turned the key in the lock. She stood at her window looking out. There was nothing to be seen but the garden and trees and fields beyond, with people working, very small and far off, and the mountains all around. When would something happen? When would somebody come?

When Brigid's hand-bell sounded she went down. Yes, the landing window was screwed down fast. It isn't logical not to do my room too, Nan told herself, thankful to find a flaw in the dreadful, purposeful working of her mother's mind.

The little dining-room with the sun full on the windows was stifling. Nan thought she could eat nothing, but suddenly discovered she was hungry. She ate the salad that Brigid had taken such pains to make appetising. When she had finished she looked across the table at her mother, who was not eating or talking at all. She stood up.

'Do you call this a way in which we can live? How long do you think this can go on?' she asked, her voice shaking.

'Six weeks, isn't it?' Virgilia said.

'Six weeks!' Nan exclaimed. 'Do you mean until Perry sails?'

'Yes.'

'I see.'

This was impossible; this was going to need action; this had to be thought about carefully. Nan checked the torrent of words that rushed to her lips and helped Brigid to clear away.

BRIGID HAD DECIDED to turn out the dark-room. It was just like her. When the atmosphere round her was restless and nervous she always steadied herself with some big piece of work. Nan said she would help. It proved to be quite a job. This long, narrow closet lined with shelves served as a store – as well as a photographic work-room. As it had doors to both the studio and the kitchen, any object that began to seem superfluous in either room was always dumped in there. The photography end was neat, with its sink under the window, which had a red blind running in grooves. The doors were edged with felt and had flaps over the keyholes to keep light out. The closet contained trunks and cases, a store of canned foods, jars of Brigid's pickles and jellies and jams, winter boots, spare lamp chimneys, supplies of candles and soap. Working amongst these homely things with Brigid was a help. A soothing incredulity began to ease Nan's mind. She began to plan a long letter to Perry, making up the sentences while she worked. Finally, she washed her hands in the kitchen and went upstairs to write it.

Her room was untidy. She had neglected it. Quickly she made the bed, her thoughts still occupied with the letter that she was going to write. Her Harlequin dress lay over the back of a chair and she opened the wardrobe to hang it up. The wardrobe looked half empty: her dance frock was gone.

Nan ran down. Her mother was in her own room; she went in there. The dress was not to be seen. It was hidden somewhere

219

– hidden in this room – in the ottoman, probably, Nan thought. She looked at her mother, saying nothing.

Virgilia was busy. She was taking garments out of drawers and laying them on her bed. She said, 'Nan, I want you to pack. We're leaving. I've decided to go away.'

'Where to?' Nan asked quickly.

'We'll cross to Holyhead this evening; then, it doesn't much matter where: London, if you like.'

Nan sat on the side of the bed. She observed that her mother was avoiding her eyes. She was bluffing. She was trying to get her way by putting on that authoritative manner, so new to her, so unlike her that it was almost ludicrous. She moved oddly, too, with a stiffness entirely different from her usual swift, free, supple way, and her eyes looked queer – as if they were beginning to squint. She wasn't mad; no, no, it wasn't that, only ... Nan couldn't remember the word. An *idée fixe*? An obsession? Yes, she was obsessed: sane about everything except – except Perry.

Was that it? She had had a dream about Perry, and it had taken possession of her mind. Just a bad dream ... Outright opposition wouldn't be the best way. Nan said quietly: 'You know, don't you, that Perry would follow me?'

'His father wouldn't let him,' Virgilia said, but her hands fumbled, trying to fold a blouse.

'His father couldn't stop him. Nobody could.'

Virgilia threw the garment aside, quite distraught.

'That's quite true. Nobody could,' she said. 'And in a strange place how could I protect you? What can I do? What am I to do?' She began to move about, saying, 'Six weeks is too long.' She was crushing her hands together and twisting them.

That, Nan thought, is what people mean by wringing their hands. She means that she can't hold out for six weeks: that her mind would give way. Nan wished that her own heart would steady itself; it felt weighted down and dragged to one side. I must be calm; I must get her to talk rationally, she resolved. She said, 'Mummie, why can't we talk about all this?'

'Because we should only torture each other,' Virgilia said. 'I would tell you lies, and you would torment me till I lost my head. There is nothing to be gained by talking. Talking won't do any good.'

'You want blind obedience from me,' Nan said bitterly. 'You always despised blind obedience. It's too late for me to learn it now.'

'It mustn't be too late.'

'You know you are making me frantic with misery?'

'Yes, I know that. I can't help it, Nan. I can't save you from misery; I can only, if you'll obey me, save your life.'

'My life?' The words were scarcely more than a breath.

'Yes, my darling, your life.'

'And Perry?'

'Don't ask me about Perry,' her mother said. She put her elbows on the sill of the small window, and laid her face in her hands. Nan saw her shudder. It was very difficult not to be infected with the horror that was in this room. With all the force of her reasoning mind Nan held it away from her.

'Can you prevent it?' she asked. Her voice was thin and high but firm.

'It can't happen if you and Perry don't meet.'

'We could meet here, where you can watch us. We must meet.'

'No,' Virgilia said. 'Because he would arrange something: he would plan some trick.'

'If you would tell me I would know what to do.'

'After he's gone, I may tell you, perhaps.'

Nan tried again.

'Perhaps if you told me I'd agree to ... to do what you want.'

Her mother turned and looked at her. She's going to tell me, Nan thought, and her heart seemed to stop, but Virgilia shook her head.

'No,' she said. 'I daren't tell you. I can't. You love him too much.'

Nan turned to the bay-window. It is an obsession, she thought again. She felt blind and stupid. She did not believe in the choice her mother was setting before her: life without Perry, or death. The sun was shining and birds were calling across the garden. She did not believe it. Simply, it was not true.

In silence she helped her mother put her clothes back in the drawer.

NAN HEARD THE CAR first, because she was listening all the time for that sound. But it was not the right sound: it was not Perry's car or the Chrysler that had gone into second gear coming up the lane. It was Pamela Ingram who drove through the gate and walked to the front door and rang the bell.

'I'll see her. I'll talk to the Ingrams,' Virgilia said.

She unlocked a drawer of her dressing-chest, took out the front-door key and let Pamela in. Pamela was looking at the flower-beds and did not seem to notice that the door had to be unlocked. As she came in she said, 'I was just thinking that you must have hard work in the spring protecting your seedlings and peas.'

Virgilia took Pamela into the studio. Nan slipped back into the bedroom and, in breathless haste, opened the ottoman, the drawers of the tall-boy, the wardrobe. Her dress was not to be seen. She tugged at the wardrobe drawer: it was locked. It must be in there. She hurried to the studio, wondering why she had been afraid to ask her mother what she had done with the dress – why she still did not want to ask … Was it because she was afraid of the refusal or the half-truth that would be the answer? Was it because, if once she knew that this dress came into her mother's tragic vision, the tragedy could not be years away?

THE ATMOSPHERE in the studio was oppressive, stagnant and hot. How cool Pamela looks, Nan thought. She was wearing a short-sleeved frock, dark blue and white, and a white hat. She said, 'Perry is at the Doyles'. He sent me to ask whether you'd both come for a drive. Mrs Wilde says you can't.' She looked from Virgilia to Nan, her grey eyes grave and questioning. She asked gently: 'Can't we do something to help?'

'I would like to see your husband,' Virgilia said. 'I would like to talk to him and to you. But not Perry. Perry must not come.'

Pamela looked at her watch. It was a quarter past four.

'I think we could come at about eight o'clock,' she said.

Brigid brought tea and Pamela drank a cup hurriedly, talked about her husband's play and the Press notices a little, then went out to her car again. Nan had tried to ask questions, to seem interested, but had not tried very hard. Pamela, she felt, had guessed a good deal. Nan wanted to go out to the car with her, but Virgilia put her hand on her arm.

Pamela turned back and opened her bag. She said, 'Perry gave me this note for you, Nan,' and handed it to her.

'Please tell him I'll write,' Nan said.

Her mother looked after her anxiously as she hurried upstairs with Perry's letter in her hand and stood by the landing window reading it.

IT WAS A LOVE-LETTER. Nan had thought Perry inarticulate compared to some of her artist friends. He was not inarticulate at all. His delight in her and his devotion flowed from the page – flowed around and over her, like fresh, singing mountain air. He was not unhappy and not afraid. He was distressed only on account of her mother's health.

> *Obviously she has had what she thinks was one of her visions* [he wrote in his free clear hand]. *She is so jumpy about them that she is probably thinking it means five times as much as it does. Very likely she saw a smash with the car. We'll have our share, I suppose, in the Bouncer and the rest, right up to the Rolls. And if she saw, for instance, you lying stunned, or with blood on your face – saw it clairvoyantly, I mean suddenly, alone there, in the dark, it would give her a terrific shock. She might easily go off the deep end, and imagine every sort of catastrophe. My father agrees with me absolutely about this. He thinks she must have tried to induce autohypnosis and succeeded too well. He also says that she has more natural equilibrium than any woman he has ever met and that she will probably recover very quickly if nobody fusses*

her. It was a bad blow that she wouldn't see him. We are hoping every hour for a call. Pamela promised to do her best, and to give you this if you can't come to me.

To know you are worried, perhaps scared, and I can't come …

Splendid, splendid, Nan thought, exulting recklessly. The same idea as mine exactly! Brigid's too. It *must* be that.

She was reading the letter a second time when she heard the horn. She could see the Austin, standing still, and Perry and Pamela waving, but she did not know whether Perry could see her or her hand pressed against the window-pane. When the car went on she went to her own room and covered pages with her first letter to Perry, telling him everything. She confessed the belief, cruel and heartless though it seemed, that sustained her: 'I think Mother is on the very edge of being out of her mind.'

2

GARRETT ISN'T LIKING THIS, Nan thought, looking at his tense, sombre face; and no wonder. Because it is his fault, partly. But it's Perry's just as much, and mine most of all. She would have held out against *them*; it was my begging and hinting – my *willing* her to do it – that made her, in the end.

The Ingrams had come into the studio straight from the garden and the door was left standing open to let in the cool evening breeze. That was a relief. The back door had been opened too, because Shuiler and the chickens had to be fed. There was air in the house. Heavy clouds lay in the west and the sun was smothered. Virgilia sat on the sofa and the Ingrams in chairs close to it. They told Nan that Perry was waiting for them at home. Virgilia was quite without colour and her eyes kept moving from Garrett's face to Pamela's uneasily. Now that they had come she seemed as if she regretted it: as if she had nothing to say. Nan sighed.

'I suppose,' she said, 'you're waiting for me to go?'

'Yes, you must go, please,' her mother replied.

Nan stood with her hands on the head of the sofa. 'Listen,' she said, looking from Garrett to Pamela, 'you will both understand. Whatever the truth is, you'll see that I have to be told and that I have to tell Perry; and ... and ...' She was going to add that Dr Franks was to come to her mother, but Dr Franks was a psychiatrist and that couldn't be said. 'You must make my mother see it,' she ended.

Pamela's answering nod was a promise to do her best.

Nan left the room. The worst part of all began now. Her mother had been quiet since Pamela's visit at teatime, as if the decision to tell these two the truth had steadied her, and the more normal her mother appeared, the tighter the grip of fear closed on Nan's heart. She was afraid at this moment: mortally afraid. It was the fear of death.

She could not stand her own thoughts, alone. She decided to sit with Brigid and went to the kitchen. The room was empty. Brigid was outside. Nan could see her back, bent over the lettuce rows. She was probably looking for slugs. The kitchen was dim except for the fire-light flickering on the blue crockery and the yellow walls. A moth flew in and began beating his wings desperately against the window-panes, trying now one, now another. Why didn't he fly out by the open door? Nan had tried everything: she had reasoned and pleaded and even confessed that she was afraid. Her fear was beating inside her madly, like the moth's wings. Her mother was telling the Ingrams now.

WHEN VIRGILIA SAID, 'I think that, perhaps, Dr Franks ought to know,' her voice came so jerkily that the words were not easy to catch.

'Dr Franks, did you say?' Garrett asked.

'Yes,' she answered, 'but I ... I could never tell him. If you think he should know perhaps *you* will.' She looked at Garrett, asking him whether he had known Perry for long. They had been at the same English school together, he told her. Their fathers were friends. Perry was his junior by six years or so, and Garrett had been expected to look after him. Garrett went on talking, trying to help her to recover her nerve.

'I liked him. He had a temper like a sky-rocket in those days. It blazed out without one second's warning, and soared to the heavens. Got him into the most unholy rows. But he knew how to apologise; I liked that, and the way he finally got it under. There's great stuff in Perry,' he said.

'A violent temper,' Virgilia repeated under her breath.

'You'd never guess it now, would you?' Garrett remarked.

'I've always suspected it.'

'Have you? I'm surprised.'

Virgilia was very tired physically. Her voice was tired. She made an effort and sat up.

'I'm sorry you're fond of Perry,' she said. 'I wouldn't throw this awful burden on you if it were for my own sake only. And you may – my great hope is that you may be able to tell me that this wasn't *necessarily* a case of prevision at all. You may tell me that I needn't believe in it.'

'I hope so, indeed,' Garrett said anxiously. 'Try to tell me every detail; all the circumstances, beginning with your own state of mind.'

Virgilia covered her eyes for a moment, looked up again and began to speak.

'It was when we came home. In the car I had decided I'd try. Nan wanted me to, and I had a premonition of danger to her. I thought I might find out how to help. I stood in my bedroom window and looked across at these windows. There was a glitter of light on them from the moon – and you see, I knew about auto-hypnosis.'

Garrett nodded. 'Dr Franks had warned you: so Perry told me this afternoon.'

Virgilia went on:

'Nan and Perry had gone down to the stream. I was sure they would be gone some time. I stood quite still, staring at the light. For a long time nothing happened, and then the light seemed to become diffused. The room seemed to grow light inside.'

'In the ordinary way?' Pamela asked.

'Yes, in the ordinary way, as it would be with those lamps. I think I forgot, then.'

'Forgot where you were?' Garrett asked. 'Became immersed, do you mean?'

'Yes. I thought I was just looking into the lighted room and that two people were dancing there. I saw Perry dancing with Nan.'

'You had seen that before, of course?' Garrett said quickly. 'In a vision, I mean?'

'Yes, and it was almost the same; not quite, I think. But Nan's dress was the same. I could see, quite distinctly, that pretty fitted bodice and flared skirt – the way the skirt flows. There are crystals at the neck and they glittered a little. She had her hair done on top. Perry's profile was very clear. I knew his mother when she and I were children and I saw the likeness – the straight line of the forehead and the square chin. His hair was a little untidy – you know the way that lock in front stands up.'

'Were there other couples?' Pamela asked.

'I don't know,' Virgilia answered. 'If there were I didn't notice them.'

Garrett asked, 'Are you sure you were standing up all the time?'

'Yes; I wasn't asleep.' Virgilia's forehead creased. 'At that moment I began to feel puzzled,' she said. 'Everything began to seem out of place – or out of time, perhaps. Not as things should be. Then I remembered where I was and that Nan and Perry were *not* in the studio. My heart gave that painful twist that comes when I'm surprised by a vision, and I turned. I looked through the other panel of the bay and saw them. I could see Nan's frock between the larches, and the glow of his cigarette. They were walking upstream and went out of sight past the house. I was dizzy for a minute and things became blurred, then I looked back at the window again.'

Virgilia shivered and stopped.

'Wait,' Garrett said. 'Please go very carefully now. At this point, what was your state of mind?'

Virgilia went on with difficulty.

'I felt sick and excited, and desperately eager,' she said. 'My head was humming. I had thought I'd heard music, but it was only the humming in my head. I was afraid of not seeing the vision completed.

I was saying to myself: It's a good omen; they will be happy. But I was only *telling* myself that. Actually, I was afraid of what was to come.'

'Yet eager to see it?'

Garrett's manner was crisp and alert – a cross-examiner's manner. He was focusing his acute mind on this so intently as to forget the state that Virgilia was in.

'Eager and frightened?' he asked. 'Both at the same time?'

'Yes, I felt it was tremendously important to see.'

'And *did* you see? Immediately?'

'No, not at once. It was as if my eyes wouldn't work. I thought I had spoilt my … my perceptive power by looking away. I saw moving shadows and blurs of light. I suppose the dance had broken. I suppose some quarrel must have sprung up. When I did see what was happening I screamed. I couldn't move. My scream didn't break it. The vision went on. I saw her fighting wildly to get away from him, and I saw him' – Virgilia drew a sharp breath and then finished clearly – 'I saw him throttling her.'

Pamela gasped. Garrett started up and his chair fell over. He left it there.

'Killing her?' he asked in a horrified voice.

'I don't know,' Virgilia said.

'What did he do?'

'He had her by the throat – no, by the shoulders, just below the throat. I could still see the glittering crystals on the neckline of her dress. He shook her violently. Her head nodded backwards and forwards like the head of a broken doll. They moved close to the window and then away and their shadows grew. Then he had her down – down below the level where the glass ends, so I couldn't see. I could only see her hands, beating about and clutching at the air. He was stooping over her, his shoulders hunched … Oh, God!'

'Horrible!' Garrett said. But Pamela exclaimed, 'It's not possible! That can't happen, Mrs Wilde.'

'I saw it, I saw it,' Virgilia murmured, her face in her hands. 'Her head flopping as if the neck were broken; her hair falling back and Perry's hair falling over his forehead. At first I was paralysed. Then I ran. When I saw that the studio was dark and empty I couldn't believe it at first.'

'So you didn't see her … afterwards?' Garrett asked.

'No, that was the end.'

'That was the end?'

Echoing her words, Garrett walked down the room to the hearth and back to the dresser and down to the hearth again. He said, 'Perry,' incredulously; and then: 'Young Perry! … Right enough, I once saw him get a grip of a chap like that … '

Dusk was closing and in the grey room Virgilia's face looked grey. While she was telling her story she had sat rigid, leaning forwards, her hands clenched in her lap. Her voice had been clear and level, scarcely faltering at all. Both hands and voice trembled as she asked, 'It could have been some … some other sort of … hallucination, couldn't it?'

Pamela, under her breath, said urgently, 'Surely, surely, Garry, it could?'

He stopped pacing and looked at his wife.

'What could it be?' he asked desperately. 'Mrs Wilde isn't deranged. Have you ever seen such self-control? This isn't dementia of any kind. And those other visions proved veridical – the tinkers' boy; the telegram; the dog; that shadow; Nan's dress. This follows the same pattern absolutely. Can't you see?'

Pamela had to admit that. She bent her head.

Virgilia stared from her to Garrett and then slowly rose from her chair. Garrett turned away from the gaze she fixed on him. Pamela rose too, thinking, almost hoping, that Virgilia was going to faint. That would be better than breaking into laughter or starting to smash the things in the room. It seemed that anything might happen, but at that moment there was a knock at the door. Nobody answered and Brigid came in.

Brigid carried a lighted lamp in her hand; she put it down on the dresser quickly as she looked round the room.

'Is she not here?' She seemed startled.

'Who?' Virgilia asked breathlessly.

'I thought Nan must be here. Ma'am, dear, she's not in the house.'

A moan broke from Virgilia.

'Don't worry,' Pamela said quickly. 'She can't possibly be wearing that dress.'

Virgilia ran into her own bedroom across the hallway; keys were jangled; a drawer was opened and locked again. She came back, saying, 'It's there. And your car's outside,' she said, breathing jerkily. 'We'd have seen her if she'd gone out by the front.'

'I was at the back,' Brigid said. 'She's not gone that way.'

Virgilia pulled open the front door, ran across the garden to the shed and saw that the bicycle was inside. She ran to her bedroom windows. They were screwed tight. She began crying, 'Nan, Nan!' but Garrett drew her back into the studio, saying, 'She must be in the house.'

Pamela was standing still in the middle of the studio, trying to think. She walked to the small door beside the dresser – a door of a cupboard, she had thought it – and pulled it open. Nan was lying huddled there on the floor.

It was only a fainting fit and they restored her quickly. She lay on the sofa looking at her mother's face. Tears were streaming down Virgilia's cheeks. Garrett went out into the garden and walked round and round the tree. A blackbird, unseen in the twilight, was still in the ash, wooing night with his song. Brigid tried to lift the lamp to a wall bracket but could not trust her hands. Pamela lifted it into its place, winking the tears back from her eyes.

'It was so stuffy,' Nan was saying. 'That's what made me faint. There was no air at all. It was so terribly stuffy. You'll have to forgive me, Mummie. I'd never have done it, but I panicked when you shut me out. I was terrified. There was nobody in the kitchen and the dark-room door was open. I couldn't stop myself. But I'm not frightened now,' she went on, her voice growing strong. 'Because there isn't going to be an accident; we're not going to be burnt or blinded or crippled. What you saw doesn't mean anything. It can't happen.' She sat erect. 'It couldn't, could it, Pamela?' she appealed.

'I can't believe it, either,' Pamela said. She turned away; it was difficult to look at that young, lovely head, poised so proudly above the delicate throat. She repeated: 'I don't believe it, Nan.'

'Mr Ingram?' Nan pleaded. He was in the doorway. He said gently: 'You put a great strain on my honesty, Nan.'

Nan loosed herself from her mother's grasp and stood up.

'You know Perry. You've known him for years, and you believe he could do that!'

Garrett drew his hand across his forehead wretchedly.

'There's a difference,' he said, 'between believing that he can and fearing that he will.'

'We shouldn't tell Perry,' Virgilia said.

'I agree,' he replied quickly. 'I agree absolutely, Mrs Wilde. God knows what the poor boy might try to do. And if ... if there is latent insanity, telling him might precipitate things.'

'That is what I'm afraid of,' Virgilia told him.

'I am going to tell him,' Nan said.

Her mother turned to her vehemently.

'Nan, that's why I didn't want you to know.' She went on, turning to the others: 'You see, I knew Perry's mother. I knew her for a few months when we were children. She was ... She had a violent temper. She was dangerous, even then – murderous, even as a child.'

Nan's temper cracked. She stood in the middle of the room, vibrant with anger, speaking to her mother and Garrett.

'I know all about Perry's mother and her temper,' she said. 'He told me all about it. She *used* her temper – *loosed* it, deliberately, in order to get her own way. She could control it perfectly well when she liked. She drove other people half demented while inside she was perfectly cool herself. She wasn't a homicidal maniac! ... As for Perry, his father has him so schooled and trained about it that he ... Oh, how can you both be so stupid, so blind? Even if you believe this is predestined to happen, don't you see that we can stop it – he can and I can – in all sorts of ways? For one thing, I needn't ever wear that dress.'

Garrett broke in quietly: 'I wouldn't rely on that.'

'Why not?'

'Because, Nan, your mother had that dress very much on her mind. She had seen it in two previsions already. She knew that you intended to wear it at your dance. The expectation – the association of ideas – might be strong enough to make her imagine that the dress she saw in this vision was the same one. Suggestion can be potent, you know.'

'Very well,' Nan conceded. 'But,' she went on, 'we need never dance.'

Virgilia said despairingly, 'You would dance, my darling. You would, some day, because you refuse to believe in this.'

'I certainly do refuse to believe in it,' Nan declared. She turned to Pamela, saying, 'You don't seem to have gone quite crazy yet. Will you go tonight and tell Perry – tell him I want us to be married at once? He must get a special licence or whatever it is.'

Virgilia cried out, and Pamela shook her head.

'Ah, no, Nan, you mustn't do that. It would upset your mother too much.'

Nan knew what Pamela meant. She had seen the blue stare in her mother's eyes. She said, more gently, 'I'm going to marry him, though.'

Garrett groaned. He said, 'Perry would believe this, you know.'

'And,' Virgilia said, 'if Nan won't give him up he will have to be told. I see, now, that he must.'

'He'll never believe it,' Nan declared.

'Nan,' Garrett said sadly, 'he will. His belief in Mrs Wilde's gift is profound. He has an honest, courageous scientist's mind. He's not going to reverse an established conviction the moment it threatens his personal life.'

There was silence for a moment. Nan sank down on the sofa again, appalled. The others looked at her.

'I don't think I can tell him,' Garrett said. 'A man who was going to be married. A man in love.'

Pamela spoke with difficulty: 'Oughtn't Dr Franks to know? He is the person to tell Perry, isn't he? He will know the ... the least dangerous way.'

Virgilia closed her eyes as if against some image of intolerable pain.

'Yes,' Garrett said. 'And it is you who will have to tell him, Mrs Wilde. Franks will have to hear it from yourself, with every detail.

He'll ask you questions and you'll answer him. And it is he who must tell Perry – no one else. We promised to go and report to them tonight. We'll just have to telephone that we're not coming; that Dr Franks is to come here tomorrow instead.'

'Yes, you're right,' Virgilia said faintly. 'That is what must be done.'

Nan was not listening. Her lips were parted and her eyes wide open. She rose slowly.

'Listen,' she said, looking from one to the other. 'Do you remember what Perry said about Mother's visions? He said, "She sees what she's going to see."'

Virgilia nodded. 'Yes, Perry said that, and it has been true.' Nan seized her hand. 'Look, then,' she said excitedly, 'suppose you never see us together? Suppose you only see me alone, and Perry alone? Or if we both go to America.' She swung round on Garrett. 'Mr Ingram, don't you see?'

Virgilia's white face became illumined. She held her breath for a moment, looking far out into the deepening night.

'Why, yes,' she said, 'that is true!'

Garrett was silent, his face dark with trouble. His wife watched him anxiously. He sighed.

'That can't be depended on,' he said.

Nan challenged him bitterly, 'Why not?'

He answered while he walked up and down. 'There are countless instances: cases of precognition where the percipient was absent from the event. They are innumerable. Space appears to be no obstacle; place to play no part at all. The explanation may lie in telepathy. Telepathic precognition seems to exist. We don't know. But the thing happens repeatedly. We have no guide in this case except the fact that Mrs Wilde has had – within the last month, isn't it? – three of these complete, detailed visions, and they have proved true. Don't try to juggle with it, Nan.'

The light went out of Nan's face and her mother's. They averted their eyes from Garrett's as if he were their executioner. Pamela said thoughtfully, 'The time element, at least, isn't fixed.'

They turned to her.

'You see,' she went on, 'there was that minute when Mrs Wilde looked away. Couldn't years go by? Couldn't the two scenes ...'

'Pamela!' her husband checked her. 'That is dangerous; it is just by means of such evasions that Nan might ... that this death-trap might be sprung.'

'Yes, yes!' Virgilia exclaimed. 'That *would* be juggling. Everything was the same, you see – the background, her dress, her hair. We're becoming too ingenious. That's the way I reasoned about Sal, exactly, and I only hastened things.'

'You are right: it is against that sort of hedging that we must guard ourselves,' Garrett said.

Nan walked down to the fireplace. She was the calmest of the four now.

'Pamela,' she asked quietly, standing there, 'in my place, what would you do?'

Pamela looked at her husband. He said sharply, 'That isn't a fair question, Nan.'

Nan ignored him.

'You'd chance it, wouldn't you?'

Pamela answered her quite firmly:

'I don't know Perry well enough to say what I'd do in your place, but, if it were Garrett, I would take all the small precautions and chance the rest.'

'And that,' Nan said, 'is what I am going to do.'

'No,' Garrett said, 'because Perry will never agree.'

'I ought never to have told any of you!' Virgilia cried. 'It has done nothing but harm. I ought to have told Perry and no one else.'

Garrett said gently, 'That will come best from his father, believe me. Simply, Perry will go away. You will have a respite, at least.'

Nan began to sob furiously. 'I think you are mad, mad, mad!'

Virgilia was sitting in the corner of the sofa in the pool of light cast down by the lamp. She said excitedly, 'Perhaps I am! Perhaps I have been insane, without suspecting it, since the shock about Timeen. That might easily have happened, mightn't it? I have done extraordinary things. I screwed up the windows. I walked in my sleep. It might be simply that. Then, what I saw would mean nothing at all.' Her excitement mounted. 'It would be just like any delusion of the insane. Yes, yes,' she cried. 'Ask Dr Franks to come, Mr Ingram; to come tomorrow as early as he can!'

Her face had brightened; Garrett's was ashen. He said, with a tremor in his voice, 'You are not out of your mind, Mrs Wilde.'

Nan was on her knees by her mother, crying bitterly. Virgilia thanked the Ingrams as they turned away. They went to the door, hesitated and looked back. Virgilia's head was bent over Nan's.

'I didn't mean it, Mummie,' Nan was saying. 'It isn't you. It isn't Perry. Things just aren't logical. There's some crazy mix-up. The world isn't made the way we thought it was. We don't know how anything works.'

Garrett looked so exhausted that Pamela took the wheel and drove the car away from Derreen.

Chapter XIV

MIDNIGHT

NAN WAS WAKENED by Brigid coming in with her breakfast on a tray. That was an unusual and pleasant way to be wakened. Nan sat up, smiling. She had slept deeply after staying up rather late adding pages to her letter to Perry: a long letter, it was.

Brigid looked tired. Nan remembered. They had had to help her mother to bed. She had become quiet and tense after the Ingrams left, but her hands shook – they shook so that she could scarcely do anything for herself, and she had stammered a little when she tried to speak. Yet there had been that strange, clear light in her eyes.

'Perry will believe it,' she had said several times, 'and he won't take risks. He'll never come near you. Tomorrow, and then never again. And you don't believe it; you won't be living in dread. Even if Dr Franks … Even if he says that I … that I didn't make a mistake …'

She had been thinking aloud, confused and half-stupefied with exhaustion, trying to comfort herself with thoughts which were torment to Nan. Nan had been glad to escape to her own room.

'Did she sleep? How is she, Brigid?' she asked anxiously, now.

'Och, not so well,' Brigid answered. 'She was dead set for some reason on being up and dressed for the doctor and seeing him in the studio, but she turned giddy and had to get back into bed. I got leave from her to open the windows before Eileen would come, but they're beyond me. Let you do it as soon as you're up.

I have Eileen busy, below, ironing, meantime. Mrs Doyle is wondering why the mistress nor you hasn't been down to visit Timeen. She wants you to take tea with her this afternoon ... That egg should be good. 'Tis new laid.'

The egg was good. Brigid made toast nicely. She stood watching Nan eat her breakfast, asking no questions; waiting to be told. Nan said: 'I'm sorry I scared you, hiding, last night.'

Brigid shook her head. 'I never thought you'd be driven to the like of that,' she responded. 'But, sure, I don't blame you. And as long as you didn't hear any fearful thing ...'

'It was something like what we guessed,' Nan told her slowly. 'Mother thought I was hurt and that Dr Perry was ... he was there. So she won't let us be together. I can't tell you any more. It wasn't one of her true visions, Brigid: I'm certain of that.'

'God keep you from hurt and harm,' Brigid said, troubled. 'So happy you were too. And now what will we all do, at all?'

'We must just wait till she's better,' Nan said.

'Aye,' Brigid said gently. 'You're right not to put any more weight of worry on her now ... 'Tis woeful the way she's changed – to see her go slow and stooping like an old woman, she that was straight as a rush. We'll not say a word to cross her now. You're right; you are my brave, kind child. I'll be praying night and day for you, asthore.'

Brigid went downstairs. Eileen's chatter could be heard from the kitchen. Nan got up and put on her yellow dress. The sun shone from a blue rift between light drifts of cirrus cloud. I'll be talking to Dr Franks in an hour or two, and then Perry, Nan told herself. She hurried down to her mother.

VIRGILIA LAY QUIET, pale and unsmiling. She scarcely spoke while Nan brushed her hair, helped her into her bed-jacket, brought her rouge to put on. Nan tried to break the heavy silence, but her own voice sounded nervous. She talked about the Ingrams.

'I wouldn't like to be in the dock with Mr Ingram as Prosecuting Counsel, would you? I'm sure he's frightfully good at law.'

'His mind has sharp edges,' her mother said.

'Too sharp. He likes things clean-cut. He's too positive. Pamela isn't, nor is Perry. And you'll find Dr Franks isn't either. You'll find things aren't as … as drastic as you imagine.'

'Shall I?'

Virgilia's eyes were fixed on the wing-chair. She asked Nan to take it away and put the cane chair in its place. Nan, puzzled, began to obey, but her mother sighed and said, 'Oh, never mind. Nothing can make any difference to this.'

The Chrysler was in the lane. It stopped about half-way up and could be heard, then, going down again.

'I must speak to him,' Nan said quickly. Her mother lay silent, watching the garden gate.

Nan sat on the stairs, the letter that she had written to Perry in her hand. If anything prevented their meeting today he should at least have that. It was she who opened the front door and let Dr Franks in. He looked into her face with his kind, searching eyes, glanced at the letter, put it into his pocket and went at once to her mother's room.

Nan ran to the landing window. The Chrysler was not in sight and she could not hear it. Perry had gone to Doyle's, she thought. She fetched a screwdriver and opened the landing window and then the windows of the bath-room and dining-room. It seemed to take a very long time. She was at work on the studio window over her table when at last she heard Dr Franks shut the door of her mother's room. Hesitantly, he called her name.

They sat by her work-table. The light was full on his face. It was in planes and ridges, like a tragic mask. He sat there and seemed unable to speak. Nan became frightened. She asked in a choked voice, 'Is she

… Is my mother a little deranged?'

He shook his head slowly.

'I do not think so. I do not think that is the explanation,' he said. Looking at the tensed muscles of his cheek and jaw, Nan knew that Dr Franks was going to fail her.

'Do you mean,' she asked weakly, 'that you believe it is going to happen?' Her hand went uncontrollably to her throat.

'I neither believe nor disbelieve it,' the doctor answered heavily. 'I am ignorant of these matters, Nan. I have spent my life studying the human mind and I find myself in an abyss of ignorance.'

She said tremulously, 'Dr Franks, it can't happen; it can't.'

'Last Sunday,' he said, 'I certified a man insane. We had been at college together. He was a brilliant, high-spirited fellow then. There had been an accident in the polo field. There are accidents; there are wars.'

Nan was leaning back in her chair, staring at him in horror. Her right hand lay on the table and he put his over it, saying brokenly, 'Forgive me, Nan; forgive me, child.'

She held his hand between both of hers; she felt sorry for him. Dr Franks had changed; he was no longer a rock; he no longer had that steadiness and wisdom that made one feel safe with him. He was shocked and shaken. He was ready to believe this incredible thing.

'But don't you see,' she said gently, 'that whatever happened to Perry – even if he did crazy things – he wouldn't do *that*? He wouldn't hurt me. That's the one thing he could not do.'

He looked at her with surprise and his face relaxed a little. 'Your faith in him is perfect,' he said.

'Dr Franks,' Nan said, 'I sent Perry a message by Pamela and it's in that letter too. I want him to marry me now, at once, before he goes away. I know it will have to be secretly, for Mother's sake, but as soon as she is better I'll go to him. I'll find a room in Pittsburgh. I'll work.'

'You mean that!' Dr Franks exclaimed.

'More than I ever meant anything in my life.'

'My dear Nan …' He was very much moved. 'If only it were possible!' he exclaimed. 'If only you could be his wife.'

'You must help us.'

'It is not possible, Nan.'

'But why, Dr Franks? You say that you don't absolutely believe in Mother's vision; then why?'

'Because, my dear, dear girl, Perry will.'

'No, no, you are wrong.'

She was so tensed against his resolve that the words could scarcely pass her throat.

The doctor said sadly: 'You don't know the strength of Perry's convictions, Nan; and his faith in the validity of your mother's visions has been confirmed. He may be wrong; I can only cling to the hope that he is. But he will believe that it is predestined – this brutal, hideous thing.'

He covered his eyes with his hand, then looked full into her face. He was looking at her with so much distress and compassion that she felt herself weakening, but she spoke obstinately.

'Even if he believes it, I won't. Besides, Dr Franks, if he does, he'll also believe that trying to avoid it is no use. He'll marry me and we'll … we'll enjoy as much of life as we can.'

Dr Franks said gently, 'Nan, you're a very courageous and intelligent girl. You are so intelligent that you must see the impossibility of such a marriage as that. Think! The grotesque precautions, the exaggerated fear at every sign of ill-temper, the ceaseless vigilance, the doubts, the boy's own unending dread.'

Nan sat immobile, her eyes, fixed on the doctor, losing their light, while her hope froze, slowly, almost to death. She said, in a dull voice, 'Then what are we to do?'

'Put the ocean between you,' Dr Franks answered. 'Make a complete break. Crowd your life with other relationships. After a time – a long time, perhaps – you may cease to think much about this, and, at length, may cease to believe in it. You may even find happiness in your separate ways.'

'Happiness?' Nan said.

She reflected for a long time, trying to look down the years. Perry, she thought, would be able to do his work, but her own would die. Her art flowed out of her pleasure in life. And Perry would become like his father – a little austere, lonely, all his own feelings shut down. Another thought came to her and she looked up.

'Perry doesn't know. He needn't. He need never know. I'll tell him a lie.'

'Marry him,' the doctor exclaimed in astonishment, 'and take no precautions and – wait! You would do that?'

Nan hesitated. She could imagine telling Perry an elaborate and convincing lie once, but not living with him, looking into his clear face and frank, trustful eyes, and keeping it up. She sighed and said, 'I don't know.'

'It would be criminal on my part to permit it,' the doctor said. 'He has got to know.'

'Even if I … give in?'

'He has to know.'

'Mother says that being told might – might have a dreadful effect on him.'

'She is right; but not to tell him would be dastardly.'

'If he's got to know, I'll tell him,' Nan said. 'Is he at Doyle's? Will you take me to him now?'

'No, my dear; it is I who must tell him,' the doctor replied. He stood up. 'And you mustn't meet yet. Your mother is very unwell. I have to add to your burden by warning you, Nan. To know that you were together might throw her off her balance.'

'You mean,' Nan said despairingly, 'that if I see Perry, Mother may go out of her mind?'

'Yes, I mean just that.'

'But …'

The doctor put his hand on her shoulder.

'Nan, listen. She told me just now that at one point she imagined for a moment that this thing could not take place unless she were alive to see it. "That would have been so simple," she said.'

Nan shut her eyes and whispered, 'I could never have been happy again.'

'That is what I told her,' the doctor said, turning away. 'In any case,' he went on, 'she has dismissed that thought. She has even consented to your seeing Perry here, just once, under her eyes, tomorrow afternoon. I dread it for her. She is at the end of her endurance now. I am afraid of the effect of the least intensification of strain. Be very, very careful, when he comes. I promised her that Perry will cross to England tomorrow evening and not return. He will wait for his sailing there. To know that the sea is between you two is, in my opinion, the one thing that will restore her now. When I tell Perry that, I am sure he will go. I will join him in America later on.'

Nan reflected. Perry would not go without seeing her alone. The doctor would not take part in deceiving her mother, and must not be asked to. Pamela will manage something, she thought; it will be managed somehow – very early in the morning perhaps. She asked, 'Are you going to live in America, too?'

He nodded. 'I may be able to help him a little, perhaps.'

'Mother will miss you.'

After a moment Dr Franks said, 'A complete break with us will be best for her and for you.'

'Give Perry my letter.'

'I will.'

As he was leaving her, Dr Franks paused in the doorway and turned to look down at her.

'My dear, if I could have chosen …' he said, then seeing the tears spring to Nan's eyes, he stopped. He went to her mother again for a few minutes, then walked across the garden and down the lane without looking back.

Nan watched from the landing window. In five minutes the Chrysler appeared in the gap. Perry stood up and waved to her. His father did not look round. Then the car was gone.

Tomorrow evening: I shall see him before tomorrow evening, Nan told herself. Her thoughts stopped there against a dead wall, because there was nothing to look at beyond.

VIRGILIA WAS A good deal stronger. She got up and walked with Nan in the wood. She asked her daughter, 'Do you think he'll go tomorrow?' and Nan said, 'I think he will. You are wrong, Mummie,' she said quietly, 'but you just mustn't be tortured any more. He will go and I'll stay and you shall have peace of mind.'

'Peace of mind,' Virgilia echoed drearily, 'when I have dragged you out of heaven into hell.'

'I'm not in hell, dearest,' Nan answered, 'though I don't quite know why.'

Her mother seemed to her perfectly sane: a sad woman; a woman worn down with sorrow, but balanced and normal and calm. She could imagine her living for years like this.

Neither of them spoke directly of the vision and neither of them mentioned Nan's dress. Virgilia built a weed fire in the garden and Nan thought it was to be burnt on that. Her mother went into the house and Nan shrank from the dreadful symbolism of what she believed was to be done, but her mother came out again without the dress and said nothing. She can't face it either, Nan thought.

Virgilia began to talk vaguely about travel. They had often made plans for going together to Paris and Provence and Italy. The cottage could be sold. The Ingrams would probably like to have Brigid and be kind to her. It was said one could live very cheaply abroad. Nan agreed with everything. None of it seemed to have any reality. By this time, she was thinking, Perry knows.

Clouds were congregating over the mountains. Showers of small rain were trailed through the glen. They put on coats after lunch and walked down to Doyle's, where Timeen received them sitting up in bed, surrounded by colourful magazines, as happy as a spoilt child could be. He displayed a picture of a boy in dungarees in a garden, saying, 'That's the way I'm going to be.'

'The doctor brought him all those,' Mrs Doyle said loquaciously. 'If the child was his own he couldn't give him more care. A lovely father he'll be in God's good time, and a great and famous doctor, I don't doubt. To see him coming in at the door, so happy in himself, does you good … Mrs Wilde,' she went on sympathetically, 'didn't the accident take a queer lot out of you? You're not looking well at all. I'll bid Eileen take you a sup of buttermilk every morning, and let you drink that. 'Twill bring the colour back to your cheeks.'

They drank tea, and walked home again, and had supper. Somehow, the long evening passed. The clouds thickened and heavier showers fell. Brigid, observing how her mistress shivered from time to time, lit a wood-fire in the studio and lit the lamps early, 'for cheerfulness' sake.' It would take more than lamps and fire to make cheerfulness in this house, Nan thought.

Virgilia seemed reluctant to go to bed. Nan wanted music and tuned in to Paris, but it was a recital of Mozart and all that idyllic joy and sweetness, just out of reach, teased the spirit too much. Virgilia said, 'Not music tonight, dearest,' and they sat in silence, trying to read. When Virgilia said 'good-night' at about eleven and went to her room she looked as if she were facing some hard ordeal. Nan thought that she was dreading a sleepless night and, halfway upstairs, turned and went to the kitchen and prepared a cup of sedative broth. When she went to her mother's door she heard bitter weeping. The white dress was spread on the bed and Virgilia was kneeling there, her arms thrown over it, sobbing in a passion of grief. Her big scissors lay on the floor. Nan could have wept herself, but she spoke consolingly.

'What does the dress matter? *I'll* cut it up. I'll do it before I sleep.'

She took the dress out of her mother's sight, leaving it in her own room upstairs. When Virgilia was in bed Nan sat by her, talking and talking, saying what she had said before – that what she had seen wouldn't happen – could not happen; that there were things nobody anywhere understood. 'Don't worry,' she implored. 'Remember, Perry is going. You have nothing to be afraid of now.' At last the storm of tears was over.

'That you don't believe it – that you are not afraid – is such a mercy,' her mother said.

She did not want to drink the broth but to please her daughter began sipping it from the spoon. Nan kissed her good-night.

'The scissors,' Virgilia said.

They were on the floor. Nan picked them up.

'I *will* destroy it. You trust me, don't you, Mummie?' she asked.

Virgilia nodded.

'I trust you,' she said.

Nan left her, shutting the door, and went up the dark stairs to her room, the scissors in her hand.

3

NAN SPREAD THE DRESS out on her bed. In the light from the lamp it glimmered like starlit snow; the crystal beads sparkled. Under a full moon in the garden it would have looked white and light as a cloud. Nan had made her own lunch over a gas-ring for three months, as well as doing without a coat, in order to buy this dress. She had never confessed to her mother how much it had cost. She had never put anything on so delicious to move in as the model from which it was copied. She loved dancing, and to dance in this would have been wonderful … To dance with Perry in this … It was hateful to have to destroy such a lovely thing, made with so much skill and care; and it was so unnecessary. It was all so unnecessary. But she had promised, and she wouldn't begin tricking her mother now. Later, perhaps, about letters; but not yet. She took up the scissors and sat on the bed near the lamp, and began to make a cut along one seam.

It was almost impossible; her fingers mutinied. She laid down the scissors and pulled off the frock she was wearing. She wanted to see herself once, just once, as Perry would have seen her next Wednesday night.

She put on the silk stockings and the silver slippers; brushed her hair up and bunched the curls on the top of her head, then, carefully, drew the dress on. The concealed fasteners were easy to manage. The fit was perfection. She twisted her curls into place with her fingers and fixed the top-knot with a comb, then smoothed the folds of the skirt and turned to her long glass.

The image that she saw there was beautiful. Even the funny upwards shadows that the lamp cast, even her lack of colour she was much too pale – did not spoil the picture that she saw. Perry would have thought … Perry would have said … Her throat contracted and tears began to stream down her face. She threw herself down on her bed and gave way to a wild fit of crying, muffling her sobs in the pillow as best she could. When that ended she lay still, while sorrow rose over her like a drowning tide. It rose and rose until she lay so helpless under the weight of it that she could not think any more. She turned and lay on her side, looking out into the night for a long time. She wished with all her heart that she were out there in the dark. Tomorrow evening was coming close; prison walls were narrowing, closing her in; out there, there would be a sense of escape. She listened and heard no more rain.

I must sleep, she thought. It is important to sleep. She believed that Perry would come in the early morning – not tonight: his father would make that difficult. He would come at dawn and throw gravel at her window to waken her, the way people did in books … Only there was no gravel. Supposing she stayed awake so late, and was so deep asleep in the morning that he was unable to waken her? He would not dare, for her mother's sake, to make very much noise. That would be their last chance of all. She wondered for a moment whether it would be possible to stay awake all night. It would not: she was very tired; it was a thing she had never done. I will leave a window open, she decided, starting up. That's the thing to do. I'll leave the studio door unlocked. Her mother had not taken the key.

She looked out. Dark mist muffled the garden. Her mother's lamp was out; she had taken the broth and by this time must be asleep. Carefully, Nan lifted her lamp with its green shade and crept down. She reached the studio without having made a sound. What a mercy, she thought, that Shuiler sleeps at the back! She set her lamp down on the dresser and carefully pulled back the bolts of the garden door, then turned the key; they were new and made no noise. When she opened the door she could hear the sound of the stream and of water dripping from a gutter; nothing else. But there was another sound in a moment – footsteps in the lane. No flash-light, no cigarette-end shone. The darkness was thick. Even when the gate was gently opened nothing could be seen. While he was still invisible he whispered her name. She ran across the grass into his arms.

Inside, with the door shut, Perry stood gazing at her, startled, then he went to the lamp and tilted the shade. She saw his face as the glow lit up her dress.

'You don't believe it,' she said under her breath. She knew then that his father had left a small stinging thorn of doubt in her mind.

'Glorious!' he exclaimed, laughing with pleasure. 'Oh, you lovely, lovely thing! I say,' he asked, 'will it crush?'

He threw his wet coat off and sat in a chair by the hearth, holding her in his arms. She made him release her and then turned the lamp out for fear that her mother might wake and look out. Among the ashes of the fire a few fragments of wood still glowed.

Perry talked very fast, but he kept his voice low. He said, 'I told Dad he ought to have himself certified.'

Nan cried a little from excitement; now she laughed too. 'He thought that you would believe it,' she said.

'They've torn you to pieces between them, haven't they?' he said tenderly. 'But you kept your head. Your letter was magnificent, Nan. There's no man alive who deserves a letter like that. I could have shouted from the house-tops. However, instead, I went and bought this – it will have to be kept hidden, worse luck. I was waiting for you to choose but ... And you've got those opal earrings ... Does it fit? Why, yes, it does!'

Three opals, two small and one large, set in a flat band of gold. She held her finger to the fire while Perry blew a spark to flame. The stones shone, celestial blue, with fire in their depths. Nan loved the ring – loved it for its beauty and its defiance of superstition, and for the utter rejection of fear that it declared, given like this, now.

'I wanted the other, Perry,' she said tremulously. 'I wanted to be married before you go.'

'Like a darling girl ...' Perry's steadiness was deserting him. 'Don't talk like that or I'll do something wild – carry you off on the morning boat and never let your mother near you again. I'll have all I can do, you know, to go ...' He broke off. Nan whispered quickly, 'It will save her, and nothing else will, now.'

'I know that,' he replied, 'and we'll go through with it. We'll give her a year.' He tried to speak cheerfully. 'You'll pretend you're forgetting all about me. We'll stage a last farewell for her tomorrow afternoon.'

'No,' Nan begged. 'No, Perry. Don't come. I couldn't do that.'

He hesitated, then said, 'Neither could I, as a matter of fact.'

He was going to England. His father might, perhaps, visit him in Pittsburgh, but was not coming to stay.

'I'll be back by this time next year,' Perry said. 'Your mother will be herself again by that time – and if she's not, well, it will be just too bad.'

'Try not to be angry with her.'

'I'm furious with the pack of them.'

'It was our fault. You made her believe in her visions, and I ...'

'I did. And her visions are fine. But, well, my honey lamb, my pretty, if I go berserk I might do in Garrett, for instance – I felt very like it this evening – but it wouldn't be you. It just wouldn't take me that way. And Dad ought to know that. I told him so. I believe I told him he was no good at his job.' Perry grinned. 'I've been telling a lot of people a lot of things.'

His laughing mood left him then and he told her that he was afraid his father might take a long time to get over what he'd been through.

'To see a man as learned and able as he is floundering and blundering in such a bog of ignorance is rather awful,' he said. 'But at least he takes my word for it now that some other explanation does exist.'

'What is the explanation?' Nan asked, not caring so very much.

'That's what beats me,' Perry replied.

'So you can't help Mother?'

'I can't. That's another damnable part of the whole devilish set-up.' He groaned. 'God, she was the only one that had sense. Why didn't we let her leave it alone?'

Nan tried to console him, and succeeded. Presently he was smiling again.

'What in the name of glory are you doing with that dress on?' he asked. 'It's magical. You're an angel in a cloud.'

She told him about her promise to destroy it. He said she should have another just the same, some day. 'Some day, Nan …' he began, and they talked of the years before them until suddenly Nan said, 'Hush!' She had seen a patch of light on the lawn. She whispered, 'Go now, quickly! Mother's awake. She may go looking for me, or look out of her window. It would kill her to find you here.'

'Which way?' he whispered.

'Through here.'

She led him through the dark-room to the kitchen, then remembered that Shuiler was out there and would growl. She went back to the studio and, standing in the corner, watched her mother's window. While she watched, the dark curtain was pulled aside for a time, then drawn into place again; a strip of light remained for a minute and then went out.

'Now!' she said, under her breath. He caught her in his arms and after a last desperate kiss was gone, without a sound, into the fog.

4

ALONE IN THE heavy darkness and silence, Nan had to fight an attack of panic. She wanted to rush after Perry. The house menaced her. To be left alone with her mother and her mother's fear was too much. Sobbing with fright and loneliness, she crossed the studio to the dresser and found her lamp. She lit it, for fear of stumbling over a floor-mat or stepping on the board that creaked. She stood in the dining-room, listening and waiting to make her own breathing quiet, then she stole upstairs.

Her ring was beautiful. The stones burned gold and red under their blue. It comforted her. It was only the suddenness of the parting and the desolation of the long months before her that had made her break down. In her heart, as in the heart of her opals, joy and new courage glowed. The nightmare was over. There was not one atom of truth in her mother's vision and no shadow of it had fallen on Perry's mind. He had even forgotten to talk and theorise about it, although he must have been thinking about it all day. He simply knew, with the whole of himself, that it was not true, and, for the present, that was enough. Only one grief remained, one problem that seemed insoluble – her mother's misery.

This dress! This beloved dress! With the opal earrings, and the ring ... It was a pity that it had to be destroyed.

She was lifting her hand to the fastening when she heard a sound. It was like the click of a latch. She remembered the studio door. She had forgotten to close it and it might bang. If it did, and woke her mother, she would guess. Once more Nan picked up her lamp and crept quietly down.

It was not until she was in the studio again and had set the lamp on the bookcase that she realised there was somebody in the room. The movement came from the corner where the log-basket and turf-basket were. It wasn't Perry; she knew that at once.

She stood quite still, collecting her courage, listening to the man's panting breath, then she lifted the shade of the lamp. The light fell on a white face with black starving eyes that seemed to want to feed on hers.

'Carlo!' she whispered. 'You! ... Hush!' she ordered at once. 'Don't make a sound.'

The door was open. She closed it, then looked at him. He was a pitiful sight: he had no overcoat and his clothes were soaked; his black hair streaked his forehead. He stood against the wall and followed every movement that she made with his eyes. On the floor beside him lay a neat, new leather case. He pointed to it and stammered, 'I b-brought your shawl.'

Nan tried not to laugh, but the reaction from high tragedy was comical. After Perry, Carlo looked like a caricature of an actor gone to seed. What in the wide, earthly world was he doing in Glencree, in muddy shoes and wet clothes, at midnight, with her shawl?

She asked him. His reply was far from coherent. As far as she could make out, he had arrived on the evening mail-boat with a few shillings in his pocket, having dropped his note-case overboard; had gone by train to Dublin, enquired for Glencree and then gone by bus to Rathfarnham. He'd spent his money on fares and on drinks, had had none left for food or car-hire and had started to walk. He must have climbed Glendhu Mountain, crossed the desolate miles of the Featherbed and tramped the whole length of the valley of Glencree. Some woman had taken pity on him and offered him a night's lodging in her cottage, but he had not had the sense to remain.

'I had to see you. Nan,' he kept saying. 'I've got to do your head. I destroyed it, Nan. I beat it to pulp, and I haven't been able to sleep since. Since you ran away from me I haven't slept a single night. You've got to let me do it again.'

Nan ceased to feel amused. She was afraid that Carlo must be drunk, though he didn't exactly appear so. She'd better wake Brigid, she thought. And he must be famished with hunger, of course. What on earth could she do with him? Make up the fire, let him dry out and sleep on the sofa? But ten to one he'd disturb her mother. The first thing was food. She had heard of eyes glittering with hunger, and there was a most ungodly glitter in his. Nan moved towards the door to the dining-room, trying not to betray the distaste that she felt, and looked back at him with a glance that she tried to make reasonably friendly and kind. Instantly, with one of those incredibly swift movements of his, he had sprung up and seized her hand. He covered it with kisses, murmuring expressions of adoration, remorse and shame.

'Be quiet, be quiet,' she said. 'My mother is ill.'

He took no notice of that at all, but continued his pleas for pity and forgiveness.

Nan's knees began to tremble. Carlo was in an extraordinary state. If she struggled to release herself he'd become more excited, and if she called it would give her mother a terrible fright. He was babbling and imploring, telling her she was the only beautiful thing left on earth. He was drawing her across the room. Her heart thudded, but she tried to speak lightly. She said, 'Let me go and I'll get you some food.' He released her, but sprang between her and the doors. She was penned in the corner between the fireplace and the sofa, all the three doors cut off. His mood had changed completely: a rage of humiliation choked his voice and burned in his eyes. His face became congested and red.

'Food!' he said furiously. 'No. You played that trick on me before! You fooled me, Nan. You laughed at me. You ran away laughing and left me. You're not going to do that again. I'll punish you for that, Nan. I smashed the bust because you did that. I wrung its neck; I beat it to pulp. I'll do the same to you if you move. You beautiful, treacherous devil – you little devil in white!'

Nan was frightened. It was time to cry out for help. She was going to call and had drawn her breath to shout, 'Mummie,' when she remembered the dress she had on. The terror that seized her then froze her voice in her throat and weakened all her muscles. She could not scream.

She swayed, trying to pass him and get to the garden door, but she tripped against one of the baskets and stumbled. He seized her by the shoulders and swung her round. She was shaken so violently that her head wagged backwards and forwards and she could not utter a sound. She tried to beat him off; his thumbs dug into her collar-bones; she thought he would grip her throat in a moment; she was shaken and shaken and everything turned red. A scream split the silence and then the red turned black.

VIRGILIA WAS NEVER ABLE to give a coherent account of what happened between the moment when she woke and the moment when Nan looked up at her from the floor, gasping, 'I'm all right.' She was in Nan's room, in the dark, clutching her bathrobe over her pyjamas, when she woke. An extremity of uneasiness possessed her – a guilty and frightened sense of something neglected.

'The dress,' she found herself saying out loud. 'I didn't destroy the dress!'

Nan was not in her bed. There was no answer. It was a scream, Nan's voice crying, 'Mummie!' she believed, that made her rush to the window, and she thought that it was Perry's shadow she saw. She still imagined that it was Perry, when she was in the studio, tearing at the man's hands, and was stunned with amazement when she saw Perry falling on him, seizing him, flinging him out of the way. Then she was on the floor gathering Nan in her arms.

That is how Brigid saw them when she came in – the young doctor standing there, panting, his hair on end and his collar pulled open; the stranger huddled over the stool in the corner, his head buried in his arms. Nan was coughing and choking, her hands at her throat, and Perry knelt down quickly, examining her.

'The brute nearly throttled her,' he said, his voice shaking.

'He nearly shook my head off,' Nan gasped.

Perry said furiously, 'You're bruised.'

They lifted her to the sofa and placed pillows under her head. She was trembling, but a smile came and went on her face all the time. Virgilia's face was as white as her gown and tears were streaming from her eyes, but they were tears of relief and joy. Perry, too bemused to know what should be done, turned to Brigid. Her face looked rumpled with sleepiness and fatigue. She murmured, 'Her throat, is it? Honey; I'll make her a honey-drink.'

'Who did it? Who is it?' Virgilia was asking, and Perry answered, 'That tramp.'

'He isn't a tramp, he's a sculptor,' Nan whispered. 'He brought my shawl.'

Virgilia exclaimed, 'Carlo!' and Nan said, 'Yes.'

'Oh, what a fool I have been, my darling, my darling,' Virgilia repeated. 'What a fool I have been!'

Nan was crying and laughing, trying to comfort her.

Perry stood looking down at the abject, penitent Carlo in disgust.

'What do I do with it?' he asked.

'If we don't feed him he'll probably die on us,' Nan said, and Brigid, turning back at the door, muttered, 'Feed him, is it? Rat-poison I'll give him!' She looked like an old witch with her fuzz of white hair and her crimson quilted dressing-gown with the down sprouting from worn spots. She went to the kitchen and Perry examined Nan again. She was not much hurt and less pale than her mother now. Virgilia sat in an armchair and gazed up at Perry as if to look at him gave her reassurance. He found a rug in the hall and tucked it round her. When Brigid came back, bringing whiskey, he made her drink some and took a stiff drink himself.

At arm's length, Brigid held out to Carlo a thick chunk of bread and meat.

'Eat it,' Perry ordered, standing over him, and Carlo wolfed the food.

'Where did you collect him, Nan?' Perry asked. He lifted the lamp, held it to Carlo's face and exclaimed, 'So that's it!'

'What is it?' Virgilia asked.

Perry answered in one word:

'Dope.'

Nan said shakily, 'He's good; I mean, he can do lovely work.'

'He nearly got some lovely work in tonight,' Perry retorted.

'Please, Perry,' Nan said imploringly. 'He must be taken care of. Please.'

'Must he? That seems a pity.' But his manner to Carlo changed. Very firmly and clearly Perry instructed him to go down the lane and up the hill at the left as far as the car which he would find there on the side of the road; to get into the car and wait. 'Go,' he advised, 'while the going's good.'

Carlo stood up and thanked him politely. He moved feebly and looked dazed. He stared at his suitcase a minute, then stooped, opened it and drew out the shawl. He kissed the shawl and, his eyes fixed remorsefully on Nan, laid it over the arm of a chair, from which it at once slid to the floor. He would have begun talking to Nan, but that Perry took him by the arm, conducted him to the garden gate and set him on his way down the lane.

Coming back, Perry said to Virgilia disgustedly, 'And that is what you mistook for me.'

She looked up at him with a wavering smile.

'You'd better begin forgiving me at once, you know, because I'm afraid it's going to take a long time.'

'Where did you come from?' Nan asked. 'Perry, I thought you had gone.'

He grinned.

'Luckily I hadn't. When I left you I got a morbid turn. I was being melancholy down by the stream. I walked along it a good bit. I didn't know a thing was wrong till I heard the scream.'

'I didn't scream,' Nan told them. 'I tried to and couldn't. So it was you, Mummie! What woke you? You didn't drink that broth after all.'

'Only a few spoonfuls,' Virgilia answered; 'but I did fall asleep. I don't know what woke me. I thought I heard you scream. I was in your room. I saw from your window … I saw everything. His shadow grew huge. And your hands! Your hands!'

Nan sipped her drink, curled up on the sofa like a ruffled swan. She held her left hand out, showing her mother her ring and told her how Perry had come.

'His faith in your visions stopped short of this one,' she said.

'Mine ought to have,' her mother said, looking at him. 'I see that now.'

Brigid was nodding to herself. She had said very little. She blew the fire up and added kindling and padded about replacing things in the room. Suddenly, her sense of outrage burst forth.

'Well, that's the end!' she declared. 'That, now, is beyond the beyonds. The outlandish heathen! If he hasn't it tumbled among the sods – Mrs Morrow's lovely Indian shawl.'

She lifted it and smoothed it lovingly. The long fringe was tangled, the fabric soiled.

'You can draw it through a ring,' she told Perry indignantly, 'and 'tis as soft as the breast of a bird. Nan was christened in that … Ah, well, I'll maybe bring it back to itself.' She looked at Perry and asked hospitably, 'You'll be staying the night?'

'It looks like it, doesn't it?' he said, smiling at her. 'But I've got to dump Nan's dear old pal in hospital. He'll collapse after this.'

'Then I hope he'll stay collapsed,' Brigid said.

'Bless you, Brigid!' Perry exclaimed gravely.

'And you'll have to tell your father,' Virgilia reminded him. 'I nearly killed him, I think.'

'Him and yourself,' Perry said. 'Well, I'll be paying a professional call here tomorrow. By the way, Mrs Wilde …' He hesitated. 'May Garrett come? And Pamela, of course?'

'For an inquisition?' Virgilia asked with a rueful smile, and consented, saying, 'I owe that much to all of you.'

Nan's eyes were closing. She opened them and said drowsily, 'Do you know what we forgot amidst all the fussation, Mummie? We forgot to cancel the dance.'

'Goodness! And what day is this?' Virgilia exclaimed. 'Thursday?'

'It's Friday morning,' Perry replied.

'And it was to be on Wednesday next. Do you think we can manage it, Brigid?' Virgilia asked.

'Is it the dance?' Brigid answered sleepily. 'To be sure we can. Why not?'

Chapter XV

PEACE-OFFERINGS

IT WAS OF GREEN CANVAS with back, sides and canopy, a long swung seat and soft cushions into which Nan gratefully snuggled her head. Her neck was sore still and very stiff.

'It's heaven,' she said. 'I shall sleep here every fine night.' The garden-couch was Dr Franks's present to Nan. Perry had arrived with it strapped on to the Bouncer, and set it up near the light shadow cast by the ash. 'My father,' he explained, 'has exaggerated ideas about Nan.'

He had offered a tribute of his own to Virgilia – a silver cocktail shaker and several bottles, including vermouth and gin. He was occupied with these, now, at a table under the tree, watched with interest by Virgilia, the Ingrams and Nan.

'A peace-offering,' he said, handing Garrett a glass.

'Two of these will be needed,' Garrett remarked. 'He told me, Mrs Wilde, that I had deteriorated – that I'd let my comparatively good brain become warped by the law. "Warped" was the word; "warped".'

'Well,' Perry retorted defensively, 'when you accuse a man of being about to strangle his wife ...'

'I wonder,' Pamela mused aloud, 'what the law ought to do in such a case? I mean, if prevision were recognised?'

A lively discussion on that question followed and a fine lot of nonsense was talked. Virgilia listened, thinking, gratefully, what a capacity these young people had for making fun of their own serious convictions and tragic experience. Where there might have been bitterness and anger and broken friendship they were throwing up an airy bridge.

Garrett, nevertheless, wanted the problem of Virgilia's error solved. His forehead was creased in thought.

'The clue to the whole thing,' he said reflectively, 'lies, of course, in that minute when you looked away.'

'The clue to the whole thing,' Nan interjected, 'lies in my precious dress. By the same token,' she added, 'it's a good deal the worse for wear. I doubt if I can wear it at the dance after all.'

'You've got to: it's predestined,' Perry said.

'Yes,' Virgilia agreed, 'and I am predestined to watch you putting it on.'

'In that case, Mummie, you are predestined to mend it, for it's beyond me.'

Garrett's thoughts were still pursuing the trail.

'But the lighting,' he said. 'Mrs Wilde, surely the lighting wasn't the same?'

'It was quite different,' Virgilia admitted. 'In the dance vision it was bright. I saw everything clearly, lit up and coloured. The other vision was dimmed and blurred. Really, it was shadows I was seeing, just as I saw them last night: the figures grew and shrank as they moved farther from the window or near it, and wavered as the silk curtains moved. But, you see, at the time I thought it was the quality of my seeing that had changed: I thought that I was visualising less clearly on account of having looked away.'

'A mistake of interpretation,' Garrett commented.

Perry said drily, 'Some mistake!'

'Honestly,' Virgilia went on, 'now that I think of it, I just didn't look at the man's figure at all. I *assumed* it was Perry.'

Nan said, 'That's what I *can't* understand. How you could possibly assume that, and stick to it as you did.'

There was silence. They sipped their drinks. Virgilia flushed. This, she knew, was the heart of the matter. Nobody was amused over this. For the sake of the future and her relationship with Perry – with Nan, even – the whole truth must be told. It would be a little distressing for them all. That couldn't be helped. Her own excessively visual memory was a part of it. That should be shown – how the dark, sharp face, hard with hate, had come between her and Perry's; between her and Carlo's; how the feeling of those hands – gripping, choking, shaking – had rushed back; how the dread of an inherited lack of control had obsessed her.

It must be told, and now was the moment, before Dr Franks arrived.

She said, 'I was quite incredibly silly, but there were one or two things.'

'My foul temper,' Perry said helpfully. 'I snapped at you the first day we met.'

'Only for a second.'

'Still, I snapped.'

'Well, you did.'

'And that damned cyclist. I blasted him to hell and shocked you. I saw you were shocked.'

'I ought not to have been.'

'Sure, you ought not. He deserved it.'

Nan was leaning on her elbow, looking with astonishment at her mother.

'Goodness, Mummie!' she said. 'And that row with the tinkers! I saw your face when Perry grabbed Sal. You looked horrified. But, you know, he was laughing. He didn't lose his temper at all.'

'I didn't know that. I thought he was in a fury,' Virgilia confessed.

'But why did you?' Nan persisted. 'It's so utterly and completely unlike you to imagine things are worse than they are, and be nervous about people and … and …'

'I think I can explain this,' Perry said.

Virgilia looked at him. He was smiling at her. It was a very sympathetic, very affectionate smile.

'I think it was your mother, Perry,' she said. 'I never told you that I knew her.'

'Dad told me.' Perry hesitated. He waited for her consent to go on. She gave it with a nod. 'A nice, classical complex out of childhood – jam for the psychoanalysts,' Perry said. 'My mother pulled her hair when they were kids, so she quite naturally thought I would strangle Nan.'

In the outburst of laughter that followed, the memory of Suzette dissolved. I shall never be able to think of her again without laughing, Virgilia thought. But the inquisition was not permitted to end there. Garrett was too keenly interested. When the whole tangle of events had been unravelled and examined Pamela commented: 'We've all been much too clever, much too logical. That's what went wrong.'

Her husband agreed.

'What transpires,' he said, 'is that one has got to allow an immense margin for error in such experiences as these. Every sort of thing seems to come in – associated ideas, obsessions, autosuggestion, complexes, memories, telepathy, guess-work. I suppose we ought never to trust such experiences at all.'

Pamela nodded.

'I think Nan was the wisest of us when she said, "We just don't know how things work."'

'No,' Nan declared, 'the wise one is Brigid. She says, "We're best after all the way we are."'

Virgilia lifted her glass, looking at Perry.

'To the unseen future,' she said.

'To the unseen future,' Perry responded, looking at Nan.

Nan held out her hand to him and rose. They emptied their glasses, then walked to the gate together. Dr Franks's car was turning into the lane.